Human by Choice

By

Travis S. Taylor, Ph.D., and Darrell Bain

Twilight Times Books
Kingsport Tennessee

Human by Choice

This is a work of fiction. All concepts, characters and events portrayed in this book are used fictitiously and any resemblance to real people or events is purely coincidental.

Paladin Timeless Books, an imprint of
Twilight Times Books
POB 3340
Kingsport TN 37664
http://twilighttimesbooks.com/

First Edition, August 2009

Library of Congress Cataloging-in-Publication Data

Taylor, Travis S.
  Human by choice / by Travis S. Taylor and Darrell Bain. -- 1st ed.
      p. cm.
  ISBN-13: 978-1-60619-047-0 (trade pbk. : alk. paper)
  ISBN-10: 1-60619-047-4 (trade pbk. : alk. paper)
  I. Bain, Darrell, 1939- II. Title.
  PS3620.A98H86 2009
  813'.6--dc22

                    2009030300

Cover art by Ural Akyuz

Printed in the United States of America.

*To all the science fiction writers,
past and present,
who helped us dream.*

PROLOG

The vagaries of chance could have gone for another billion years before such an occurrence happened again, indeed if it ever did. The Cresperian species were cautious in thought, and deliberate in handling the huge exploration ship. They were almost always alert to even the slightest changes in the timeless unreality encapsulating their ship while traversing untold distances at many times the speed of light. Had a rare, almost unheard-of controversy not been taking place that captured the perceptive senses of the two senior navigators at the time, all would have been well. Unfortunately, a long, tenacious debate among differing groups of explorers became extremely interesting at just the wrong moment. Both navigators were using their perception to follow it, amused at how even merging perceptions of the pro and con and status quo contingents could still come to no agreement.

A tiny spark of contained plasma leaped a gap from one instrument to another, warning of an approaching reality region in the path of the present dimensionless, timeless containment enclosing the ship, a reality where none should have been possible. It was such a rare phenomenon that for long, uncaptured seconds the navigators let it go unnoticed while they followed the debate in another part of the ship. By the time they realized how derelict they had been in their duty, it was too late. They knew such an event was theoretically possible but not in their wildest waking dreams had they ever thought to encounter one.

The ship shuddered as the navigators frantically caused it to reach out with tentacles of the space-time harnessed in its bowels, trying to deflect the piece of reality and sideslip into a dimension where they might possibly save the ship. It was too late. Reality tore at the fabric of controlled nothingness and began ripping it apart, exposing the body of matter necessary for life itself.

A silent scream of alarm penetrated the perception of every being aboard, warning of imminent disaster. Another, greater convulsion shook the ship as the navigators made a valiant effort to change their direction toward the only possible salvation, whatever planet might be near enough to support life, for they already knew the ship was beyond saving. Their very lives were forfeit as they remained in place while the rest of the crew scrambled for emergency escape pods. Some made it to the dubious safety of the lifeboats before the last rumbling spasm tore through the ship, breaking it into pieces against the sudden barrier of reality. Most couldn't find a lifeboat in time and the navigators didn't even make an attempt, holding true to their profession as they sacrificed their lives in a desperate attempt to save some of the others.

A dozen small craft of the hundreds that emerged from the wreckage were still intact and escaped the explosions, collisions and punctures that doomed the other lifeboats. Two of this dozen failed to reach the green and blue and brown globe of the planet where they might possibly survive, and at least one more broke up upon entering the atmosphere. Some of them were scattered across the star system, due to the uncertain nature of the unreality drives. The hibernation systems might function for a while, keeping the crews alive, but it was unlikely that another ship would pass that way before the systems finally failed. It would be unlikely that those craft stranded orbiting the yellow star or crashing into the more harsh planets of the system would survive. Very unlikely.

Of those which reached the earth, some contained only one passenger and none held more than three. Even then, one more ran into a problem which might have killed its inhabitant had it not been for where it came to rest, just before its pilot slipped into a non-perceptive state from the hard impact of landing. A crucial component damaged during the breakup of the mother ship failed while the boat was still fifty feet in the air. The small lifeboat careened through the canopy of the tall slender green vegetation of the planet with thunderous claps of sound. Systems within the craft continued to fail as the extreme impact forces of reality relentlessly pounded on it until it slammed into the surface. The occupant was more than dazed by the impact, and the reality-unreality generators still tore at each other and at the very fabric of spacetime on the outside of the lifeboat. Finally, the reality generator failed, causing a collapsing rift into unreality. The ship slowly began to disintegrate into the nothingness of the void.

Chapter One

What the hell was that? I looked up from my book, out the window and across the pine thicket in the direction of the loud *thud* and then reached over to the end table, gripping my glass of iced tea carefully. The condensation on the glass drooled down, forming a pool in a perfect ring. I took a couple swigs of the cool drink, careful not to let it drip on the page, before setting my book down and rising from my chair. *Might as well go see*, I thought. I winced from the old battle wounds as I stood up. Anyone watching would think I was an old man instead of in my thirties.

My first notion was that a rather large limb must have fallen off one of the tall pines in the thicket surrounding the small home, up in the mountains of northern Arkansas, I had bought a few weeks earlier. Some of the trees were huge and the older ones often had dead limbs on them thicker than my thigh, and sticking out like some ghastly appendage. They dropped every now and then and caused quite a ruckus when they did. I'd made a point to keep my things out from under the trees that had them, but sometimes the wind would toss them into the most inopportune directions.

"The book wasn't that captivating, anyway," I half-heartedly hmmphed, and frowned. Come to think of it, the noise had sounded peculiar. I hoped it hadn't hit the Hummer. Or worse, the hybrid car. It was flimsier.

I went to the door and opened it, then peered through the screen where a nice breeze chilled the light sheen of sweat on my face. Time to close the doors and windows and turn on the air conditioning, but first I wanted to see what had fallen. I frowned when nothing appeared out of the ordinary from where I stood. I opened the screen door and stepped outside. I walked a few feet forward and then noticed several limbs that had been thrown asunder from high up in the pine tree canopy. There was a gouge through it that tracked at a slight angle downward to the ground. Then, I saw it.

A shimmering light blue egg-shaped apparition a dozen feet long lay before me in a short furrow a couple feet deep in the pine straw covered earth just beyond the old Hummer. The egg glimmered faintly with a red glow near its point and I could feel heat washing over my face as the glow quickly faded. For a moment I stood frozen, with only my mind moving, but it was racing like a jet on afterburner. The thing resembled nothing I'd ever seen. At first I thought it must be an errant weather balloon, then I reexamined the upturned earth where it hit. No balloon was that heavy or that hard! Was it some kind of amateur built aircraft? But that didn't match any of my preconceptions, either. All I could come up with was that the light blue color suggested it must be one of those government drones so prevalent now, perhaps an experimental type.

"You must've been booking to have heated up like that," I said to nobody in particular. "I didn't know we had hypersonic drones." But even as I formed that thought, the thing began dissolving right before my eyes the way Styrofoam does when you pour acetone on it, or more like ice melting when doused with hot water.

I thought it was just becoming transparent at first, perhaps part of a stealthy design, until I looked closer and saw that the material was disintegrating into smaller and smaller fragments until they were tiny enough to be blown away by the breeze. I watched the course of a portion of them and saw even those bits fade into nothingness, as if the material was breaking into even smaller bits, down to its constituent molecules and atoms.

"So much for the drone hypothesis," I mumbled to myself, scratching my head as the shell continued to fade and the interior was revealed, looking like nothing so much as the pilot's compartment of an aircraft. And then…"Holy shit!"

There was someone inside, wrapped in a translucent cocoon that crumbled into nothingness even as I stood there like a dummy, trying to make sense of what was happening. That lasted only the few seconds it took for the last tiny bits of the cocoon to blow away on the breeze. What I saw then finally impelled me into action, for the being inside the still-disintegrating shell of its craft resembled nothing human. Well, it was vaguely humanoid, if four upper appendages and an upper portion that was more like a rounded pyramid attached to the body than a head and neck were taken into account.

I don't remember feeling any fear. I was still too stunned to feel much of anything other than an overwhelming sense of unreality, like an extraordinarily vivid dream. My first really coherent thought was concern for the being once I saw it was in trouble. Its two lower appendages disappeared into a crumbled tangle of unfamiliar, varicolored material, where that end of the egg shell shape had impacted the earth. The being trembled, then twitched, as if attempting to free itself. Anyone with a lick of sense could see that the thing was hurt and needed help. I stepped forward, then climbed over two featureless suitcase-sized bundles that had remained after the shell disappeared. As I passed the upper portion of the being I glanced down and took in the wide, bifurcated mouth set in a lumpy sort of face with two very large round green eyes. A thin vertical line bisected each of them. Even as I looked, a nictitating kind of membrane slowly descended over the eyes. Was it dying? I had no way of telling. I continued on to where I could get a closer look at where its feet were caught in a tangle of thick fibers and crushed portions of the shell. I bent down, but for some reason hesitated. The shell had completely vanished all the way to the end and now the wreckage was beginning to crumble and blow away, including where the fibers disappeared into the bowels of the morass. I decided to wait until it was all gone, then I should be able to either lift or drag the being into the house and see what I could do for it there.

I jerked upright as a cry issued from the alien. That's right, alien, I told myself. What the hell else could it have been? It would have been plain enough in any language that it was making a sound of distress, and a second later I saw why. The thick fibers holding the lower part of its feet, or what served as feet, were dissolving and taking them with it in the process! A portion of one leg was already partially gone. I could see that the other would follow it in seconds if I didn't do something. I backed up, then reached down and grabbed two of its upper appendages and jerked forcefully once, twice, then gave a harder pull. It came free of the wreckage. I drug the creature farther away, then watched as the last of what had obviously been a spacecraft of some kind finished disintegrating and its particles wafted away like clouds of dust. All that remained were the two rectangular bundles, looking almost like luggage except for being featureless. I ignored them and stooped to get a better grip on the being, sliding my hands in under the two upper appendages and lifting. It was surprisingly light for its size, bigger than me, but slippery. At first I thought it had skin like a reptile but then saw it was more of a pelt, an exceedingly fine one, so sleek it felt almost like satin. I wondered vaguely why the thing wasn't bleeding from its injured legs. If it was built anything like us it should have been spurting blood, or whatever it used for blood, all over the place.

Wonder about it later, I told myself, and then "Aren't you a freaky looking sucker?" I grinned crazily at the alien and realigned my handhold.

"Ersquaaack." The thing made a squawking sound, but who the hell knew if it was grunting at me, in pain, or just generally spitting some alien curse about getting itself into a pickle of a predicament.

"Right, whatever you say pal. Just don't eat me or give me some form of alien pox that I can't get rid of. And this don't mean we're dating." It's amazing some of the stupid things a person will say in a situation never encountered before. And I'm certainly no exception.

Once I found that I could probably lift the creature into my arms, I did so, grunting a bit and ignoring the pain it caused in my bum hip. I carried it back to the house. One of its arms folded against my chest in the process, as if it were either boneless or broken. It dangled almost limp, like a wet spaghetti noodle.

My first attempt at getting inside ended with a breeze slamming the screen door against one of the alien's damaged legs. I guessed they were legs. The thing eeked with a shrill noise that was most likely its way of calling me a dumbass.

"Sorry."

I had to stop and prop the screen door open to maneuver my way inside. I took the creature over to the big couch and deposited it as gently as possible. Seeing it there gave me a better perspective on its size. My length fit the couch easily when I grabbed a quick nap on it, but I had to cant the alien's lower legs, what was left of them, off to the side. The membrane still covered its eyes and it still squawked in low tones every now and then. I doubted if it was trying to talk; the noises it was making were probably involuntary, since its eyes were still closed. I scanned the length of its body more closely now that it was out of danger. Or was it?

"Think I should call 911?" I asked it and shrugged. "I doubt they'd believe me if I did."

One end of a leg was still missing and a small portion of the other. Yet it was making a semblance of breathing, its middle portion moving in on each side then back out, an inch or so at a time.

"Hmm, looks like you breathe our air."

It wore no clothing that I could see, though its four arms and waist were adorned with what looked to be metallic bands, the one about the waist wider than the others. They were a darker green than the pale lime color of its pelt, but like the bundles still outside, featureless. The damned things could've been anything from an alien doomsday explosive to a ray-gun to a Zippo cigarette lighter. There was just no way of knowing what the little featureless boxes were.

Suddenly I felt a presence behind me, perhaps a movement of air that alerted my senses. I turned and saw both the rectangular blocks I had left outside floating toward me—or rather toward the alien; I was just in the way. I stepped hurriedly aside, while making a mental note that I had to find out how that was done! At the same time, I wondered what would have happened if I hadn't left the screen and door open.

"Is that superpowers or tech?" I asked and continued to observe closely.

One of the cases passed me and came to rest precariously on the end of the couch beside the alien's injured lower legs while the other settled gently to the floor. I slid the coffee table in under the overhanging part of the one on the couch just in case. *Survival packs? Medical apparatus?* I had no way of knowing and was fearful of prying into what I didn't understand. I waited to see what would happen next, while a million questions raced through my mind, none of them particularly original. For someone who gobbles up science fiction novels like rednecks going after free beer, you'd think I would've done something more than stand there like a statue, or at least *thought* of doing or saying something useful, but I didn't. I had done my part by pulling the thing from its dissolving ship. A moment later the pack on the couch divided along an invisible seam. The top half flipped back and separated, leaving two smaller, but still featureless rectangular cartons. From the one nearest the alien, a bulge appeared at one end. It grew into a tentacle that in turn grew a cluster of smaller tentacles at its terminal end. The part growing from the box stretched like taffy even as the little snake-like ends of it began exploring the body of the alien.

It was fascinating to watch. Some of the terminal tentacles divided again and again, becoming smaller and smaller in the process until I could no longer see them, but I suspected they had become microscopic in size and were delving into the very body of the motionless creature. Before long, the exploratory tentacle appeared to be satisfied with all but the missing portion of the alien's legs. It bifurcated and each part settled over a limb, with the smaller parts of it making a mesh over where its legs had been caught in the wreckage and inadvertently dissolved along with the rest of its craft. I thought the tentacle from the box must be starting a healing process. In time, I was proven correct, for the feet were slowly reconstituted, growing back into six slim toes forward and two larger ones at what would be the heel in a human. Those folded back under as if designed for that position while at rest, sort of like the arm had folded against my chest while carrying it in.

A tingling in my feet brought me back to reality. I glanced at my watch and was startled to see that almost an hour had passed since I heard the noise of the spacecraft hitting the earth outside the house. After hauling its passenger inside, I had been standing all that time as if mesmerized, and in a sense I suppose I was. I had bought the house out in the country, barely in range of even the local electric co-op, in order to get away by myself for a while. Then to have something like this interrupt my solitude—well, it was more than ironic; it was the height of absurdity, and I guess that's how I reacted.

After the death of Lyle, my twin brother, I lost my wife Gwen, the only woman I've ever truly loved. I found that I was having all kinds of problems adjusting to life without her. My intent had been to take a year's sabbatical from research and writing and live alone, where I could drag my soul out in the open and examine it. There was just all sorts of touchy-feely shit that I felt I needed to figure out or wad up into a tight ball and bury it away, never to think of it again. I wanted to find out whether a life without Gwen and my brother was even worthwhile. Gwen's death had come while I was still grieving over the loss of Lyle. We had been close, as only identical twins can really appreciate, and his illness had been hard to take. He died slowly, in great pain, from some kind of incurable tropical disease he caught on a trip to Africa. He suffered and cried for six long weeks while it ravaged his body, and I cried with him. Toward the end, he begged me to help him end it and I did, with Gwen's support and without consulting anyone else.

After losing the only two people in the world I loved deeply and without reservations to an uncaring universe, I had to get away, from everybody. Everybody. I wanted to think deeply on this and other matters, like where humanity was going with its burgeoning, ever-expanding technology that was growing at almost logarithmic rates but still couldn't stop a microbial onslaught to my womb-mate. I was questioning life and hating life and even wondering whether all of humanity even *had* much of a future. And if it did, was it one that I cared to be part of? The conflicts of the world were almost more than I could even consider at that point in my life. My mental and emotional state was a total wreck. I was, plainly put, a mess.

But in order to avoid thinking about the picture that really mattered then, namely me, I avoided it by thinking and worrying about more global issues enveloping humanity. What could I do about it, anyway, and did I care to, if I could? It appeared to me that the conflict between fundamentalist and secular Islamic practices was going to be decided in the fundamentalists' favor. I could see that coming as plainly as any good historian, even if our leaders seemed blind to the fact. And in opposition, hard-core Christianity was seeing a revival to brighten the hearts of any suspenders-snapping Baptist preacher or Pentecostal dogmatist. Even the Catholics, and Hindus with their pantheon of Gods, were falling prey to evangelical moralizing.

The isolation I'd sought had barely begun, less than two months ago, but I thought I might be coming to terms with my present life sooner than I'd imagined, although it was by no means certain yet. It was Gwen's loss that was so brutal to my sense of well-being and happiness. I'm not much of a socializer and certainly had never thought anyone as lovely and intelligent as she would ever look my way, but she did—and my real life started then, as if I had been only partially existing before meeting her. She made me happier than I ever thought possible. Just being in her presence was a continuing delight. I don't know to this day how I ever got through that awful night when a police officer showed up at the door and told me Gwen was dead, the victim of a drunk driver. I saw the world through a haze of grief and unutterable loneliness after that until I finally exiled myself to the country, hoping I could somehow use the isolation to get my life back on track. And now this.

I thought about a drink but decided to keep my mind clear and set some coffee to brew. While it was dripping, I began pacing the confines of the big living room, loosening up my cramped leg muscles and aching hip and feet and trying to decide what I should do. With every circuit around the room that went past the bar separating the kitchen from the rest of the room, behind the two easy chairs and back again, I glanced at the alien still lying quietly on the couch. Apparently the healing process was nearly complete. The leg with the least damage was already back to normal and the amputated leg had grown back. The stump where long flexible toes with what looked like sheathed claws should be was beginning to sprout buds front and back.

I poured coffee and sat down in one of the easy chairs where I could watch my uninvited guest and sipped the hot brew, trying to decide what to do. Should I call the authorities and report it? That's what most people would think of doing, I knew, but I also knew what would happen should I make that call. The alien and its two boxy possessions would be spirited away by either the military or some security arm of the government and never heard from again. In fact, as I considered my options, I decided there was a good chance I would be taken away as well, and stuck in some out-of-the-way place the rest of my life. Some of the agencies might even think it safer to simply have me eliminated and be done with it. The terrorist mania was causing congress to pass outlandish laws governing homeland security and the Supreme Court wasn't objecting very strenuously. But suppose the wounded craft had been tracked to earth? I thought about that possibility for a moment, then decided it hadn't been; otherwise, helicopters and patrol cars and men in black suits would probably already be swarming around, taking control and enjoining me to silence at the least, and wiping me from the face of the earth at worst. No, I wasn't going to call anyone, especially as the alien's equipment appeared to be taking adequate care of it. Once it awakened, if it wanted to apply the age-old cliché "Take me to your leader," then I'd help it do so, but only after warning it of the probable consequences—assuming we were eventually able to communicate with each other, of course.

On the other hand, it was possible the descending craft *had* been detected and even now the government was cordoning off the area before moving in. The thought bothered me. I voiced the big screen on the wall into action. It was already set to a news channel. I watched for a few moments, especially the scrolling text along the bottom of the screen but nothing untoward appeared to have happened. Just to be sure, I went to a news search and tried several different combinations of wording to see if a meteor or crash of an aircraft or anything at all resembling what actually had happened was being reported. I found a couple of suspicious sources but after going back for some in-depth reporting found that they were all innocuous happenings, easily explained. Then I got smart and changed channels to one I liked to peruse in idle moments, *Strange Events*. And there I did find two items. First was a report of some sort of unexplained astronomical event that was 'being studied'. The other item told of an area in Scotland that had been cordoned off and where a news blackout had been put into effect. I got a satellite view but the area was covered with clouds and neither infrared nor other wavelengths told me anything new, except that what looked to be a large tent had been erected near the center of the excluded area.

I found a couple of other places where some incident had triggered the *Strange Events* monitor but I couldn't find out much more than I had from the first one. And right then it hit me, and damn my stupid mind for not thinking of it earlier. Maybe I should have had a stiff drink right off and got some of my brighter neurons to functioning. *My God! Have more than one of these spacecraft come down?* Were we being invaded and had the vessel that landed in my yard simply malfunctioned? No, that didn't make sense. An invasion wouldn't start this way, not the kind we'd been envisioning in literature and movies ever since H.G. Wells' *War of the Worlds* was published, well over a hundred years ago. But if there was more than one...hell, I just didn't know. Better to wait until I had more data before getting into wild speculation. Gwen used to tell me I had thought patterns resembling a drunk physicist when I got going good.

I got up again and resumed pacing, unbearably anxious for the rejuvenation process the alien was undergoing to be finished. Absent-mindedly, I began straightening the room here and there, then sat down to go through yesterday evening's mail. I had left it lying on the kitchen table where I usually sorted it before taking anything important into the room I was beginning to turn into an office. Halfway through the stack of mostly junk, I found my own face staring back at me from the cover of a trade journal. It looked as if the picture had been touched up a bit. I had more gray in my dark brown hair than that and the scar above my right eyebrow had been smoothed over. The end result made me look almost handsome except that I was a little thinner now than when the photo had been taken, making my high cheekbones inherited from a Cherokee ancestor visible. Beneath the photo was a caption: *Kyle Leverson, Making Science Intelligible.*

I had one of those odd professions that pays well but that hardly anyone knows anything about, or has even heard of in most cases. I've been freelancing for years, taking science articles and rewording them into intelligible English. You'd be surprised at the number of high grade geniuses in the science fields who can hardly tell a verb from a vampire and need people like me to rewrite their papers for them. That means I have to do a lot of research, keeping up with the latest in studies in such diverse fields as amoebic diseases and how atmospheres form on other planets and so forth, but I've always been a science bug anyway, so that was no hardship. That doesn't mean I'm an expert in any of the professions like zoology or molecular biology or genetics or particle physics and the like—just that I know enough about them, or can find out enough, to transcribe the authors' gibberish into something readable by their peers. I also was well known (in professional circles) as a pretty fair science writer for the masses: everything from Sunday supplement type articles to more serious ones in national magazines and on the internet. With my disability income from the army, the result of gunshot wounds to the shoulder and hip, and what I earned freelancing, plus the payoff from the insurance company of the drunken driver that killed Gwen, I was very well off economically. I still got the pension even though the old wounds didn't bother me too much now, so long as I was very careful and assiduous with my non-impact exercise programs. The only thing I had regrets about is that I could no longer practice karate. It was just too much for the mess the bullets made of my shoulder and hip.

I had just finished another circuit and was pouring a second cup of coffee when I heard a noise over the newscast I had left on. I turned around and the alien creature's eyes were no longer covered by that membrane; their bisected orbs were clearly turned in my direction. An old soldier's instinct washed over me for a fleeting second, an impulse making me want to run for my pistol.

Chapter Two

What do you do in a situation that no human has ever experienced before? I sure as hell didn't know, but while I stood there like a dunce, the alien moved its upper trunk and switched its gaze toward the big screen on the wall. There was no possible way to gauge its reaction. All I could do was try to picture how a human from another epoch might act in a similar situation, say like a Cro-Magnon with a time traveler dropped in front of its cave, and even then the circumstances could only be remotely compared. They would at least have their humanity in common, while we were two wildly different species. I might have been nothing more than technologically advanced kibble to this thing.

Luckily for me, the alien took charge. It levered itself upright and leaned against the cushioned backrest of the couch. Its gaze left the screen and traversed the room in a slow arc, as if studying each object in the room—including me, for that's where its eyes rested after the circuit around the room. Only momentarily though, for then it pointed one of its fingers—it had six on each hand, along with two opposable thumbs—and the box sitting on the floor opened just as it had done earlier, prior to the healing of the amputated foot. The gun idea was still twitching at the back of my mind as an inch-thick fiber uncoiled from the depths of the box. The fiber was topped by a small globe no more than a couple of inches in diameter. Evidently it was some kind of interpretive device, for the alien began speaking to it and it answered, but in a gabble that made no sense at all to me.

This went on for several moments while I brought my fresh coffee over to the easy chair and set it on the side table. I started to sit down but then wondered if my alien guest might be hungry or thirsty. I went over to the refrigerator and poured a glass of cold water. Very slowly, so as not to alarm it, I crossed the room and held out the glass.

There was no hesitation on its part. It took the glass and raised it to the lipless, bifurcated mouth. A tongue as pink as my own lapped at the water at first, then somehow formed a tube and suctioned the rest of it up. It held out the glass to me, a clear signal that it wanted more. I set the glass on the coffee table and fetched the water pitcher. I demonstrated how to pour, probably an unnecessary gesture. I watched as it drank almost the whole pitcher of water. After that it placed its mouth over the globe at the end of the upright fiber that had risen from the box. It made swallowing motions, leading me to think it was probably taking in some nourishment, or possibly medicine. When it seemed to be satisfied, I decided to get busy.

"Kyle," I said, touching my chest like Tarzan as I uttered my name.

It repeated my action and said, "Cresperian," speaking slowly. If it had said, "Take me to your leader" instead, I would have headed for the nearest funny farm and checked myself in faster than a cat having sex. At that point a piece of useless knowledge popped into my head about tomcats. I was lost on the thought that a tomcat has barbs on its penis and ejaculates in less than ten seconds. Then I cringed, thinking about the sight of a poor pussycat being mounted. I've got more useless facts like that running around in my mind than are in Wikipedia. Gwen used to show me off at parties, having people ask me odd questions, the odder the better. Sometimes stress causes nonsense like that to just pop to the front of my brain. Perhaps I developed it early on as some sort of coping mechanism to make up for being shy.

"Kyle." The alien snapped me out of my wandering trivial pursuit by pointing in my direction and repeating my name.

I didn't intend to try putting over the fact that humans usually went by two, and sometimes three names, but even so I confused it. By the time I realized it was speaking of species while I had given my individual name, it took several minutes and finally showing it a picture of a crowd before it got the idea. After that the session went easier, even though I learned later that they had no permanent names of their own, but changed their designation as they changed professions or specialties. Nevertheless, we began making rapid progress, I by talking and demonstrating, and it by what turned out to be an eidetic memory and use of its boxed assistant that seemed to have as many functions as the contents of a woman's handbag, maybe more.

Time passed and eventually I played out, while it appeared content to continue the language and culture lessons indefinitely. It was midnight by then. We hadn't gotten around to discussing sleep but I was really feeling the need. Finally I hit on a bright idea. I had already managed to explain the idea of what a computer was, so I showed it the basics on my spare (not being willing to risk a neophyte with the main one). It caught on quickly, and we had already gone over the association between words and the text in books. I left it with a dictionary, a connection to one of the simpler encyclopedias on the net and a general science site to play with, and Google, and then I pointed out the bathroom in case it had needs along those lines. I lay down on the couch, instead of my bed, to sleep. I wanted be nearby in case it needed me.

For the time being I was calling it Jerry, for no particular reason other than it sounded like the first couple of syllables of what it gave as its designation when we decided it needed a name in English, and it seemed satisfied with the shortened form. After I'd sleepily watched Jerry for a while, I thought he could navigate by himself (herself? We hadn't gotten into that yet, but I decided on him for the time being) and closed my eyes at last. Just as I was dozing off I heard a cat "raoow" out behind the shed, causing me to dream of an alien tomcat mounting a poor little kitty.

ஐ03

A sunbeam making its way through the shade of the big pines around the house woke me well after sunrise the second day after the alien's arrival. Jerry was still at it, apparently as happy with what I had given him to play with as a pup with a roomful of squeaky toys, and to all appearances he had been busy the whole time I slept, breaking only once to engage me in conversation when I woke up for an hour. Occasionally while I was awake, I saw him take a drink of water or sustenance from the case still sitting on the floor, which I had concluded must be the lifeboat survival kit. When he heard me yawn and sit up, he turned around.

I was so short on sleep that at first I had trouble remembering what was going on, then I blinked and it all came rushing back into my mind, just as it did every time I woke up. *An alien!* I had an alien in my home, an intelligent, reasoning creature from the stars, a phenomenon we humans had been dreaming of for the better part of a century! And, it hadn't as of yet made the slightest motions toward eating me alive. That part I was happiest about.

"Good morning, Jerry," I said.

"Good morning, Kyle. Your sleepness was…noisy at times but not disturbing. I thank you for the generosity of your computer and of your home."

I do snore occasionally, especially when I'm tired, so I guess that's what he was referring to. His language had improved considerably overnight, enough so that we could converse easily. There were plenty of misunderstandings, circumlocutions and cultural differences that occasionally took a long time to overcome, but I won't try to reproduce any of that. Apparently he (I went on referring to it as he for a day or two until we got that straightened out) had no need of sleep, at least not in the sense we did.

"Thank you. Are you tired? Do you need to rest?"

"No, I have no need to sleep at the present time."

"Uh huh." Right then, I had no idea of the implications *that* simple statement held for the future. I simply assumed he needed less sleep than we did and would rest when he felt the need.

"How about some food? Are you hungry? Do you think you can eat what we do?"

"Yes, when I begin to need food, I believe it will be compatible with my body."

Again, I had no inkling of what his statement really meant, but if it didn't need food, I did, as well as a shower and some coffee to get me going. I started the coffee brewing, then said, "Excuse me. I need to shower and brush my teeth, and then we'll talk some more while I make breakfast."

"I will be content until you return."

The formal way he spoke soon disappeared as he picked up the nuances of slang, along with my southern accent, and began working deeper into the incredible versatility of the rich English language.

He turned back to the computer as I left the room. It was one of the fastest showers and morning ablutions of my life, for I could hardly contain myself until I could get back and talk some more with him. Whatever else I had expected of an alien, I never thought I'd meet one who learned so rapidly or was so agreeable with whatever I happened to suggest.

Not wanting to waste time cooking, I pulled down a box of sweetened Cheerios for breakfast. While I spooned them into my mouth we talked, with me sometimes having to finish a bite before answering.

Once my bowl was empty, I poured coffee for myself, and then offered some to Jerry.

"Not at the present, thank you, but I believe by tomorrow or perhaps the next day I'll be able to partake," he told me.

And again I missed the implications, but of course there was no possible way for me to understand what he meant. Once the coffee quieted my caffeine addiction and got my mind into gear, I decided to bring up the subject of sex, taking a chance that I might be broaching some taboo of his species.

"Jerry, I've been referring to you as 'he', implying not only that you're male but that your species has two sexes like ours. Am I correct or way off base?"

"Off base?" He hesitated before continuing. Just as I opened my mouth to explain, he said "Yes, I understand now. A sports analogy. Your communication mode is extremely versatile for being so limited."

"Limited how?"

"We have what you would call a perceptive sense. It allows us to discern many more nuances of meaning than speech alone."

"You mean you're telepathic? You can read minds?" Great blazing balls of fire! What must he be thinking of me if he knew everything that had gone through my mind since he fell to earth in my yard? If I were the alien I'd probably be the one wanting a shootin' iron!

"No, just that we 'see' with more than our eyes, even down to the small molecular level or even to the atomic. When communicating with a companion, speech is only part of the message. In time I will be able to explain in more detail."

I breathed a huge sigh of relief. "Okay," I said and gladly left it at that, now that I was assured he wasn't reading my thoughts. Aliens using my computer and drinking my water was one thing, but if they got into my mind that was an entirely different matter. What if the thing had seen my crazy dream about the alien tomcat raping that kitty? Humanity might be looked at as really freaking weird, were that to happen. Fortunately for humankind, Jerry wasn't telepathic, as far as I understood it. "But back to your sex. Are you male or female?"

He seemed to muse for a moment before answering, making me wonder for a moment if I had touched on a taboo subject. I was just thinking of how to phrase my apology when he put my fears to rest. "In our culture we have two genders, just as you do, but we're not limited as you are. In the course of our lives, we may have one sexual identity, then change to another, just as we change specialties of interest from time to time, and eventually two of us may propagate through what you would think of as…a third sex, perhaps. One who bears the young."

"Hmm." That must be a nice arrangement, I thought to myself. One sex just to have the babies while the other two have all the fun. Of course, I had no idea of their sexual practices at the time, or even if they had sex in the fashion we did. For certain I could detect nothing at Jerry's crotch that looked anything like genitalia. Anyway, his sexual organs didn't necessarily have to be placed like ours. His outward appearance was sort of like a cartoon animal—sexless. And who knew what he had hiding under that pelt?

He must have taken my little utterance as a signal to continue with the subject, for then he said, "I've already instituted the necessary biomolecular and genetic revisions of my structure to become female. However, if that is unsatisfactory to you, I can reverse the process with little problem at this stage."

I was curious, I'll admit. Besides, men are always thinking about sex. "Why did you decide to start the change now, on a strange planet and in what must be an even stranger environment for you? Or is it something that happens automatically?"

"Oh, no, Kyle. Long ago we progressed to a stage of biotechnology where the changes may be done at will. Of course we don't usually switch back and forth very often. Our lifespans are extremely long compared to yours, so there's no necessity for hurry in most matters."

"Of course not," I said, and immediately hoped he hadn't picked up on the sarcasm. Damn it, he could have gone all day without saying that. The fact that we had to die was one of my pet peeves. At the very least, I thought our lifetimes were far too short. I hated the thought of death, the negation of my ego, and being non-religious, I had no anticipation of an afterlife. And while I'm still relatively young, I can remember how bitterly resentful my Dad had been as his life neared its end, not only because he knew he was going to die, but also at all the aches and pains that old age entails. And he didn't believe in an afterlife either. Frankly, I doubt that most people really, deep down, believe in a heaven, or they wouldn't struggle so to keep on living, even in pain and misery and conditions where death should seem welcome if they really thought there was something nice waiting afterward. And just look at how we misbehave. Would we really act the way we do if we thought our chances of going to heaven were based on our actions while alive? Hell no, we wouldn't.

I shook my head to get the random thoughts out of my mind. "So I take it you're male now. Will you look the same after you change to a female or will the differences be apparent, like our sexual characteristics?"

If an alien with a face like a cross between a cat and an owl could look troubled, Jerry did. I apologized, thinking I shouldn't have raised the issue so soon. "I'm sorry, Jerry. I think I must have troubled or embarrassed you. I didn't intend to." Damn my big mouth. Why can't I ever learn to keep it shut?

"It isn't that, Kyle. You've mistaken my meaning, most likely from my incomplete comprehension of your language and culture. I'm becoming a female because I thought that would please you, since you're alone—that is, you have no companion present. Wife? Partner?"

"I was married," I told him. "My wife died in an accident several months ago. If you're becoming a female simply to please me...well, I don't see what difference it would make. I'm sure I could continue to relate to you in your present form just as well as whatever you look like as a female."

A long moment of silence ensued and again I thought I had said something wrong.

"I see that I still have failed to make myself understood. I apologize for that. What my transition means is that when it is complete I will look like a human female. In fact, in all respects I will be able to function as a human female, retaining only my perceptive sense and my knowledge."

ଋଠଓଷ

That floored me. An alien changing into a functional human female? I didn't see how it was possible and said so.

"Jerry, how can you do such a thing? Unless you've been studying us more thoroughly than you've admitted, I don't see how you can possibly do it."

He, or I guess I should say she, answered, since I began thinking of the alien as female from that point on. At any rate I changed the wording of its name to Jeri in my mind and thought of her like that from then on. She responded to my question with wording she had used before in somewhat the same context, but it had passed me by then, just as all the indirect references to the coming change had failed to penetrate. Some days I'm dense, I'll admit it.

"My perceptive sense goes down to the molecular level, Kyle, and even beyond if necessary, as I've mentioned to you. I've already done a thorough analysis of your gene structure. As I'm sure you know, all the aspects of both male and female are contained in the chromosomes of every cell of your body, particularly as you possess both the X and Y chromosomes. Had you been female, I would have been unable to successfully change or perhaps even gone off on a false highway. Road? Path?"

"Path. You mean you've been able to look inside my body without me even knowing it?"

"Not look, as you interpret the term, Kyle. Perceive is the only English word I can use to describe what I did. As I've said before, our perceptive sense goes down to the molecular level." She stopped for a moment, then continued. "Was I wrong to look inside your body without your permission?"

"No harm done, but if you truly get to where you look like a female and can pass for human, it wouldn't do to go around looking through people's clothes, for instance. If you ever forget, for God's sake don't mention it! We like our privacy and the nudity taboos are rather strong in our culture."

"Yes, I've gathered that, but what you suggested I could do would never be detectable. Even so, as human, I shall practice the same mores as you do, so far as possible."

"Hmm. Maybe this is the time to ask if any more of you are on earth." I think I kind of held my breath until she answered. It turned out that my suspicions were correct.

"I believe so, although I can't say how many. As our ship broke up, hundreds of lifeboats escaped, but very few survived. I perceived several before distance became a factor. Perhaps as few as two or three of us made it to earth but certainly no more than two dozen, in somewhat less than a dozen boats."

I should have figured it out without her help by then, but I hadn't. I had been picturing the spaceship she arrived in as an interstellar craft that had crashed because of a mechanical failure, but in retrospect it was a sillier assumption than thinking you can drink boilermakers all night without consequences the next morning. Considering its size and the way it disintegrated upon touching earth in order to free its occupant should have enabled me to figure out that it was a survival craft of some kind, but I guess my brain had been overloaded right from the beginning. Anyway, knowing the truth brought up another question.

"Did you manage to send a distress signal? Will another ship be coming to rescue you?"

"No. I fear I shall never return to my home planet."

"Never? Why not?"

"Several reasons. First, this galaxy is huge, as you well know. While many planets bear life, we've found only three or four others so far in hundreds of years of exploration that have intelligent species and all of those but humans are subtechnical."

I'm glad she included us among the intelligences. Some days I have my doubts about just how smart humans are despite being able to invent such things as fast food and pantyhose. But maybe she was overlooking something.

"How about if one of your navigators survived, wouldn't they know how to get back? Or is that all pre-programmed?"

"No, that's one of the few things that weren't completely automatic, but I know for certain that our pathfinders all perished when our starship failed, so even if it were possible to build another ship here, which it isn't, it's doubtful that I or any of my fellows who escaped could find the way back."

"You don't know how a spaceship, a starship I should say, works?"

"Only generally. You know in a broad sense how a nuclear reactor works, but could you design and build one using the technical aid of south sea islanders?"

"Uh, no." I got the point. We were barbarians compared to them, but personally, I think she could have thought of a gentler way of putting it. "Won't another ship ever come this way again?"

"Perhaps, but again using an analogy, in the course of your life will you ever travel to London, to a particular street and house number you've never heard of, much less seen?"

"No, I guess not. So you're stuck here. Is that why you're planning on assuming human shape?"

"I see no other recourse. Judging from what little I know yet of your culture, it's impossible for me to go out in public in my present appearance. Fortunately, in our own culture, assuming other body shapes, including the mental processes, is commonplace. I myself have taken the shape of, and lived for a short time as, one of our nearest cousins in the animal world. It's no inconvenience for me to become like a human. In fact, again judging from what little I know, it should be an extraordinary experience, since I will assume the characteristics of a human female. But before that happens, I'm going to have to impose on you for some assistance with the change. May I?"

"Certainly. I'll do whatever I can to help you. We sure as hell don't want the military or one of the security agencies to get their hands on you." That made me pause for thought. "You said you can perceive others of your kind. Do you have any idea at all of where the others might be?"

"I was so busy trying to keep my boat operational that I only remember flashes of a few trajectories. I know of one that probably came to rest hundreds of miles east of here and I believe another ship probably landed in the United Kingdom, although I can't be certain. Other than those, I have no idea, since even though we were all on the same general trajectory, some of the survivors lagged behind me and some were ahead, like the two I mentioned, but there must have been a lot of divergence. They could have come down most anywhere, although the lifeboats would have guided toward land masses."

"I see." And I had to wonder if anyone else was in the same predicament as me—offering aid to that old bugbear of humans: a bug-eyed monster. BEM in science fiction parlance. We had gotten off track. "You said you needed my help. What is it you want me to do for you?"

"In order to assure a successful transition, I'd like you to convey me to the vicinity of the nearest young female that you know of. Could you do that?"

"Sure," I said, thinking momentarily of Gwen. As if this alien could ever match her! I didn't say that, though. No sense in getting her aggravated at me. "In fact, I need to go shopping in a day or two, anyway, and the little store where I buy groceries and gas has a young lady working there in the afternoons and evenings. I could cover you with a blanket in the back seat and you can do what's necessary while I'm inside. How would that be?" You know, I didn't feel a bit of guilt over Jeri preparing to look inside Bridgett. Heck, I wouldn't have minded a peek myself, at least beneath her clothes. I had a sneaking suspicion she didn't wear panties all the time, but I could be wrong. Just my evil self doing the speculation.

"Yes, that would work very well. Actually, I only need to get within a couple of hundred feet to…zero in, I think is the term, on the anatomy I'm interested in. In case you're wondering, I want to observe the uterus and ovaries and the other sexual differences, and look more closely at the X chromosome as it is expressed in a female."

"No problem. Hey, what kind of woman will you look like when you're finished?"

The bifurcated mouth opened wider in what I think was an attempt at a smile. "I can look like any of the ones I've seen while watching the newscast, but I'd rather you do the choosing."

"No shit?"

Chapter Three

If ever a man wanted to play God, here was my chance. I thought almost constantly about what she wanted me to do. When it was first mentioned, a picture of Gwen popped into my mind, as she had been back when we first married, as young and fresh and precious-looking as a just-unfolded spring flower in the morning, dew drops on the petals sparkling with little pinpoints of fire from the morning sunshine. It took only a moment for me to realize that trying to recreate Gwen would be the biggest mistake of my life. Every time I would look at her, I'd be hoping to see the love of my life again, but it wouldn't really be her. I decided that it would be much better to keep the memories the way they were and to start fresh. That was if I could ever be attracted to an alien masquerading as a human female, as Jeri apparently thought I would be. Hell, she probably understood humans better than I did at that point.

"Well," I ventured, "if you can do what you're saying, and trust me to help pick out your form, the best thing to do is to let me show you shapes and colors and descriptions, then you mold yourself to the woman you want to look like."

"If that is what you wish," she said.

Jeri was amenable, but then I had to peruse some pictures of nude females to give her an idea of what I considered a nice face and figure. Inevitably, that meant seeing some pornography. I tried to keep it to a minimum, but it was no use. Looking for nude women on the internet meant you were going to see some porn, regardless. For that matter, looking for dishwashing detergent on the internet meant that you'd probably come across a come-on to a site where men and women were doing wild things to each other that had nothing to do with dirty dishes. Once, back before pop-up blockers came along, I got a into window of MILFs that wouldn't go away no matter how many times I "clicked X" on it. I didn't even know what the crap a MILF was until the site came up. Each time I'd click X, it would close and another would take its place, announcing that they had the hottest nude teens or the best library of nude celebrities or the nastiest women on the web or, you name it, it was there. And once there was even a site for very, very, *large* women. I quickly noted that Jeri was captivated by some of the acts pictured, even though I hurriedly scanned past them or closed them out. Finally, I just stopped fighting the flood of internet porn and tried to explain one of the most oddly fascinating, strange, and weird aspects of human nature—sex, and as a consequence, internet porn.

"Jeri, some of the things you're seeing here aren't what most of us would call normal or mainstream. Humans are subject to innumerable neuroses, almost all of them at least partly sexual in nature. And a lot of them will do almost anything for the right amount of money or fame. If you get confused about any of this stuff, please ask, or better still, try to ignore it until later, when you're better acculturated. Okay?"

"Yes. Shall we continue looking at nude females, then?" she said. Jeri was truly an alien after my own heart.

"Yes, but I've got a better way of doing it. If you're determined to do this, you may as well do it right. Just wait here a minute."

I had a stack of old Playboy magazines inherited from my father, some of them collector's items now. And, yes, of course I had added to the pile myself over the years, but before I was married. I had gone through them once or twice and separated out the ones I thought I might like to look at again sometime in the future, either for the particularly pulchritudinous young women or for an article I might use sometime in my writing. And for the pictures of the young women, or did I mention that already?

I brought the ones with the best photo displays (in my opinion). I like boobs as well as any normal man, but I like them proportional to the rest of the body, not oversized (although if a pair of extra large naked boobs just happened to be in front of me, I certainly wouldn't shy away from them). I showed Jeri some examples of what I considered to be ideal figures and coloring, then gave her a height limitation of no more than five feet six inches and preferably an inch or two shorter, which was probably a subconscious hangover of mine from Gwen. By the time we were finished, she had a good idea of what I liked, but none of them really resembled Gwen (who had been very pretty, verging on beautiful) other than their height. And I was not only as embarrassed as a kid caught with pornography by his parents but had a pretty fair erection besides. Call me old-fashioned, but looking at naked women for that prolonged a period of time did get my blood pumping.

Those pictures at least gave Jeri something to shoot for. I still had my doubts about whether she could accomplish it or not, but I figured if she was going to do it, she may as well try for something I liked, since she was living with me. If the process came out anywhere near what I envisioned, she would turn heads by the score, which brought up another subject we had touched on here and there over the last three days but hadn't tried to explore yet in any depth.

Once we were seated (and it turned out that my couch suited her about as well as any earthly furniture, so long as she sat upright), she began the conversation. I wasn't quite ready for it. Hell, I was even trying to avoid it. I mean, come on, sex with an alien, a very *alien*-looking alien at that, was not something even the free love hippies from the last century would've been up for.

"Kyle, human sexual practices appear to be something I shall have to experience in order to even begin to comprehend. They bear little relation to what our species thinks of as sexual bonding. I've gotten the impression that much of your sexuality is exceedingly pleasurable, yet somehow associated with deep subconscious feelings of guilt. These in turn are very closely related to your religious beliefs, of which there are many. Am I correct so far?"

"Well, yeah, religious and moral beliefs. All morals aren't necessarily derived from religion, though. I mean, even atheists have morals based on what they think is right and wrong." I had to admit she was mostly right, though, much as I hated to. We're a weird species, no doubt about it.

"Therein lies the confusion for me. We have nothing at all like religion in our culture, since our mathematicians have proven beyond doubt the non-existence of a Supreme Entity which orders how the universes work, much less one that takes a personal interest in our everyday affairs. I'm sorry if that offends you, but I have no other way of looking at it."

"You're not offending me, Jeri." In fact, I felt a huge sense of relief. Religion has caused enough grief on our old earth already, without bringing in new ones from other parts of the galaxy! I wondered about her species' history, though, but didn't have a chance to ask right away, because she continued almost immediately. And had I truly understood more about the underlying math of quantum physics and the connectedness phenomenon, I would have argued that any good mathematical proof can eventually be overturned with a new understanding or axiom. But I didn't, so I didn't.

"Oh. Then I assume you belong to the ten percent or so of humanity which has lost the genes governing a belief system in the supernatural?"

"Uh, well," I started to say but then hesitated. Up until the loss of my brother and my wife I thought I was pretty sure about things, religion-wise. But these days I wasn't sure I knew anything about anything. But

Jeri perhaps knew more than I did about humanity as she had really been researching our species. I was already pretty much aware of how much she'd learned. "That's one way of putting it, I suppose, although I'd sure like to see that proof you say you have. But yes, that's about right. Maybe as much as one in ten of us, or thereabout, apparently are born without a need to believe in a higher power. Of course, our scientists are beginning to think there are a number of interrelated genes associated with the belief genes, or any genes for that matter, and environment governs a good deal of the way most genes are expressed. It's extremely complicated. For us, anyway."

"I'll be able to shed some light on it for you once I've become human. Perhaps by publishing my findings?"

The statement was in the form of a question. I wasn't certain if it was rhetorical or not. And I thought about it briefly. There were two problems with that. One was just a hunch that being human might change her mind. Seeing and "feeling" the universe from a human's perspective would be a new observation that might throw a monkey wrench in that proof of hers. The second was pure logistics of the Spanish inquisition of scientific publishing.

"It's not that easy, at least if you can't show the research to back you up. If you don't have that, and credentials to match, a reputable genetics journal, or any other science journal for that matter, won't publish you." I grinned. "Of course, there's always the internet. That's made a considerable change in the ways we make information available to the common man." I thought for a moment. "In fact, I could probably do it for you. It's right up my line and I have a good reputation for not going off the deep end. Well, not too often, anyway."

"If I understand your similes correctly, you're involved with the publication of scientific data?"

"That's right. And I think I have a pretty open mind. You know, Jeri, you were very lucky you came down in my bailiwick rather than some hillbilly preacher's or someone that's ignorant of anything outside movies or the pabulum you find on television and so-called internet entertainment. You might have been shot or tied up and beaten to drive the devils out of you." I shook my head, thinking of all the different prejudiced, opinionated, dogmatic and downright mean-minded people she might have come in contact with first, rather than me. Not that I'm free of some neurotic quirks and beliefs with no foundation in fact; all of us have them, and some cultures are more subject to them than others, but

I did think I was relatively free of the most objectionable kinds. I said so and Jeri tried to nod with the very beginning of a neck separating her head from her trunk. So far it was just a little indentation at the base of the pyramid shape her trunk ascended into, where her brain resided, the same as in humans. The thought of human xenophobia didn't even cross my mind.

"I understand," she replied.

"Well," I started, remembering that I wanted to know a little of their history. "Did your species ever have religious beliefs or was there some other method your primitive ancestors evolved to reconcile their fear of the unknown and of death with their regular lives?" I asked.

"Kyle, I can't say. We have such lengthy lives now and have had for such an immeasurably long time that our cultural sense of history is different from yours. We pay much less attention to our past. Ordinarily, we go for long periods while considering subjects before ever acting, other than in an emergency, which of course I classify my present predicament as. To put it more simply, we have no reckoning of whether our species ever had religions or wars. We don't even know how far in the past we deciphered our genetic code and began altering it to our present protean nature, where we can modify our bodies in many different ways simply by using our perceptive sense to initiate and control the process."

No wars, no religions, and I suspected their civilization and culture weren't driven by their sexual nature as ours is, and that sex wasn't nearly as important a part of their lives as with us. They had evidently lost most of their genetic disposition for territorial control in the past as well, if they ever had one. They were truly alien in every sense of the word. Jeri was blank on the subject of history and sex, but very interested in my take on it.

"You think your territorial nature, the impulse to control domains, is the result of your sexual drive, then?"

"Probably," I nodded. "Or more likely the other way around, although very few of us will admit it since the territorial genes haven't been very well identified yet, nor the interrelated genes or environmental influences on them. The religious teachings ignore the obvious fact of our territorial nature when they preach peace and turning the other cheek and so forth." I had to explain that metaphor, and that led to more talk of religion.

"It's all very strange to me, Kyle. You do know that even when my human shape is complete, I'll still retain all my knowledge and beliefs and they'll be applied to the expression of my genes a human, even though my body may contain some contradictory genes, such as the religious ones, if I find it impossible to weed them out. Also, I may find that my actions and beliefs become at least partially subject to hormonal influence and other behavior dictated by the type of proteins some genes code for, just as I believe yours are. That might be the most difficult"

"How will that be possible to believe the opposite of what your genes dictate if—oh, I get it. You'll be like a blank slate in some ways. You may have the genes for lots of undesirable characteristics but they'll never have been subject to environmental modification in their expression. And vice versa. Whew! You're going to be like no other human in history. And that's probably going to cause both you and me problems when we go out in public." My mind was working as though I were outlining an article. It made me go into my lecture mode. "You'll have the look, but you're going to have to learn not only how to act like a human but how to act like a *female* human. In case you haven't figured it out yet, we're almost like separate species in many ways. Our brains don't function exactly alike; they even use the two hemispheres in dissimilar fashion, and that leads to different ways of viewing the world and interacting with others, particularly the opposite sex. Just as an example you've already run across, men are much more visually oriented than women, who are driven more by emotion and closeness. So far as sex goes anyway. That's why pornography is designed and produced much more for males than females and why sexual aberrations take such bizarre forms. Religion and sex and our separate sexual natures are all tangled together in relationships so complex we're probably still centuries away from even beginning to understand them."

"Yes," she said and again tried to nod, already attempting to mimic human mannerisms. "I'm beginning to see the enormous challenge this process will involve. You mentioned that you were married but your wife died in an accident. Since you've lived with a woman, I'm hoping that you'll be able to help me learn the human mannerisms associated with being female, the ones I can't discover from reading."

I stood up and walked around the room, suddenly realizing how little I actually knew about women. I tried to imagine myself as a woman and simply couldn't do it, not with any assurance of how I would feel. It was the age-old conundrum, Mars and Venus; we act one way, they act another, and both of us all too frequently misinterpret the other's intentions. Just as small examples of what I began imagining then, I wondered how I would feel, existing in a culture where almost a hundred percent of the other sex was twice as strong as me, where I would be the undersized one, where even such little things as how tightly jar caps were screwed on and how furniture was almost always made to fit men rather than women would be (or so I thought) constant irritants. How would I like it if my body and face were constantly being scrutinized while I was out in public, and an immediate judgment of my worth was being made on that basis? How would I feel if I had to sometimes act contrary to my nature in order to get along? Hell, I didn't even have a clue about what women talked about among themselves when they let their hair down.

I quit pacing amid all those thoughts and decided to have a drink and, for a change, a stiff one rather than coffee. It made me wonder whether Jeri's species used stimulants of any kind, but I put that aside for a moment while I poured some rum over ice and opened a Coke to dilute it. I brought it back over and sat down.

"Jeri, you're going to be surprised at how little I know about women. Christ, they even button their shirts opposite from men. I'll help you all I can, but you're simply going to have to get out in public, among women, and observe. Perhaps you should watch some television and chick flicks, too." It took her a moment to gather what I meant by "chick flicks."

"You speak as if your species have little interaction with the opposite sex, other than sex itself, yet from my perusal of text and literature, that appears not to be the case. Can you explain?"

"Uh, sure, it's, uh," I couldn't, not in a million years but I didn't tell her that. "I guess it's just that we're so different. Sure, we talk and work together and live together and love each other, but that still doesn't mean we understand our opposites. Shucks, we can't really get inside another male person's head, much less a woman's."

"I'm sure I'll learn but I'm certain to make mistakes along the way. Hopefully, they won't be too serious."

"As I said, I'll help you all I can but don't expect miracles."

"Good. We'll manage, I think."

I had no idea then, nor had I even considered, how much help Jeri would expect from me. For one thing, there were several periods during the transition where she had to concentrate so intensely that she went into an almost death-like comatose state. One lasted a full day as she prepared the human genome within her, and the other almost as long when she switched from her original to the human. She left instructions for me on how to care for her during those occasions, which she told me helped by not having to worry about her safety. She could have done it alone, but would have had to divert a portion of her attention to avoid becoming prey to interruptions which she said would hinder the process. I didn't quite understand that but let it go, thinking she must know what she was doing. If not, we were both in trouble!

I sipped at my drink and remembered the bottle was almost empty. There were other items I was getting low on, too. "Are you about ready to take that trip into town with me?"

"Yes. Actually, the sooner the better."

That suited me, too. I needed to get out and see some other humans just to assure myself I wasn't dreaming!

"Is there anything you need to take with you from your survival kit?"

"Anything I need, I'll carry."

"Good. It wouldn't do to have a suitcase trailing along behind you, propped up by air so far as I can tell. How did they know to follow you into the house, and for that matter, how do they work?"

"They're attuned to my perceptive sense and 'knew', so to speak, that I was in trouble and couldn't use my perceptiveness just then. As for how they work—let's just say some...magnetic repulsion is involved. We haven't built up enough of a technical vocabulary yet for me to really explain it."

"That's good enough for now," I said.

⅒⎄⅓

It turned out that I didn't need to conceal her under a blanket. The military was already working hard on that long-sought "invisibility cape" of legend and magic and was actually coming nearer to success all the time. Jeri's survival kit included one for just such purposes as intermingling with alien species should they have the need, or to observe alien life on the planets they explored. It wasn't a cape as such, though, but a little gadget about the size of my thumb she attached to one of the bands around her upper arm. She simply stuck it there and it clung as if by magnetic attraction. It was amazing to watch her seemingly blink into and out of existence as she turned it on and off to test it.

"That will work great," I said, then asked, "Is that thing very complicated?"

"It's far beyond your present technology."

And that made me wonder just how long her species had been civilized, but before I could ask I remembered she had told me already. She didn't know. And that created a nagging thought in the back of my mind that just wouldn't go away. I couldn't keep from thinking what an old history teacher of mine had drilled into me when I was in the eleventh grade in high school. He told us every single day that people who didn't know their history were doomed to repeat it. How could such an advanced civilization not know their history? And how did they manage not to recreate problems that they had solved in their past? It all sounded too, well, alien.

"Well, I hope none of your other people got captured and some of our enemies get hold of that thing. Or other gadgets you may have, too."

"It wouldn't work for anyone but a Cresperian, Kyle."

"Good. That reminds me, though. Have you any idea about what your companions might be doing? No contact yet?"

"None, other than I know some survived. Most likely, even if they were seen, they would have used their cloaking device and escaped capture once their lifeboat dissolved. On the other hand, they're likely to be doing the same as I, assuming human shape as rapidly as possible."

"Would they purposely try to find humans to help them?"

"I imagine so, after they learned enough of the local language to ask."

I could just picture what a spectacle that would be, a four-armed monster tapping someone on the shoulder and asking if they could assist it in turning into a human. They'd either faint, run screaming or try to shoot it. Or maybe they'd help. My expectations of humanity might be lower than reality.

Something was troubling me but I couldn't get it to come to the surface of my mind. Actually, there was a whole hell of a lot troubling me, but there was more still trying to form into real troubles in the recesses of my cerebrum. I made a mental bookmark to try thinking about it later, and began writing up a grocery list. While I was doing that, one of the things I'd been wondering about came to mind.

"Jeri, just curious, but why did you have to have a first-aid kit to repair your body if you can manipulate it to such an extent as to turn into a human? Couldn't you have fixed your injuries the same way?"

She tried laughing but it didn't come out well. Not human enough yet. "I could have, if I hadn't been injured and taken a blow to the head that affected my perceptive sense for a while. In fact, I could have freed myself, too. The kits are designed to assist in cases like that—although this is the first I've known of them being used. In fact, ours is the first spacecraft that's ever been lost, to my knowledge. If by chance I ever return home, I must tell the designers about the dissolving process of the lifeboat trying to do the same to me!"

That was my first indication that they weren't omniscient. Somehow, it made me feel better.

୫୦୦୫

My home was located up in northeastern Arkansas in the thinly populated Ozark Mountains, near some little towns with the picturesque names of Ash Flat, Evening Shade and such. The county seat was Hatfield. The Strawberry River wasn't too far away. Since moving there, I've driven through the mountains occasionally to try relaxing but I found you have to pay too much attention to the traffic on the winding, up and down roads to think about much else.

Jeri was astounded at how I could maneuver the old Hummer all by myself, as she put it. All their conveyances at home were automatic, she told me. Talking to what looked to be empty air beside me as I drove was so strange at first that I kept wanting to reach over and assure myself there was really someone beside me, but after a while I got used to it. I took us to Hatfield, the nearest town with a super Wal-Mart, a pretty fair drive from home. I wanted to give Jeri a chance to see a lot of human activity from up close. She asked if she could go into the store with me but I suggested it wait until she was human. I did roll the windows halfway down so she could hear the conversation as people passed back and forth and get an idea of what other people talked about in the normal course of their affairs.

Jeri had told me that she'd soon begin taking earth food, although only small amounts at first. I had neglected shopping since she arrived, so I had a larger than usual list, including a greater variety of food than I normally bought. And looking to the future, I thought I'd get both the junior and regular size of tampons for her to take care of that problem, just in case she hadn't thought of it yet. I had to just take wild guesses when it came to buying clothes for her. I felt downright ashamed that I couldn't even use Gwen's sizes as a guide, because I didn't *know* any of them, which goes to show how much attention men pay to things like that. Anyway, all the clothing was just to give her a start. She'd select her own after becoming completely human, but the whole episode certainly made me think of what a state of affairs it is when men don't know things that basic about women, even ones they've been close to.

I got back to the Hummer just in time. My mind must have been in park or even sound asleep for me to leave the window open with no passenger to be seen inside. It was an open invitation to theft and two sleazy-looking characters were already attempting to equalize the wealth, one acting as a lookout while the other obviously had some means he thought would get the hummer started. He already had an arm inside and as I watched he flipped the locks open and slid into the driver's seat.

"Hey, you son of a bitch!" I yelled as loud as I could, cursing myself for not bringing the pistol I was licensed to carry with me. Once I'd gotten the permit I packed it for a while, feeling like a wild west cowboy, then started getting careless. I might as well have saved the money I'd spent for the permit for all the good it was doing me the first time I needed it. I abandoned the cart and began running as best I could toward the car and stopped a few feet away from the young, rotten-toothed, anorexic idiot trying to steal the Hummer. The rotten teeth and frail figure along with the wild stare in his bloodshot eyes told me that he was a meth-head. The homemade drug had become so damned prevalent across the country that us law abiding citizens could no longer buy nasal decongestants at the local pharmacy. The idiots were using it in their home factories so much so that they had been buying them in large quantities. So instead of cracking down on the druggies, us law-abiding citizens could no longer buy decongestants with pseudoephedrine in them anywhere. If you got a sinus cold, then you were damned to some newer version of a medicine that you couldn't make meth out of. And that newer stuff didn't work for me at all. Goddamned junkie bastards.

"Back-off, gramps," he said, turning a rotten-toothed snarl towards me. He flashed a multi-tool pocket knife in his right hand.

"Hold on there, sonny. I don't want any problems," I told him as I shifted my weight onto my good left leg in back with my good right arm forward.

"Give me the keys, old man, and nobody gets hurt." He continued to wave the little pocket knife side-to-side.

"You know what? You are so spaced out of your dumbass head that I don't think you could hurt me even if you tried. So, no. Get the fuck away from my car, you piece of methed-out shit." I taunted him just enough so that he made an angry and horribly off-balance lunge toward me.

I hopped sideways on my good leg just out of the way and grabbed a handful of his long, matted hair with my right hand. I used his forward motion and yanked him by the hair forward and down with all my strength. He did a wild off-balance face plant into the parking lot asphalt that probably broke his nose and some of those nasty teeth. The knife flew from his hand and skittered underneath an adjacent car. I kicked him in the side with my nearly worthless right leg to add to the insult.

Fortunately, the druggy was an idiot and his buddy was a coward. They were more interested in making a getaway than staying to fight. The man crawled up to his feet holding his bloody nose and they both ran away. Normally, I would probably have muttered something about how my tax dollars would end up paying for his hospital bill because I was certain he didn't have medical insurance. I'd probably have bitched about the fact that even though the sonofabitch couldn't pass a drug test or might be an illegal alien—that's right, alien, not immigrant—he would still get free health care at the emergency room paid for by Mr. and Mrs. Middle Class America. Normally, I'd have cussed about that and spat at them. But I quickly realized what I had just done and how plainly fucking stupid it was.

I didn't give chase. Hell, I couldn't give chase. Had they been more than dying, cowardly, meth-heads, I'd have been in trouble. I didn't think just how stupid I had been. My ego just wouldn't let me accept my permanent disability.

"Not sure what the hell I was thinking," is what I finally muttered to myself. "Good thing they ran." Then it hit me. "Jeri!" That's why I had faced them down. I was way more concerned for Jeri than for my own safety, and I sure didn't care to give chase just for the sake of corralling a couple of car thieves who were gonna die pretty soon from self-inflicted poisoning, anyway.

"Are you okay?" I asked and poked my head in the window.

She didn't reply and I thought for a moment she must have abandoned the vehicle when the man started to get inside. Instead, she had the good sense not to answer me because she noticed what I hadn't. A few male shoppers who had seen what was going on after I yelled came running to help. Another young man had pulled my cart out of the middle of the driving lane and now brought it to me. I could tell that one of the men was carrying a gun from the slight bulge under his left arm.

"Who are you talking to, Mister?" asked the young man pushing my shopping cart over to me.

I turned around with what must have been a very stupid look on my face, an expression that appears there all too often. It wasn't intentional, but for once it did some good instead of causing whispers about how retarded I am. That brainless stare managed to put over the first remark that came into my head.

"Oh. Those bastards flustered me so much I forgot that my wife didn't come with me this time. Thanks. I'm calming down and will be okay now. Seriously, thanks." I took my buggy back from him and started putting the groceries in the back seat. The men looked at me the way younger men look at older men who are getting senile, but I guess they decided I had just forgotten to take my meds that day, for they helped me unload my groceries and then they left.

"You take care of yourself, you hear?" one of the men said.

"You handled those two pretty good if you ask me," the one carrying the gun added.

"Thanks, gentlemen. I appreciate the help," I told them and smiled as they turned away. Then I rushed into the car, nervous that Jeri might have been scared out of her mind. Once into the driver's seat, I rolled up the window and said quietly, trying not to move my lips, "I'll explain in a minute."

"It's probably not necessary, Kyle. I believe I've had my first encounter with thieves. A strange process, one I'll have trouble adjusting to, I fear."

"Yeah, me too," I said shakily. By then I was pulling out of the parking lot and felt I could talk without attracting attention so long as we were moving and not stopped at a light next to anyone. "That was more unusual than you might think, Jeri. It's the first time in my life I've encountered thieves, other than during the war."

"Oh. I'm glad to hear it. I was afraid it might be more common than I had thought from my studies. You saw such things in a war? Were you an observer or a participant?"

"I was in the army."

She was quiet for a moment, then asked "By chance is that where your scars came from?"

"Yes," I admitted. "The one you've seen on my shoulder is from a bullet wound and the one above my eye from a little piece of shrapnel. I've got one on my hip, as well."

"Did you have to kill any of your fellow humans while you were in the army?"

"Here's a lesson for you, Jeri. Men and women who have been in combat generally don't talk much about it, and that question is something you just don't ask a veteran. However, in this case, you deserve an answer. Yes, I did have to kill other humans. I didn't enjoy it. Hardly any of us do, although there're always a few who seek it out. They're sometimes called psychopaths or sociopaths, though the definitions do differ. I prefer just to think of them as crazy bastards. Some psychologists say about five percent of the human race are utterly amoral. I suspect they're pretty close to right, and probably up to as much as twenty percent of humans have less than the normal ethical sense. Or maybe they were never properly taught ethics. I dunno."

We discussed that unfortunate aspect of behavior all the way home, but Jeri had a hard time understanding it. I told her my own thoughts about it, which were that most antisocial behavior is tied in with the survival instinct somehow and that environmental influences have altered the way the genes are expressed. I also admitted I might be wrong, even in my contention that the true psychopaths are simply born that way or their brain is wired in such a way that the psychopathic behavior is inevitable. But then again, a perfectly healthy baby could be tormented on a regular basis until it formed into an adult that was nothing short of shithouse rat crazy.

She was quiet for a while, then finally said "Kyle, it's become obvious to me that my species altered our genetic makeup so far back in our history that there's no way of knowing whether we were ever subject to such behavior. For certain, I have a difficult time grasping all the aspects of human culture I'll have to adjust to while living among you. However, I still believe becoming human is my best option. I'll simply have to learn as rapidly as possible."

Again I assured her I'd help, and I meant it. It was just that my idiot self still hadn't figured out how she was intending to learn. I didn't doubt for a minute how quickly she could absorb information, though. She could read almost as fast as she could change pages on the net and remembered virtually everything. The big problem for her was resolving all the contradictory views that differed according to which authority or pundit espoused them and that appeared to change as often as my unneutered cat used to have kittens before I had sense enough to let a vet take care of it. Bobo had been in the car with Gwen, on her way to be neutered, when she died, along with the cat. But I'd managed to bring two of the kittens with me. The ungrateful things went native as soon as they got here and haven't let me pet them since. I see them from time to time and hear them out behind the shed. I fully expect to see more of them in the future because one of them was female.

Once I turned onto our lane, Jeri dispensed with the invisibility cloak and put it away. It was a mistake, but I wasn't expecting company, either. Who would believe their eyes if they saw us, anyway?

Chapter Four

There's a sharp curve in the gravel lane just before my home comes into sight. It is well hidden from the blacktop county road by the pines, and the area of the curve is grown up with brush and young saplings. A person in a car is practically on my doorstep before he sees the house, which is why the driveway curves around it, making a complete circle. I had no desire for a vehicle to join me at the dinner table some evening. The UPS truck was stopped in back of the house and the driver had gotten out to come to the door but been distracted by the gouge in the earth and the broken pine limbs caused by Jeri's lifeboat when it crashed. She turned around as I slammed on the brakes and stopped the Hummer just before hitting her truck.

I saw her raise her arms and open her mouth to scream. At first I thought it was because of how close I came to having a mashed UPS truck cluttering up the backyard. Then I remembered Jeri. I turned, intending to tell her to get invisible quick. She vanished before I had a chance to say anything. The woman closed her mouth with the scream unuttered.

When I got out of the Hummer and began walking toward her, she shrank away from me, a fearful expression distorting her pretty young face.

I stopped walking and did my best to play the innocent, putting concern in my voice. "What's wrong? Are you in pain?"

"Uh, uh…" She was still staring at the passenger seat of my Hummer. "What on earth is that thing in the car with you?"

"Thing? What thing? What are you talking about?"

"I saw a…a monster in there. Don't tell me I didn't. It's still in there!"

"Ma'am, I don't know what you're talking about. Monster?"

"I saw it!"

Acting like a patient parent trying to soothe a confused child, I walked back to the Hummer and opened all four doors and the end gate.

She brushed her hair back and very cautiously approached, peering inside from every angle, then circling the vehicle to be sure she had seen every nook and cranny. I waited on her to satisfy herself there was no monster hiding inside, but damned if I know what I would have done if she'd started feeling around on the passenger seat. Fortunately, she let what looked like empty space do her thinking for her. "I…I'm sorry. I must have been hallucinating or dozed off while standing up for a second and had a nightmare."

"No problem," I assured her. "Are you tired?"

"Well, yes. I didn't get much sleep last night." A faint blush suffused her face as she spoke, giving me a pretty good idea of the reason for her lack of sleep.

"You need to be careful driving, then. You sure don't want to fall asleep at the wheel."

"No. I'll be careful, thanks."

"Did you have something for me?"

"Huh?" The blush that had been fading reappeared. "Oh. Sorry. I really am out of it today. I'd better drink some more coffee. I keep a thermos in the van."

I was glad she said that or I would have felt obligated to offer her some. She brought me the package, some books I had ordered. I signed for it and she drove slowly away. As she turned the corner of the house I saw her shaking her head. She looked back once at the disturbed earth and then was gone.

"It's okay now, Jeri. She won't be back and we'll hear if anyone else comes up."

"I'm sorry. I overlooked the fact that you might have visitors."

"No problem. It's a rare thing, but I should have warned you, anyway. However, we'd better be careful from now on, just in case. Any time we're outside, use that gadget of yours, at least until you look human. How long will it be?"

"Another three weeks or so, now that I've perceived females, but remember, Kyle, I won't just look human. I will *be* human in every aspect other than my previous knowledge and having a perceptive sense. Of course, an X-ray machine would notice something like a small tumor residing in my abdominal cavity, where I'll retain a biomass containing the core of my present abilities and genome of my former self. Would you like some help with the articles you bought?"

"Sure. Give me a hand and I'll let you help me put 'em up, too, so you can see where everything goes. You're going to have to learn at least the simpler aspects of cooking. It's still expected of women, even in this country, the most sexually liberated in the world."

We discussed the meaning of sexual liberation, while bringing in the groceries. She'd been thinking sexual liberation referred to sex alone, just another in the long string of things she'd have to learn or unlearn despite the tremendous amount of knowledge she was accumulating. It made me feel like I was in the presence of an *idiot savant* at times.

ଃଠଓଃ

As the days passed, her lower set of arms shrank into nubs and finally disappeared entirely. The indentation grew into a definite neck and the beginning of a waist was forming. Her sleek pelt was also being absorbed and her color beneath was fading from the light lime green to tan, which she assured me would become even lighter.

She also continued to do without sleep, absorbing huge quantities of data while I was dreaming away. I found that she was able to divide her attention, perusing the net while leaving the television on. Mostly she watched news to help with understanding what she was learning (though I was doubtful about the utility of that) or talk shows to see how humans interacted. I was damned glad Jerry Springer wasn't around any longer or I really would have had some explaining to do. If she watched shows like that, I might wind up with a bipolar, overweight lesbian, sleeping with her father and brother at the same time as she was having a secret affair with a polygamous man who had a toenail fetish. Well, you get the idea. I advised her to stay away from that kind of drivel until she had a better grasp of normal behavior, or as normal as we contrary humans ever get. To my dismay, she did seem to be involved in several daily soap operas. She had found something on the web about women and entertainment and began observing the oldest female stereotypical action around. She was, for all intents and purposes, hooked on soaps, but I don't know whether it was because she read that they were watched mostly by women and wanted to do what they did or if she was truly interested. I advised her not to interpret them as the model of normal everyday life, and left her to them.

She also learned to record everything, and then erase all but the items she liked to question me about. That included commercials, which gave me a hard time explaining, but eventually we got through their relationship to the economy. And that led to discussions on capitalism and so on—that was how things went on in my house for a while. One morning she seemed concerned about something she had seen. It was clear she wanted my opinion on it.

"Kyle, I'd like you to look at something I saw on the news last night."

"Sure. Let me get some coffee going and I'll be right with you." Stimulants were something else her species didn't use, which made sense if their brains were already stabilized to work at their most efficient level.

Besides, I assumed they could probably have used their perceptive sense to get high had they cared to.

I sat down on the couch and Jeri joined me there after first running her hands against the back of her thighs to smooth out the robe she had begun wearing a couple of days before. She found the segment she wanted quickly and started it running. It was one of the fifteen minute "in depth" specials that were becoming popular with those more interested in expanding their mind than being entertained with the pabulum most programming resembled.

The announcer was a pretty blonde, the norm for most news readers. She was getting to the age where she would probably be replaced and would move into higher realms of journalism before long, which was a shame because she was good at her job.

The story was from South Georgia, where news of a "monster" sighting had previously been ignored, but now a sharp little investigative journalist had needled out the fact that it was being "ignored" because of pressure from political sources.

The reports of the apparition suddenly stopped after a conference with Admiral Jones and Senator Trehan, the Democrat from Georgia, assured the press that there was no cover up. It was explained that what was seen was not a monster, but a field test of "flexible armor" of a new type. However, Janice Forliter and her daughter Caroline swear the thing was no soldier and that they definitely didn't see any armor. Others questioned about the sightings agree with them.

Further investigation revealed that some unexplained electronic interference in a military AWACS plane, the type used for controlling wide areas of combat at sea or in the air, occurred shortly before reports of monster sightings began. The military definitely scrambled a squadron of Raptor all weather fighter bombers at that time, but we were told by a military spokesman it was simply the result of a combat exercise and in no way connected to the electronic static. A source tells us the interference seen on their radar was of a type never before encountered.

The special continued on to the end without divulging much more hard data, but what we saw was evidence enough for both of us. I guess I can mention that the Admiral and Senator were both investigated over the affair. Their roles were suspicious, especially considering the Admiral was in procurement and the Senator had accepted heavy political contributions from a certain tycoon, but nothing was proven. Not then.

"I think the military or a security agency must have captured at least one of your people, Jeri."

"That was my interpretation, too. Will they be mistreated, do you think?"

"It'll probably depend on which agency gets final control, but I suspect your friend or friends will never see daylight again."

"How do you mean?"

"They'll never be freed unless they manage to escape by themselves. What I'm worried about is how much they'll tell whoever has them. Will they spill the beans about the rest of you?"

"Hmm." She had heard that expression before. "It's hard to say." Her face was beginning to take on some human expressions now. She looked sad, I thought. "As I learn, I'm beginning to see just how fortunate I was in landing near you. They'll be subject to mendacity, having never encountered it before. And I suspect they allowed themselves to be taken into custody by listening to misinformation, if what you say about the authorities is right."

"Oh, it's right. Any of the intelligence agencies or the military would love to get their hands on you or another one like you. Believe me on this."

More bad news. And at last that little nagging notion I hadn't been able to bring to the surface of my mind finally emerged.

"Jeri, just how much are you people susceptible to mendacity, as you put it, although it's more commonly called lying? For instance, suppose one of you comes in contact with a fundamentalist Christian first. Could they be subject to proselytizing? Or could the military convince them they ought to divulge every bit of technical knowledge they possess?"

She had to think for a moment. Again, I believed her partly-human face was expressing sadness.

"Kyle, I don't know for certain. None of us have ever been in this type of situation before," that you know of, I thought but said nothing, "and you have to remember that even though we're the same species, we're still individuals, and as individuals, we'll each do what we think is best for us. I'm sure the others will consider how their actions will impact on the rest of us, but they can't possibly know what's the right thing to do at first. Fortunately, most of us are what you might call conservative in thought, so, hopefully, we'll all keep quiet about some things. But again, I'm guessing. If I knew which of us survived, I could be more helpful, but unfortunately, I have no way of knowing. There were some other relative youngsters aboard and I believe if any deviant action occurs it will be among our group. We haven't lived long enough yet to always be able to judge matters as ably as the older ones." She appeared to consider what she'd said, then amended it slightly. "I have to admit that a small number of the young ones I knew well might, if they survived, go in almost any direction under the right, or perhaps I should say the wrong, circumstances."

I'd already had some vague thoughts on the subject, but now I began to seriously consider the idea of some kind of identification for Jeri. Even after she looked completely human, she was going to have to have an ID if the authorities got a hint of anything else unusual out here. We'd have to do a lot of explaining about her presence without it, but with some really good papers, as convincing as possible, we might be able to sidetrack them rather than having to run. These days it's not easy to get lost. I had only one pertinent question. "Jeri, are long periods being cloaked by your gadget uncomfortable in any way?"

"If it's kept working extensively, the power source will eventually wind down but it will last for hundreds of hours, minimum. And yes, after several hours, any of us would have a need to turn it off for a time. It has an oppressing effect if used constantly."

"Okay. I had to ask, because we need to take a trip." I explained the need for personal identification and eventually got it over. It was a subject we hadn't covered yet.

Not only did I need some ID for her, but it had to be unchallengeable. The most common, almost foolproof, method is to take the identity of a child who had died who would, at the present time, have been about the same age as the person as an adult, then build a background from there. Even that wouldn't produce an unbreakable cover, not if the authorities really bore down hard. Just the fact that you had to construct a complete life history entailed a lot of risks. The best way was to find some parents who had lived in out-of-the-way places, then died, and the child was placed in foster care, and subsequently died. Or, find parents who had worked overseas. The better the ID, the more expensive it was going to be, but I wanted the best. Fortunately, my work in the 902nd Military Intelligence Group, "the Deuce" we called it, before I was wounded and discharged, gave me a lot of knowledge and contacts. Also fortunately, I could afford the best, which meant hiring a trusted hacker to break into a lot of government and municipal data storage sites, then create the identity almost from scratch, and make it seem as if the new person has had few social contacts.

Even the name I had given her, Jeri, would be easy to fix, if I gave her an identity where she had been "adopted." All this involved the trip I asked her about. It was an occasion where the contacts had to be made in person, because e-mail is so easy to trace, and this in turn meant a trip to Little Rock, the nearest city where I could have it all done.

I debated with myself over whether we dared to wait until her transformation was complete. Finally I decided it was best to get it done now, then remain in Little Rock somewhere at a cheap motel until she was fully human. That way, I could explain to anyone who asked that we had met there, fallen in love and decided to live together until we were sure we wanted to get married. Not that I ever intended to marry Jeri even if she did turn out to look human. Marry an alien? Sex with an alien? Forget it. That was for books, not real life. I pushed the subject aside, not sure why I was even thinking about it, but all too frequently my mind goes off on tangents like that. Besides, we needed to get packed and get gone.

∞∞

Jeri said she was only ten days or so from completing her transition, so I had her bring the clothes I'd bought for her, along with the two robes I'd also bought to make do with until then. That was just in case this took longer than I thought it would. It had been a number of years since I had dealt with the Little Rock underground and my old contacts might no longer be active. I also had to round up some money, in cash. Fortunately, with the financial situation like it was in America, where an overwhelming debt load and atrocious balance of trade had been building for years, a lot of my money was in gold and silver now, in a safe deposit box in Little Rock, where Gwen and I had lived before I sold out and bought this place. While we were packing, I told Jeri how I was planning on creating the ID for her, another idea that was foreign to her. She hadn't quite understood when I'd mentioned it before, since Cresperians never concealed their identities from one another. Their perceptive sense meant that no disguise was possible and they had no desire for subterfuge anyway. "Jeri, do you have a pretty good idea of what you're going to look like in the face once your transition's done?"

"Oh, yes. Here, I'll show you." She pulled down the old *Playboy* we had looked at and pointed to one of the side photos of the centerfold girl.

Wavy auburn hair reaching below the shoulders, what looked like hazel eyes although the color had faded a bit over the years, and a classically pretty face, with even features and a gorgeous smile.

I hated to destroy the value of the old magazine, so I packed it with my other luggage rather than cutting out the photo. I didn't trust my ability enough with digital manipulation to try making a facsimile.

After it cooled off that evening, I got out and did what I should have already taken care of—getting rid of that furrow in the ground beneath the pines. I leveled it out with the little tractor I'd bought, then used a chain saw to cut the limbs into smaller pieces. I carried them a good distance away, then scattered them about. The stark white of the broken limbs in the trees was already fading and the breaks could always be attributed to some high winds we'd experienced before Jeri's arrival. With that out of the way, I got a quick shower while she did the same, and we were ready. In her original form, her pelt had been pretty well self-cleaning but now she was washing every few days. She could have taken care of accumulations on her skin with the power of her perceptive sense but it turned out she liked the feel of a hot shower. I suggested we turn in for a few hours' sleep before the trip and she agreed. She was also beginning to require a little sleep as her brain became more human and needed to dream, and her body had to eliminate fatigue poisons, just as ours do. She did mention that she thought she'd never require nearly as much sleep as humans, though. That perceptive sense again. I was starting to get the impression it was all-powerful, which it wasn't. Eventually she set me straight on what it could and couldn't do, but the knowledge came in bits and pieces rather than all at once.

We left the next morning.

Chapter Five

The distance to Little Rock, the capital of Arkansas, wasn't that far as the crow flies, but it took most of the day to get there on the secondary roads I had to use almost all the way just because my place was so isolated. I stopped fairly frequently at deserted spots along the road to let Jeri get out from under her cloak now and then. I also decided there was nothing wrong with staying at a decent motel. With Holiday Inn, at least you know what to expect, and they usually have double beds. I brought along a notebook computer so Jeri could study at night while I slept.

The only real problems were being careful not to let anyone trip over Jeri and giving her a chance to eat, but she said fast food would do her as well as anything, so that's what we lived on mostly. Her human taste buds obviously weren't well developed yet.

I slept the first night. Then I left Jeri alone in the room while I ventured out to see if any of my old contacts were still around. I found one, Mack the Knife he was called. I know that was extremely cliché, but I didn't name him. I found Mack in the same old haunt where he'd been doing business for years and years. He recognized me but didn't let on. I gave him the high sign, had a quick beer and left. A few minutes later he followed me outside and over to my car, a big sedan and damn global warming. I liked the protection a big car offered in case of an accident and had taken it rather than the Hummer, which was a little uncomfortable on long trips. In the meantime I wished I'd bought tinted windshields so Jeri didn't have to stay cloaked so much. I quit thinking about it soon enough because I know it's an exercise in futility to wish you'd done something different in the past. The butterfly effect might have changed things in ways you'd never imagine and you'd be worse off, not better.

I unlocked the car and slid into the driver's seat while Mackie took the other side.

"Long time, Kyle. What's up?"

"I need a top grade ID, female, about twenty years old. Here's what she looks like." I raised the console lid and took out the Playboy and showed him what I wanted.

"She looks just like this?"

"Close enough not to matter."

"Top grade, huh?"

"Absolutely. Something that can't be broken under any circumstances you can think of."

"Whew," Mackie whistled softly. I'd never gone that far with him before. "No dead baby, huh?"

"Right. Or if you just have to go that way, make damn sure you cover the background right from the start."

He rubbed his chin and scratched his head. "You still married?"

"No. My wife died almost a year ago."

"Okay. Sorry to hear it, but that makes it easier. How about we bring you an Albanian bride? Their record keeping is still chaotic. It won't take much to build a background for her. The big expense is faking the passport and flight to here, but it can be done. I'll fix up a history at one of those singles match sites that offer European brides. I'll need your email address and your comp password so I can go in and put a history of your e-mail back and forth on it. And I'll need this magazine and one of your credit cards. What do you want to call her?"

"I've been calling her Jeri. J-E-R-I. The last name doesn't matter."

"Good deal. There's bound to be a first name that you'd automatically shorten to that. You're sure you don't want me to take a pic? It would match exactly."

"Sorry. There are reasons."

He shrugged and quoted me a price that merely made me bite my tongue rather than threaten him with ten different kinds of mayhem, then asked, "How soon?"

"As quick as you can," I told him.

"Okay. Records will show she'll arrive in a couple of days with a six-week visa. Get yourself married before it expires, then notify the state department and immigration service. Better still, just let me know when and where, and I'll do it. It won't cost much more and it's safer that way."

Mackie never made idle promises. I asked him if he'd take gold and he grinned. "You shitting me? Of course I will. Our paper is heading for the bottom of the ocean if the goddamned politicians don't get off their fat asses and do something."

"Don't hold your breath. They're all too busy feathering their own nests to worry about anyone else."

"Motherfuckers. Ought to all be shot. Every goddamned one of 'em."

Mackie seldom curses, which should give you an idea of how strongly he endorsed the idea. I couldn't disagree that much myself. I rate most politicians right up there with skunks in the obnoxious department and I don't think they can help it any more than lawyers can resist overbilling their clients when working by the hour. There's just something about elective office that corrupts the soul of anyone who stays with it past one term, and most of the time it doesn't even take that long. Maybe a person has to have the kind of character, or lack of character, that draws them to politics in the first place. Hell, I don't know. All I can say for sure is that most of them are some of the sorriest bastards on earth. Maybe they started out with good intentions and maybe they didn't. One thing for certain is that they can rationalize their behavior to almost unbelievable lengths of self-deception while screwing the people who elected them.

Mackie asked where I was staying. I gave him my room number and he said he'd call when the goods were ready. "Just hang around your room every morning and evening between seven and eight so I won't miss you."

ഇൗരു

When I told Jeri what I had done, she gave me a smile that looked gruesome on her still-forming face. It was all I could do not to flinch.

"It sounds as if you've taken care of everything. When will we get married?"

That's when it hit me. I actually *was* going to be caught up in that old science fiction cliché "I Married an Alien." I almost laughed out loud but managed to hold it back for fear of hurting her feelings. Of course, it would be a marriage in name only and I could always arrange for a divorce after she got her citizenship. Her voice made me realize I had been spaced out with the thought of us being wed.

"Some time in the next six weeks," I said. "That ought to keep the men in the black coats out of our hair. Do you want to go walk around or have me bring you something back for supper?"

"Let's walk. The more human contact I have, the better."

We crossed the parking lot, stepped over a concrete divider and were in a small shopping mall, the kind with individual stores laid out on three sides of a square with sidewalks in front. It was late afternoon by then and the shoppers were out. Jeri had to step lively a couple of times to avoid being run into. She waited outside while I bought some junk food at a little convenience store on the next block, then we walked back. I purposely moved slowly so she could do a lot of observing. I guess we shouldn't have tried it. A kid loose from his parents came running along the sidewalk from behind us and hit Jeri in the legs. I didn't see it, of course, but she tumbled to the ground and momentarily lost the concentration necessary to keep her cloaking device active. For five long seconds she was visible, while the kid began screaming like a berserk banshee. I was used to her but I can just imagine what others must have thought when they saw her partly human appearance. A terrible accident. A genetic disease that turned a human into a cross between an animal and something out of Star Trek. No telling what else they might have imagined but it couldn't have been very complimentary.

There were gasps of surprise when she appeared and cries of shock when she vanished again. All I could do was act like I hadn't seen anything and tell bystanders of my conviction. Others hadn't noticed either, so before long an argument ensued between those who'd seen her and the ones who hadn't. It allowed me to slip away and trust Jeri to follow. She did, easily.

Once in my car she apologized profusely. "I'm sorry, Kyle. I shouldn't have slipped like that, but it was such a startling event I couldn't help it."

"I don't think it matters. The crowd was pretty confused by the time we left and I doubt anyone will remember my face." At least that's what I hoped, but we decided then and there to take no more chances until she looked altogether human.

ʊᏨ

One evening three days later there was a knock on our door. I opened it cautiously, thinking it might be a maid, even though it was late for the cleaning crew.

It was Mackie. "I've got your papers," he said. He handed me a large brown envelope and quickly walked away. I closed the door behind him and brought the envelope over to see what we had. He had done his usual thorough job, even to receipts for the plane ticket and a charge for gas at a station near the airport to indicate I had really gone there to pick her up. He also left some instructions for us. I read through them.

"Jeri, you've already been practicing the Albanian language. How're you coming along?"

"Fine. I'll be able to read and speak by tomorrow, although I'm sure I'll have an accent, not having an Albanian to converse with."

That phenomenal memory. She could learn the basics of a language overnight but it took her a bit longer to get the slang and idioms down. "Shucks, that's good. Now you need to learn to speak English with what you imagine an Albanian accent might be like if you can manage that."

"I can try. Is it really necessary to be so thorough?"

"You bet it is. I know how some of the NSA gets information from prisoners and damned if I want either of us to go through that."

She didn't say anything but I knew she was troubled by the thought of torture. Of all the concepts she tried to understand about humans, that was one of the hardest. It was so foreign to her people as to be comparable to deliberate cannibalism for me. Unthinkable, yet she had to consider the possibility.

"You do understand what I mean, don't you?"

"Yes, Kyle, theoretically, I do, but practically, no. It's too barbaric to comprehend. I suspect that if it were tried on any of us we would either terminate our lives or go into a depressive state so deep it might become permanent. Of course, that assumes our original shape."

"How about if you or some of the others have taken a human form, like you're doing?"

"I believe the core of our abilities I mentioned would still allow termination, though the depression might not happen, or happen differently."

I left it at that. And I still hadn't gotten around to asking just what her perceptive abilities consisted of, other than being able to read at roughly the speed of light, and not only having an eidetic memory, but being able to comprehend what she read, barring cultural differences—but that covered a multitude of sins and allowed plenty of room for mistakes. I knew she'd make them and I knew I could do only so much to prevent them. I just had to hope any blunders we made didn't get our heads chopped off. I decided we'd be better off back home until she was completely human. Besides, I was sick of fast food and living in a single hotel room.

80G3

Once we were headed home, I asked her not to go outside until her transition was complete and I could take her out into the world. And get married, of course, though that would just be a formality, a means of allowing her to stay in the country. I mean, the actual consummation part might appeal to some weirdoes on the Internet or some overzealous trekkies, but I wasn't either of those.

I wanted to take a trip eastward and see if we could happen upon any others of her fellow survivors. She'd said she knew that at least one and possibly two lifeboats came down somewhere hundreds of miles east of us. That was probably Georgia, although that didn't mean a captured alien would still be in the vicinity. She said her perceptive sense could pick up the presence of another of her kind from a good distance (but not that far), though it wouldn't amount to any more than that. From very far away, she wouldn't be able to identify who they were, or even how many of them there were. I hadn't told her, but I also intended to start carrying my little S&W .40 caliber automatic, and hoped I could convince her to take some firearms training and be able to use at least a few of our basic pistols and rifles, even though she'd told me she had something of her own that was better. But no point in advertising them, I thought. When we left, I'd map out a route that took us only through states where concealed handgun permits were reciprocal. I hoped I'd never have to kill anyone again, but I didn't intend to see Jeri get hurt while she was still learning to act like a human, either. It would be nice if I could get her a concealed weapons permit but she'd have to apply for citizenship first.

"A trip with you sounds like a good idea, Kyle. I could see some more of your country and mix with many different kinds of people."

"You're going to have to be careful, Jeri. You'll have a very attractive female shape. Men will stare at you. Probably even some women. If you're by yourself, you might be approached in a sexual way, wedding ring or not."

"Is there a chance I might be assaulted?" The even tenor of her voice wavered for the first time at the possibility of being raped.

"For a woman, there's always that chance. It hasn't been all that long since women almost everywhere were little more than slaves, and still are in some parts of the world, especially in Muslim countries. And you have to remember that our species evolved with men as the dominant sex. It's still in our genes, even though most men today have grown up in an environment where the genes are expressed quite differently than they would have been thousands, or even hundreds, of years ago.

"It's a hard concept to grasp. I'm so grateful to you, Kyle. From my studies, you're apparently one of a small minority of your species that not only could accept an alien in your home, but do everything in your power to help her cope."

"You don't have to thank me, Jeri. Having you here is more interesting than anything else I could ever have hoped to run across the rest of my life. I'm the one who should be grateful." I didn't realize then just how interesting things were going to get! I was beginning to realize how depressed I had been in my self-imposed isolation, though. Looking back on it, I hadn't been suicidal at all, but I had been ready to give up on life being fun anymore. Jeri was almost like an angel dropping from the heavens to save my tortured soul. Oh, bullshit, I don't even believe in angels. I was bored and depressed and now I had something to take my mind off that and to keep life exciting.

೫೧೮

I spotted the intrusion the minute we drove up. There was a piece of crime scene tape across the entrance. When I got a little closer, I could see a business card attached to the tape. It belonged to the county sheriff. There was a little handwritten note on it. *Call me*, it read. I told Jeri to sit tight and pulled out my phone. It took a few minutes to get through to the sheriff, but he knew what I was talking about immediately.

"Uh huh. Mr. Leverson, a UPS driver reported a...well, a monster out at your place. She said it hid after she saw it in your car. Then when she told her boyfriend about it, he insisted on coming out to your place to see. She also said there had been a big hole by your house before and it had been covered up. And state records said you owned a car, but it was missing. Well, Mr. Leverson, I had to come out and take a look, just on the face of it."

"Sheriff Morrison, you had to break into my house because some crazy woman said she saw a fucking monster out here?" I raised my voice, putting as much indignation into it as possible.

"Mr. Leverson, when you weren't there and didn't return a call after I left a note on your door, I decided there was a chance of foul play, considering the hole and all." I glanced over to where I had leveled it out and saw it had been excavated again. I must have really been preoccupied not to have noticed it at once.

"Oh, hell," I gave a big sigh. "Sheriff, I think you went overboard, but never mind. I guess you were just doing your duty."

"Glad you feel that way. I'm going to be coming out to your neck of the woods this evening and I need to get your signature on my report, so don't go anywhere, okay?"

"Whatever." I treated him to another big sigh, as if disgusted at all the bureaucratic nonsense, but I judged there was no point in arguing. "I'll be here today, but I planned on going in to town later to get some stuff, so don't keep me waiting too long." The last was an impromptu lie, with no idea of why I'd told it. Nervousness, probably.

"Right. I won't," he said and hung up.

Jeri's acute hearing had picked up both sides of the conversation. "Is there going to be trouble?" she asked.

"Probably nothing we can't handle here, but it's sure going to screw up our cover story about your new identity. I can't think of a single reason why you wouldn't have come back with me, can you?'

"Of course not, Kyle. I'm not familiar enough with what you're attempting to be able to evaluate the situation. I simply trust you."

That was nice to know, but it wasn't going to help if the authorities got suspicious right now. There was no way to cover up that discrepancy, because the feds usually talked to the locals first before an investigation. When and if they came, and heard about a "Monster" at my place, it would all be over. I didn't see anything to do but return to Little Rock after the sheriff had come and gone and get Mackie to alter the records, and even that was risky. The sheriff was probably going to ask what I had been doing in Little Rock to begin with, much less why I was going back. "Let's get unpacked," I said. "I want a drink. And I need to think."

ଞଔଔ

Jeri was silent while we got things put away. Her change was far enough along now that she was using the other bedroom, the one where I had originally set up my office. I had planned on altering that when we returned, after getting the new computer I'd bought linked into my network. "Oh, shit!" I said aloud, and then apologized.

"What is it?"

"I hope your memory is as good as I think it is, because just to be on the safe side, I want you to eliminate all the sites you've been visiting from the comp records. Delete all your bookmarks and...no, crap. There's a bare possibility he uses a hacker and had him go into our computer. He'd notice the deletions if he asked to see what I've been doing since I got back. I'm probably being way too paranoid here, but believe me, Jeri, the more I think about it, the more I doubt there's a limit to how far the feds would go in trying to pry information out of an alien, especially if they know there's no help coming." I muttered an expletive I seldom use, then said, "I guess the best thing to do is play it by ear." I was talking as much to myself as to Jeri.

"Is there anything I can do to assist you, Kyle?"

I laughed. "Not unless you can hurry up your transition."

According to what she'd said, she still had a week to go, but I had noticed during our breaks on the way back that she was looking more and more human. Her hair was growing out and her body was well on the way to its final form. Most of that could be disguised, but her face still wouldn't pass.

"I can do it if necessary, if just the external changes will suffice. It will be rather painful, but I believe I can bear it."

"How about just the face and neck? Would that hurt you?"

"Not nearly as much."

"Okay, here's what we'll do. Get your face into its final form, then when the sheriff arrives, you get into bed and cover up and pretend to be sleeping. Your body will be fairly well concealed by the bedclothes, but rumple them up so he can't tell what your figure looks like. He may not even ask where I've been, but I think it's best to volunteer the information anyway so we'll be covered."

"May I leave the television screen on?"

"Sure. You can leave whatever you want to on and we'll pretend you fell asleep while watching. I'll tell him you have a real bad case of jet lag."

"And suppose he insists on questioning me?"

"Just use broken English and tell him what a nice man I am." I grinned.

Chapter Six

Fortunately, the sheriff got tied up and didn't arrive until the next morning. He did do me the courtesy of calling and telling me he'd be delayed until then, which spoke well of his professionalism, if nothing else. I still didn't see the need for me to sign anything, though. As with the UPS lady's boyfriend, I thought the talk of a monster had aroused his curiosity. Anything bizarre always attracts humans, like bears racing toward a new salmon run.

When I saw Jeri the next morning, I was amazed. Her face was perfectly human, and pretty as a hummingbird in the sunshine. In fact, sitting at the breakfast table in her robe, she could have been taken for human if she didn't stand and possibly even then, except for her body. The lumpiness under the robe didn't fit at all with the attention-grabbing face and hair, already shoulder length and a beautiful auburn color. The speeded up change must have taken a little out of her because her face looked drawn, just as a human's would have. It made a perfect match for the jet lag story.

I left some windows open both to air out the place after being gone and so I could hear the sheriff coming. We had just finished breakfast when the sound of a car pulling into the drive alerted Jeri. She heard it well before I did.

"That's your cue, Jeri. Into bed."

"Yes." She smiled at me and left. For some reason I still had an image of her face in my mind as I stepped outside. I waited on the porch as he approached.

"Mr. Leverson?"

"Sheriff?" I held out my hand. "Call me Kyle, please."

"All right. I'm Buddy Morrison, County Sheriff," he said as he shook my hand with a firm grip.

"Of course. Would you like to come in? I have some coffee, just brewed."

"That sounds fine." Unlike some of the big-bellied parodies of southern sheriffs, Morrison was tall and slim. He removed his hat as he entered the house, displaying totally white hair, incongruous over a face that didn't appear old enough to warrant it.

I poured coffee after asking him how he took it and we sat down at the kitchen table, almost a requirement for conducting business in the rural south.

"All right, Sheriff, now what can I do for you?" I was a little short with him intentionally, reinforcing my supposed exasperation at the incident of "the monster."

"It's like this, Kyle. Miz Moletta is well thought of in this neck of the woods. Nice, hardworking family woman, raising a little girl by herself and not given to hysterics. She swears she saw something horrible in your jeep, then it looked to her like it suddenly disappeared."

"How could that be? A disappearing monster? Come on!"

"Who knows?" He shrugged. "You mind telling me what that hole was for?"

"Humph," I plopped my hands down on the table, exasperated. My tone of voice became irritated as I tried to act like a normal person would if confronted with such a tale. "Yes, I do mind. I don't think it's anyone else's damn business, but I'll tell you anyway. I got tired of hauling my trash to the dump and decided I'd just bury it instead. Then after I had it dug, I got to thinking about it and decided it wasn't that good of an idea, after all. This is really a nice place. No point in burying a bunch of junk on it when it can go to the landfill. Hell, it's not that big a deal."

He nodded, unable to refute my logic. It *was* a troublesome chore and a good number of the locals did what I told him I had planned, if for no other reason than to avoid the yearly fee of sixty dollars for use of the county dump. I watched him sipping at his coffee as he thought it over. The only hole in my story, no pun intended, was that it looked more like something heavy had landed at an angle than what a person might have dug. Apparently he decided to let it pass because I could see from his expression he was considering his next question and how he was going to put it.

"I was looking around to see if there was any evidence of foul play while I was inside your house t'other day. There's a couple of odd-looking boxes you got in one of your bedrooms."

"So?"

"Don't guess they're big enough to hide a body, but all the same, I'd like to see them again, if you don't mind."

"There's someone in the bedroom sleeping. I'd rather not disturb her."

"Really?" he said, with a raised eyebrow. He took another sip of his coffee and patted his phone clipped to the top pocket of his shirt. "I guess I could call Judge Best and get a warrant to do a real search, but you could save some time 'n trouble if I just had a peek inside that room again."

"Damn it," I said. That UPS driver and her friend must have really laid it on thick. I stood up. "All right, come on, but you'll see they're just a new kind of European luggage designed to make it hard to get into if you don't know where the latch is. Try to be quiet. She's still got a bad case of jet lag. The only time she can sleep is mornings and early afternoons."

"I'll be quiet."

I led the way and eased the door open far enough to let him look inside. The sun lit the room well enough even through the curtains. Jeri was lying on her side facing the door in a sort of fetal position, her hair tousled and the sheet all wadded up on her in a rumpled mess. It did a good job of concealing her odd body shape. She must have practiced a bit while I slept. As we stood there, her eyes blinked open. She closed them then opened them again.

"It's okay, Jeri. Just a visitor."

"Sorry to disturb you, ma'am," the sheriff said.

"Is okay. I sleep wrong. Aeroflot noise make him." Her voice had a thick accent.

"Are you okay?"

"Am okay. Kyle nice man is him."

The sheriff backed out and I gently closed the door.

Back in the kitchen, we sat down again.

"Who's the lady? Sounds like a furriner."

"She just arrived from Albania. That's where I had gone when you came out before—to pick her up."

"She some kind of relative?"

"Uh, you might say that." I made an effort to look guilty. "She's here on a six-week visa. We're probably going to get married. That's if I think we can get along."

"I see," he said shaking his head knowingly. There were no flies on him. "One of those gals looking for a rich American, huh? You want to be careful. Some of them are prostitutes just looking for a way to stay in the country. You'd better have her checked for STDs."

"I had her checked by an agency. They were supposed to take care of all that. She's just a woman wanting an opportunity to better herself.

I've been lonely since my wife died and I'm not much for the single bars scene. Not much of a socializer either."

"Jerry? With a R R Y or an R I?" He asked how her name was spelled.

"R I," I gave him the one we had picked out. He wrote it in a little notebook and allowed a lazy smile to cross his face as he rose, preparing to go.

"Good luck, then. Sorry to've bothered you."

We had little else to say to each other as I walked him outside. When he reached out to shake hands I reinforced my story, doing my best to act as if I was embarrassed. "Sheriff, I'd appreciate it if you'd, uh, keep this to yourself. It's no one else's business, after all, and before my wife died I'd never have thought I would do something like this in a zillion years. It's just so damned lonely these days."

"Do my best," he said ambiguously. He tipped his hat and slid into his patrol car. A moment later he was gone. Either he had forgotten that he told me he had forms for me to sign or had just used that as an excuse to investigate. I strongly suspected the latter. And he hadn't mentioned Jeri's survival kits again, either, so I guessed he thought they weren't important enough to bother with. If there's a force watching over us, it was surely with us then. But, of course, I don't believe in such things.

I had no earthly idea what I'd have done if Morrison hadn't been distracted by Jeri and decided to check those "peculiar cases." I might have tried to explain they were some newfangled suitcases I'd lost the key to, but I doubted it would have gotten by him. He was no dummy, not by a long shot.

I didn't know whether or not he'd keep my affairs under that white Stetson of his. Maybe he would. He wouldn't last long in office if he made a practice of gossiping, not in this part of the country. On the other hand, I fully expected him to check and see if Jeri really did have a visa. In the age of terrorism, a new foreigner with an accent was automatically suspicious, especially arriving less than a year after Gwen's death, and visiting a newcomer to the area as well.

As I walked back to the house I suddenly realized I had thought very little about Gwen since Jeri arrived. It made me feel truly guilty, not just the play-acting I had done with Morrison. It's funny how you can be so broken-hearted you think you'll never get over it, and then find that your emotions are fading, even though the past memories are intact. I guess it's a survival trait. I know it's not healthy to grieve for long periods or you begin living in the past.

Jeri heard the sheriff driving off and was waiting on me at the door. She still had that jet lag appearance on her face. I wondered why but she told me before I could ask.

"Now I know what it is to lie, Kyle. I don't care much for it."

"Don't worry about it." Despite her appearance below the neck I gave her a comforting hug. "But you see where it's necessary on occasion?"

"Yes, but..."

"I know. It's not something you've ever done. I'm sorry, Jeri, but you'll just have to get used to it. We couldn't function as a society without a certain amount of mendacity. Some of it's meant as a kindness, like not telling a friend he's stupid for believing in astrology, for instance. Or when a person desperately needs their job to support a family, they aren't going to tell the truth to the boss when his wife is wearing a dress that makes her look like a whore and he asks you whether you like it as much as he does. Telling the truth all the time just isn't possible. When it's done to spare someone's feelings, to keep them from being hurt, it's called a 'white lie'. It's all part of our culture even if it isn't talked about that much."

"It's still wrong to lie deliberately for no good reason, isn't it?"

"I think so. Some businessmen might disagree. A lot of them think anything they say or do to make a sale or get a contract is legitimate business, but I personally believe they're wrong. As the old adage goes, man is not a rational animal; he is a *rationalizing* animal. Our brains are wired somehow to rationalize a hell of a lot of behavior we wouldn't even consider if we thought about it logically. Hormones and our sex drives play a part in that, as well as our territorial instinct. I guess what I'm trying to say is that in the long run, if you always try to be as truthful as you can without upsetting people's apple carts, you won't go too far wrong."

"You said it's not talked about. You must be right because I don't find many references to it in entertainment or popular culture articles, other than surveys."

"Lying isn't the only thing we don't talk about. Do Cresperians daydream? Or have you begun daydreaming as a human yet?"

For the first time, I saw her blush. It wasn't much, probably because all her internal changes weren't complete, but it was there. She started to reply but I held up my hand to stop her.

"Don't tell me about it," I advised gently. "Everyone daydreams and some of the dreams are really wild, but no one talks about the subject. If we all suddenly confessed to what we've daydreamed about over the last week, our whole civilization would probably collapse." I chuckled, thinking I had hit on a not too obvious truth. "Come on, let's get inside and have a drink and I'll tell you a story."

While I was pouring a shot of bourbon over ice for myself and a glass of wine for Jeri, I began talking. "Okay, the story goes like this. I was at a party once with Gwen. There must have been, oh, maybe twenty or thirty people and we were playing a game, each of us asking the rest of the group a question about human behavior and trying to stump them. When it came my turn, I asked, 'What is an activity that we all spend a significant part of our waking lives doing but no one ever talks about, not even to their spouses or lovers?' Know what? Not a single person got the answer right. No one thought of daydreams, even though we all spend a lot of time doing it, because we never talk about daydreams to anyone else. Never, even if they're perfectly innocent and not about sex or violence of being a hero or poking an obnoxious boss in the nose."

"How curious."

"Isn't it? But we're a damn weird species, or at least I think so. You'll just have to get used to it."

∞∞

Jeri's changes progressed rapidly after that. A few days later she was looking entirely human. She had dispensed with the robe and was dressed in jeans and t-shirt when I came into the kitchen to brew my morning coffee. She had told me the day before that there were still a few changes going on internally but even those would be finished by the end of the week. They were out of sight, and mostly had to do with adjusting and fine-tuning her prioperceptive senses, the ones that take care of those thousands of little automatic movements we make without having to think about them, and putting the finishing touches on her immune system so she wouldn't have to spend so much time using her perceptive sense combating diseases. From what she had told me up until then, with her running a human body, it wouldn't be susceptible to illnesses. No colds, no genetic diseases, no cancer. For the first time I had a real view of the woman I was now living with. And what a view. It was enough to wake me up without my usual morning coffee.

"Good morning, Jeri," I greeted her. "You look good in clothes." I averted my eyes from her bust. She hadn't put on a bra and the t-shirt was a light-weight summer cotton. Her nipples were partially erect and clearly limned against the fabric.

"Thank you, Kyle. I made the coffee already."

"Huh?" I said, very intelligently. Sure enough, it was already in the carafe where I kept it hot through the mornings. I drink a lot of coffee. I poured a cup, then thought of her. "Would you like to try some?"

"Um, yes, but not much. Remember, while my external body is completely human now, my taste buds aren't quite ready for some things." I could understand that. A lot of food and beverages we eat or drink are acquired tastes and differ tremendously according to ethnic groups, cultural habits and so forth.

"Here." I poured a half cup and handed it to her. "Just drink what you want. I take mine black but you may like cream or sugar. Many people do."

I was feeling distinctly uncomfortable. Jeri had constructed an extremely attractive female body, just judging from what I could see, but I had no doubt that beneath her clothing she would look pretty much like the model from the magazine. I hadn't lived with any woman other than Gwen, although my experience wasn't limited to her. We'd married after I'd been in the army several years and had decided to take the commission I was offered and make a career of it. We moved down to Fort Rucker, Alabama, where I went to Warrant Officer Candidate School. Then I did the Warrant Officer Basic Course at Fort Huachuca, Arizona, and from there was moved back to Huntsville, Alabama, with the 902nd Counter Intelligence Group. I was away a lot even then. Before long I was promoted up to a Chief Warrant Officer Two (CW2) and then I got promoted to CW3 just before I was wounded. We had five years together after my medical discharge and she had just gotten pregnant when she was killed. They were happy years, too. Once we married, I barely looked at other women. She was all I wanted and then some. Pretty, intelligent, a great figure, and a career of her own, not just an adjunct of my own life. She was a book editor, which was how I met her, at a science convention she was attending to get a feel for a science book she was editing. And it was her who made the approach. She was too regal-looking for me to even think about making a pass at her.

I shook the old memories out of my mind and took my coffee over to the big lounger in the den, just as I normally did. I liked to have several cups before breakfast. She followed me and sat down, curling one leg under her and sitting half turned toward me just as a normal woman might have. It stretched her t-shirt tight, causing me to avert my gaze again. Damn. I knew right then that I hadn't correctly anticipated how much her face and body would appeal to me. Or any other halfway normal man, for that matter, despite her alien origin.

"You're being very quiet this morning," she commented.

I looked at her. Even without makeup, something I'd neglected to buy, she was disquietingly pretty, on the verge of beautiful. This was going to take some getting used to.

"I'm sorry. You're so good-looking that it's distracting me, but it's all right. I'll get used to it." I looked at her bust again. "Did I get the wrong size bra?"

She laughed, a pleasant-sounding tinkle. "I don't think so, but I found it a little uncomfortable. I think I probably need to have you help me adjust it." I realized that to her it was a perfectly innocent request, and that she didn't yet understand how much men are visually oriented in sexual matters despite my explanations back when she'd first run across pornography on the net. I didn't even know if men were attractive to her as a female human now. Theoretically they should be, but she was a blank slate. However, hormones should take care of that problem to some extent, I thought. I didn't know yet just how much she would be affected.

For a moment I wondered why she would have had problems with the bra, then thought of how girls start practicing wearing one even before they've properly begun to develop breasts. But helping her? I felt a twinge in my groin, then remembered her original appearance and it deflated. Still...

"Maybe you need to have a bra fitting done by a professional, except I doubt we could find one closer than Little Rock."

"You couldn't help me? I think the cup size is okay, it's the straps giving me trouble." She was fast losing her formal English and picking up my way of speaking.

"I could try but...Jeri, remember you look exactly like a very attractive woman. I couldn't help but, uh..." I floundered, as embarrassed as I'd been the first time a girl allowed me the opportunity to unhook her bra and I couldn't manage it.

"Good." She smiled sweetly. "I was hoping I'd have that effect on you. I believe my hormones are already near their proper level."

That took care of my wondering how men affected her. Of course, I was the only man she'd known yet. I was in pretty good shape, but I wasn't all that handsome to begin with. The best that can be said is that Gwen told me I caught female glances because my face had the characteristics of an adventurer or a pirate, whatever that meant. My premature gray hair made me look older than my years. People seeing us together were going to think she was my daughter or I was her sugar daddy, or perhaps had gotten me a trophy wife. Or so my thoughts went then.

"Whoa," I said. "We're going to be living together, but I didn't intend for you to, uh, feel that way." Me and my big mouth. It got me into trouble more often than I like to admit.

She looked stricken, already using appropriate facial expressions without having to think about it. I wondered if this one was real or just for effect. She quickly set me straight.

"You didn't? But…" For the first time since her arrival, I saw her at a loss for words.

"Jeri, remember you're an *alien*." That got her going again.

"No, Kyle, that's no longer true. I'm a human *woman*, or will be within a few…a few more days." She seemed to be having trouble getting the words out. There was a tremor to her voice that made me hurt inside to hear until she got it under control. Then she explained. "I'm going to be as human as you are. The alien part of me will be reserved for necessary adjustment of my human aspect, allowing me to make the very most of this body. And for defense if it becomes necessary, of course." A faint shudder coursed through her body at the thought but it was quickly stilled. "And of course my perceptive sense remains intact, but I already know I have to be careful about when and how I use it."

"You see? You're still an alien at heart. How could I…" Again I floundered. I felt a blush suffuse my face.

"Why, Kyle, I do believe you're embarrassed."

"Maybe so, but…never mind. Let me think about this. Okay?"

"Certainly, although I must admit, I thought you were going to help me in every way you could. I see now that perhaps I was assuming too much."

The look on her face was so pitiful it would have evoked sympathy from a sociopath. I saw wetness forming in her eyelashes. Oh, Damn. Tears already. I always was a sucker for tears.

"Jeri, please, wait. Don't judge me too harshly. I'll still help, but think of what you looked like before. I still have that image in my mind, even though now you're such a knockout you could stop Adonis in his tracks."

"You think?" She knew the reference. Again she smiled. I'm a sucker for smiles, too. "Then maybe you'll grow used to me like this?"

"Maybe. No, cancel that." I stared frankly at her, letting my eyes rove over the length of her body. Of course I'd get used to her. Whether or not I'd want to go any further than that was still problematic. I tried to convince myself of that but I don't think I fooled my subconscious even a little bit. "Yes, I'll get used to you. That's how the human mind works. And I promise I'll help you through the learning process as much as I'm able to, but how about we wait a few days on the bra. You don't really need to wear one around the house, anyway." I thought that took care of the problem, but then she threw me a curve.

"All right. But Kyle, won't we still have to get married in order for me to stay in the country?" She gave me a hopeful look, her eyes practically begging me to agree.

I guess I could have arranged for Mackie to fake that part of her background as easily as he had done the rest of it, but the look in her eyes held me back. And just because we "married" didn't mean it would have to be consummated.

"Yep, we'll still go through with it."

"Oh, wonderful!" She leaned forward and kissed me on the cheek, then waited to see how I'd react. I had to grin. She must have done a hell of a lot of reading and observing on television and the net already. I began to wonder just how much help she was going to need, then remembered what a neophyte she was as a human, much less a woman. There were a million little things about behavior she was going to have to learn, not only theoretically, but the actual practice.

I poured myself more coffee. It had become a morning ritual, me having my two cups before breakfast while she turned off the comp so it wouldn't distract me while we talked. She could still split her attention easily, which was going to either get her in trouble or help her adjust; I wasn't sure which.

"How do your clothes fit otherwise, not counting the bra?" I asked, more to have something to say than anything. I was still discomfited by her appearance and assumptions on our future relationship.

"The panties are too large and I think the jeans are too tight. I had trouble getting them on."

"Stand up for me and let me look."

She did, and I had to agree. They fit her like the proverbial glove, only tighter. "If they're uncomfortable, why don't you put on something else? We'll go shopping soon as you're ready and let you try on some different things and get what's right for you."

"But I don't know what's right!"

"Oh, yeah. Well, you're so pretty that anything you wear short of a tent is going to make you look sexy, so you sure don't have to force that part of it. Besides, we'll go into one of the little towns near here that has sort of a general store and they don't mind assisting customers. I've talked to one of the sales ladies a few times. She seems pretty nice, so I'll ask her to help with selecting. How does that sound?"

"Good, but don't you want to have a say?"

"Sure." I nodded. "You can show me as you try things on. It's not something a male normally does, but we can make an exception for you."

I was getting to like her smile. It was sort of a cross between little girl and sultry seductress. She was going to have to learn to be careful how she dispensed it, but I was sure she'd learn. She had told me she'd still retain her phenomenal memory and ability to absorb and comprehend tremendous amounts of knowledge, by our standards. It was perfectly normal where she came from; she was just adjusting her human brain to have the same capacity, aided by her perceptive sense. It wasn't even giving her human brain new powers. Some people here and there have eidetic memories but scientists still aren't sure how they work. Just like some autistics have fantastic powers of concentration that are a puzzle. She'd be able to teach us a lot if we ever got into a position where she could.

"Time for breakfast," I said, draining my cup and standing up.

"Let me help. You said I had to learn."

"Okay. D'you want to change first?"

"Please."

I couldn't help watching as she retreated to her room. I don't think that motion which always catches the male eye was intentionally exaggerated on her part, but with those ultra-tight jeans it sure as hell drew my attention to her ass. I couldn't tear my eyes away until she closed the door behind her. What in hell had I gotten myself into? Whatever, I could just imagine how I'd feel if I were stranded a jillion miles from home, among a wildly different species, with no way to ever get back. It must be devastating to her, even if she had concealed it well.

Chapter Seven

She came back wearing the same t-shirt but had disposed of the jeans and put on a pair of shorts. Her long slim legs were as attractive as the rest of her. I found myself wondering what she would look like in a skimpy bikini and felt a surge in my groin. Damn, I was going to have to be careful around her.

"Do those feel better?" I said, forcing my gaze up from her legs to her face.

"Much better, but now it's just the opposite. The shorts are a little large."

"Which size did you put on?" I had bought sizes, but had forgotten which was which.

"Oh, I didn't look."

"Then the other pair will be either much too large or just about right, but don't bother changing again right now. I don't know about you, but I'm hungry."

It turned out that Jeri had been very observant as I was cooking, while I thought her attention was on the kitchen wall screen. She knew the details of what to get out and how to prepare bacon and eggs over easy with toast, but when she tried to transfer the eggs to a napkin to soak up some of the butter they were fried in she broke both yolks.

"Don't worry about it," I chuckled. "I'd hate to tell you how many I broke before I got the technique down. Let's try again and let me do it. I'll talk my way through it as you observe."

"Won't the bacon get cold?"

I covered the saucer where she'd put the bacon on a napkin on a plate, again to soak up grease, with another plate.

"Simple," I said. "There's lots of little techniques like that you'll have to learn and some of them you'll have to experiment with by yourself. Gwen did most of the cooking."

"Do you miss her a lot?"

"Of course I do. We were married almost ten years and I loved her deeply."

"What…" She pulled up on whatever she was going to ask but I pretty much guessed what she'd intended to say.

"You'll find that intense emotions associated with memorable events fade rapidly with time, although the memories themselves remain intact."

"I suspected as much. I think I'd better use the next week or so to peruse more of what's been written about the psychology of human beings."

The eggs were ready again. I talked her through transferring them to the napkin, then said, "Just be careful, Jeri. Psychology and psychiatry are far from being exact sciences and there's damn near as many theories as there are practitioners or professors."

"I'd gathered that much, but you have a very succinct way of putting it; much better than I could have done." She laughed, her amusement demonstrating how she was already developing a sense of humor.

"You'll learn," I said. That little phrase was already becoming tediously repetitive, but it seemed to always reassure her, so I kept using it. "Now let's eat. That bacon smell always gets my juices flowing."

&O&&

Three days later, Jeri announced that her internal changes were complete and that she was ready to go shopping for new clothes and "feminine" things.

"Okay, may as well get you started intermingling. We'll go this afternoon, if that's okay. Why don't we sit down and I'll help you make a list?"

"You can just tell me. I won't forget."

"I'm sure, but lists help me remember and stay organized."

By the time we were finished, I was not only flabbergasted but chagrined over how little I'd ever thought about women's necessities for everyday living.

The first thing on the list was tampons, even though I'd already bought some. She'd probably seen them but I wanted her to get used to keeping a supply.

"I saw the ones you bought, and I tried one this morning even though I haven't had a period yet. My first one should start in a few days."

"Did it, uh, work out all right?" This was a subject that embarrassed a lot of men, me included, mainly because it simply wasn't talked about much between men and women, even married ones.

"Yes. I'll use the junior for now, I think. Once I start having sex, it might change, but I'll have to wait and see."

I didn't comment but that settled one question in my mind. She intended to be a woman in every sense of the word, and I strongly suspected I was going to be the object of her first experiments, if she had anything to say about it. Oh hell, no suspecting about it. I knew she'd want to try it with me first. I pushed the thought away for the time being. Then I looked at her tits again.

"I've read where women can now limit the number of their periods or eliminate them completely, but I'm going to have my first two, just to be certain I have my body regulated correctly. Besides, I need to experience what every other woman has gone through."

"You'll need to see a doctor and get a prescription," I told her.

"Yes. That won't be a problem, will it?"

"I'll give you the name of one of the local doctors, but eventually you'll probably want to find a gynecologist. That can wait a little while, though. Let's move on."

Makeup. I had as little knowledge of the stuff a woman uses, and how she applies it, as I did of what women talk about when they go to a restroom together. When Jeri asked for my advice about lipstick, all I could tell her is that I didn't care for the bright reds or the exotic colors some of the teens were wearing, but with her auburn hair she'd probably want something slightly darker than pink.

She gave that tinkling laugh again. "Kyle, from what I've read, the names of lipstick colors don't match regular colors. I'll never be able to figure them out by the descriptions."

I remembered once Gwen had asked me to pick her up a tube of "French Gloss" and I didn't even know she was asking for lipstick!

"Oh, yeah. Well, I'll still have to let you handle the makeup, because I don't know beans about it."

"I've seen several makeover shows on television that explain the basics of makeup. I think I can handle it, really." She smiled that smile again. "Clothes and shoes are going to be a bigger problem, I think. From what I've seen of style shows compared to what women wear in net videos or photos or on television, I don't think I want anything I've seen modeled on a catwalk."

I breathed a sigh of relief, because I knew exactly what she meant. One of my big chuckles every week was looking at the style section of the newspaper and what was being touted. I've yet to see a woman out in public wearing anything as bizarre as most of those creations. It's a complete mystery to me why they even bother showing them.

"There I can help," I said. "Gwen said I had good taste in women's clothing. Let's just make a list of all we think you'll need to start with, and after we pick them, you'll probably be able to manage in the future."

"Right now I'm doubtful, but go ahead."

We started with undergarments first. Since I knew little about sizes, and remembered Gwen telling me once that you can't depend on size labels with women's clothes anyway, all I could do was tell her what I liked.

"You can take your pick of bras of just about any type. I think the bras and panties are usually matched by color but I wouldn't bet the farm on it. Hip hugger panties, but not too skimpy. Maybe you should start with front closure bras and a few with the hooks in back so you can get used to them."

She nodded, and I went on describing my taste in several styles of nighties, robes, gowns, slippers, casual outfits and so on and suggesting how many of each she might want. From there we went on to clothing for spring, for evening (it still got kind of cool at night this high up), and for summer, both casual and dressy. By the time fall rolled around, she ought to be able to handle the selections herself. We settled on a wardrobe for the time being, including several items I wouldn't have thought of if she hadn't mentioned them. It got to be fun, sitting with her on the couch and picking out clothes for her. I found myself laughing and smiling with her, just as if she were a normal woman who'd recently arrived from the boondocks of Europe.

All the time, she left the big screen in the living room going on a news program I liked as well as she did. It covered state, national and world news and concentrated on events normal people like me were interested in. I guess I'm normal, although from the frequency I'd heard television programs and movies discussed when Gwen and I socialized, sometimes I doubted it. My tastes were eclectic but didn't run to the currently popular entertainment, either in movies, music or TV programming. I had suggested Jeri watch some of it so she'd have an idea of what our popular culture was like. I was amused when it turned out that she enjoyed the soaps and do-it-yourself programs. Like me, she had little use for the typical prime time shows.

From clothes we went to shoes. I advised her to stay away from real high heels, but otherwise suit herself. It seemed to me that she was more the athletic shoe type, or at least that is what she kept picking out on ebay. She added pantyhose for dressy and then we got into jewelry, which led to piercing of ears. I would have done that for her except I wasn't real sure where the hole in the earlobe should go. "A beauty shop can do that for you, though."

"Have you forgotten? I'm changing my whole body. Surely I can manage a couple of little holes in my earlobes." She laughed merrily. I joined her, while confessing I hadn't even thought of her doing the piercing herself.

Uh oh. Mention of a beauty shop caused us to stray from jewelry and into shampoo, lotions, soaps, oils and other things I couldn't help with, but then it segued into the subject of body hair and the American aversion to it on women other than on the head and the pubic area. And from modern pornography it looked like hair on the pubic area was removed or kept to a minimum, too, although I told her to do what was comfortable and still let her look good in a bikini. Lucky girl. She wouldn't have to shave; she could just use her perceptive sense to rid herself of unwanted body hair—and keep it gone. Nevertheless, she put a lady's razor on the list. She was determined to have the same experiences as a normal woman, just so she could take part in a conversation without giving herself away.

Whew! By this time it was already well past noon. I recommended that we postpone the trip until the next day because we still weren't finished with the list yet.

"And how about a break for a snack? Something light and a glass of wine?"

"I've been anticipating that, Kyle. It seems to be a common mood enhancer, other than in Muslim countries, and if I've interpreted what I've read correctly, there's a good deal of use even in those places."

"You're right, but humans are big hypocrites where religion is concerned," I said, as we got up and began making sandwiches. Or rather Jeri insisted on preparing them, while I opened a bottle of White Zinfandel. We brought the snacks and wine back to the couch.

Jeri sipped tentatively at the wine. I watched her closely. At first, she made a slight nose wriggle but she seemed to accept it after that.

"What do you think?"

"I think it must be like what I said about other food and beverages—an acquired taste."

"Right. And most people drink liquor of any type much more for the buzz than the taste." Good thing I didn't try to start her off with beer.

"Do you enjoy the…buzz?"

"Buzz, high, euphoria, whatever you call it; yes, I do. I don't care to take it too far, although I'll confess I've done so on more than a few occasions, especially when I was younger."

"Producing a hangover, I take it?" She grinned like a little elf at me.

"Right. Unless you become a problem drinker, it doesn't take too many of those to learn your limit."

"I think I could negate the effects on myself, but I'm afraid I couldn't help anyone else."

"If you could, you'd make a fortune, quick."

"Ah, that," she said sheepishly, and suddenly frowned. "Kyle, it just occurred to me that you're planning on spending a great deal of money on me. Can I help you with the expenses?"

"It's really not much considering what I'm worth, Jeri. Anyway, you have no way to earn money yet and I'd rather you didn't try. It's too much of a risk right now."

"So I'll be a kept woman until we marry?" That smile again. It was damn near irresistible, yet behind it lay real mirth. I didn't know about her little fabricator yet.

I returned the smile, although I was serious. "Don't look at it that way. I'd do the same thing whether you'd become human or not. You're fascinating."

"As an alien or as a human or as a human female?"

I opened my mouth, then closed it again. She waited demurely for me to answer. Damn it, the whole situation was becoming much more complicated than I'd ever imagined, and I was already learning she wasn't one to mince words. Finally I gave what I thought was the correct answer.

"Eh, all of them, I guess. I have to admit it's fun and likely to get more so, watching you learn to act like a woman. Don't get aggravated if I laugh at you sometimes."

"I wouldn't. Not ever." I'm not sure she liked my answer, though. I think she was hoping I'd emphasize the human female angle more than the others. She went on, "My survival equipment includes a small fabricator. I could duplicate as much money as you need. Or even make gold, but that would use up its power rather quickly."

Naturally I declined her offer, and furthermore gave her a short lecture on the penalties for counterfeiting. I finished my sandwich and glass of Zinfandel. I poured more for myself and raised my brows at her. She knew what the gesture meant.

"Yes, I think so. The effects are curiously pleasant."

"You bet," I said, grinning. "Just don't get carried away. This stuff sneaks up on you. It also lowers inhibitions and alters your judgment." It took her a moment to interpret the slang in the middle of the sentence.

"I'll be careful, but from what I've learned about spirits, I thought it also lowered reaction speed as well."

"Yes, it does, but not all that much, not until you really get a load on. That's just one out of a horde of so-called facts that most people think are true but aren't. What it does do is affect your judgment and you take longer to make up your mind."

She nodded reflectively, and I knew she'd learned one more peculiarity about humans. Then she asked, "Shall we continue with our shopping list?"

"Sure. Where were we?"

"Jewelry, I think."

She was just being polite; she probably remembered our conversation perfectly.

"Okay. Just a hint, though. These days gold and diamonds are likely to get you robbed if you're not careful."

"I could probably sense an evil intent from a person nearby and avoid it."

That brought on another change of subject for a while. I asked, "Just what does your perceptive sense entail? Can you explain how it works in terms I can understand?"

"No. I'm sorry, Kyle, but it would be like you trying to explain colors to someone blind from birth. The best I can do is…" She paused to think a moment. "Let me put it this way. The universe is made up of something. Only a few of your scientists, as far as I can tell, have begun to accept that the actual space between things is not just a vacuum. Your quantum vacuum fluctuations, or zero point energy as I've seen it called, are close to what is actually there. Everything in the universe consists of an amalgam or a convoluted superposition of these spacetime fluctuations. One day, when your scientists and mathematicians get smart enough, they will be able to describe everything as a multi-dimensional tensor of these energy waves superimposed on each other and coupled through these different dimensions to generate what is perceived by you in the four dimensions humanity can detect."

"Uh, I'm not a physicist, but that sounds a lot like string theory."

"Well, it is more like a combination of your quantum membrane theory, general relativity, and polarizable vacuum theories. But none of those are quite correct, either."

"Hmm, I never heard of polarizable vacuum theory," I replied.

"It's kind of esoteric and not really the point, anyway." She giggled a bit and continued. "Way back when we began rearranging our genetic structure, we learned how to attune to these quantum vacuum energy fluctuations and how to understand the immensely convolved waveforms. From there we developed our sensory system, which not only detects the process, but can manipulate it in certain ways. It is by manipulation of spacetime on this scale that we can rearrange atoms and even atomic structure, but that takes some doing. Of course, we no longer have a history of the discoveries and I have no idea how long it took us to figure all this out. That's one area of human culture I really admire, the yearning to understand and retain the facts of your evolution and past civilizations."

Well, her finding something to admire about us as a species made me feel better, but I was still floored. I mean that almost literally. I damn near fell off the couch, I was so excited. I don't even pretend to understand quantum mechanics, beyond having just enough general knowledge to write intelligently about it. The math is way beyond me. And the damned theory is so counterintuitive to normal thought that even Einstein had trouble believing it at first. "God doesn't play dice with the universe" is the way I think he put it.

She gave me a moment to recover before she continued. "I can tell you some of the things I can do with our perceptive sense as a human, if that will help."

"Sure. This should be interesting," I replied—about as inadequate a statement as I've ever uttered.

Chapter Eight

I didn't know how fascinating it was until she began rattling off the things she could do that a normal human couldn't. And after hearing them I was just as excited as a schoolboy, but a little bit apprehensive as well. What if some of her buddies that survived and crashed around the world became whackos and used the enhancements against us?

"I have enhanced hearing and sight. I'll be able to see in the dark, although it isn't really seeing. I can't be knocked off my feet easily, although a blow to the head could render me unconscious. My reactions are at the optimum of a human body, which would put them somewhere near what your elite athletes can accomplish, and I can go well beyond that by using my perceptive sense. I can use it to alter the genetic constituents of my chromosomes, and have already done so to a certain extent. My perceptive sense can operate at the molecular level, although I can't tell you exactly how it works, because it's become so instinctive. For instance, I noticed that it's entirely possible to greatly slow and perhaps even halt the aging process in my human body completely. I can..."

"Whoa," I stopped her right there. "Jeri, let me warn you now. Don't ever let that knowledge get out. The one universal fear shared by humans everywhere is the onset of aging and death. If you ever come under the control of a government, or even some corporations or wealthy individuals, it's likely your body would be torn to bits while you're still living, if you couldn't explain how you do it."

"Oh, my! I knew biologists and geneticists were actively seeking the cause of the aging process, but I had no idea such strong feelings were associated with it. My studies have most humans assuming they'll have an afterlife."

"Where do you think the religious idea of an afterlife came from?" I remembered the thoughts that ran through my mind when I'd first learned of her long lifespan and related them to her right then, vocally, even the story of my Dad's death, then continued, "I firmly believe religion was invented to compensate for fear of death, and fear of the unknown, pure and simple. If you can explain how to prolong life, the best thing to do would be to disseminate it to the world right now, even though I doubt we're ready yet to deal with such a boon intelligently." Even before meeting Jeri, I've sometimes had doubts over whether we're really a sapient species or not. Most of the time I give us the benefit of the doubt, but some days I think it's a tossup.

"I don't think I can explain, Kyle, at least not yet and probably not for a long time to come, if ever. I don't have the words to describe how I do it with my perceptive sense. Besides, even if I did know how to explain it, you might not have the scientific and mathematic background to follow. Perhaps we can work on that, but it's going to be difficult. Our species has become so accustomed to controlling the inner workings of our bodies and nearby objects that it's almost at an instinctive level by now."

I looked at her and realized I was already coming to think of her as a human rather than an alien. Almost immediately, I felt a bitter resentment beginning to build up inside me at her potential immortality. It must have shown on my face, because she suddenly moved closer and put her arms around me and pulled me to her. I resisted for a moment, then held her while my body shook with the realization that I was holding an age-less woman in my arms, one who would still look much the same while I grew old and died. That, to me, was still alien. So many thoughts were competing for my attention that I couldn't speak. Lyle dying after suffer-ing such a horrible, lingering illness, followed so closely by that drunken driver killing Gwen, had made me realize all too clearly our vulnerability to death, whether it comes early or late in life. Nothing mattered but the fact that we *died*, damn it all to hell. I'd never live long enough to see real space flight, to learn how the great religious upheavals taking place would turn out, or even whether we'd survive as a species. I wanted so much to see where we humans would go in the future, how much we'd learn. I'd never know if our species would realize its great potential or waste itself in a useless spate of wars over all that religious crap.

And for all the biologists' and geneticists' talk of how far they'd ad-vanced in anti-senility research, it wasn't likely to come in time to help me, and possibly it wouldn't happen at all, not only because of the distinct possibility of nuclear warfare but because it was so complicated. Death is built into every creature on earth. We've all *evolved* like that, and it was going to take a hell of a lot of doing to unravel two or three billion years of genetic programming. Crap. I know most people my age don't think that much about dying, and youngsters hardly at all—they think they're immortal—but I knew older ones did, from talking to Mom and Dad and knowing how much they hated aging and losing their youth and vitality. And some of my older friends felt exactly the same way, despite their professed religion. Besides, I had been beside good friends in the military when bullets and explosions chewed their bodies to mush, so I'd seen more of it up close than most people.

I think Jeri murmured some soothing platitudes while she held me. I think I may have even cried. Hell, I know I did. At any rate, when I finally came back to my senses my face was wet and my vision was blurred with tears.

ಶುಲ್ಕ

"Kyle, please, it's not that bad," I heard her saying some interminable time later.

I drew away and looked her in the eye, unable to curb my emotional resentment even then. "I'll get old and wrinkled and feeble and die while you'll still be young. Tell me what's good about *that*, damn it."

"Give me time and I'm sure I can use my perceptive sense on anyone I know really well and remain close to, like you. I'll be able to alter their body just as I do mine. It wouldn't be an immediate process because I'd have to institute repairs as well as new processes in your body, but I see no real reason why I couldn't do it, over a period of time."

My heart was suddenly thudding in my chest like a runaway drum, going a mile a minute. I had never realized how close to the surface of our minds the fear of death lies, not until I suddenly ran through that gamut of emotion, first thinking Jeri had the secret most people would kill for, and then hearing her tell me she could grant it to me.

"You said it would be a long process. How long?"

"As much as a year, but that's the upper limit. As we're becoming so close, I think it could be much less. Is that okay?"

I lost all comprehension of events again for a while. I swear, I've never been on such an emotional roller coaster in my life, not even when Lyle and Gwen died. I came back to reality and found I was wiping away tears and emptying the last of the wine into our glasses. Jeri was still sitting beside me, her hand on my other arm.

"Hmph," I drooped my head and turned smiling weakly at her. "My reaction doesn't say much for our species, does it, Jeri?"

"How can I tell, Kyle? I have no conception of what it's like to fear death. We live so long that most of us eventually tire of our existence and terminate it."

"Just how old are you?" I took two big gulps of wine, taking my glass down by half.

"Me? Oh, I'm a youngster by our standards, only a few years past two hundred."

Only a little past two hundred? God, even that much extra lifespan was enough to start wars, and if it came to light, a hunt for the aliens would make the search for the perpetrators of the smallpox outbreak on the east coast a few years ago pale by comparison.

"Please don't dislike me for this, Kyle. It's something we're born with. I feel sure that given enough time, I or one of the others will solve the problem of giving a long life to everyone rather than just individuals, like you." She squeezed my arm.

"Me?" I said, like a perfect dummy. I had gone senseless when she said something about applying her abilities for my benefit, and was still reeling, not truly able to comprehend it.

"Of course. My husband? How could I not? I couldn't stand for you to grow old while I stayed young. I'll begin the process very soon, within a week or so; there're only a few of the genetic mechanisms left to unravel. That's with your permission, of course."

"Thank you," I said quietly. "Start anytime you're ready." My head was still swirling. It made me want something stronger to drink than the wine, but right then I wanted to keep my mind clear. I'd already had three glasses of Zinfandel. Come to think of it, Jeri had had two. I wondered how it was affecting her. "How do you feel after the wine?" I asked.

"It's rather pleasant, in a strange way. I feel...very good. Elated." She hesitated, but continued. "When I look at you I have a desire to be close to you, in an amorous manner, I think. It's like the emotion was described in studies, but experiencing it is an entirely different thing, just as I understand that reading about sexual relations gives a person very little preparation for the actual event." We had certainly strayed a long way from our shopping list!

"I think I've told you before that reading about humans and women and being a human woman are two different things."

"You have, but I think I understand it better now. Intense emotions in particular are of that nature. Like my reaction to your dismay at the potential difference in our life spans. I felt a sensation akin to pain, yet it wasn't painful in a physical sense. And now I'm feeling...elated, I guess is the term, since you agreed to let me work on stopping the aging process of your body. It's all very strange and like nothing any of our species ever experiences. I think we have as much to learn from you as you do from us. I only hope that someday I can return home with you and pass this information on."

Well, shucks, I hoped that too, but right now I was more concerned with our personal relationship. Did she care that much for me already, enough that it upset her when she thought I had been hurt because of her? And what were my feelings toward her now? I knew I was over-joyed at the thought of a long life and I could sense an attraction to her that I hadn't consciously realized was there until now. But was her gift to me coloring my emotions? I just didn't know, not yet. The whole scenario of an alien turning into a human woman and becoming close to me, and me to her, was so bizarre that there wasn't anything to compare it to. It was like being adrift in a trackless ocean. I did what I could to explain it to her, and probably made a botch of the job, but I did get over to her that emotional pain among humans was sometimes much worse than mere physical hurt. If we weren't able to eventually distance ourselves from it, we'd go insane. Upsetting emotions made many of us act like we were crazy, anyway.

"Well, I'm awfully glad I can make amends to you this time."

"Ha," I laughed, a bit hysterically. "Believe me, you've more than made up for it."

80C8

After a while we got back to the shopping list. It kept growing. Hand mirror, curlers, and I didn't have a clue as to the kind she'd need with her long hair, but she could ask the beauty shop lady when she got around to it. Douche equipment, the little version like Gwen used, I thought. Combs, brushes, deodorant and perfume, a couple of purses, a couple of wallets to go in them, nail polish, and new toothbrushes to replace the old one of mine she'd started to use. Innumerable other items, and even after neither of us could think of anything else, I felt sure we'd overlooked some necessity or other, and most likely a whole other batch of things she'd want but we hadn't thought of yet.

Whoops! Back to jewelry. Necklaces, bracelets, earrings and so on. A watch, if she wanted one. I knew I'd feel lost without my own, but Jeri probably had a perfect clock in her head. She stopped me there.

"Kyle, haven't you noticed I'm wearing a pendant and bracelet? And a ring?"

Damn me for an outright unobservant fool. Of course she was! The one bone of contention between Gwen and me was that my mind was so frequently up in the clouds, I hardly noticed whether or not she had bothered to dress that day. Well, maybe I wasn't that bad, but you get what I mean.

"Where did you get them? Oh, they must be some of Gwen's old jewelry."

"No." She shook her head. "I wouldn't have worn anything of hers without your permission, Kyle. Remember the bands around my arms and waist when I first arrived?"

"Oh, yeah, but they didn't look anything like what you're wearing now. Somehow, I assumed you didn't wear jewelry in your original form." Drat. I hadn't even noticed when she took them off. Well, Gwen had told me more than once that men were unobservant idiots about things like that.

"We didn't. The bands you saw are functional equipment, meant for incorporating some of our survival equipment and a great amount of engineering, technical and general data we ordinarily don't have in our memories. I put them on immediately upon entering the lifepod. I changed their appearance with the fabricator I mentioned and with my perceptive sense so I could keep the most important things on my person at all times without attracting attention, just in case we somehow lost the cases you've seen. Or if they were taken from us by force, although that would be extremely hard to accomplish except under some of the circumstances you've mentioned. Certainly a non-technical species could never get them away from one of us, but it's possible for you. Not just you personally, but humans in general."

"I understood that much. Pretty neat. I guess you just copied some of the types of jewelry you saw in town, huh?"

"That, and what I've seen on the net. I did want to consult you before going any further, though. For the time being, most of the rest of it is on leg bands, up high where they're covered if I wear shorts."

I had to laugh, thinking of her beautiful legs marred by something like garters. Some men may think they're sexy, but I'm sure not one of them. My chuckle puzzled her.

"What's funny?"

"Uh, nothing important," I said, feeling myself blush. "But let's try to find something that looks better than leg bands, okay?"

"Sure. I trust your judgment and I can change the form pretty much at will. The material is pliable and responds to my perception and fabricator in rearranging its molecular lattice." More of that perceptive sense that I wanted to get back to later, but right now we still needed to finish our shopping list. It got to be downright funny when we had to stop for dinner and I still didn't think we'd covered it all.

We did take a break in the middle of the afternoon to let me call and make an appointment with Dr. Brown, even though Jeri told me she now thought her perceptive sense would allow her to control her periods without medication. I figured a normal woman would want birth control supplies, and whatever else we did, we had to impress on the townfolk that she wasn't different; just very unsophisticated. Besides, she'd have to have a pre-marital blood test. After that, I took a deep breath and called to find out what time the courthouse opened, in order to apply for a marriage license and to find out when the local judge or Justice of the Peace would be available to perform the ceremony.

Jeri watched me as I conversed with the officials. Her long-lashed, hazel-colored eyes were open wide, like a little girl's would be, I supposed, when she heard her parents calling to find a puppy for her. We were still sitting side by side while I made the appointments. When I hung up the phone, she put her arms around my neck and pulled my head down. I resisted only a moment before surrendering. Her lips were soft and pliant under my own, yet within a moment or two they were open and questing, her tongue sliding gently around mine. I felt her breathing speed up. I couldn't keep my hands to myself. I stroked her back and the curve of her hip and began to move toward her breasts before I knew what was happening. I had completely forgotten her alien origin.

I broke the embrace first, pulling away from her before it went any further, but there wasn't much doubt now. Even if I did still have the jitters about it, Jeri was determined that our marriage was going to be more than just a formality. After that kiss, and after her telling me what she had planned for my shot-up body over the next year, I doubted I could resist whatever she wanted. By then I didn't really want to stymie her, anyway. Call it bestiality, if you like (and I was certain a great number of religious types would be all too ready to do exactly that if they discovered Jeri was an alien), but so what? I'm an adult, and so far as I'm concerned, I can do as I damn well please so long as it doesn't hurt anyone else.

"Why…why did you stop? It felt so wonderful I wanted it to go on." Jeri could hardly speak afterward, and when she did her voice was shaky.

"Let's wait," I said. "If we're going to do this, we may as well do it the old-fashioned way and save it for our marriage night. Okay?'

"Yes," she said simply, and smiled in that enticing way I was beginning to love. But she did hug me again, pressing her body as close to mine as possible for a moment. "I'm so glad, Kyle. You've been so good to me. I know, just from reading so much about human prejudice and aversion to things outside their range of experience, that there are very few other people who would have gone as far as you. That's not even considering the religious factor, and I know what a huge role it plays in human affairs. The only drawback is that it makes me fear for the other survivors of the wreck. It's highly unlikely any of them landed practically on the doorstep of someone like you."

I have to admit that made me feel good. And I was amazed how far I'd come with her, so fast. It made me hope the future would work out as well. I delved into my mind as we sat there, trying to make myself believe I would have come to the same decision, to treat her as a woman in every sense of the word, even if she couldn't extend my life. I think I would have. Maybe it would have taken a little longer, maybe not, but I was sure the end result would have been the same. Other than her kind of stilted way of speaking, she was about as human as anyone could wish for, and she was rapidly losing that speech pattern. In fact, as I contemplated all that had happened, I found myself unable to recapture the initial revulsion and the constant assault on my senses at the sight of her in alien form. We had talked so much and done so much together already that even before she was very far along in the conversion to human form I had become comfortable with her. Of course, it wouldn't have been possible to be attracted to her in a sexual fashion until she changed. It had only been the fading memories of her previous appearance that delayed the reaction by a few days. We were so compatible, I thought, that it would have happened anyway. It wasn't until later that I learned just how compatible.

As we ate our evening meal, a news segment came on that spoiled some of the euphoric revelation I was experiencing in knowing I was going to have her as my wife soon.

80CB

We hadn't heard anything else about the "monster sightings" in the eastern states. The military had pulled out without ever saying why they had been in the area to begin with, and the story gradually died a natural death when no further news was forthcoming. This time, that part of Jeri's attention which was monitoring the news caught something new.

In Baja Mexico, southwest of Mexicali, an army unit had somehow surprised one of the surviving Cresperians and opened fire on the being before it had a chance to use its cloaking apparatus. The remains were bloody and so badly shot up that one of its arms was dangling by only a thread and both its legs had been completely amputated by converging swaths of machine gun bullets. That was according to an unnamed source. There was no doubt about the body being something not of our earth. The Mexican media and as many international reporters as possible were converging on the city, going after the story and more photos, if possible. At first the government tried to keep the event secret, but by the time media control went into effect it was far too late. Too much of the account had already leaked.

Someone high in the Mexican hierarchy of politicians took charge and reversed the secrecy, but according to Jeri, much of the ensuing story was completely false. It was claimed that the alien had attacked the soldiers with a "ray-gun" first and they had to fire in self-defense. Its ship, they said, had flown back into the sky, trailing smoke. A search was underway for a possible crash site. In the meantime, highly qualified Mexican scientists were studying the remains in a series of contamination chambers to prevent alien microbes from getting loose and possibly causing an epidemic of incurable diseases. There was more of the same, with the stories getting wilder and wilder.

"Turn it off, Jeri," I said.

She did. I could see that she was baffled and upset by what had taken place. "Oh, how could that happen? I don't understand."

"What part of it don't you understand?" I asked gently, knowing she must be grieving at the loss of one of her former crewmates.

"How the crewman could have been caught unawares, to begin with. He must have been hurt when his lifeboat landed. No, if he lived, he would have repaired his injuries by now. I just don't know how..." Her voice trailed off.

"Well," I put my arm around her. "That's desert country, where they said they found him. Him? You could tell it was male?"

"Oh yes. I saw that much, but his head was torn up so badly I don't know who it was."

"Could his survival kit, like those boxes you used, have been ruined in the crash?"

"Maybe." She tilted her head and thought for a moment. "Yes, that's certainly possible. And with no water, eventually he would have become disoriented. He was either wounded or couldn't find any water. Perhaps both. I'll bet he's been wandering around all this time, trying to survive and becoming weaker and weaker. The ray gun is nonsense, though.

The survival kits do carry a defensive weapon, but it's not like a cartoon blaster or laser."

"I'm sorry. I wish there was something we could do."

"Thank you, Kyle. It's best to just forget it now. There's no way to change the past."

"The only good I see coming from this is that he hadn't begun changing to a human. Otherwise, there'd be worldwide hysteria. The old 'aliens among us' cliché," I mused, rubbing my chin with the hand that wasn't resting on her shoulder.

"If he was isolated and without a survival kit to tune in on broadcast wavelengths, he wouldn't have known about humans—or at least what they look like."

"Too bad. Damn it, I feel rotten about this, and not just because one of your friends died, although I'm sorry about that. What bothers me now is that every government in the world is bound to start looking for more of you. Is there any sort of radar signature the lifeboats may have made as they came in? I hadn't worried about it before because I thought that if there had been, they'd have been all over us at the start, like a swarm of mosquitoes with a warm body in their sights."

"I don't know, really." Jeri had to think about that one. Finally she said, "My current profession was analogous to what you might think of as a mathematician. I guess there might have been some kind of electrical interference or static, but I can't really say, because I wasn't involved with that kind of work. Besides, we have no history of lifeboats from an interstellar spaceship ever entering the atmosphere of a world where a species is advanced enough to detect such a thing, or ever being used at all, for that matter."

"Never a spaceship wreck in all your history?"

"Not that I know of, but bear in mind we haven't had interstellar craft all that long and there are only a few of them, at that. Supporting an expedition like I was with was terribly expensive in terms of the resources necessary to build and launch it, but the real problem is finding crews interested in manning them."

Somehow I had been assuming they had a great number of spacecraft plying the galaxy. I could see now why she had said, after first learning English, that there was little chance of her ever returning home. The odds of one of their few ships coming to earth were so prohibitive that they weren't worth considering. The only way she'd ever get home would be if we could build her a spaceship ourselves.

ꙮꙮ

The next day we headed for the County Seat courthouse and all the other places we needed to go in order to get Jeri lined up. We couldn't do everything in one day, of course, but I intended to get the most important things taken care of.

Chapter Nine

One of the first people we ran into was Sheriff Morrison. We were just leaving the room where we'd applied for the marriage license and almost bumped into him.

"Well, hello there, Kyle," he said, then glanced at the office we'd just departed. He grinned. "I see you're not wasting any time."

"No, we've decided we're going to get along fine, Sheriff. Jeri, this is Sheriff Buddy Morrison. You've met him but you may not remember it. You were sleeping off some of that jet lag at the time."

"I'm glad to meet you, sir. I'm very apologetic at not remembering name, your."

I was proud of her. She sounded just like someone who had the vocabulary of a new language down pretty well but was still unsure of its structure at times.

"Not a problem, ma'am. I'm glad to see you looking so chipper. I guess the jet lag must be behind you." He touched his hand to the brim of his Stetson.

"Yes, sir."

"Well, I wish you folks a happy marriage," he said, and went on down the hallway.

I breathed a sigh of relief. Morrison kept some pretty sharp brain cells under that Stetson, and the fewer encounters we had with him, the better I'd like it.

From the courthouse we went to see Doctor Brown. I told the nurse I'd like to be present during all but the pelvic exam, since she was from a very isolated part of Europe and not familiar with doctors. She told me she'd call me in as soon as it was over.

I hadn't met the doctor before. He turned out to be a pleasantly gregarious old man who didn't seem to be in much of a hurry, but nevertheless patients moved into and out of the bowels of his clinic in fairly rapid succession as we waited. It was only a little while after Jeri went in until my name was called. I'd brought my reader along because I was expecting the usual long wait at a doctor's office. It seemed to me Jeri had hardly had time to undress, much less have the exam when I made my entrance. City doctors could well take lessons from the old man. Jeri was dressed and sitting in a chair. I introduced myself and told him I was her fiancé.

"Congratulations, then. I'm happy to tell you that everything looks normal. The nurse will call you about the pap smear." He was writing on a prescription pad as he talked. He handed it to Jeri, along with her lab results, and asked us if there was anything else he could do for us. He acted just as if he had all day to attend to us and no one else, but he was gone in an eye blink when I told him no, we were satisfied.

Once we were outside his office, I laughed. "Jeri, don't ever expect things to go that fast in a doctor's office, if by chance you ever have to see one again. That old man is a pure delight to watch working and the time we spent waiting must have set some kind of record for a family practitioner."

"He acted a little bit surprised that my hymen was still intact." She returned my chuckle, but for a different reason.

"What did he say?" I was surprised, too. I hadn't even thought of that aspect of her human form.

"He just asked if I wanted him to take care of it. I assured him you were perfectly capable of doing the job."

I think I blushed, right there on the sidewalk in the middle of town. Hell, I know I did.

&)(&

The last of our stops after taking the lab results back to the marriage license office (we should have gotten the pre-marital blood test first, of course) was Wal-Mart, where we could get just about everything on our list, including having the prescription filled, not that it was necessary, but I wanted to cover all the bases. Jeri was fascinated with the cornucopia of goods Americans felt they had to have for everyday living, especially all the clothing. Her culture had no nudity taboo, nor did they need all that many separate items for everyday life. She told me their homes came with fabricators that took care of most necessities, not that there were that many, she said. I'd already gotten the impression of an old, a very old, and nearly static, culture, a natural result given their tremendously long life spans. They saw little need of changing most of their customs.

I felt very much out of place when Jeri began changing into different outfits and coming from the dressing room to show me. I had cornered a female associate and explained Jeri's problem regarding new clothes to her, then slipped her some folding money to induce her to stay and help. She glanced around, then pocketed the money. She was much more helpful to Jeri than I could have been. She had very good taste in clothing, even down to a couple of bathing suits, along with undergarments and such. She even helped her with the bras, adjusting them for her much better than I could ever have done, and which I'd never gotten around to. She hadn't worn one yet and didn't try to even when we came to town. She just put on a blouse that wasn't even close to being translucent. Her breasts swayed some beneath the garment as she moved, but very little, indicating how firm they must be.

I had to put my hand in my pants pocket to conceal an erection when she showed me what she looked like in a bikini. She could easily have replaced the centerfold she was modeled after and then some. I almost laughed out loud when I saw a couple pass, reflected in a mirror. The man's gaze held fast to Jeri in that bikini while the rest of his body kept walking. He stumbled against his wife, almost causing her to fall down. She let out an exclamation of surprise, and then saw what the problem was. She yanked on his arm and got him moving again.

The rest of the shopping went quickly. We had one basket filled with groceries and two piled high with the other goods by the time we finished, buying the groceries last. Once we were checked out and had our goodies stowed in the car, we headed for home.

₧∓

As I pulled around back I saw a strange car there. The back door and screen were propped open. I thought almost immediately I was being robbed. The thieves must have been really intent on their business because no one came up at the sound of us arriving. I do have a very quiet car, though, an electric hybrid and I was using the battery right then.

"Stay here," I said to Jeri. I handed her my phone, glad now I had taught her how to use one. "Get in the driver's seat and if I get in trouble, get out of here and call 911 and tell them what's going on." I had begun teaching her to drive, and as with everything else, she learned quickly because she never forgot anything.

I opened the car door as silently as I could, and as soon as I was standing upright, I drew the little automatic I'd begun carrying again. I was walking toward the doorway when a man in a coat and tie walked out, a phone in his hand and in the process of dialing. I raised my gun as he saw me.

"Just hold it right there, bud," I said quietly, thinking there must be more than one of them. "Lay down flat on the ground, on your back, and stretch your hands out behind you. Then drop the phone."

"FBI," he said, but he thumbed the phone off and raised his hands to shoulder level.

I looked him over carefully. Thieves don't normally wear ties and sports jackets. "All right, let's see some ID, but move very carefully. I don't mind shooting if I have to."

He pulled his jacket wide open to let me see the pistol he carried in a shoulder holster, then very carefully reached into an inside pocket of his jacket and withdrew a little folder. He flipped it open, displaying a badge and what was probably his identification but I wasn't close enough to see. All the time I was watching for others. Agents don't usually work alone, though they sometimes do.

"Closer, but move slow." He nodded and took a couple of slow steps, holding the opened ID holder well in front of him. "How many others are inside?"

"I'm by myself. We're short-handed." His voice was level, not afraid at all.

"Come a little bit closer, just one more step, so I can see your badge and photo plainly."

He took another slow step, holding it stretched in front of him. I was satisfied, almost. But why? No, I knew why. How had they gotten suspicious of me? Then I remembered. That damned UPS driver. She must have seen the news from Mexico and told the Sheriff that what she'd seen out here matched the picture of the alien still being displayed in the tabloids at the Wal-Mart checkout counters. Then he must have called in the feds. There was only one because they must have been investigating a thousand supposed aliens at the same time. That was my immediate thought, and I was glad of it. Damn. I didn't see how I could let him go, but I didn't think I could kill him in cold blood, either. Shit. My mind raced, trying to come up with a solution to the quandary. I kept him at bay while my mind whirled with wild scenarios for getting us out of the fix.

"All right. Now I want you to take your gun out, using two fingers only, and put it on the ground. Move very slowly."

"Didn't you see? I'm an FBI Special Agent, here on official business. Don't make it hard on yourself."

"Do what I said."

He did exactly as asked, while telling me I should be cooperating with him. As he squatted to lay down his gun, I saw him hesitate, and knew what he was intending to do. "Don't try it," I said. "Lie down on your back, raise your legs and pull up both pants legs."

"You're making a mistake," he said, but again did exactly what I told him. By then, I had no real doubt he was a real agent. I was just playing for time while I decided what to do.

"If I am, I'll apologize, but there are too goddamn many terrorists and crooks with phony ID to take chances these days. Now spread your legs way apart and put your hands under your butt."

I guess he thought I was a professional. I had worked in military intelligence and been in combat but mostly I just read a lot. I knew all about ankle holsters. I approached from the side and pulled his other gun from its holster, then stepped back.

"Okay, Jeri, come on, but stay well behind me in case I have to shoot. What's your name, bud? I couldn't read it plainly."

"John Lester."

"Okay, John, while I decide whether you're legitimate or not, let's go inside and get out of the sun. Don't move fast whatever you do. Hear?"

"I got you."

He moved very carefully as we followed him inside. There, I made him shuck his jacket and toss his phone over onto another chair, then sit down in one of the easy chairs with the foot rest up so he couldn't put any fast moves on me. I took Jeri over to one side of the room and kept my eye on him as we talked very softly.

"What are you going to do, Kyle?"

I leaned close to her ear and spoke in a whisper. "Damned if I know yet, but it looks as if we're going to have to run. The thing is, they'd be sure to catch us eventually. You can't avoid capture for long, when all the law officers in the nation are concentrating on finding you. Any suggestions?"

"I don't want to see you kill him. Does that matter?"

"Of course it does. I don't want to kill him, either." Suddenly the image of Sheriff Morrison popped into my mind, maybe my subconscious at work. I decided the only way to get out of the jam and keep the authorities off our back was to play innocent. That meant taking the offensive. We came back and sat down on the couch facing the agent. I grinned, causing a puzzled expression to cross his face.

"Look here, I suspect you're legitimate, but I'm new to the area and my fiancée is *really* new. She's from eastern Europe and you've scared hell out of her. She thinks you're the secret police."

That drew a faint smile but no comment. I began pretending I was pissed off.

"Who in hell put you up to coming out here and bothering us?"

"Sorry, I can't say."

"You don't have to—I think I know. That crazy lady driving the UPS truck. I've already had the sheriff break into my house over that wild tale, but he had a halfway decent excuse. What's yours?"

"There was an official complaint." He put his hand on the lever to lower the foot rest, thinking I was going to relent.

"All right, I can go along with that. Just show me your warrant." I waved my little S&W and he froze.

A blush began at his neck and worked its way up to his face.

"Oh ho! No warrant. I've had about enough of this crap. Just because I'm a newcomer here doesn't mean I'm not a citizen. I think I'd better call the sheriff, and my lawyer too, while I'm at it. Just sit tight, John, and don't try to get up. I've got a perfect right to kill you already."

I called Sheriff Morrison first. Fortunately, he was in. I described what was happening and asked if he knew anything about it. He told me he did, but when I asked about a warrant, he went silent.

"You mean you sent this guy out here, knowing he was going to break into my house, and you knew he didn't have a warrant? What in hell is going on around this place? Are you all crazy?" I made my voice sound like that of a very irate citizen, one who's just about had it with intrusions of my privacy.

"I didn't know he was going inside unless you were there, Kyle. I think he had cause, though."

"Are you talking about that imaginary monster again? Look, sheriff, I'm a reasonable man, but enough's enough. Was it that same lady?"

He admitted it was.

"Damn it all, I don't care how well thought of she is, she's crazy as a loon if she thinks I'm hiding monsters in my closet. Crap, she told me herself that she was practically asleep on her feet when she was here. I bet she saw that fake picture in the tabloids at Wal-Mart and decided it would do for a backup to her story."

"The agent, Lester's his name, seems to think the thing in Mexico was real, but I have to admit he didn't come right out and say so."

"I know what his name is. I'm holding a gun on him right now and I'm going to call my lawyer and press charges. No, wait a minute. Was that lady's boyfriend with her when she came back to you again?"

He admitted that he'd been with her.

"Well, I bet a dime to a donut he's the one that put her up to it. Probably one of those goddamn crazy, jealous types. Is he?"

"I wouldn't want to talk about a man behind his back, but I guess I can say he doesn't have the highest IQ in town." Behind that remark, I could almost read his mind over the phone and thought I'd guessed right. A jealous boyfriend with a Neanderthal mentality who liked to intimidate any other male he thought he could bully, especially strangers.

"Okay, sheriff, I know you have to cooperate with the feds in this day and age but I sure would appreciate it if you'd help put this crazy story to rest. I'm new here and don't want to make trouble for anyone, but I guess you can't blame me for consulting an attorney, considering all that's happened."

He agreed with only a shade of reluctance in his voice. I thanked him and hung up. "Jeri, why don't you make us some coffee while I call Arlene. Do you drink coffee, John, or something else?"

"Coffee's fine." Again, he started to lower the foot rest.

"Just a few minutes more, please. I'm not quite finished yet."

Arlene Andrews was the lawyer I'd used to help me close on the property. She had a general practice in Hatfield, doing a little of everything. She was also a feisty little brunette in her thirties and struck me as a lady who would love any kind of chance to show this rural, male-dominated community just how far women had come in the last couple of generations.

I was on a roll because she was in, too. I gave her a quick summary of what had gone on from the time the UPS driver first "imagined" a monster at my place, and asked her to quietly pass the word around that I'd had all I was going to take of the nonsense.

"You bet, Kyle. No warrant? Hell, I don't care what Homeland Security thinks, there are still limits on how far they can go. I'll let Morrison know I'm getting a restraining order from Judge Best and also sue hell out of anyone who even thinks of bothering you with this crap again. Monster, my ass. I know that village idiot Lisa runs around with. He's trouble, and I've told her so."

"Okay, thanks, Arlene."

"Sure. Anything else?"

I thought for a moment. "Uh huh, one more thing. You might contact Senator Brad Benchley and mention my name, then tell him I might need a favor."

"I certainly will," she said in a soft, extremely respectful voice.

I saw Lester wince when I mentioned a senator's name. That ought to do it. I didn't know the Senator from Missouri that well, but he knew of me, all right. His son owed his life to me for quick thinking in a really bad situation we'd gotten into when he was in my unit, back during the last war. He wasn't likely to forget that.

"The coffee is ready now," Jeri announced. "Can him get up?"

"He," I corrected, as if I were still teaching her English. "Yes, pour him a cup. How do you take it, John?"

"Black, please."

He put his hand on the foot rest lever of the easy chair, and raised his brows. I nodded and slid my gun back into the side pocket of my jean jacket. While he was getting his feet to the floor, I pulled out my wallet and went over to show him my concealed weapon permit.

"Thanks," he said. "That makes it easier, but...oh, hell, never mind."

I could tell he was embarrassed over me getting the drop on him. I grinned.

"Tell you what, you help stomp on this goddamned crazy story for me and I promise I won't tell anyone how careless you were."

"All I can promise is that I'll try—that's if you'll run through it all for me, so we can be sure it really was that woman's imagination."

"You don't mean that story out of Mexico is real, do you?" I frowned, as if puzzled.

"We haven't taken an official position on it, but...never mind. There are some things you're better off not knowing, Mr. Leverson."

"Be damned," I said, as if truly astounded but still not believing him.

An hour later, we were using first names and talking together like old friends. Jeri even joined the conversation occasionally, once I'd assured her that Lester didn't belong to any kind of secret police. By the time I'd told him my story, including the fib about changing my mind on burying my trash because of guilt feelings over spoiling the environment, I was fairly certain I'd put it over. Anyone interested in Jeri and me ought to be convinced by now that we were just what we appeared to be, a lonely widower who'd imported a pretty young European woman to keep him company. I even embellished the story by confessing to having a good portion of the "bashful" complex of genes, my reason for not trying harder to find a companion at home. Fortunately, Lester had heard of the discovery and understood, sort of. Actually, I don't think anyone who hasn't been born with those genes can really understand how they affect a person. I can understand it because I really do have them. Gwen had to practically knock me off my feet before I got up the courage to ask her for a date.

Finally we shook hands and he drove off.

As soon as he was out of sight I asked Jeri if her perceptive sense could spot a bug. After I'd explained the slang, she told me she was almost certain she could detect the ambient electrical aura of one of the little gadgets, but the place seemed to be clean. I began to breathe normally again but it still took a good strong shot of bourbon to counteract the adrenalin that had kept me tensed up for so long. That was getting to be a habit, but I needed a drink. The long pretense had pretty well exhausted me.

Chapter Ten

Before we retired for the night I explained to Jeri what had happened, just in case she had missed some of the byplay I'd indulged in. There was very little she'd misinterpreted. In a way I was glad of what had happened, as she'd now have a better idea of how the authorities worked.

"We were lucky," I told her. "Had there been more than one agent, I don't know what I'd have done, but I doubt it would have come out as well as it did with just Lester there."

"Would you really have shot him?" Jeri asked.

I saw how concerned she was. I patted her knee.

"I doubt it, not unless they threatened you, and even then it would have been hard. It's too bad I can't do karate like I used to before getting shot up. Even if there had been two of them, I might've been able to take them. Remember, those people are mostly honest and just doing their jobs. I hope I would have come up with an excuse to keep them from taking us into custody right away, but I think the way it happened was actually better. We shouldn't be bothered again."

"So we don't have to leave here now?"

"No, especially not now. Leaving immediately would just arouse suspicion all over again. Eventually we will, though. I'd sure like to find out about the others, and I know you would, too."

"More than anything." She smiled at me. "Except getting married. That's what I want most now."

I put my arm around her and drew her close for a long, intimate kiss. I touched her breast and once we broke the embrace I continued to caress her gently.

"You can leave off the bra again if you want to."

"It's not as uncomfortable now, and I suppose I should get used to wearing it, shouldn't I?"

"Yes, but I like it when you don't. It makes you even more enticing."

"Then I'll remove it."

She began unbuttoning her blouse. She had no more bodily modesty than if she had been raised as a nudist. It took all my will power to have her stop.

"I can wait to see you naked a couple of more days, sweetheart." It was the first time I used an endearment with her.

"Anticipation?"

"Exactly. And you're going to discover that sometimes the right kind of clothing on a woman is as sexy to a man as complete nudity—or more so."

"I don't quite understand as yet, but I'm sure I'll learn."

"I'm sure you will." I kissed her again and we got up to continue the cooking lessons, with a cookbook now. I didn't have a very elaborate repertoire. Neither did the cookbook, as I discovered, at least not in the way of things I cared for and were easy to prepare. I grew up eating nothing but brown, white and fried. Gwen had to teach me to appreciate other food, like steaks that weren't well done and seafood and the like. One more thing to add to the new list I was making for when we went back to town for the marriage ceremony was an introductory cookbook. Oh, we could have downloaded tons of them, but I still liked to visit bookstores in person every now and then. Jeri suggested she should start watching more cooking programming on television also.

I knew I didn't have to write anything down, not with Jeri's perfect memory, but for the time being I had decided to act the same as I would if she were an ordinary woman living with me. Not only would it help with me knowing her as a woman, but it would show her how most people lived. People like me, anyway, who were as absent-minded as a cartoon professor.

Besides the cooking, I had an inspiration. Just because my shoulder and hip were too torn up to practice karate, I couldn't see any reason not teach Jeri a few moves. When I mentioned it, she was enthusiastic.

"Good! I want to learn, because I'd hate to have to kill a person."

"Well, I'll show you as best I can," I told her. We started the lessons that day, both study and practice, with me as her tutor. She made rapid progress not only because she never forgot instructions, but also because she was determined to take care of the superb body she had made for herself.

"Oh, this is fun," she said, and grinned at me while holding a side-kick in place head high like a black belt martial artist would in a kung-fu movie after administering a whole bunch of whup-ass. "I think I'm going to like being attractive, so I want to stay that way."

I couldn't agree more.

ജാരു

Our government tried to downplay the story from Mexico with statements which said they had no proof that either the news reports or photos were genuine, but they didn't work that well. Most people seem to have an inherent desire to believe in aliens from other worlds or other dimensions, and the fact that the government of our next-door neighbor kept insisting it was factual made it hard to suppress. Despite the tabloids' propensity for making up news, a lot of hard scientific speculation began percolating through the internet and that led some investigative reporters for the major newspapers to begin delving into it. I have no idea what kind of pressure our government used on Mexico, but they must have leaned on their leaders pretty fiercely to gain access to the alien corpse. When reporters got wind of that, they really got busy and nosier than ever. Before long, it became pretty well accepted that a real alien had been found and killed. That in turn stirred the pot up even more, until aliens were being seen in bushes and backyards and forests all over America, and the rest of the world too, for that matter. Fortunately, all of those were proven to either be false or eye witness sightings that couldn't possibly be verified. The only one, or group maybe, we suspected might be in government hands was from that incident in Georgia. It sounded authentic.

The hysteria gradually died down over the next few days, but I knew that didn't mean the federal and state agencies had stopped looking. I came close to asking Jeri to postpone the marriage, but she was so eager I couldn't do it. Besides, I discovered that I was excited about it myself. I made an appointment with Judge Best and four days later we headed for town.

ಬಂಡಿ

The judge was a relatively young man and appeared to enjoy performing the ceremony. Just to try cementing a good relationship with the sheriff, I asked him to be my best man. He accepted graciously. His wife, Mona, accompanied him. We spoke with her a few minutes while Judge Best was taking care of some last-minute court business. It turned out that she had read a few of my articles written for the general public. She complimented me on them.

"It takes a good writer to make science intelligible for the layman, Kyle. I teach general science at the high school here."

We could probably have spent the rest of the day talking about the general public's apathy concerning the very science that provided for their wellbeing, but it was time for the ceremony.

I managed to get through it without stumbling, other than dropping Jeri's ring, a beauty if I do say so, but she had picked it out herself. It was faceted platinum with gold trim. Jeri used her lightning-fast reflexes to catch it, drawing a laugh from the witnesses, a deputy and the court clerk. I tried again with trembling hands, hoping no one noticed just how fast Jeri had reacted. I got the words out somehow, and then turned back to the judge.

"...I now pronounce you man and wife. You may kiss your bride."

I don't think Jeri quite understood that the kiss wasn't supposed to go on and on. I gently drew back from her after a few seconds, then we accepted everyone's congratulations.

"Where are you going on your honeymoon?" Mona asked when her turn came.

Just as we'd discussed it, I told her that we were going back home for a few days, then we'd take a leisurely trip west so Jeri could see some of her new country. Well, we were going home for a few days because that's where she wanted to begin our married life, the place where we'd met. Speak of becoming human—she was already getting sentimental! We weren't going west, though. We intended to head east, toward where Jeri thought at least one other lifeboat had come down.

Just as we left, Mona invited us to have dinner with them when we returned. Jeri accepted for us, doing a good job with her accented English.

She sat very close to me all the way home, using the center seat belt. I didn't complain.

&⁂☙

I won't say too much about what happened after we'd gotten back and split a bottle of wine, more to calm me down than her, except in general terms. An account like this needn't give a detailed description of our sex life. Let's just say that when she undressed, I saw that she was even more beautiful than I'd imagined her to be.

I never thought once about her having had an alien body only a few short weeks ago. Men are visually stimulated creatures. I'm a visually stimulated creature, and Jeri was visually stimulating. Hell, she was hotter than a damned firecracker on Independence Day, and the sight of her naked body not only lit my fuse but damned near shot me into orbit. As she slid into bed and into my arms, and the length of our bodies touched, a tide of desire swept over me like the first adrenalin rush of combat. I felt alive again. I loved her. I had a fierce craving for her and never wanted to let her go.

We caressed and explored each other's body with our hands and lips and tongues, moving together almost as if our minds were as united as our bodies soon would be. Jeri was as eager as any new bride, but completely uninhibited. She hadn't grown up with any cultural baggage about sex, making her as responsive and willing as a barnyard animal in heat, to put it crudely. None of those women on the porn websites could have done anything better if they'd tried, not that we got into many variations at first.

It was Jeri who pulled at my shoulders, telling me how eager she was to get on with it. She was ready, her warm moisture guiding the penetration, with only a passing resistance from her hymen and that was over in a moment. I didn't notice her wince in pain, even briefly. Our bodies merged and she wrapped her arms and legs around me, clinging so forcefully that for a moment I feared a cracked rib, even as I moved in the age-old rhythm of love. A very short while later, she climaxed. Her body shuddered beneath me in a long-drawn-out orgasm, all the while holding me so tightly that if my mind hadn't been elsewhere, I would have wondered how we could even draw breath. We both cried out incoherently as my own body went into its spasm of release. *Not bad for a shot-up old man*, I told myself.

৳০৫�৪

The next few days were spent mostly in bed, with only a few hours used for sleep and other necessities. Jeri was as fervently enthusiastic as only a woman not born and raised on earth could be. She was completely agreeable to anything I suggested and was soon taking the initiative as often as me.

Sometime during that first night, when we were taking a break, we just cuddled together in an exhausted, happy daze and waited for me to recover some stamina. She began talking in a soft voice, a kind of reminiscing tinged with regret that her species had nothing to compare to our sexual union.

"It's so wonderful, making love with you, Kyle. The Cresperian species has nothing even close to what I've just experienced—and it's only the beginning! I really can't fathom how the whole human species has somehow been brainwashed into thinking that there's something sullied or grubby, even dirty, about sex. I know religion has a lot to do with it, but it's so ridiculous that anything so beautiful could ever be thought of as something not to be talked about in public or taught in schools or…well, you know what I mean."

"Yeah, I do." I pulled her a little closer, wondering how on earth I had gotten so lucky as to have her land in my back yard. I know I'm nothing special, and I don't believe in some supernatural being that orders every little detail of our lives. It almost had to be chance, pure and simple, like buying a winning lottery ticket. But whatever it was, I'm damn well grateful for it! "Sweetheart, smarter people than me have tried to explain that very point to the masses, with not much success. I think we were on the verge of gradually losing such stupid ideas, until the fundamentalist revival. Now I just don't know. I'm very much afraid that we're in the midst of one of those great religious upheavals, a paradigm change in religious philosophy. If it succeeds, we'll be back to the olden days again, where the priests and shamans begin preaching against enjoyment of sex except under their rules, and forcing politicians to make more laws governing how we practice sex. You've read what it's like in some Muslim countries today, haven't you?"

"Oh, yes. It's cruel and barbaric and horrible. Kyle, after tonight, even if I could go back home and change into my old form again, I wouldn't want to. Not and give up loving you."

"Now that is just something special. I can't even fathom how to respond other than to say, thanks." I drew her into an even closer embrace. Our lips touched and the fire began building again

Were those few days the final process of falling in love? I really don't know. Later, Jeri told me it was, for her. I guess it really doesn't matter, because the moment I put my life on the line for her I knew I loved her as deeply as I ever had Gwen.

She still didn't require nearly as much sleep as a normal human, and probably never would. She continued to spend many hours a day on the net, but according to what happened before we started our trip, she must have spent at least some of the time while I was asleep practicing her karate.

⋙⋘

A thought occurred to me as we first began packing. How in hell would I have explained the English labels on her clothes if the sheriff had thought to look? I couldn't have, because they should have been in Albanian or Russian script. Now that Jeri had some new duds that fit her, I decided to burn the other clothes I had bought, and if we were ever asked, just claim that Jeri's foreign attire had been so tacky she wanted to get rid of it.

I was out poking the ashes when Jeri came running out the door. I had never seen her so upset. Her expression alarmed me.

"Kyle! Come quick!"

She didn't wait on me but turned and ran back into the house.

I followed as quickly as I could, ignoring my bad hip. She was in the living room, sitting on the couch and bent over the keyboard I usually keep on the coffee table. I slowed down, or at least my body did. My heart was still racing. I thought something dire had happened. "What is it?"

She looked up. "I've found one of the other crew."

I sat down beside her, wondering how she'd managed that with the computer. Then when I saw where she was, my heart began thudding in my chest again. My God, she had somehow wormed her way into an ultra-secret web site maintained by an offshoot of Homeland Security, either CIA or NSA; I couldn't be sure which. Hell, I had done a lot of really clandestine intelligence work when I was with the 902nd and all I knew about that group was a few whispers I'd overheard by accident. If they traced her link back to us, we were dead! I didn't see how to avoid it, though. Crap and Shinola, why hadn't I warned her? I knew she had already surpassed my expertise with computers by a wide margin, and had a nearly eidetic memory, but hadn't given a thought to her ability to hack passwords. And not just passwords, for I recognized the little icon that meant the data was encrypted so well that only a few techs in the business knew how to turn it into readable data.

"Jeri, how did you *do* that? Don't you know they'll be able to back-track to our computer and arrest us?"

"No, no," she replied, with a wave of her hand. She looked up at me again and must have seen the concern on my face. "Please don't worry, Kyle. I just had to see this once I found a reference to it."

"But I do worry! Jeri…"

"You worry too much." She interrupted me without bothering to be polite about it. "Sweetheart, trust me. Computers operate far above a quantum level of understanding. I can back out as easily as I got in and not leave a trace. Now, look here. See?"

I saw all right. They had a Cresperian prisoner but were apparently having problems getting it to cooperate with them, after it first acted friendly. That gave me a world of information all by itself. Someone had gotten in a hurry and abused it while trying to dig the secret of star flight out of it, probably.

"All right, I see. But memorize the rest off it and back out of there! Find the user's log if you can and change it to show you weren't there."

The pages on the monitor began flickering past almost as fast as a high-end laser printer spits out copies. It was hard to believe she was capturing all that data, but I knew she was. She had shown me once and I just shook my head in wonder. A few minutes later she had it all. She shut down and stood up, practically dancing with excitement.

"Come on, Kyle, let's go for a walk while I tell you about it, then we're going to have to leave."

I wasn't about to argue with her on that point. Despite her having altered the log, I knew there were other ways to catch unauthorized users of a computer holding those kinds of secrets.

My place was heavily forested not far from the house, but there were trails running through the woods, making it a good place for walking, so long as you applied some insect repellent before going out. I grabbed the jean jacket I wear almost all the time, the one with the little automatic I carried, and we stepped outside. I picked a trail wide enough for us to walk side by side while she briefed me on what she'd found out.

"There was only one blurred photo but I think I know the one being held. He was a friend, though not in the same sense as you think of a friend. I know him fairly well. He's still in his Cresperian body, but it really doesn't matter. They're treating him horribly after someone punched him. He's refusing to cooperate at all except when their handling becomes unbearable."

"I thought you told me your people would go into a trance or something under those circumstances." I brushed at a deer fly that was annoying me even though it refused to land.

"Ordinarily they would, but someone inadvertently let it slip that some of our people are still loose. He's hoping for a rescue. That's one reason I was so excited. Right at the beginning, I found a reference that wouldn't make sense to anyone except a Cresperian, asking for help if any of us were able and discovered that site." She frowned. "Still, I wouldn't have thought that remote hope was enough to keep him going. He must be getting support from someone, somehow."

"Okay, I've got that, but what made you go to that site in the first place? And for that matter, how in hell did you get into it? And if you could get in, how come he couldn't send word out? Those kind of computers are supposed to be sealed off from any possible intrusion."

"They run on electricity, don't they?" She smiled and took my hand as the path widened.

"Sure."

"Then they should have taken my fellow Cresperian to a place with its own generators. I came in through the power lines. He's using his perception to send out a quantum encrypted beacon over the power cables of the facility he's being held in. The beacon sticks out like a sore thumb, if you know what to look for. Even if the place had its own source of power, I'd have found them eventually anyway, since they receive so much data from the satellites. He could have piggybacked the beacon on an uplink but it would have taken longer to find."

Wow! Boogram help us if Russia or China ever got hold of a cooperative alien! Even some of those funky little Mideast countries could soon run us in circles with the kind of knowledge Jeri carried in her bracelets, pendant, rings and purse.

"Where are they holding him? Did you get that?"

"Uh huh. It's in Virginia, at a secret facility built just a few years ago."

That didn't tell me much. There were numerous little hidey-holes various government agencies had created in the Virginian hills.

"Can you pinpoint it a little closer?"

"I think so, once we're nearer. Anyhow, when we get close enough, I'll be able to sense him."

"You keep saying him. Does he have a name?"

She rattled off some Ceresperian I knew I'd never be able to pronounce. The first part of it sounded sort of like Ish followed by a string of syllables. "Ishmael? Could we call him that?"

"Is that a human name?"

"It's from an old novel. That was the protagonist's name."

"Good enough."

Well, the honeymoon at home had been great while it lasted.

We headed back, not saying much. I was up in the clouds, thinking about packing and making arrangements for someone to watch the place, and I guess Jeri was lost in her own thoughts. As we rounded the last bend in the trail where it widened out, we damn near ran head on into three very nasty customers.

Chapter Eleven

I think we surprised them as much as they did us. The moist earth had softened our footsteps. A good thing, too. I don't remember stopping to think. It was, *Bad guys! Attack!* There was something about the one in the lead that told me without my stopping to analyze it that he and his companions were after our hides.

"Run, Jeri!" I shouted, even as I hurried my last few steps to where they stood with a look of astonishment on their faces. The one farthest forward tried to step back as he was going for his weapon. My jumping front-kick caught him under the chin while he was off-balance. He went down like he'd been hit in the face by a heavy iron bar. I spun quickly, catching the second one in the eye with my elbow, disabling him momentarily. I saw the third man raising a pistol. I had no idea where Jeri was by then, other than a glimpse I'd caught of her still standing as if frozen to the spot, but his gun wasn't being pointed at me.

Jeri! I threw my body in front of the line of fire without the least hesitation, thinking he was aiming at her. It almost got me killed. A fraction of a second later, his head disappeared as cleanly as if it had been lopped off by an executioner's axe. His body fell backward, neck arteries spurting fountains of bright red blood with each heartbeat.

I didn't pause to wonder what had happened. I was still concerned about Jeri and I knew my elbow hadn't hit the second man hard enough to put him out of action for more than a minute or two. I needn't have worried. By the time I spotted him, Jeri had already put him down for the count with a blow to the solar plexus. He was writhing on the ground, trying desperately to draw a breath.

A glance at the one I'd kicked told me he wouldn't be going anywhere. I must have broken his neck with my blow because he was already turning the waxy color of death. I bent over Jeri's victim and frisked him, removing an ankle gun and retrieving the one he'd dropped when I first hit him. Only then did I stop to see about Jeri.

She came into my arms, tears streaming down her face. I held her close.

"Are you hurt? Did that last guy hit you somewhere?"

She shook her head, unable to speak yet because she was still crying. I breathed a sigh of relief. Crying wouldn't hurt a thing. I know. I've shed plenty of tears in my life.

"We're okay now." After she'd quieted, I couldn't contain myself any longer. "What on earth did you do to that guy's head? It disappeared like a magician waved a wand at it."

"It…it was my finger ring." Her voice was still shaky. "That's where I decided to keep my defensive weapon. Oh, Kyle, I almost killed you!"

I remembered then how close I had been to the death ray or whatever the hell she'd used and shuddered.

"Why didn't you tell me you had something like that? I wouldn't have been so eager to throw myself in front of his gun if I'd known about it." She was still clutching me around the waist, with her head resting on my shoulder.

"I did tell you I had a defensive weapon, didn't I? But I…didn't know I was going to…to have to *kill* someone with it!" Another sob escaped, along with a sniff.

I thought back. Sure enough, she'd said something about having one, but this was wildly beyond anything I had imagined.

"Yeah, I guess you did tell me. I just didn't know it was so good for offense. What is it?"

She gave a weak chuckle in response. "I guess you could call it a disintegrator gun, like you see in comic strips. It disrupts the molecular and atomic bonds and dissipates the released energy into the quantum foam. But I think it was intended to create a hole in the ground between the individual and a threat, just to stay out of range of danger from wild animals or perhaps a belligerent native. I've never heard of it being used to kill. In fact, I've never seen it actually used."

"Ha," I laughed, almost hysterically. "Well, you certainly took care of one belligerent native with it." I blew out a breath of air. "I'm damn glad you had it, but if you've got anything else like that up your sleeve, tell me."

She started to speak, but I pushed her back enough so I could see her face. It was streaked where tears had made a path down her cheeks. I got out my handkerchief and wiped at her eyes. If she was deliberately acting like a woman would in a situation like that, I sure couldn't tell the difference. Not that I think women are any less brave or willing to fight than men; they just react differently—with tears, for example. I have no idea whether it's cultural or inherited, but females just cry more than males do.

"Don't tell me now. Later. Right now, we've got some things to do. I sure hope I didn't make a mistake by attacking first or we're gonna be in a world of hurt."

"You didn't," Jeri stated emphatically. "I could sense the evil intent."

She let me take the lead and we got to work. I trussed up the guy that Jeri had punched real well, then began going through their belongings. There wasn't much, just some cash and drivers' licenses that I felt sure were as phony as Jeri's passport. No other ID at all. One phone. I found the car keys in the pocket of the body with no head.

"Come on," I said.

We were just out of sight of the house. Their car was parked in back, just as blatantly as you please. There was no ID there, either, but while I was looking, I began to get an idea. I hated to phone the sheriff. It would just call attention to us, big time. Better if he never knew it happened. That's why I left the Beretta machine pistol I found under the front seat just where it was. I made sure there were no other phones anywhere, though.

We dragged the two bodies to their car and tossed them into the back seat. By that time Mr. Breathless was beginning to come around. His right eye was swollen shut where I'd hit him. His face was pale and drawn. I guess he wasn't used to being on the receiving end of a beating.

I loosed the bonds on his feet and told him to get up. He did but I had to help. Once he was upright, I steered him toward his car, a late model sedan. I put him in the driver's seat, his hands still tied behind him. I got in on the passenger side and motioned for Jeri to come close.

"Can you tell if this guy is lying when I start asking questions?"

"I don't see any problem. There'll be enough physiological changes for me to know."

"Good." I turned toward our prisoner. "Okay, listen up, bud. You've got two choices here. Answer truthfully and you live. Lie to me and you die. Got it?"

He didn't say anything.

"Got it?" I took out my pistol and tapped him on the nose.

"Yeah." His voice was surly enough to fit nicely with his uncooperative attitude.

"Okay, I don't care what your name is. Just tell me who you work for."

"A government agency. It's secret. You don't let me go, they'll bust yer balls."

"That's rich!" I laughed out loud. He didn't even talk like an agent. "Try again."

"It's the truth."

"He's lying," Jeri said.

"Yeah, even I can tell that so far. What were you here for?"

"Yer 'sposed to know where one of them space critters is."

"How...no, never mind. Tell me who wants to know."

"I told ya. A government agency."

"Really?" I put the barrel against his temple. "You're real close to death, Mr. No-name. Who sent you here?"

"Uh." Sweat began rolling down his face, not all of it from the heat. "I don't know his name for sure."

"Take a guess."

"Uh, Sam Jones."

"Lie," Jeri corrected.

"Bitch! How d' you know?"

"Don't call her a bitch, asshole." I rapped him hard this time. His nose began to pour blood profusely down his face from both nostrils. "The name, bud. Last chance." I ground the barrel of my gun into his good eye, not being gentle.

"Ow! Awright, awright. It's Boris Kavinski. At least, I think so. Honest, that's all I know. You killed my boss. He woulda known more."

I looked at Jeri. She nodded that he was being truthful, then she looked away. I didn't blame her. I always hated interrogations, but...oh crap. How in hell had that gangster found out about us? He was the reputed head of a major segment of the Russian Mafia.

I didn't see any sense in taking it further. The one we had questioned was just a thug, a strong arm man. He wouldn't know much more, if anything. I got out and urged Jeri back to the house, leaving the door of the car opened so No-name wouldn't roast.

"What are we going to do now, Kyle?"

"Well," I held the door open for her as I answered. "We're going to rescue your friend if we can. As for that plug ugly, much as I hate to say it, we can't leave him alive."

"I was afraid you'd say that." Jeri blanched. "Do we have to...kill him?" She had trouble even saying the words.

"I don't like it any better than you do, sweetheart, but I'll bet we've got the whole Russian Mafia after us. If I turn him loose, they'll know I have a woman with me and what you look like. They won't stop until they find us. Maybe you've read about them."

"I have. They're ruthless, according to what I know, which isn't much. I've been concentrating on the good things about human culture rather than the deviants. I guess I should have learned more about them."

"It wouldn't hurt. Let's start packing. I'll tell you what we're going to do when we're ready."

ଔ

It wouldn't have taken near as long if I hadn't had to dispose of as much evidence as possible. We had already stuffed the bodies into the back seat of their car. After loading our luggage in my car, we made a final check of the house, then locked up. I put the Hummer in the garage instead of leaving it outside like I usually did, and used the old-fashioned zapper to close and lock it. I got a wheelbarrow and shoveled the blood-soaked earth into it and carried it way off into the woods, scattering a little of it at a time until it was gone. Then I filled the hole with some branches that had fallen since the last time I'd picked up, as if preparing to burn them. I took a lawn rake and obliterated all their footsteps and tire tracks where they'd gone off the pavement of my driveway. Their car was parked on it now. It was only then that I told Jeri what I had in mind. She nodded agreement but I could tell she still didn't like it.

"It's no loss, Jeri. The world will be a little better place with him out of it. All three of them have probably killed more people than I even know, and that's not counting what they probably did before the killings. You don't even want to read about that stuff."

That seemed to make her feel a little better. She got in the passenger seat of my car while I went over to theirs. No-name was drenched with sweat, even with the door standing open.

"I'm burning up, Mister Leverson. Turn on the A/C for me."

"What's the magic word?" Not even a please, damn his soul. And he knew my name. "You can turn it on yourself in a minute. I'm letting you go."

"You are?" He couldn't believe his good fortune. I was amazed that a fellow in his line of work was so trusting.

"Yeah, but here's how it goes. I want you to drive out of here up to where the pavement starts, but *don't* drive in the ruts when you get to the gravel. Keep to the grass. And don't get more than ten or fifteen feet ahead of me or I'll shoot your tires out, then kill you, too. When we get to the paved road, turn right, but don't try to get in a hurry, because I'm going stay right behind you. Once we get to the main highway, you head to the right and we'll go the other way. Don't try to follow us or I'll put a rifle bullet through your head. *Capise?*"

"Yeah." He had a crafty look on his face but I knew what he was thinking. Very deliberately, I reached under the seat and removed the clip from the machine pistol. The crafty look disappeared.

The son of a bitch was still surly, even with a black eye and blood running from his nose and dripping off his chin. I think he actually believed I was going to turn him loose. Dumb bastard. He probably started his criminal career as a kid by palming the coins his mother gave him to put in the collection plate.

ଽଠ୦ଷ

It hit me as I drove off, following the thug's car as close as I dared. I hadn't felt any pain at all when I made that first kick, almost instinctively just like it's supposed to happen. My shoulder hadn't bothered me, either, when I got that lick in with my elbow. Either of those moves should have been very painful, especially the high front-kick. I couldn't figure it out at first, but then I remembered that secretive mirth I'd noticed in Jeri for the last couple of weeks. No wonder she was laughing up her sleeve.

"You fixed my hip and shoulder, didn't you?" I asked.

She laughed for the first time since she'd run out of the house, calling my name. "I wanted it to be a surprise, but I guess those awful men spoiled it."

"Don't worry. You surprised me all right. I just didn't realize it until now. What did you do?"

I eased up closer to the gangster's car as we began climbing a small mountain, trying to concentrate on driving and her at the same time.

"I gradually removed all the metal pins and the artificial ball joints while I speeded up production of your osteoblasts to take their place. And I removed all the old scar tissue and damaged cartilage, muscles and tendons and stimulated healthy tissue to replace them. You were a mess in both those places. You must have had a great deal of pain while they were healing."

"Yeah, but the VA took good care of me. The best they knew how, anyway. Too bad you can't do that for more people."

"Someday you'll be able to do it yourself, and then you can teach others."

I left it at that because we were coming up on the switchbacks near the top of the mountain. There were three spots I had picked out in my mind. Any of them would do so long as no other vehicles were near.

"Is it all clear behind and in front of us?" I asked.

"As far as my perceptive sense and hearing can reach."

"Okay, brace yourself."

Just as we reached the sharp turn where I knew there was no guard rail, I stomped on the gas pedal. We surged ahead. I guided my car into the rear of his, hit his bumper, and twisted the wheel savagely to the right. His car slewed off the road and into the air as neatly as a bird taking flight, except he went down, not up. I kept going, around the switchback and into another, where I could see the Strawberry River in the canyon below. The only evidence of the thug's cars was a series of ripples, already dying down.

"He's dead," Jeri said in a low voice.

I reached down and touched her hand, which was resting on my knee. She still liked to use the center seat belt. "I'm glad it went quick," I said, "but I'm not sorry, knowing what they probably had in mind for us, especially you."

"What do you think they'd have done to us?"

"Probably killed me before long, then tried to wring you dry before raping you and selling you to the highest bidder. That's if they knew Cresperians can change into human form. Otherwise, they'd probably have tortured us, thinking we knew the whereabouts of the aliens they've obviously learned are loose on earth. After that, they'd have killed both of us."

Surprisingly, that cheered her up as much as anything else I could have said. If there's a clear, clean-cut motive justifying it, Cresperians can kill, despite loathing the thought far more than humans do. I went on musing.

"What gets me is how the Russian Mafia got word before anyone else. They obviously have a connection into one of our security agencies or DoD."

"DoD?"

"Department of Defense, and there are several intelligence agencies controlled by them, as well. There's bound to be a leak in one of them. Damn, I knew the Russian Mafia had a long reach but I had no idea it went that far."

"Does the Mafia use computers?"

"Hmm. Good question. I'll get you to find out when we get a breathing spell. And if you can, find out which agency spotted us and how close on our trail they are."

"Okay." She patted my knee, then removed her hand from it. "I'll try. In fact, I'll start now. Maybe the satellites will work on either the phone or notebook here." She was carrying the laptop and smartphone I'd bought her. She got them both going simultaneously.

That reassured me. I had brought my own high-end laptop and a handheld with us, and our smart phones of course, but left the desktops at home. What bothered me was how much time we had to spare before the government started looking for us. It couldn't be long. When I mentioned the matter to Jeri, she didn't appear as worried as she should have been. Either she trusted my ability to keep us out of the hands of goons and any of the agencies that would split us up, or she had some more tricks up her sleeve. I guess that was the reason that I headed for Hatfield instead of the other way when we came to the next intersection. I decided to take a chance in order to create a little diversion and possibly make anyone looking for me think I wasn't involved. Wrong move.

Chapter Twelve

I know I've left a lot out about Jeri's conversion to human form (much of which I couldn't understand, anyway) and how she acted at first, but I can't tell everything. Just as an example, despite all Jeri's theoretical knowledge, she was continuously making little errors that a human woman wouldn't have. Almost all of them would have drawn curious looks, perhaps, but nothing more. Still, it was disconcerting, like when we were shopping and I asked her to try on the first selection. She headed for the ladies room to change. I had to run catch her before she got in trouble. The fact that department stores had changing rooms had completely escaped her study of our culture. And I still had the feeling that she was being condescending toward me despite all her endearments. Sometimes she'd ask me a question when I thought she must already know the answer. I figured she was trying not to make me feel inadequate when compared to her. I think she sensed that I *did* feel that way, despite my earnest efforts not to let her know, and even though I tried my best to suppress the feeling.

But I'm as human as anyone, and didn't always succeed. And then there were the sneaky little doubts over whether she really loved me that I couldn't keep from intruding into my mind despite my happiness at being married to her. Maybe she was just pretending, keeping me happy as a reward for all my help. Despite my occasional uncertainty, there was no question that I was head over heels in love with her, desperately so. I knew that, from the moment I threw my body between her and that thug, even though I was certain I was going to take a bullet in the gut for my efforts.

I did notice that my memory was much improved, no doubt due to her tinkering, but I didn't ask. I was content to let her work on me and enjoy the changes, especially after I found that I no longer had a bum hip and shoulder.

೮೦ೞ

I doubted anyone would even notice a car had gone off the road at that switchback. Drivers would be paying strict attention to their driving at that point, and passengers probably shrinking away from the unrailed side where they could see how far down they'd fall before hitting an obstacle, if they went off the road. It was far enough from my home that I didn't think there would be any suspicion I was involved when the car was discovered during the summer after the river went down. That headless body was sure going to rouse some curiosity if it hadn't been thrown from the car, though.

"Where are we going now, Kyle?"

"Into Hatfield to see the Sheriff. If anyone asks questions, just tell them we're heading west for our honeymoon and haven't picked a destination yet. I'm going to try throwing the bad guys off our trail. I sure as hell hope we have time for this."

She didn't ask any questions. During the rest of the drive she stayed busy with the laptop and phone, dragging data from satellite broadcasts with only an occasional interruption of reception when an overhang shadowed us.

෨ଔ

I checked my watch and drove directly toward the Sheriff's office, hoping I could catch him before he left for home. I did, barely. He was coming out the door of the courthouse as I drove up. I spotted his car and pulled into a spot right beside it and waited. He grinned when he saw me standing there and noticed that Jeri was sitting in my car.

"Hi, Kyle. How're the lovebirds doing?"

"Just fine, Sheriff," I answered, with a grin of my own. "Hey, could I ask you a favor?"

"Uh, sure." The grin disappeared. "You can always ask. Won't say whether or not I'll do it."

"Well, we're leaving for our honeymoon now and I was wondering if one or two of your deputies would like to earn a little extra money off duty by checking on my place a couple of times a day? What with all the nonsense lately with monsters and such, it would make us feel safer if they did."

"Shouldn't be a problem."

"Good Thanks. Here, I'll write you a check and let you divide it up however they want to work it."

He nodded. I always keep a few extra checks in my wallet to avoid having to carry my checkbook around. Gwen used to keep it, but now Jeri had it in her purse. I wrote a check for a thousand dollars and handed it to him.

"Hey," he said with raised eyebrows. "That's too much, son."

"Oh?" Son. He wasn't that much older than me, despite his white hair. "It's all right, Sheriff. I can afford it and it'll make me feel better. Besides, we may be gone quite a while. If that's not enough, I'll make up the difference when we get back. We're driving to the coast and stopping in Las Vegas for a few days on the way."

He shrugged and pocketed the check. The smile returned as he said, "Good luck." He shook my hand, tipped his Stetson at Jeri, and we drove off.

I explained to Jeri what I'd done and why. She just nodded, busy with the notebook again. We left in a direction indicating we'd be going west, but as soon as I could, I cut off on a side road and headed for the Interstate.

It was well after dark when we pulled into a little isolated quick stop type of place to buy gas, take a bathroom break and get something to eat. I didn't want to stop too long for fear we might be followed. Don't ask me why I thought that. Every now and then everyone gets those hunches or feelings, whatever they're called. I'm pretty well convinced there's something to psychic phenomena. The big boys say there's a probably a quantum connection to the whole universe. Some even say the entire universe is what we collectively *think* it is. It's too deep for me, but I do know some things happen that are too strange for coincidence. Once I dreamed Gwen bought an odd type of lamp at that miles-long garage sale, in Kentucky, I think, when she and her sister went on a trip together. I visualized the lamp clearly in my dream, and it was one of the rare kinds of dream you remember almost completely. When she got home, she showed me an exact duplicate of the lamp and told me she had bought it at that garage sale. See what I mean? Anyway, I was antsy as hell and wanted to get gone.

ଚଓଷ

The car was out by the gas pump. I noticed someone else had pulled in after us and left their car at the end of the tarmac. I wondered idly why they'd parked so far from the entrance, but gave it no further thought. We had passed through the door into the muggy air outside and taken only a few steps when Jeri grabbed my hand and yelled at me.

"Kyle! Run!"

I knew better than to doubt her now, but it still took a second or two to get my feet going while she tugged on my hand. We ran toward the car, but suddenly she stopped, turned and pointed a closed fist behind us. It took me a step or two to come to a halt and turn around. I was just in time to see an overbalanced man of the same type who had assaulted us at home plunge into a massive hole in front of him.

Once I get in gear, my mind works pretty fast. "How many were there?" I asked while glancing back toward the lighted interior of the store. The clerk was busy with his interactive comic book again, paying not the slightest attention to anything else.

"Three," Jeri said. "They all have guns."

I stepped a little closer to the hole, but still kept out of sight. "Toss out your guns! Quick, or you're going to go to the same place the tarmac did!"

I have no idea what they were thinking, but two handguns rose from the hole and landed at my feet.

"The other one!" I shouted. A moment later a third gun hit the asphalt, bounced once and came to rest. In retrospect, that was sort of a stupid move. Any one of them could have gone off from the impact. Fortunately they didn't.

I looked around. There was only one other parked car. The clerk must have someone coming for him. "Disappear that other car, Jeri," I ordered while I gathered the weapons. An instant later it was gone, along with a little more of the asphalt. Why I hadn't thought of that with the previous thugs I don't know. Maybe I just didn't want Jeri to have to kill again if she didn't have to.

"Okay, let's get out of here." I purposely headed back in the same direction we'd come from for a few miles, then pulled over to a stop. All the while, after Jeri had done her magic, she sat quietly while I drove.

"Is there any way for you to tell if there's a radio signal of any kind emanating from our car?" I asked Jeri.

"Yes." It took only a second or two. "Under the left rear, right back of the tire and in a few inches."

I got out with a flashlight I always keep in the glove compartment and removed the tracer. No wonder that bastard I'd run off the road had looked so smug. They'd put that thing on my car before we ever came out of the woods!

"Damn bastards." I tossed it into the grass and started back the other way. "You're a sweetheart," I said to Jeri. Man, what a weapon! And what our military could do with something like that!

"I'm sorry, Kyle. I should have noticed it before, but I wasn't even looking for that sort of thing, and I've been kind of preoccupied with the searches you asked me to do."

"Never mind, you did great. Maybe we have a chance now."

Famous last words.

ಜಂ೪

We didn't stop again until we reached Little Rock. I hoped we could get lost in a big city, because despite removing the tracer, I still had a vague sense of danger that I couldn't put my finger on. I thought maybe when we stopped for rest I could coax it to the surface of my mind and find out what was bothering me.

"I was wondering," I said once we were on the outskirts of the city, "is there any way you can wipe out someone's short-term memory?"

"Hmm." She frowned, just as a human would have when considering a new problem. "I don't know for sure. I guess I could try if it was really important, but I wouldn't like doing it to an innocent person."

"Suppose it helped us out and wouldn't really hurt the person?"

She shrugged, just as a human woman might have. It was amazing how quickly she picked up little mannerisms like that. My only fear was that she was getting too many from me and not enough from other females. Somehow, I'd have to try to remedy that.

"As I said, I could try. It's not something I've thought of before. Why do you ask?"

"I'm still antsy but I can't explain why. Well, I can in a way. Whoever's feeding information to the Russian Mafia already knows how important you are—or rather, that there are definitely aliens on earth. I have no idea how much else they know—only that they've tracked us down. Somehow, the lifeboats must have left a signal that at least roused the suspicion of some agency, and they tracked yours either directly to my house or to the general area. I've got to get some sleep sometime soon, and I want a chance to think. Maybe whatever I'm worried about will come to mind. I'm going to find us an obscure motel and stop for a while, but it would be nice if the night clerk forgot we were there."

"I think I can do that much."

I'd been driving while we talked. Soon enough I found what I wanted, remembering the area from the six months I'd spent under cover in Little Rock, trying to trace a pipeline of stolen military weapons.

It wasn't much. I paid cash and hesitated over signing the register until the clerk produced the room cards. Then he suddenly got a blank look on his face and quit moving; he just stood staring into space. I grabbed the cards and we vamoosed. As soon as we were out of hearing, I said, "I take it you made it work?"

"Uh huh. He'll come out of it in a moment and have no memory of us checking in. It took a few minutes to accomplish, as you noticed, so don't depend on it if we're in a hurry, at least not until I know more. I don't want to injure innocent people. Having to hurt or kill vile ones is bad enough." She paused for a moment while I parked and got what luggage we'd need out of the trunk. As I unlocked the door, she continued, "Kyle, until now I had no idea of how ruthless and cruel humans can be, even though I've read so much of your history. It just didn't seem real to me." She smiled. "You've been too much of a good influence on me."

"I'm glad, sweetheart. But you're just going to have to keep in mind that there's a tremendous variation in human beliefs and behavior. And if I remember right, you told me that some of your younger crewmates may be influenced by whichever humans they contact first."

"I said I think that may be the case. In fact, I think it will be. I just can't tell to what extent and see no way of finding out. I suppose it will depend a lot on how much information they're allowed access to."

"Got it. Let's grab a shower before going to bed, just in case we have to leave in a hurry. Okay?"

That smile again. I had a suspicion our shower would last longer than it normally would. I was exactly right. We washed off together and made love in the little alcove, then again when we climbed into bed. Jeri had learned to make the byproducts of our unions disappear into the quantum foam, so there was no need to use the bathroom again. I fear we disturbed our neighbors, but I didn't worry about it. Anyone staying in this sort of place would probably expect noises such as we made.

We lay with our bodies close together afterward, all nice and snug and contented. Just before I dozed off, Jeri whispered in my ear. "Go on to sleep, Kyle. I'm going to do some more research." I barely heard her. My memory was improving and I thought I was needing less sleep than before, but I definitely still needed several hours a night in order to be at my best.

She had told me she could go several days without sleep if necessary, but rather enjoyed the experience when she did sleep and presumably dream. Just one more new thing she was finding enjoyable as a human. Too bad there's so much that's deplorable about our species.

Chapter Thirteen

Jeri was still hard at it when I blinked my eyes open. I was lying on my side and could see the appearance of both concentration and concern on her features. She must have sensed that I was awake. She stood up and came over to sit on the side of the bed. She bent down and kissed me and stroked my face while I let my hands wander over her waist and breasts. I could very easily have drawn her into bed with me, but that look on her face when I first woke up deterred me.

"Finding out anything useful?" I asked when our lips finally parted company.

"Yes, and you're probably not going to like it."

"Can it wait for me to run to the bathroom and shave and brush my teeth?"

"Go ahead. I sensed you getting restless and started getting ready to leave an hour or so ago."

It only took five minutes or so to get me looking much better than I had a few minutes earlier—too much better. My wrinkles were fewer and there wasn't quite so much gray in my hair. And I felt younger, and had more energy than normal. Jeri at work. I was going to have to ask her to slow down the process, at least so far as my appearance went. There would be nothing so apt to get the wolves baying on our trails as the hint that she had a means of restoring youth. And it wouldn't do a damn bit of good trying to convince the masses, or the agencies, that she didn't have a secret that would work for everyone. Aging and death are the two great fears of mankind, whether most of us admit it or not. Just looking at all the nostrums advertised to slow the aging process and all the books written on the same subject should be enough to tell anyone that, even though a majority of people deny it.

When I came out of the bathroom, Jeri already had some of the snack food I'd bought at the quick stop on the little table and coffee ready. Even dumps like we were in had net connections in case of low batteries and coffee machines with pre-measured little bags of grounds nowadays. While we were eating sugar-loaded pastries and I was getting my caffeine fix, she told me what she'd been up to.

"You were right about the leaks, sweetheart. I found at least two. One is from the chairman of the Senate Select Committee on Intelligence, Senator Jack Wellgood. He's where the Russian Mafia's been getting their data. The same information is going to Alvin Grayson, a very large contributor to Congressman Moses Tarryall, who's on the House Permanent Select Committee for Intelligence, HPSCI. It's Tarryall who's feeding it to him."

Good God and Boogram, too! All three of those men were very well known and respected, although rumors of unethical business deals trailed Grayson like a string of tin cans on a newlyweds' car. None had ever been proven, though. And no one would ever guess those congress critters were funneling information from their committees to anyone other than those who had "need to know." Both the SSCI and the HPSCI dealt with extremely sensitive information relating to "black" funding, items so secret that spending on them was buried deeply in other bills coming from both chambers of congress. It was hard to believe, but I had to. Particularly when my and Jeri's lives and freedom were at risk because of it.

I didn't have to think much to know what Grayson was after: more money and power. He was already a billionaire many times over, but was one of those kinds of men who were constantly seeking to expand their wealth, power and domain and had very few moral scruples about how they did it. The other two were the ones who flummoxed me. I wondered how they passed the lie detector tests. Or were they even given to politicians? A moment of consideration, and I thought, nah, not a goddamned elected representative in Washington would ever stand still for it, and few appointees. They had too much sleaze to hide. It really didn't matter, though. I trusted Jeri.

"What else?"

"Both of the committee members have not only given out the position to which one of the NSA satellites tracked the location of two of our lifeboats, including mine and the one where at least one Cresperian was captured, but they've just now informed those higher up in government. I don't know why they delayed."

"Humph." Jeri still didn't really get it. "I do. They're traitors to their country. Somehow they were able to sit on the data long enough to tell their goddamned friends first and give them time to come after us, before notifying the proper authorities. I'd be willing to bet your friend in the hands of the government was reported by outside sources right from the start and captured quickly, though I still don't know which agency or sub-branch of an agency is holding him. But if they know about us now, they are bound to be on our trail soon, if they're not already." I thought over her news for a moment. "I suspect it was only after your friend was killed in Mexico that radar and other data were backtracked and gone over with a fine tooth comb, trying to pinpoint anomalies enough to get landing points. That must be one reason why we weren't tackled right away, although certainly not the only one. Those congressmen had their committees sit on the data long enough to inform their friends—the Russians and Grayson."

"All this violence and extreme competition between individuals and nations still seems insane to me, Kyle. I'm beginning to think we should have kept better records of our own development. Even so, it's one of those things, uh, right under your nose?"

"Can't see the woods because of the trees?"

"Yes, that's it. It's so obvious in retrospect from life we've found on other planets, and even on our own for that matter, that we should have realized we'd been through the same evolutionary and cultural developments that humans are experiencing now."

Jesus H. Christ! How old were they, anyway? But I doubted we had time to go into that now. Again. We had to hit the road, and I needed a little quiet time to think about what to do with the information Jeri had found. I was beginning to doubt our ability to stay out of harm's way without government protection, but I damn sure didn't want to see Jeri picked up by whatever agency was already holding at least one of her stranded friends. I had to let someone in the government know about the leaks, soon, though, or I'd feel as guilty as they already were. I asked Jeri to slow down the repairs of my face but to keep the rest going if she could separate the two, and also to get back on the net and find the name of the specific agency holding that other Cresperian. I wanted to avoid falling into their hands! And I began to ruminate on two sources of possible help. One was the senator I'd mentioned to Lester and the other was an old military contact.

But it wasn't government agents who got to us first.

☜☞

We had barely finished loading our luggage. I was preparing to open the car door for Jeri and she was smiling at me in anticipation of the gesture, when another car came zooming into the parking lot and rammed into the back end of my vehicle, barely missing me. Mine slewed sideways a few feet, causing the front to go the other way. It knocked me off my feet and staggered Jeri. I fell backward. My head hit the cement hard enough to momentarily knock me senseless. The whole thing happened so quickly that by the time I got a few brain cells working again after the blow to my head, Jeri was already in action.

Two men had jumped from their car right after banging into us, and obviously had managed to disconnect the air bags because I saw no sign of them having discharged later. One had just reached Jeri. She shrank away, as if afraid. Her assailant made a move to simply shove her aside in order to get to me. He was holding a pistol in one hand. Jeri quickly moved inside his guard, what he may have had of it. A hard slam of her elbow batted his pistol from his hand. She grabbed his other arm with one hand and brought her other up in a hard fist, snapping the elbow joint with an audible *crack!* He screamed at the excruciating pain as she shoved him into the advancing form of the other man. It was intended to knock both of them down, but somehow they managed to stay on their feet, even the one with his forearm dangling backward. He was out of it momentarily, though, blinded by tears of pain already streaming down his face.

I had my little S&W automatic out by that time, but I fired in such a hurry at her other opponent that I missed with my first two shots and by then she was in the line of fire. I never saw the third man. Obviously, they didn't yet know that the aliens could change their form to human. It was me they were after, thinking I had information about where the alien spacecraft was hidden. I spotted him just as he aimed at Jeri's back, clearly intending to kill her.

The gun exploded, blowing his hand off. Some shrapnel fragments hit him in the face. One of them put out his right eye. He yelled and tried to clutch his face, then doubled over and vomited when he saw the mangled strips of flesh and tendons and bits of broken bone where his hand had been a second ago.

I didn't know why Jeri hadn't used her disintegrator on them, since they were so clearly bent on murder and mayhem, other than her aversion to killing. I had no such qualms. Still in a sitting position, I saw the one with the broken elbow scrabbling for what must be a weapon in an ankle holster. I didn't miss this time. Two quick shots both hit him in the head, one snapping it back, the other catching him in the chin and exiting the back of his head in a shower of blood and gray matter.

I got to my feet and stepped over to the only one still alive. He was just straightening back up. I pointed my pistol at his face.

"Two seconds to tell me who sent you or you're dead!" I shouted, partly because I couldn't hear very well from the effects of the explosion and gunfire.

"G...Grayson," he stammered. His face was bloody and spotted with black marks from bits of metal embedded in his skin.

That told me all I wanted to know. I killed him with a shot between the eyes.

Heads were beginning to poke from doors of a couple of rooms.

"Police! Get back inside!" I yelled, waving my gun. They disappeared. This wasn't the kind of place where anyone wanted to become involved with the police, even as a witness.

I went over to Jeri. She was trembling and looking around like Bambi without his mother. I pulled her against my chest and comforted her for a moment, but there wasn't any time to lose. We had to go. That explosion and gunfire was sure to invoke calls, from the motel clerk if no one else.

One look at my car and I saw it wasn't going anywhere. The front bumper of the other heavy sedan had crumpled the rear fender up against the tire. Jeri could probably have fixed it, but I had no idea how long it might take and I suddenly decided we'd better get rid of it, anyway.

I took a quick look at their vehicle and saw the keys dangling from the ignition.

"Jeri, disappear the bodies and our car, but be careful not to hurt theirs. We're going to use it. Let's grab our luggage first, though."

She nodded, catching on immediately despite her distress. She pulled herself together and took care of the bodies while I grabbed our suitcases and threw them into the back seat of the Lincoln they were driving. Our car went next. We jumped in the Lincoln and got the hell out of there. I drove away, just at the legal speed limit. The last thing I wanted right now was to get pulled over. And damn my soul, I realized I should have killed those other Russian thugs who tried to jump us at the convenience store. More of them would be after us, too. I had been trying to assuage Jeri's feelings, knowing her attitude about killing.

The Lincoln didn't have a console. Jeri moved over close to me. I put my hand on her thigh, hoping my touch would reassure her. Poor thing, events were moving a little too fast for someone thinking in terms of centuries and who'd never been exposed to interspecies violence. I hardly knew what to say to her, but I tried.

"I'm sorry, Jeri. I'm doing the best I can, but I realize now that we're going to have to have some protection, despite all your magic. Someone's bound to get lucky sooner or later. Oh! Is there a tracer on this car?"

"No," she said and wiped a tear off her face. "Not that I can tell. But Kyle, I don't *want* to go to the government, not if I'll be treated like my friend is."

"I don't either, sweetheart. Let me think, okay?"

I glanced at her. She nodded and tried to smile. I patted her leg, then had to grab the wheel with both hands to maneuver in the morning traffic. But I got my thinker busy, anyway. After a while I came up with a plan that might work, but it still had a flaw or two that Jeri might object to. We were fairly near a good spot to get started, and the first part was necessary whatever else we did.

"Jeri, I have a friend from my time in the army. He was in the intelligence service with me and a career commissioned officer, not a warrant officer like I was until I got shot up. I think he'll help us if I put it to him right. In fact, in hindsight I should already have called him. I'll explain in a few minutes but first we need to change cars. That damn Grayson has enough pull to have roadblocks thrown up and get the police looking for this car when his hired help doesn't report back. Let's make sure we have that covered first."

"All right. Can I help?"

"You sure can, babe." I explained what we were going to do and she agreed readily enough, especially after I told her we could take care of compensation for a stolen car later. It would still be theft but wouldn't really hurt anyone.

I drove to a medium-sized factory I remembered that was on the outskirts of the city in the same direction we wanted to go. The day shift was just arriving. I pointed to a woman driving a SUV only a couple of years old, who was just pulling into the parking lot. Jeri went into her concentration mode. She was attempting a trick she hadn't tried before. The woman parked, then just sat in her seat, not moving, while Jeri toyed with her short-term memory. After almost a minute she got out and walked off toward the plant entrance, leaving her keys dangling in the ignition. I got into that car and had Jeri follow me to a Super Wal-Mart. I left the Lincoln there and transferred our luggage to the SUV.

"Shew." Once we were back together, Jeri shook her head. "I just found out there are limits to what I can do, Kyle. It's not that difficult to dispel a short-term memory, but planting a false one in its place is beyond me, at least for now."

Oh well. I had wanted her to try making the woman think she'd sold her car and accidentally left her key chain in it and intended to hitch a ride home. I was going to have Jeri rearrange some banking records to compensate her for the car soon as we had time, and had hoped she'd never put out an alarm. We'd still have an eight-hour head start, though.

I'd settle for that. Once we were on the road again, still heading east, I told Jeri exactly what I had in mind.

"As I said, I think my friend Bill will help us, but before turning ourselves in, I want a guarantee that we make the rules about questioning you. Not only that, I'm going to insist on a lot of private time for us and full contact with the rest of the world over the internet if we can swing it. Also, I want them to let me bring some of my old buddies and their families to wherever they keep us, so long as they're willing. I want you to start having a social life, especially with some other women, rather than spending all your time with me. Okay so far?"

"It sounds good, but can your friend guarantee all that?"

"Hell if I know?" I shrugged. "But we're not going unless he can agree to the terms. Most of them, anyway. There's a problem, though. Ishmael is still being mistreated and I'm not sure he'll be able to swing enough weight to make the agency holding him turn loose." As I mentioned, when we decided we needed a name for Jeri's friend, my often weird thought processes caused the opening line of Melville's book to pop into my head. *Call me Ishmael.* And Ishmael he was from then on, or Ish for short.

"You must have some kind of plan, though." She made it a declarative sentence. I was relieved she had so much faith in me. I just hoped I could live up to her expectations.

"I do. First, I want you to see if you can determine the agency that's holding Ishmael. Then if you agree to the risk, I still want to try grabbing him."

"How? And why? I mean why not let Bill help us?"

"Well, those places are usually designed more to keep other people out than for the ones already there to leave. So with your ability to erase short-term memory and spot bugs and things like that, I suspect we can get in and out. As for letting Bill help, I'm all for it, but I don't know if there's enough time. Ishmael is being hurt and there's a chance they may move him if we wait on Bill. However, it's possible we'll get caught if we try it alone and you might have to kill again to get loose. I probably wouldn't mind so long as I knew which ones were the real bad guys, but…hell, even if you can tell me which are which, we still might have to eliminate some innocents. Or possibly get blown away ourselves."

I sure as hell hoped not. I don't think I'm afraid to die if it's for a good enough reason, but now I had a chance of living a long time with a woman I loved, and seeing a lot of the ideas I'd read about come to fruition. I wanted that. *Space. Going to Mars and the other planets. Maybe even heading for the stars eventually. And Boogram's backside, think of all the technology and scientific endeavors just getting started. I might live long enough to see real nanotechnology working for us. Or fusion power. Maybe I'd even be on hand to watch some of the more exotic ideas be realized. I had always been a fan of those teleporters from science fiction shows and books. I'd like to see them. Real artificial intelligence would be cool, too.*

I shook my head to stop my skittering mind. It was acting like a drop of water bouncing around on a hot stove.

"Tell you what. Let's keep driving east and you get back on the net and see what else you can pick up about your friend, especially the agency holding him. In the meantime, soon as we're out of state we'll be relatively safe in this car. That's when I'll try getting in touch with Bill. Heck. When the car's reported stolen, you can get into the records and wipe out the report, can't you?"

"Which agency. Police?"

"Uh huh. Little Rock Police. Even better, if you can go there now and rig things to where our e-mail gets a ding when the license plate and description goes up, and do it without them knowing, you won't have to waste time monitoring them. You can erase it right then. With me so far?"

"I think so. I'll ask if I need help."

I glanced over at her and grinned to show how much I appreciated everything she was doing, even if it was on her behalf.

"Okay, love, now first thing, I want you to get into the Officers' Personnel Records at the Pentagon and see if you can find where William J. Shelton is stationed now. There may be more than one person by that name, so go by his age. He's..." I had to stop and think a moment. He had been my boss and was a light colonel then. "...somewhere in the mid forties, maybe early fifties. I don't know what his rank will be now, but he's probably a Colonel. Or possibly still a Lieutenant Colonel, but I doubt it. He was on the colonel's list for promotion last time I talked to him. That ought to narrow it down enough. See if you can find out his home phone number or even his work number. Otherwise, get his address and everything else about where he is and what he's doing. If that doesn't work, I think there's an index somewhere that has a list of cell phone numbers with names. It's not public knowledge so, you may have to work at it."

"Anything else?"

"Uh, let me think." Man, did I love her attitude! "That ought to keep you busy for a while. Oh—his address and phone number might be classified but it'll be somewhere. You should be able to track him down unless he's in deep undercover and I kind of doubt that."

She leaned toward me and gave me a quick peck on the cheek, then got busy.

Chapter Fourteen

"Kyle, I think I found him." It turned out to be surprisingly easy. Hardly any time had gone by when she said, "I have a Brigadier General named William S. Shelton. He's fifty-one. Does that sound close?"

That had to be him. Old Bill was doing pretty well for himself. We'd gotten on a first-name basis after I was discharged, but I'd still feel kind of funny addressing a general by his first name after my time in the military.

"Have you got a home phone number for him?"

"Uh huh. It's not listed in the Post Directory, but it was easy enough to find. I have his home and work number both."

"That's my girl. Write it down, just in case you're asleep when I call. Where's he stationed now?"

"Stationed?"

"Where does he live and work?"

"Oh. Military jargon, I guess. It said his assignment is in the Pentagon and his job title is Commanding Officer of Special Affairs Intelligence for Technology. It's abbreviated as SAIT. Is that good?"

I laughed, causing a couple of tiny puzzle lines to form between her eyebrows.

"Sweetie, in the intelligence community, titles can be awfully misleading. Sometimes the title is a cover for something entirely different. And acronyms were probably invented by the military about the same time writing was, if not sooner. However, maybe we're hitting a bit of luck for a change. The technology part sounds interesting, at least. I think I'll wait and call him at home, though. Sometimes it's hard to get through the flappers at that level."

"Flappers?"

"Uh, a literary reference. *Gulliver's Travels*, if I remember right. Someone who speaks to you in place of the important person you really want to talk to. The English language is filled with references like that. A lot of them come from Shakespeare, but there're others. You can get into old English literature later on when we have more time if you like, but I found most of it boring. *Gulliver's Travels* was one of the few books I liked. When you have time for poetry, start with Coleridge. He was good." Damn. I was getting off track again. That happened with Jeri for a long time. One thing always seemed to lead to another, and that to a third and forth and so on. "Moat dragons, some people call them that. They are the dragons in the moat that keep you from getting into the castle to see the king."

"I like that one better," she replied.

"Anyway, I think we'll have an easier time talking to him at home than at the Pentagon, and if he can help at all, he'll tell me so. He won't lie to me. Besides, last time we served together we had a little code we used over the phone."

"How can you be so sure he won't lie, Kyle? Lying seems to go with being human, like uh, pancakes and syrup."

"Good enough analogy." She was doing her damnedest to learn when to use all the little idioms and slang expressions so common to the English language. It's part of what makes English so rich and versatile, but it's also the portion that causes so much trouble when others try to speak it. So much depends on the context, dialect, age and educational level of the audience, among many other factors. If she didn't have a perfect memory she would be fouling up constantly, especially not being human originally.

"To heck with analogy. I want to know."

"Don't worry." I glanced her way and grinned. "These wounds I have—had, I mean—were from bullets meant for him. He'd be dead if I hadn't pulled him out of the line of fire. That's something a person doesn't forget. Ever."

"Kyle, I believe you, but you seem so...so nonchalant about how you almost got killed in order to save someone else. I know it's common in human warfare and some other situations, too, but...well, given your pitifully short lifetimes, it's hard for me to fathom. I can understand to a degree dying in order to save someone you love, like you were willing to do for me, but..." She suddenly stopped speaking. I glanced over at her again for a moment. Her eyes were opened wide, and a strange, almost *alien* expression had replaced that of a young, pretty woman trying to decipher a puzzle. Even after I turned my attention back to the traffic, I could still feel her staring at me, almost as if it was the first time she'd ever laid eyes on a human being. I sensed her shifting in the seat and then she was pressed close to me. She kept one of her hands on my shoulder and slid her other across my waist and clutched my side, trying to get as close to me as possible. I felt her body heave with a great intake of breath, then she was sobbing uncontrollably, so hard that my shirt was soon soaked with her tears.

I spotted a break in the traffic just ahead and pulled off onto a side street. I loosened both our seat belts and took her into my arms and held her while she cried her heart out. I knew almost instinctively that right then was the moment when she became wholly, irrevocably human.

I said nothing other than murmuring little unintelligent words of comfort while I held her tight, which is just about all that's possible in situations like that. It's best not to talk until the other person is ready.

Eventually her crying tapered off into lighter sobs, then sniffs, and finally it was over. Still holding her with one arm, I searched blindly in the side pocket of the door for the little packet of tissues I always kept in the car. It wasn't there. It wasn't my car. Then I remembered the tissues I'd stuck in my shirt pocket. I let her go and handed them to her.

"Don't look at me." She sniffed one more time, then blew her nose. "Oh hell, what a mess. And I must look awful." See? She was as human as any woman on earth.

"You're beautiful," I returned, always the right thing to say to a woman whether it's true or not.

"I'm still a mess. Kyle…"

"Shh. You don't have to explain. I already know what happened."

"You do?"

"Uh huh. You've finally grasped right down to your very bones what it's like to be a human being. I don't think you completely understood all the implications before, but you do now. You *are* a human, and I don't think you could go back to being a Cresperian if you tried."

"You're right. I could, but I'd never want to. Please kiss me, Kyle, even if I do look awful. And oh my! Look what I did to your shirt!"

"Never mind." I kissed her, as gently and thoroughly as I possibly could.

After a while, we drove on, still heading east. Jeri was very quiet, when usually she could browse the net and carry on a conversation at the same time. She must have been going over all the ramifications of what it meant to be human. How we could both love and hate so deeply. How we differ so much individually, yet mostly have the same basic characteristics. What a wide range of emotion we're capable of. How we manage to govern ourselves, even if we do it badly most of the time. How we fight and go to war, then become friends with our previous enemies. How emotion and bias and the way genes are expressed and culture and ethnicity cause so many problems, yet give us such deep rewards. How we rationalize most of our decisions, and how loyalty to family and clan and city and nation originates and how it enriches our lives as well as causing misery for others. And how those and all the million and one other factors like religion and education and hormones and upbringing and environment merge into a giant indecipherable tangle in our minds, and create our personalities and make each of us a unique person. In one way I could almost feel sorry for her at having to try sorting all that out, yet in another I envied her for being able to learn it as an adult. She hadn't been subjected to all the idiocy, misinformation and harmful, unnecessary baggage we get as children while our personalities are being formed.

଼ଠଔ

I had driven south after leaving Little Rock, so we crossed the bridge into Mississippi at Vicksburg a little past noon. I could have taken a more northerly route, but I knew this way better and thought it might fool anyone tailing us about where we were heading. There were no road blocks. For the first time since Jeri found where her friend Ishmael was being held, I thought we were relatively immune to any more trouble. Of course, we were heading toward a very risky encounter, but that was still a few days off. And what the hell, maybe Bill—General Shelton, that was—could even help with that problem. Shucks, very shortly I was going to be more important than he was, even as Jeri's paramour if nothing else, so I might as well keep on calling him by his first name, privately, anyway. Maybe he'd even have to say "sir" to me while around other people, just the opposite of how it used to be. I chuckled at the thought, causing Jeri to look up from her notebook for a moment. I smiled at her and she got back to work. It was a good thing it was equipped with the new powercells that had just hit the market, as she was using it so much. I planned on having her take a break tonight in the most pleasant way possible, though.

I said I thought we were safe. Goes to show what happens when I start thinking of good stuff instead of danger. That's when the shit usually hits the fan.

଼ଠଔ

At least I got to talk to Bill, and managed that, um, break I had been anticipating ever since we crossed the bridge before the stuff started flying.

Again we checked into a ratty hot bed motel where they were unlikely to ask questions. Jeri sniffed at the odor as we opened the door to our room. I had long since gotten the impression that Cresperians liked a clean, orderly environment, and Jeri hadn't changed much in that regard. When I noticed her reaction I immediately told her to hang loose a minute. I walked back up to the desk and gave the manager an extra fifty for some fresh linen and a can of air freshener, then twenty more for immediate service.

While the maid was busy changing the sheets, Jeri and I stepped outside, where I used one of the disposable phones I'd bought in Little Rock that day we did all the shopping.

Bill's wife, Esmeralda, answered. She was an army brat he'd met in his teens, a third generation Hispanic and cute as a bug with her black hair and liquid brown eyes that could melt a man's heart with a single glance.

"Hi, Essie. Is Bill around?" I asked as casually as I could. "This is Mansom." I hoped Esmeralda would remember the old code Bill and I had worked out years ago so I could call him at home and not cause a ruckus if his phone had been tapped.

"Oh, hi, Manny. No, he's a little late today. Probably gassing up the car. Do you want him to call you back?" Great! She remembered, and didn't make any comments about how long it had been since we last talked.

"No, that's all right. Just have him give me a call when it's convenient."

"Okay, will do. 'Bye, Manny."

" 'Bye, Essie," I answered. That completed the message. In five minutes Bill would step outside with their phone and I'd call him back. Esmeralda would know it was important because no one but me would ever shorten her beautiful name. I only did it because it was part of our private code.

I checked off the time on my watch nervously while waiting. Jeri helped me pass the time by snuggling up against me, making us look like the typical couple who met at motels like that one.

I kissed Jeri one more time for luck, then dialed Bill's number. He answered immediately.

"Hi, Bill. This is Manny."

"Hi, Chief. Long time no hear! What's up?" His voice was louder than usual and I could visualize him trying to contain an explosion of questions. Instead he kept it casual, calling me Chief, even though it's not an official designation and I was no longer in the army.

"Oh, not much, Bill. I just need a little help with a problem I'm having and wonder if you could spare a few minutes."

"I've got plenty of time. What can I do you for?"

Great. That was his way of telling me there was no way his end of the conversation would be tracked. Not only did he have an encryption package attached to his phone that I was sure he'd activated, but it also hopped through several routers and a couple different satellites. And on his end there was a handshaking device that stripped off any IP packet information that might enable the signal to be geolocated or decrypted without the key code. And I was pretty sure Bill's key code revolved on some sort of random generator every day or so. At least it used to.

"I have a throwaway," I said. "Okay?"

"Yeah, I'm having it washed through several quantum processing algorithms for anyone who might be listening. Go ahead, and Chief, this better be good. Your name is like a big red light in the sky right now. How in hell you've kept from being caught already is beyond me."

When he said "washed" the encryption handshaking program on his end would automatically garble then untangle our messages going back and forth. If anybody actually did intercept our call, it was very unlikely they could decrypt it without knowing *a priori* the quantum algorithms and the key-codes both.

"It's been difficult, but I've had a lot of help, if you get my meaning."

"You have? Good God, Kyle, where are you? I'll have someone pick you both up before the bad guys grab you."

"Slow down, Bill. There's more than one group of bad guys after us."

"What? Who else besides the Muslim confederation and China?"

"Great Gold Gods of Gooshmail! I don't know anything about them! I was talking about the Russian Mafia and Alvin Grayson, that fucking tycoon that wants to own the world. Bill, you've got traitors on both intelligence committees on the Hill. Maybe even in the military, but I'm not sure about that yet."

"Tell me who the fuck they are before you do another goddamned thing, Chief!"

I could practically see steam coming out his ears.

"Bill, I'm not a Chief anymore, remember? I'm retired."

"We'll see about that. But that's beside the point. What's going on? And how can I help?"

I gave him all the information I knew.

"Goddamned politicians!" He cursed some more and almost hung up in his hurry to plug the leaks and perhaps do something unwise, but I stopped him in time.

"Wait up, Bill. I've got more and we desperately need help. One of our agencies already has an alien captive and we need to break him out before they kill him or he kills himself. Wait one."

I covered the phone with my hand and queried Jeri about the agency holding Ishmael. I'd forgotten to ask before calling.

"It's a branch of the CIA operating under cover as an Israeli Consulate and funded through several different fly-by-nights. It's referred to in the documents we saw as BLAT. I don't know why."

I repeated that to Bill and he cursed again. I could tell how irate he was by the simple fact that he seldom used profanity unless he had a very good reason. After he calmed down, I heard him sigh.

"I know that BLAT group. They're operating illegally as hell. The NSA, SecDHS, SecDef, and the DNI would never allow this inside the borders, not to mention that they should have been closed down long ago, and would have been if not for the very same politicians you named. Okay, who else?"

"I was questioned by an FBI agent named John Lester. He's about my age, maybe a little younger. I think I convinced him the stories about a monster at my place in Arkansas were pure bullshit, being spread by a hysterical UPS driver, but the fibbies may have caught on later."

"Arkansas? When did you move there?"

"Eight or nine months ago. I wanted to get away by myself after Gwen was killed and my brother died."

"Yeah. I hated that, Chief, and kind of figured you'd gone into isolation and that's why we haven't heard from you. Is that where you are now?"

"No. We're a ways past Vicksburg, heading east on I-20 to where our friend is being held and tortured. We call him Ishmael, since we had to give him a name. We're going to break him out."

That brought on another round of cursing, not so much over my plans as over the mention of torture. Well, maybe both. I could imagine how important the military thought getting their hands on some alien technology was. Shucks, a good many would kill their own mother with bare hands and nary a quiver just to have an alien who had traveled the stars to talk to! When he finally stopped cussing, he told me that the acronym of that little sub-branch of the CIA didn't exist and that it was a rogue group pretending to be government operatives, that the FBI and the CIA had been trying to round up for years. There was even some hint that the BLAT group was funneling information to various international terrorist organizations, most of which were Muslim or Chinese. He asked how he could help right now and with the rescue as well. That told me all I needed to know about the reputation of the Blats, as we called them from then on.

"There's more, Bill. Before we let any agency get their paws on either of us, we want some guarantees." I ran through them, and then added a couple more Jeri and I had come up with. "Think a minute, then tell me whether or not you've got the moxie to stand off anyone or any agency trying to break the promises you make to us. Otherwise, we're going to have to look further."

That was enough to tell him how deeply we felt about each other and how serious we were. I was, anyway. He had no method of judging an alien, so he had to go by what I told him. I didn't mention I had already decided he was our only hope of staying free. Senator Bentley could help but the military had the muscle.

"You still there, Bill?" The silence told me how hard he was concentrating on what I'd told him.

"Yeah, I'm here. Look, I'm in the military and I have to follow orders, but if push comes to shove, I'll take a court-martial or resign before breaking my word. I owe you my life, Chief, and I'll never forget that. I'd even try to help you escape if I had to."

I knew how much Bill loved the army and our country, same as me. Maybe more, so he wasn't just mouthing off. And I'd never known him to back down or desert a friend when he felt strongly enough to take a stand over a matter. He'd faced a court once rather than do what he thought was wrong—and been vindicated. If we were ever betrayed, the ones who did it better not ever turn their back on him. Or even come face to face with him. Ditto for me.

After a pause he said "There's one thing that would help me out, Chief, and that's reactivating you. I'll get waivers going on your disabilities but I'll start the help now."

"Wait one." I told Jeri I'd probably have to go back into the army but it was okay and she said go ahead.

"Okay, General Bill, where can you send me some help? And I mean tough help and soonest. I'll call you back later. Just get a team together and get them moving. In fact, get whoever's the closest to us that you trust utterly and head them this way in front of your team. We need to rest up a few hours but I don't want to stay here long. We're at the Hideaway Motel on the eastern outskirts of Vicksburg, about a half mile from the interstate. Oh yeah, one more thing. The woman I'm traveling with is more important than I am. If push comes to shove, save her first. Understand?"

"Um, I'm not certain but I'll put that in my orders, anyway."

"Okay." I gave him a quick description of Jeri, the make and model and license plate of the SUV we were driving, told him how long we'd be staying, and which direction and highway we'd be on once we left. He said he had it, then gave me his personal phone number at the Pentagon to call for emergencies, and broke the connection before I could mention I wouldn't need a medical waiver now.

By then, the room was ready. We had only brought in the essentials: our two little handbags of underwear and bathroom accessories, the computers and phones, Jeri's purse, and the little touristy-type tote she'd bought at one of our stops, that held the rest of her survival kit. If we lost the car with the rest of our luggage, it wouldn't hurt that much. Even the tote held the less important parts of her equipment.

Chapter Fifteen

We each grabbed a quick shower and crawled into bed. After Jeri's epiphany earlier that day, she was more fervent with desire than ever before. When our bodies came together, the first touch of flesh was like a capacitor releasing a burst of electricity, shocking in its intensity. Moments later she climaxed twice in succession, crying out in short bursts of sound with such agonized emotion that they were akin to pain.

That first encounter released some of the tension we were both suffering. A little later we made love again, slower this time but no less delightful.

It happened near the end, just as we were both on the verge of another explosive orgasm. Jeri was straddling me, leaning forward but with her head thrown back and her mouth open, while I held her breasts and strained my hips upward, holding my breath and feeling ready to fly into pieces if I waited much longer for release. The door to our room crashed open. The flimsy wood splintered from the impact, leaving it hanging by one hinge.

"Freeze!" A man in a dark suit screamed. He shuffled to the side, allowing another man and a woman to enter. The second man holstered a big automatic of some kind and pulled a pair of plastic cuffs loose from his belt, while the woman sidled into position to fire if need be. She had a pistol with a silencer attached, holding it in a half-raised position so as not to point it at her companion while he secured us. She had on a dark brown windbreaker that hung on her like a sack. It was obviously used to conceal her weapon while traveling.

I couldn't even reach for my S&W lying on the bedside table. While we were occupied with each other, we'd shifted over to Jeri's side of the bed, and it was out of reach. Jeri very carefully removed herself from atop my hips, drawing an evil leer at her nakedness from the dark-suited man who'd been first through the door. I was tempted to try for my gun right then but I was still fearful of her safety. I had no idea whether they knew she was an alien or not—they could still think she was my Albanian wife.

"Watch the woman, she's dangerous. Kill her if she moves," the second man told his companions. To me he said, "Roll over and put your hands behind your back."

"Fuck you," I said. I wasn't about to put myself in a helpless position while Jeri was still alive.

"Kill the woman," he retorted. It was their death knell.

Jeri had gotten off on the other side of me but was still on her knees, sitting back on her heels and facing the door. She must have sensed a finger tightening on a trigger because she didn't take time to aim her finger ring disintegrator. It took out the one holding the gun on us and part of the wall adjacent to the door. He and the wall just disappeared without a sound, along with part of the door jamb. Some bugs attracted to the light shining through the curtained window near the door flew into the room.

The female agent evidently saw her companion and part of the door and its frame blink out of existence from her side vision. It startled her for just an instant but no longer. She was good, and fast as well. She got off a shot at me as I was reaching for my little automatic, but hurrying threw her aim off just enough that she missed my arm which she must have been aiming at. When they ordered Jeri to be killed, I figured they still thought I held the key to the stars. Nevertheless, the bullet smashed into my hip with blinding force, rolling me onto my back. Just like the first time I'd been hit there, it was more shocking than painful at first. I sucked in a breath of air and clenched my teeth, again reaching for my gun. The woman had simply disappeared after firing her first shot, leaving only the man with the cuffs. "Don't kill him yet," I managed to gasp. The pain was just beginning to hit but I had to speak up.

"Why not?" Jeri asked, as calm this time as if she were at a tea party. She was staring directly at him, fire in her eyes. While he hesitated, not sure whether to try for his gun or not, she realized I'd been hit. Only her anger at the attempt on our lives had kept her perceptive sense from noticing it at once. "Kyle!" she screamed. "Goddamn them!" She disintegrated the last man's legs from just below the knees before turning her attention to me.

I saw her victim collapse, then suddenly felt woozy, even though I was lying down. I could still see, though. The guy had the cuffs clutched tightly in one hand, as if they were talismans that might stave off impending death. He watched stupidly as arterial blood pulsed from his stumps, turning the worn carpet a bright red color.

"Save him if you can, Jeri," I said through gritted teeth, my vision blurring. I wanted to know who this group belonged to, just in case we managed to get out of this. I had no doubt there was a backup squad outside.

These looked and acted like professionals. And thugs don't usually use women for this kind of work.

"You first," she said, still calmly, but I had the impression of a raging anger, barely held in check and only subdued by her worry over me.

I stole a glance at my hip and saw that it wasn't bleeding, and then suddenly the pain went away. At the same time she must have done something for the one whose feet were gone, or he would have bled to death while she was helping me.

My vision cleared as the pain faded. Within a moment or two, I felt almost normal, although I knew I must have a lot of damage to my hip. I just hoped I'd be able to get out to our car.

"There's more of them outside," Jeri said.

"Are they coming in?"

"I can't tell from this distance."

"Then just keep watch. But you'd better grab that fellow's gun while he's still out of action."

She took the weapon. She didn't bother to put any clothes on—nudity never bothered her under any circumstances, especially when more important business took priority.

I tried to move closer to the side of the bed in order to see our fallen miscreant. The action caused a stabbing bolt of pain in my hip. I gasped and held very still.

"Damn it, Kyle, don't move until I tell you it's okay. I'm still working on you." It was the first time Jeri had ever raised her voice with me, but I knew it was out of concern rather than anger. I stayed where I was and questioned him from there.

"What agency are you with, bud? Make it quick, we're in a hurry."

He shook his head and kept his lips closed. I could tell he must be hurting, but he was doing a good job of holding it in. Whatever else, he had guts.

"We can take both your hands off just as easily as your legs, and blind you in the process if that's the way you want it," I said. "No arms, no legs, no eyes, but we'll leave you alive."

He didn't take any more convincing. Thoughts of being a total cripple are worse than any amount of torture for most people. "Homeland Security. NSA. There's more of us outside, so you may as well give up," he declared, answering my next question at the same time. "You're not going anywhere with your hip shot off, anyhow."

"You'd be surprised," I told him, forcing a smile to maybe give him the idea I wasn't as bad off as he thought. "How many more and where are they?"

"We've got both entrances to the motel blocked. Three agents in each vehicle. You can't get away. We've got orders not to kill you, but there's nothing saying we can't touch your woman. Think about that."

I was, whether he knew it or not. Damn it all, we shouldn't have stopped, but...well, fuck it, I told myself. Can't change the past. You do what you think is best at the time and that's all anyone can ask. I knew one of the turncoats must have finally given information to the NSA and now they were here. But some way or other, we had to hold out until Bill's people got to us. How long had we been here? I didn't know; my watch was on the table with my gun, but it had been at least an hour, probably longer. Not long enough. Help might be close but it also might be several hours away.

"Scoot over to the door, no matter how much it hurts you. Holler at your buddies and tell them to stay back for the time being."

"That won't help."

"Maybe." I grinned. It must have been more like a grimace, because he looked away from me. "Tell them you've a gun to your head and we'd rather commit suicide than be captured."

He thought for a moment, trying to decide whether we had a way out or not. He was tough. I think he might have sacrificed himself rather than let us get away if he thought we had a chance. I guess he didn't think we could escape, because he carried out my orders, right to the letter. Jeri must have blocked some of his pain, because he was able to call out in a loud voice.

"You're doing fine," I said. "Now crawl back out of sight."

"I think the one who ordered the woman to kill me was the worst," Jeri said. "I'm sorry I couldn't save her."

"It's okay, sweetheart. You do what you gotta do when the time comes and hope you're right. Now hand me my phone and gun, and you keep an eye on things while I call Bill. Okay?"

She nodded but didn't speak, apparently still concentrating on my hip. I could feel things going on inside, but it was like a dentist working on your mouth with your jaw deadened. No pain, just a creepy crawly sensation where repairs must be taking place.

Bill answered on the second ring.

"We're in trouble," I said immediately, then went on to tell him we were still at the little motel and described what had happened.

"Can you hold out another twenty minutes?" he asked.

I glanced at Jeri.

She shrugged and reflected for a moment. Her acute hearing had caught both sides of the conversation. "If they don't do anything unusual, it won't be a problem."

I repeated her statement to Bill and added, "Just remember I can't walk or hardly even move. We don't know how long they were given to capture me, but I suspect as long as it takes. They may decide on an odorless gas, or something like that. Oh yeah, they still think I'm the one. Keep it that way, or rather make sure anyone you have to tell or who knows differently is taken into deep custody and not allowed contact with the outside world again."

"Understood. Don't try teaching an old dog tricks he already knows, Chief," he said, and then told me to hang on. Help was on the way, lots of it. "A man by the name of Sam Haley will be leading the team. He's Afro-Italian and a big mother, with short curly hair. Watch for him. And keep this line open so I can monitor events."

"Got it." I laid the phone down. Jeri moved so that she was sitting sideways, allowing me to prop my head on her thigh for closer contact. I felt a wave of assurance course through me. It felt good, whether it was induced by her or came from my own mind. She stroked my face and bent down to kiss me, making me feel even better.

The NSA agent lay quietly on the floor, not sure of what was going on but I could tell he was beginning to get worried over our apparent unconcern. That was easy to fathom, especially after what Jeri had done. He had to be disconcerted after seeing the power he thought I had wielded, and sickened by what had happened to his feet, but he was a professional. I would bet money he was already beginning to regret the decision not to kill me immediately. I doubted malice on his part—just an unpleasant duty he would have performed in service to his country. I hoped he lived. If help arrived in time we could take him with us, but if they had to hurry, someone might make the decision to simply kill him and be done with it. I didn't like the thought. It would get them off on the wrong foot with Jeri, and with me, too.

If I've been making Jeri sound like a superwoman in this narrative, it wasn't quite like that. She could be killed easily under the right circumstances. She wasn't a mind-reader nor could she work miracles, and there were limits to what she could do with her survival kit, as I found out a moment later.

"Kyle, my ring is pinging. It's telling me it needs to be recharged before long. I've had to use it too often."

"Can you do it now?" Shit, that didn't sound good.

"No, not until we can rig up some kind of energy conversion system. I thought I'd better tell you so you and your friends won't depend on it too much. It still has enough power to keep those people out there at bay, though. And to help with the rescue."

"Thanks, sweetie." It was good to know, but didn't make me feel any easier.

She had given me my watch while retrieving my phone and gun. I glanced at it. Ten more minutes, at least.

The waiting was like the movement of a supercooled liquid, dragging on forever. I'd read once that an upright pane of glass would spread at the bottom and sag in the middle from the pull of gravity if given enough time. Say a few hundred years or something like that. I didn't remember exactly, but time seemed to be passing just that slowly, made all the worse by the tension of not knowing exactly what was going on outside.

"Hello in there?" Eventually a voice called to us, a woman's voice. "I want to come in and talk! I'll be unarmed! Don't hurt me!"

"Damn," I said to Jeri. "Can you spare enough attention to tell if she's lying or hiding a weapon?"

"Yes."

"I'll stall," I whispered so our friend on the floor couldn't overhear me. Shucks, I barely heard my own voice but she had no problem. She nodded her head minutely, trying not to give anything away.

"Tell her to come in, moving slowly and with her hands on top of her head," I said to the man on the floor.

He nodded and shouted the instructions.

A moment later an attractive middle-aged woman with shoulder length blonde hair came through the entrance, taking baby steps, and going slow, as we'd ordered.

"Easy." I waved my pistol at her. There was one chair in the room. It was occupied by our clothes. "Go sit on the chair. Put our clothes in your lap so they don't get blood on them."

She complied. Then when she was seated, replaced her hands on her head, with fingers interlocked. She wasn't taking any chances after she glanced at her legless compatriot and blanched, despite trying to maintain control.

"Hello." She started the conversation. "My name is Carolyn Blanchard. I'm the senior NSA agent on the premises. Anything I tell you or anything we agree to carries my guarantee that I'm not going to try deceiving you. Okay so far?"

"How about your superiors? You can't give them orders."

"Ha," she nodded and sort of laughed. It looked funny with her hands still on her head. "That's true, but my orders here will stand and anything I tell them will carry all the power and influence I'm capable of exercising."

Well, she was honest, anyway. Or it sounded like she was. I hated to bother Jeri while she was concentrating on my wound, but I needed her help.

"What do you think, hon?"

"She's being honest. I believe I could like her under different circumstances."

That made it a little easier, and the NSA woman raised an eyebrow at the comment. I decided to start out on a first-name basis, and assumed she already knew who I was.

"Listen closely, Carolyn, to everything I tell you. This is too important for you to try anything fancy. First, are you carrying a bug?" I waived the pistol slowly back and forth in front of her.

She hesitated, then nodded. "Yes."

"Tell your friends you're going to disable it for the time being. But first, move your chair to where they can see you from the outside, so they'll know we're not going to harm you."

I could tell she didn't want to do that but she also wanted this to end peacefully. She worried the problem over in her mind for a full minute before deciding to obey. Jeri told me when the bug went silent, drawing a peculiar glance from Carolyn. Then as she set back down in sight of the ones outside, her mouth dropped open. She suddenly realized that Jeri was the alien they were after, right here in the room with her. She closed her mouth and stared.

"Aha," I smiled at her. "Disconcerting, isn't it?"

"Yes." Her lips twitched in what might have been a wry smile. "Very."

"Okay, now I can tell you that I have help on the way. Everyone outside is going to be taken prisoner. If they resist, they'll be killed. I'm sorry, but it has to be that way. It's Military Intelligence that's going to be in control, not anyone else. You don't have to worry, though. Come along peacefully and you and the guys outside can be in on it. If any of you lie to me or my friends, or try to escape, Jeri will know and..." I gave the age-old thumbs down motion from the days of the Roman arena, depicting death.

She swallowed, but nodded. Her eyes were bright with intelligence and a burning curiosity. I agreed with Jeri—I could get to like this woman if we were given a chance.

"Okay, now hold on for a minute. You can put your hands in your lap if you want to."

She sighed with relief. Try holding your hands on top or your own head for a while and see how tiring it becomes.

"Hello," I said into the phone. "Bill, I may have the situation partly under control. How close are you and how many are coming to start with?"

"I have a squad of ten, no more than five minutes away, and more coming. They have orders to take over peacefully if possible, but to take control and get you out of there. Period."

Man, he really was putting his career and life on the line, giving orders that might result in the death of several NSA agents. I repeated to Carolyn exactly what Bill had told me.

"Do you think you can go outside and defuse the situation? Try to keep anyone from contacting higher-ups for now. Even better, you contact them and report that you have the situation in hand and will be reporting back in an hour or so. Can you do that? It means saving your life and those of your team, and the results will still be about the same. Our country will have Jeri, and we know the location of one of her friends as well that we're going to rescue."

It took her only a few seconds to analyze the situation. She decided we had the best hand, and folded her own. A fast thinker, and a decisive one. I wouldn't want to play poker with her.

"I'll do my best," she said.

"Good enough. Get started. You've got about five minutes before the fireworks start." I thought that might be a good time for Jeri and me to get dressed. In my case that just meant pulling on my shirt.

ഇന്ദ

Again time slowed to a crawl. It was worse than waiting on a slow freight train at a crossing with a sick child in the car. The time was just running out when I heard a shot from outside, then another in quick succession. Uh oh.

"Jeri, please get down. Behind the bed. Better yet, go to the bathroom and wait there."

"No. I won't leave you."

"Please. I've lost one wife. I don't want to lose you, too."

"No. I love you. I won't leave."

Damn, hell and other dirty words, but I quit arguing and began watching the door, my S&W ready. I just hoped one of us could tell the good guys from the bad. Well, crap, these weren't bad people, like the Mafia or Grayson's goons, but I knew Bill and I didn't know them.

There was one more shot, then silence. A second later I heard the sound of cautious footsteps near the door. I got ready. My pulse speeded up but my hand was steady.

A voice called out.

"Inside there, Kyle Leverson! Speak up!"

"Who is it?" I yelled.

"Sam Haley. My boss is General Shelton." He lowered his voice this time, but spoke in such a deep bass tone that even when he was talking normally it sounded loud and commanding.

"This is Kyle. Come on in, but slow. No weapon showing."

A shadow crossed the sidewalk in front of the entrance, then it was filled with the bulk of a big dark-skinned man with short graying hair, and curly, like Bill had said. His hands were by his side but he radiated alertness, like a quarterback in the midst of calling signals in the last seconds of a tie game.

"He's okay, Kyle."

"Good." I lowered my weapon but hung on to it. "What was the shooting about?"

"One of the NSA boys didn't want to obey orders."

"I see." I didn't ask what happened to him. "Where's Carolyn?"

"The lady is waiting outside with two of my men. Do you need her?"

"Yes, and I want all these people taken with us, and get us out of here quickly, far away, but head east, toward Virginia. I'll need a stretcher, and so will the gentleman on the floor."

Sam glanced at him, but scarcely raised a brow, nor did he waste time asking a lot of unnecessary questions. He was one cool dude, with that innate sense of priority all good leaders have. He tapped at the subvocal microphone on his throat and began giving orders over the wireless.

Chapter Sixteen

Even though I thought I was going to play only a minor role in the next event, I went along for the ride because they needed Jeri to help pull it off, and even that caused an argument at higher levels. I learned later that some of the trusted associates of General Shelton didn't want to risk her, but in the end it was her call and she couldn't be dissuaded. She insisted on helping rescue Ishmael. Then with that settled, I demanded to go along even if I had to be carried. I can imagine someone in the Pentagon finally throwing up their hands and saying, "Let them go, goddamnit! Maybe they'll all get killed and we can quit worrying about it." Of course, that was before they were truly aware of Jeri's tremendous importance. Not many at that point had been let into Bill's circle of advisors.

Jeri had managed to set up a communication system with Ishmael even though he was no longer allowed access to a computer. Some young genius had snapped to the fact that Crispies could manipulate our internet as easily and instinctively as a baby going after a nipple. All it took was Ishmael agreeing to a limited amount of cooperation and insisting on reading transcripts of all the data concerning him, both going and coming. Of course no one saw any harm in that, or believed their self-contained computers could be accessed through the electrical connections so long as they stayed off the internet. The scheme fooled them completely. Ishmael worded his replies to questioning in a fashion that Jeri could spot and she inserted a few changes in the manuscript before it was given to him to read in order to keep him posted. No one remembers every single sentence they utter, and if a few changes pop up, they'll tend to blame it on the transcriptionist. Human nature at work. If they'd been using generators for power, they might have been safe, but I wouldn't put it past Jeri to have figured out a way to bust even that kind of security. I was beginning to learn she had a *very* high intellect, even among her fellows. As it stood, those renegades may as well have set up their operation in Times Square, for all the good it did them.

When I mentioned that to Sam a little later, his skin damn near turned as white as mine. He got on the phone to General Shelton and let him know the facts. That quickly stopped any possible leaks from Bill's command, but no one knew how much damage had already been done. It was entirely possible that some of the other Crispies were actively working for China or the Islamic Confederation already. It wasn't long before all doubt was eliminated, because we ran into a hornet's nest in Virginia. Oh yeah, it was somewhere in that time frame that Cresperians began to be referred to as Crispies. Human nature again. We love shortening long names into nicknames, although sometimes the shortened or changed versions became epithets. That wasn't the case here. Crispies or Crispy just flowed more smoothly from the tongue than their full name, and never mind the crude jokes that popped up here and there. We've still got cavemen in our ranks. You can prove that by downloading a newspaper from any big city in the United States.

All this began with me being trundled out of our motel room on a stretcher while Jeri gave orders on how to handle me to keep from undoing her repair work. Our legless friend was also carried into the ambulance, and was placed across from me, with Jeri, Sam, Carolyn, and another man, who introduced himself as Major Randolph Seabrook, crammed in between. During the trip to Virginia, I learned that Seabrook normally commanded the counterterrorism intelligence office with the Corps of Engineers there. He had been on leave when this came up, and he hooked up with the team that had been hurriedly put together when Bill called him. They all sat on the floor, with Jeri in front, holding my hand, and Carolyn squeezed in next to her. Despite the shots and commotion outside, not many bystanders were about. It was still dark, and anyway shots and sirens were probably as common in that area as alley cats. The siren came on and away we went.

The siren was silenced after a few minutes. Sam said he wanted to get us to safety without attracting any more attention than he already had. I can just imagine what the NSA thought at the time, when their six-person team disappeared in an ambulance, leaving their vehicles behind and a big hole in the wall of the motel room. For certain they weren't going to be very happy about it, especially not about the two agents who had been killed, but I figured Bill could straighten it out later. Anyway, damn it, they shouldn't have come busting into a room like that. Carolyn told me she'd arrived on the scene too late to stop it.

In the meantime, we drove for a half hour or so along a smooth highway, giving us all a chance to get acquainted. Sam Haley turned out to be a full colonel, but the only reason he admitted it was that he knew no one in the ambulance would be allowed to mix with outsiders again. Ordinarily he stayed out in the field, under deep cover. Carolyn Blanchard didn't have as many superiors as I thought. She worked under Jonn Enlake, one of the assistants to the NSA Director. He was a career specialist in electronic warfare. I didn't know much about him, other than I'd bet a silver dollar he would raise a ruckus over losing her. She knew more about fighting with electrons than her boss did. I never learned why she was sent into the field and told to catch up to that team, but I got the idea from talking to her that she rubbed the Head of Homeland Security the wrong way sometimes. I didn't worry about it. Those political appointees were there for show and to make speeches. The undersecretaries and deputies did the real work.

The NSA agent who had lost the lower part of his legs took all this in with a grim look on his face at first. He was probably wondering whether or not he'd done the right thing, and had to be a little sick when he rose up far enough for a last look at his stumps before he was strapped in and Sam began wrapping them in bandages.

Jeri was still concentrating on my hip, so she didn't talk much during the first part of the ride. Once she glanced over at the man on the other stretcher. She noticed how despondent he was and turned enough so she could speak to him.

"What's your name?"

"Bruce O'Brian," he muttered.

"I'm sorry about this." She leaned close to him and placed a hand on his shoulder. "Don't worry, I'll repair your legs as soon as I get a chance," she whispered. I don't think anyone other than me and possibly Carolyn overheard her. After that he perked up.

I had no idea of who had "need to know" status for all kinds of things we were certain to be doing later, so I kept fairly quiet, too. I explained it by telling the others my hip hurt, even though it didn't. When Jeri did speak it was almost always to Carolyn. I could tell already they'd get along fine.

Abruptly the ride became bumpy, and then my hip really did begin to hurt, but I didn't complain. Ambulances aren't the most comfortable vehicles, anyhow, as I knew from past experience. The bumps continued for another fifteen minutes or so.

The back doors were already being flung open before we came to a full stop. All I saw while I was transferred to a large van were moonlit woods and the faint outline of other vehicles. They all had their lights on dim, or turned off completely. The van had a single stretcher rack. Once I was secured in it, Sam and Carolyn climbed inside with me, along with Major Seabrook and three other agents, two men and a woman.

Major Seabrook told us to call him Randy. The others didn't give their names just then. All they did was sit and listen alertly. Randy himself appeared to be just a wee bit in awe of what he'd stumbled into from being one of Bill's trusted cohorts and also close enough to the action to be called in.

The van rode much easier than that boxy damned ambulance and my hip quit hurting.

"Where did you take Bruce?" I asked Sam, then immediately knew I shouldn't have, not yet. "Sorry. You can tell us later. What's next for us?"

"We'll be picked up at a little airport and flown into another just about like it, right on the border between Virginia and West Virginia, about fifty miles due west of Washington, D.C. I suspect Jeri's friend Ishmael is being held somewhere in that general area. She'll have to direct us from there."

"She will, if we're anywhere close."

"How close?"

"Less than a hundred miles," Jeri spoke up.

Sam didn't even blink. He acted as if rescuing beautiful alien women was as common as going to church on Sunday in rural Mississippi; just an everyday part of his job. He pulled out his phone and began punching numbers.

"Sam, wait!" I said.

"What is it?" He looked up.

"I'm not sure just how capable the other aliens are at tapping into our networks, but it's easy as pie for Jeri. I know you had to make that call to stop any more leaks, but I'd stay off the phone as much as possible until we get to a safe place."

"Okay." He nodded and put his phone away. "I'll contact some locals when we get to the airport and have them use new coding to arrange for backup, one with no mention of aliens in case the others have broken our old one. We'll spin up a new code-key and go from there. With a minimum amount of talk, it should be good for a few days at least."

The way he then described the code made me wonder briefly if he was a Heinlein fan, but there were more important things to talk about. On the other hand, I dared not give away too much information just in case he or Carolyn was captured. I think the only reason Sam mentioned his rank was to let everyone know he was completely in charge—if they hadn't already realized it. With Sam, anyone near almost automatically assumes he's the man.

After asking Sam's permission, I ran through as much of my and Jeri's history as I thought was necessary for the rescue operation, including the fact that she possessed a gadget capable of rendering her and one other person invisible to every form of radiation likely to be used in a defensive system. I only gave that away after Sam assured me that none of the others with us would be allowed contact with anyone else for a long while. Randy's face tightened when he heard that.

"Relax," Sam smiled at him. "You'll have your family with you as soon as we can arrange it."

The other agents didn't seem to mind. They appeared more excited at the prospect of being involved with us than anything else.

Once we got off the bumpy road and out of the forest, the van speeded up. We arrived at the airport five minutes later. I don't know how Sam arranged for a jet with a comfortable little bed in it for me so soon, but he had. Maybe it was on call. I didn't ask. I was just grateful to get off the litter and onto some memory foam.

Several more of Sam's people joined us in the jet, increasing the team to more than a dozen. And once we were in the air, Jeri spoke to me.

"Kyle, baby, I'm going to put you in a kind of trance. You'll be able to hear us, but I don't want you moving or talking for the next hour or two. Don't say a word unless you feel it's absolutely necessary. Okay?"

"Sure, sweetie. Shucks, I may even take a nap."

That brought a good round of laughter and tended to ease some of the tension already beginning to build, like homemade bread slowly rising at room temperature, getting ready for the oven. I didn't know how apt that metaphor was right then.

I entered a curious state where I could hear and think as normally as always, but had no desire to move or speak. I had the notion that I could if I really had to, but for the time being I was content to just lie there and listen to Jeri and Carolyn talk while Sam briefed the rest of the team as thoroughly as he knew how with limited information.

"I'm sorry about your agents, Carolyn. It all happened so fast we didn't have much choice. Why..." Jeri's voice broke and it was a couple of seconds before she could continue. "Why did they have to come bursting in on us like that with no warning? We didn't want to kill anyone or hurt Bruce like that. It was so...unnecessary."

"It's me that should be sorry. I had no idea Burley Turnis would be in charge of the detail. Had I known, I would have gotten here sooner. He's a hothead I tried to have removed earlier, but the Director overruled me and my boss, too. He had some kind of political connection."

"That's one aspect of human affairs I just can't fathom, how persons truly unsuited for positions in government or business get their way despite being incompetent. Or how people like Kyle learn to live with it. He's such a good person and he loves his country despite how awful the government is sometimes. I know the arguments, that this is the best political system invented so far, but its faults are going to lead to its downfall." She sighed as if accepting a heavy burden and gathering the strength to bear it.

"I wish I could help, Jeri. About all I can say is that we humans are incredibly complicated. It's been such a short time since we evolved intelligence that we still carry remnants of our past in our genes, garbage if you will, that will be with us for a long time to come. We're just now developing methods of understanding and bettering our nature, but I'm afraid they may come too late to save us. There's a huge amount of religious resistance to the kind of technology that can affect us at basic and crucial levels. The way our brains work, a lot of it is disguised, sublimated and rationalized in a way where we're able to deny the influence of a particular culture in our thinking, but the genetic disposition for belief is still present in the majority of us. Religion aside, we may think we're being reasonable, but at an unconscious level our minds are being influenced by millions of little factors we're almost totally unaware of."

Sam had been listening with half an ear. He glanced our way with a little half smile on his face, as if indicating he was one of us. I could only agree with Carolyn. Wow. A philosopher, psychologist and student of history in the NSA, all rolled into an attractive blonde package. It made me wonder if she had a family. A lot of people who think like that don't fit into the herd, same as me. I've often felt like an alien in the presence of savages, when friends and acquaintances start talking nonsense without even realizing what they're doing. If you're that kind of person, you have to be really lucky to find a fit with the opposite sex, like I was with Gwen and now with Jeri. You also have to learn to stand still and keep your mouth shut on some occasions when every fiber of your being is urging you to either walk away or tell the ones around you what fools they are.

"I know, Carolyn. After all, I have the same kind of brain as anyone else now. My advantages are having much more knowledge and starting with a clean slate, but I'm as susceptible to human emotions as others are. Perhaps more so in some instances, like loving Kyle and appreciating his love for me. Plenty of men will be sexually attracted by my appear-ance, but very few would be capable of setting aside their innate fear of the strange and unusual and truly falling in love with me in the romantic sense of the term. Did you know that not long after we met he threw his body in the line of fire, intending to take a bullet himself rather than let me be hurt? He didn't hesitate for an instant. I found it hard to accept at first, but it is actions and feelings like those that make some human behavior so admirable. The willingness to die for your family or your country. Sacrificing your own comfort and security to make the environ-ment better for your loved ones. Fighting to preserve your way of life, however mistaken we may think some of it is, such as a religion or the political system in power. I think that was the instant I knew I loved him, when I saw he was willing to die to keep me alive." She looked down at me. The corners of her lips lifted in a tender smile that carried a wealth of emotion to me.

"There's the opposite side of the coin, too, Jeri," Carolyn said. "We're far from perfect, even the best of us."

"Of course. You don't know yet how much I've studied the human species, almost every aspect of it, and then compared it to what I once was, what my former species still is." She sniffed, then went on, "I could change back, but I have no desire to. I love Kyle with all my heart. I love what he stands for and how he dreams of a better tomorrow for the race. I want to help him achieve those dreams, and those of others like him. You see, I'm not just a human now. I'm a human *by choice*, and I'll never give it up. I'll never give him up."

I could feel the tears beginning to trickle down the side of my face but had no desire to wipe them away. It's barely possible Jeri could have faked the emotions that go into making us human and mimicked them beforehand, the way we laugh and cry, love and hate, fear and doubt. She might even have been pretending to love me but I had never doubted her. Even if I had, the way she gazed tenderly down at my tear-streaked face now left no possible room for doubt. I knew she loved me with all her heart, with all the emotion a woman is capable of giving. I knew it right down to my very bones. She gently wiped the tears away with her fingers, then bent and kissed me. It went on for a long time. When she finally rose back up, I could see that Carolyn was crying, too, openly and unashamedly.

Chapter Seventeen

Shortly before we began our descent, Jeri suddenly started acting excited about something. I could see on her face that there was something making her anxious.

"Sam! I can sense Ishmael!" There was excitement in her voice.

"Which direction? How far? Can he detect you, too?" Sam had just finished chastising one of his troops for taking his little submachine gun out to check the action and loads, and the man was returning it to its odd-shaped holster beneath his jacket.

Jeri laughed at the explosion of questions from the previously taciturn colonel. "He's about thirty miles east of Front Royal. We'll pass almost directly over his position," she said, displaying that phenomenal memory. Somewhere on the net she'd seen a map of that area of the country. "It's—"

"Wait," Sam interrupted, holding up a hand. "You can give me details later. Right now, just tell me whether or not he can sense you, and if he can, tell him not to let on."

"Uh," Jeri explained again. "Sam, I can *not* read minds, not even the minds of other Crispies." Even she was using the shortened version of our name for them. She thought it was amusing. "It just doesn't work that way."

"Sorry," Sam said. "It's so easy to make that assumption. I'll remember in the future."

He would, too. He didn't have an eidetic memory but it didn't miss by much.

"That's all right. I've already warned Ishmael not to show any signs of excitement or agitation when we come in range of each other. Besides, I doubt his inquisitors could tell, anyway. He's still in his original form, remember?"

Sam and Carolyn's faces both showed expressions of disquiet at the term she used for his captors even though they both tried to hide their feelings. Sam continued with his questions.

"Oh, yeah. I did remember, but...never mind. Let me put it this way: will he know when our team is getting close and will he help them when they find him?"

"Oh yes, he'll know almost to the nearest inch where I am as we get close enough for the rescue to begin."

"Too bad he doesn't have one of those Harry Potter cloaks with him, like you do."

He lost her with that one.

"Harry Potter cloak? I've seen some references to the name, of course, but I haven't read the books yet."

"Oh. The gadget you can use to make yourself invisible."

"But he does. At least I'm pretty sure one of his commos referred to him still possessing it even though he's been deprived of most of his other survival equipment. We've had to be very circumspect to avoid detection, so I can't be absolutely certain."

"Well, we'll go in assuming he doesn't, but if we find he does, it's just icing. Okay now, let's try pinning down where he is before we land, to save time." He took a United States highway atlas from one of the seat pockets and opened it to the Virginia/West Virginia map.

Jeri took one glance at it, then put her finger on a spot. It was a little hamlet that probably wasn't even incorporated. "Just about five miles northeast of here. We'll be passing over the location in—how fast are we going?"

"We've probably slowed to about 400 kmh by now."

"Then less than five minutes. I'll tell you when."

Everyone waited tensely until she said, "Mark! We're right overhead, deflected due north about a half mile."

Sam nodded and began studying the map, holding the atlas with one hand and reaching out his other without saying a word. One of his team produced a binder with plastic page holders, already opened to the correct place. He mouthed his thanks and scrutinized it intensely. His face brightened into a real smile.

"I think I may know the exact location. There was a big redoubt built there back in the sixties by a wealthy businessman who wanted a good shelter in case of nuclear warfare. After he died, it was sold by his heirs and passed through a number of hands until it was taken over by the feds under eminent domain laws. I believe all the county records have been erased to keep its nature secret. Now it simply looks like an old country house, but it's a warren beneath. I have no idea how well it's rigged for security or what part of it he's being held in." His expression changed from cheerful to worried. "This may be more difficult than I imagined."

"Would it help if I guided our team directly to him?"

"Help? Hell, yes, it would help!" Sam practically shouted and he started grinning again.

"Ishmael will remember exactly every part of it he's been in as well as the routes taken and he'll know pretty much what kind of security apparatus is being used."

"Can he disconnect them?"

"Probably, but it's possible the very act of doing so might set off other alarms. However, between the two of us and your team we can probably manage everything except a streak of bad luck."

Murphy was sticking his ugly little gnome of a head up already. No one can predict when that evil gremlin will make an appearance, but you can always bet he'll pick the very worst moment when he does.

"This is off-subject," Carolyn said, "but I'm wondering how they managed to capture him in the first place, if he could make himself invisible."

"Oh," Jeri answered. "The craft he was in probably was seen by some of those people as it came down. I'd bet he was surrounded and didn't realize at first how unfriendly those particular humans were likely to be. By then, it was too late. I'm surprised he managed to salvage as much as he did."

See what I said about Murphy? Even aliens aren't immune to his appearance.

"What else does he have?" Sam wanted to know, not from curiosity, though. Anything that would help with the rescue and hold down casualties was important.

"If we're lucky, he still has his disintegrator, but probably not. He wasn't able to indicate much."

"Well, you've still got yours, fortunately."

"Yes, but as I told Kyle, its power supply is running low. I can use it about a dozen more times if I have to, but that will be about it until we can get it recharged."

"Then save it until we get in a bind. Anything else you know that might help?"

"Only that he's very anxious to get away from those people. They've been treating him abominably, some more so than others, but they're all guilty." Her lips thinned into a tight line and her face set in a rigid expression I hadn't seen before. I thought right then I wouldn't want to be one of the men or women who'd been particularly cruel to him during his captivity.

We landed at the other airport, almost a duplicate of the same small isolated one we'd left from, even to the wooded area. Sam told us it wasn't marked on any FAA maps and was "Privately" owned, meaning it belonged to Military Intelligence through a dummy. We were met by a covey of vehicles, a mixture of vans and cars and a couple of heavy SUVs, all carrying more men and women, well armed and ready to go where they were told—and prepared to do whatever was asked of then. All but a few were in the army and had job classifications of Intelligence Specialists. They wore no rank insignia, so I couldn't tell which were officers and which enlisted. It didn't seem to matter to them, anyway. Sam picked up some supplies there and distributed them, including syringes of a powerful anesthetic.

ဆာ၀ၵ

Again I was carried to a van and my stretcher racked into a slot built for one. Sam, Jeri, Carolyn, and several troopers who weren't introduced, joined me, some taking seats and others sitting on the carpeted floor. Very shortly a convoy was on the road, but the vehicles were separated by various distances, making the caravan resemble a night of heavier traffic than usual on those back roads. On the way to our final stop where the operatives would embark on foot, Jeri took the opportunity to give me some final instructions and encouragement. Some of her words were intended to be overheard, but other parts were for me alone.

"Kyle, love, I want you to try remaining still for another half hour, especially the lower part of your body. The trance will wear off very shortly and you'll be able to raise your arm to check the time or take a drink of water, things like that, and I'll prop your head and shoulders up, but don't move about unless you absolutely have to. It might be okay, but I'd rather not take chances with my favorite husband." She winked at me and I found I could grin, even talk.

"Be careful, sweetie. Those guys won't be amateurs like some of the ones we've encountered, or near as dumb. And you come back to me, hear?"

We were both making an attempt to keep it light but not making much of a success at it. I felt moisture forming and blurring my vision. I could see gathering tears being trapped by Jeri's eyelashes, and hanging there, sparkling in the dim lighting. Abruptly she leaned down and laid her face on my chest. I put an arm around her and could feel the trembling of her body, while the pent up-tears escaped and wet my shirt. I didn't mind. Not a bit.

"I love you," she said. Then she rose up and was all business. "I've got to go. The rest are waiting on me. She kissed me, quickly but thoroughly, and was gone. I lay there for long minutes with my eyes closed, listening to the sounds of gear being adjusted, shells being racked into the chambers of weapons, and a low mutter of voices as the final briefing took place. It was done swiftly, and soon thereafter the crunch of footsteps on gravel faded away. I would have given every possession I had in the world to be able to go with them. I felt desperately alone. I was crying inside at the thought of Jeri going into danger and my not being able to accompany her. I knew it had to be done but that didn't make me feel any better. I was living in that special hell of having a loved one going out to battle the barbarians and being forced to remain at home.

For the first time, I could appreciate what it was akin to, what Gwen and millions of others like her had faced throughout history. These days it wasn't only men going off to war and leaving their women behind. When the hidebound politicians and military finally faced the fact that women were just as good in combat as men, perhaps even better, some of the male half of our species got a taste of their own medicine. They had to suffer through the uncertainty and horror of warfare with their wives and lovers in just as much danger as them, and sometimes more. I can tell you from experience, it is a sobering and humbling experience. Never again would I tell anyone not to worry when their loved ones were sent off to war or on clandestine missions that could turn into situations as hairy and violent as those encountered in more formal combat, if there is such a thing.

After Sam, Carolyn, Jeri and the others departed, there was one trooper left in the van with me. A number of others waited outside as a combination backup and rear guard. One of their duties was to protect me and get me to safety at all costs if the party going inside screwed the goose and wasn't able to fight their way out. The mission of those going into the redoubt was much the same. Protect Jeri first and get her back at all costs. Next came Ishmael. Only after those two were accounted for were they allowed to worry about their own safety.

Chapter Eighteen

What happened inside was told to me later at a series of debriefings, and described by Jeri herself when we finally had a chance to be alone. It scared the shit out of me, to put it bluntly, and I hadn't had that easy a time of it myself.

ᏒᎧᏣ

The first problem was removing the outpost guards without raising an alarm. That was relatively easy. Using her cloaking device Jeri and Sam snuck up and disabled both of them. After a hard whack on the head with a sap, an anesthetic put them out of business for several hours. They were robbed of their identification cards. The problem was there hadn't been time to find out how often or what time the shifts changed, so at least one man had to be left at each post in case relief guards showed up before the inside team returned.

The next step wasn't nearly as easy. When they got closer to the disguised old house, Jeri was able to provide a fairly accurate census of the number of renegade CIA agents inside. There were more than Sam had expected, but he wasn't about to stop now. A little guard shack with gates barring entrance to the grounds by vehicles was the next objective. Jeri and another agent wore the stolen ID. They took one of the vans and drove up, leaving Sam and the rest of the vehicles waiting just out of sight. The agent drove, leaving Jeri to concentrate her talents on removing the short-term memories of the two guards there. She got out of the van and kept the guards occupied while they raised the barrier and allowed four more vehicles to pass, but an unanticipated trouble spot developed right there.

They found it took a call to the house before the locks would open and allow anyone inside the guard post. Jeri couldn't just order them to do that. She could keep removing their short-term memory, but she was needed inside.

Sam made the decision when his van drove up. He listened for a moment, then shook his head. Nothing to do but kill them. Disposing of these men, even though they were government agents, wasn't a worry. He knew they had to realize they were operating outside the law, and might even know it was on behalf of traitors. Nevertheless, he had intended to limit casualties to the bare minimum, but when it became necessary, he did the dirty work himself. He had Jeri divert their attention, then used a special heavy caliber silenced pistol to shoot both of them in the back of the head right through the glass. Even if the glass had been made of bulletproof material, that gun would have punched through. It was designed for just such purposes. Jeri flinched and turned away when they were killed. Sam leaned close and whispered into her ear. She nodded but still didn't look happy. Later she told me he needn't have bothered telling her the men were evil. She already knew both the guards were as bad as the worst ones inside. She just hated the necessity for killing. I can't blame her. We could spend the rest of our lives wiping out miscreants and hardly make a dent in the numbers.

Sam left two troopers there with orders to find a way inside even if they had to blow out the door lock with a small explosive charge, then to change into the dead guards' shirts. They were told to use delaying tactics to assure the ones inside that all was right with their world. Failing that, they were to disable every video possible if it could be done from there. One of them was a security specialist. He told Sam he would try but gave no guarantees.

Meanwhile the advance contingent was just pulling up in front of the main entrance. Sam picked up Jeri and raced to join them. One person rang the door bell while the rest waited to the side for Jeri and Sam to arrive. They got there a moment later, just as the door swung open, but by then the operation was already out of sequence, held up by the locked guard house.

Sam and Jeri were in the back seat of their car. It was pretty well concealed by the others. They immediately got together and Jeri cloaked them both. There was no indication of their presence other than a couple of pebbles on the sidewalk disturbed by their passage.

The person at the front door was arguing with two of our men who were wearing the ID taken from the dead guards. He didn't know what was going on but he was alert and suspicious. He barred entry while calling for assistance, probably by stepping on an alarm button on the floor. A man and woman joined him, both armed.

The words being exchanged grew louder and more heated. Jeri and Sam hurried before it got out of hand and talk changed to action. If shooting started there, it was going to make the intrusion into the stronghold much harder, perhaps impossible.

Sam's sap appeared to materialize out of thin air, reaching just past the limits of the invisibility shield. It swooshed around in a short vicious arc and hit with a dull thud, like the sound of a cantaloupe being crushed with a hammer. It probably cracked the man's skull; there was no time to be gentle. He collapsed without a sound. The woman's eyes opened wide but she didn't panic. She turned in the direction where the sap had come from, intending to shoot into what looked like empty space.

Jeri knocked the gun from her hand with an invisible blow that must have been a dilly. Bones in her wrist and hand broke with an audible crunching noise. She started to scream but Sam already had his sap back in action. He hit her squarely in the mouth, disintegrating her front teeth and splitting her lip.

The two men holding the guards' ID cards hadn't been idle, but they'd had little room for maneuver once Jeri and Sam arrived, and were afraid to do much in any case for fear of getting in the way of their invisible comrades. They hadn't forgotten their mission, though. When the last of their opponents from inside threw caution to the wind and bulled his way forward while his finger tightened on the trigger of an old Uzi, one of them smothered the weapon with his own body, taking three bullets in the stomach but keeping the shots from making much noise.

Sam killed that man with a maddened blow from his sap. There was no doubt about it, not from the distorted shape of his skull where he was struck with such brutal force.

They were inside, but didn't yet know if an alarm had gone off or not. "Which way?" Sam asked.

Jeri pointed.

Sam motioned for a dozen or so men to follow him into the house, while four more waited at the entrance as a rear guard and such backup as the limited communication allowed.

"Surround her and let's move. You're in charge, Jeri. Don't wait for me to ask, just tell us which way to go and whether anyone's in front or back of us. If you can do it, disable any cameras or infrared beams. Anything that might sound an alarm. Let's hurry, while we still have the advantage. It won't last long."

It didn't.

Jeri led the way confidently, but had them pause at intervals in order to disable sentry cameras with her perceptive sense. Once she led them down a flight of stairs in order to avoid the elevator, where she said a half dozen armed men and a couple of women had begun congregating in an ominous group, clearly on alert and ready for a confrontation.

"How much farther?" Sam asked quietly.

"We're on the right floor now, but let's step it up. We have two long hallways to traverse and I can sense people moving in them."

"Are they armed?"

"Yes." Jeri began walking at a faster clip, almost trotting, while Sam kept urging those in front to move faster but stay close to her.

The hallway they were in held numerous doors, but she ignored them. It branched at right angles going both ways. A hundred feet before the T Jeri called them to a halt with a soft but urgent command.

"We need to go right, but there's two men just around the corner. Let me use my cloak and go first."

"No," Sam said. "We can't risk you getting hurt. You men in front, have your weapons ready. Try to use silencers, but shoot to kill."

Jeri looked appealingly at him, but he shook his head, and spoke softly.

"I know how you feel, but we have to. You hold fast. Front rank, go!" Sam ordered his men. They moved out, stooping low, weapons ready. Sam motioned his hand for the rest to follow, indicating he wanted two more in front of Jeri. As soon as the corner was turned, the sounds of gunfire echoed in the hallways, loud in the confined spaces.

"That does it," Sam said. "Everyone, stay with Jeri. Protect her with your life if you have to. Let's move!"

They ran forward. The two enemies who had been waiting were dead. One of Sam's men was down, the top of his head blown to bits.

"Ishmael is free. He's coming this way, but there are more closing in behind us, and they know he's loose. The ones behind Ishmael know it, too, but he's recovered his cloak and got it working," Jeri said.

They were boxed in. Sam glanced down at the thick carpet. There was nothing to do about it other than hope none of the rogue, misguided agents noticed Ishmael's footprints.

"How far away is he?"

"One hallway over. We'll have to...wait! Hold up. He knows a short-cut. He'll be here in a few seconds."

"You and you!" Sam pointed at a man and woman. "Back the way we came. Hold them up or divert them as long as you can." He gave the or-ders calmly, but Jeri could sense how he was hurting inside. He was most likely sending them to their deaths.

The two he designated turned and ran, knowing they were probably on a suicide mission but showing no hesitation. Just as a doorway down the hall in front of them opened, the sounds of gunfire to the rear broke out. The clatter of another Uzi was unmistakable, even when mixed with firing from a machine pistol.

"Don't shoot! That's Ishmael!"

The alien came into the hall, uncloaked so they wouldn't shoot him by accident. He was holding one of his middle arms with an upper on the same side. A trickle of pale greenish fluid dripped through his fingers and spattered the floor. Jeri had known already that he had gotten hurt making his escape, but she also knew it wasn't a debilitating wound and hadn't mentioned it. His appearance very nearly resulted in disaster as Sam's subordinates paused to gawk.

"Watch out!" Jeri shouted. "There's a whole gang of men running this way behind him! They're all over the place!"

Deafening bursts of gunfire erupted again in the hallway as Ishmael's pursuers rounded the corner. Several men from both sides fell with mortal wounds. The circle around Jeri thinned, and now they had Ishmael to guard as well when Sam pushed him inside the protective barrier of bodies.

Jeri grabbed Ishmael's free upper arm and tugged, urging him to follow her. Instead, he resisted and said something in their native tongue. She listened and spoke to him briefly in the same indecipherable language. I can only imagine what Jeri looked like right then, but it couldn't have been pretty. As soon as she and Ishmael were close they were able to exchange a huge amount of personal information in a very short period of time. Her face set in a hard, grim expression, and thereafter she and Ishmael showed no mercy to the ones responsible for torturing him.

"Wait," She turned to Sam. "He says he knows a better way out. Let him lead the way."

"We'll go with him, but he can't be in front."

"He knows that. I just told him. Now let's go! Hurry! The two you left behind died to give us this chance!"

Her tone of voice brooked no argument. She directed their movement to a door. One of the leaders opened it and they began running from room to room. Each time they passed through an exit, the rear guard locked it behind them. Several times they came to rooms occupied by scientists or staff workers. Those who offered no resistance were left alone, except for the ones Ishmael pointed out. Each time, Jeri nodded approval. Somehow he had managed to grab part of his survival pack, including the disintegrator. He used it to wipe the first two from the face of the Earth without a qualm. The only thing left was one shoe with a foot in it. After that, Jeri told him to save his power. Three more times, as they ran from room to room, they encountered agents or staff who had tormented Ishmael, two men and one woman. She was an overweight dirty blonde with cruel eyes, who looked as if she had been teleported directly from the pitiless labs of Nazi Germany, the ones where medical "experiments" were performed on human victims. Jeri simply pointed to them as they passed and told Sam, "Kill him," or in the case of the woman, "Kill her." Silenced handguns were used. The blond faux Nazi managed one short scream before she died. The men seemed resigned to their fate and went quietly, as if confessing their guilt and accepting the consequences.

Once, they encountered a couple, a man with his arm around the woman, ready to protect her even though he wasn't armed. Jeri stopped for a moment, almost causing a pileup.

"Bring those two with us," she said, an order. Sam shrugged and motioned them to come along. An alarm suddenly began warbling, interrupted briefly by a voice from loudspeakers.

"Intruder alert! Intruder alert! Lock down, lock down! Security personnel, report to posts! Non-combat personnel remain in place and secure your quarters!" The alarm began blaring again. The sequence was repeated over and over. There wasn't time to wonder why it had taken so long to be broadcast, as Sam kept the group together urging them onward, relying on Jeri for guidance.

She led them into another hallway and shoved the man in front of her.

"Hurry! Run! To that exit!" Her voice became shrill, telling Sam pursuit was right on their tail. The hallway must have seemed a mile long and the red exit sign a tiny beacon of safety that took hours to reach, even running at full speed. It was two hundred feet in front of them.

"It's locked!" The first man to reach it shouted. He went into a frenzied panic, trying to kick the door open. When that failed, he aimed his gun at the lock.

"No! Move aside!" Jeri shouted.

He appeared not to hear. Sam grabbed his hand just before he fired, forcing it down. The bullet spanged off the armored door and plowed into the floor by his foot. Sam wrenched his weapon from him and struck him in the face with it, leaving a bloody furrow in his chin. He shook his head, flinging droplets of blood, but came back to his senses. Ishmael tried to disintegrate the door, but his weapon was out of juice, having been used too much by his captors trying to figure out how it worked. It only heated the metal.

"Behind you!" Jeri screamed. She took out the section of the door containing the lock, without looking around. She backed up and front-kicked it open.

Sam and the two others in the rear exchanged fire with three men emerging from a doorway in the hall. They were off-balance as they came through. One of them managed a three-round burst from a machine pistol before he died, but two of the slugs found targets. The first got Sam in the fleshy part of his left thigh. The second killed one of his men by hitting him in the throat just above his vest, going on through and shattering his spine. Ironically, he was one of the few wearing body armor. The team had been put together so quickly that it hadn't been available for everyone. Sam let out an oath, not at his own wound but at the loss of another good man.

Jeri bent and picked up the dead man's machine pistol, an MP-5 similar to the MP-10 I owned and had showed her how to use.

"It's clear for the moment. Go!" she said loudly. Her front guard was already through the exit and moving up the set of stairs it exposed. The stairs led to a ground-level door in back of the house. It was locked, stopping them momentarily.

"Get back!" Sam ordered. He stepped to the side, glanced back to see that everyone was free as possible from ricochets and shot the lock off. He kicked the door open with his wounded leg, not letting it slow him down at all. With the way clear, he led the sparse phalanx of guards outside. They began running around toward the front of the building, where the assault had begun, but the sound of helicopter blades slowly revolving in ready mode, mixed with the noise of machine gun and rifle fire brought them to an abrupt halt. Sam rapidly considered his remaining options.

Chapter Nineteen

Waiting in the van, I chewed on my lip hard enough to draw blood, as I listened to the faint sounds of gunfire coming from the house. I was already heartsick with worry over Jeri, when I realized a noise I had been hearing in the background was a helicopter. It clattered to the ground just to the other side of the cars Sam had left parked, in plain sight from the van. A machine gun was already stuttering lethally as it landed, aiming for the troops guarding me. There wasn't a goddamned thing I could do about it. The little S&W I still carried was like a popgun compared to the 50 caliber MG in the helicopter or the Kalashnikovs the three men who jumped from it were carrying. I got it out and sat up, anyway. I damn sure wasn't going to die lying on my back. I could see most of the action from inside the van, but I held my fire for the moment.

"*Allahu Akbar!*" "*Allahu Akbar!*"

Muslims! I heard the throaty shout during a momentary pause of the MG, even over the *thwok thwok* of the slowly revolving chopper blades, and the voices were drowned out by the roar of more gunfire. My guards had taken cover behind the cars as soon as they saw the helicopter coming in but they were poor protection against 50 caliber slugs. They were riddled. Even the van got a few bullet holes in the paneling and I don't think they were even aiming for it. Nevertheless, at least one of my guards did exactly the right thing. He was armed with a compact XM8 automatic rifle. He ignored the Kalashnikovs and went for the helicopter MG and the pilot. That dude was a damn fine shot. He silenced the MG, shattered the chopper canopy, and killed the single pilot before one of the bearded Muslims took him out.

"Stay down!" the trooper in the van with me ordered as he crawled to the driver's seat, leaving a trail of blood behind. I hadn't even known he was hit.

I ignored him. The S&W was leveled with both my hands and supported by my knees. I felt my body tremble with the fear of approaching death, but I wasn't going quietly.

"*Allahu Akbar!*" The cry came again, this time from nearby. The bearded head and shoulders of another Muslim came into view, limned by the still-open rear door of the van. My first shot plastered him right between his stupid fucking eyes.

The van lurched and screeched as it burned rubber on the tarmac of the driveway. The rear door swung wildly as my guard drove toward the back of the house. I knew he was hoping to find refuge in the woods if he could get us that far. There had to be more than just the helicopter crew and its three gunmen. They wouldn't have attacked a redoubt like this with so few men.

The guy driving the van damn near ran over Sam, Jeri and the others still with them, along with Ishmael. I couldn't see what was happening in front, but he must have jumped halfway out of his skin when he caught a glimpse of the alien. Crispies have that effect at first. We came to such a sudden stop that I was thrown backward. The fight ended for me the same way it had begun, lying flat on the stretcher. Jeri clambered inside and smothered me with her body. Tears were flowing freely down her cheeks. She held me with an excruciatingly rigid grip that was as sweet as it was painful. She didn't loose her taut hold on me until she sensed my difficulty in breathing. The others had piled in by this time, and we drove away at a speed the old road behind the house wasn't designed for. The van bumped and swerved, flinging us this way and that as it careened around curves and over ruts made by larger vehicles. Sam ignored the blood still streaming from his leg as he talked on his phone. I couldn't hear what he was saying but I sure as hell hoped he was calling for help!

ৰওন্দ

Sam's team was simply the first and fastest one he had been able to gather. Others were on their way, but I'd bet the farm there were other Muslims heading our way, too. We didn't know it at the time, nor know how they did it, but a clandestine network of well-armed and well-connected terrorist groups under the hand of the Islamic Confederation had gotten wind of us. They were ordered to drop all other plans and follow us to the renegade CIA group. Senator Terhune might have been a worse traitor than Congressman Tarryall, but it was hard to differentiate the two. Both did enormous damage to the country. They were under arrest, as I learned later, but Alvin Grayson had covered his tracks well; he was still free.

Just as we thought our van had made a clean getaway, the driver relayed word back to us that he saw a pursuing vehicle in the rearview mirror, a big SUV of some kind.

"Probably some rebel Boy Scouts or a gang of French Peaceniks after us now," Jeri said, attempting a joke. It got more laughs than I expected, considering the circumstances, but sometimes humor is the only outlet from the tension of violent combat.

"I wouldn't be surprised at anything," Sam retorted. "Not at this point. I've got some help on the way, though."

"How close?" Carolyn asked.

"The first ones should be here soon. There's more behind them, but I don't know when they'll make it. Major Seabrook is working his tail off rounding up troops who can be trusted and are combat ready." He began punching numbers on his phone again.

Randy had been left behind at the airport for just that purpose, over his fierce protests. I sympathized with him at the time, but I was happy as a mustang with his new commission that he had stayed after the shit hit the fan.

My mind wandered for a moment, imagining what must have happened inside the armored compound disguised as an old house. So many had gone in and so few returned. What kind of hellacious conditions had they found in there? And the CIA agents. Had they all been working for Grayson and Tarryall with full knowledge of what traitors they were? Or were some of them simply misguided into thinking they were doing the right thing? I decided I'd rather not know, so I never asked.

Chapter Twenty

I noticed Sam shaking his head and frowning. It made me wonder just how much aid he had been able to gather. I didn't like the looks of that frown. I decided to try for some help myself. In retrospect, it's probably what I should have done earlier, but Jeri's fear of government agencies and her worry over Ishmael had convinced me to go it alone at first. After that, events kept overtaking us, one after the other until it seemed as if we had done nothing but run and fight for eons. And at the moment, having my call traced was the least of our worries.

I had Senator Brad Benchley's home phone number memorized, just as he had asked me to long ago. I had spoken to his son, Caden Benchley, at home once or twice while he recovered from his wounds. Every time the senator spoke to me, he insisted that I call him if I was ever in need of help. I always told him Caden would have done exactly the same for me, had our roles been reversed. Right now, I hoped I hadn't been too convincing.

His wife answered on the second ring.

"Hello, Mrs. Benchley. This is Kyle Leverson."

"Kyle! Where are you? What—never mind! You stay on the phone while I get Brad. Don't you dare hang up!"

Benchley's voice was gruffer than normal, as if he'd just been woke from a sound sleep or had been talking too much lately. Maybe both.

"Kyle, where the hell are you? We've been worried stiff and half the damned country is after you."

"Senator, I don't have time for a lot of explanation, but I'm in trouble and I need help, quickly."

"Tell me." I always did like the way he cut to the chase, same as he did in the senate, never mincing words and never afraid to speak his mind, unlike most of those idiots in Washington. It's no wonder he kept getting re-elected.

I explained about having two aliens with me, and how one had been tortured by a rogue element of the CIA controlled by Alvin Grayson and Moses Tarryall, and that neither of them had much faith in the government after that.

"Goddamned those bastards! I hope we shoot them." I guess he was talking about Tarryall and Grayson, but he might have had enough of

Washington's officialdom in mind to fill a stadium. "Tell me where you are and I'll guarantee you'll be placed in good hands."

"We're in good hands now, Senator. General Shelton, CO of Special Affairs Intelligence for Technology. He sent a crew to help us rescue the captive alien. We got him out, but then were attacked by some Muslim terrorists who must know all about the aliens here. We got away from the first ones, but there's bound to be others on the way. And we're being tailed right now by unidentified parties."

"Give me your location and phone number."

I hurried through it, scanning the wrinkled map Sam handed me when he heard what I was up to. I gave him my number as well as Sam's.

"Okay, got it. Hold on while I get the FBI moving."

I winced, but he was gone before I could say anything. Of all the government agencies under the umbrella of Homeland Security, the FBI was the most bureaucratic and turf-conscious. When he came back on the line, I put it to him quick and plain. "Senator, we'll take any help we can get at the moment, but make it plain that General Shelton stays in control of us. Period. His chief field agent is with us now, Colonel Haley. The aliens trust him, and they trust General Shelton because I do. Can you make that clear to the FBI?"

"If I can't, the President can. I'm due at the White House in an hour for a meeting. He's been worried stiff over the IC and Chinese having their hands on some of the aliens while we don't. Even the British are playing games with us. That damn socialist Prime Minister thinks he can make England king of the world again. I've met General Shelton and Colonel Haley, by the way. Shelton has testified at some secret hearings and had Haley along to back him. Good men, both of them."

"Great." That made me breathe a little easier. "Thank you, sir. But hurry them up, please. And if you can talk to the President in person, and maybe privately, that would sure help."

"No problem. I'm heading for the hill in a bit but I'll have my phone with me. And let me give you another number, just in case. Don't let this one out, please."

"I won't, sir." He gave it to me and kept talking.

"Okay. Stay safe, Kyle. Our country needs you."

He killed the connection. All the time I was on the line Sam was looking at me curiously, especially when I mentioned the President.

"Maybe I should have let you call for help to begin with, Kyle."

I shrugged. Jeri had told me I could sit up and move around now.

"Most of us know someone who knows someone else. I helped Senator Benchley's son once. He thinks he owes me a favor."

"Well, I sure as hell hope he comes through. The pick-up team Randy has on the way now is mighty slim from the 308th out of Fort Monroe. Military Intelligence is spread all over, and a lot of it operates overseas. Rapid response isn't one of our strong suits."

"I can sense vehicles ahead of us," Jeri broke in to say.

"Ah, shit, we're boxed in," Sam said. It was the first real curse I'd heard from him.

Chapter Twenty-One

"How far ahead, sweetheart?" I asked.

"At the next crossroad. About…a mile or so."

The van slowed. I put my arm around Jeri, knowing she needed all the comfort I could give her, and then some. It had been a hard day for her. Hell, it had been a hard day for everyone, but she was more vulnerable than most of us.

"I hate this." She leaned into my embrace. Her body trembled with fatigue tension and worry that she hadn't bothered to dispel with her perceptive sense yet. "When is it all going to end, Kyle? I don't think I can stand much more of this. And Ishmael is near the breaking point. He needs a safe refuge to recover from those…those…" For once she was at a loss for words.

"Those cretins," Ishmael supplied them. "Those evil, malignant people, especially the female. She was the worst."

"Most humans aren't like that, Ishmael," I said, the first time I spoke to him.

"I can assure you of that," Jeri added.

"We tried to stop it, but there was little we could do."

The voice came from the very back of the overcrowded van, from the female of the couple Jeri had ordered to be brought out.

"That's true. Martha and Robert were extremely helpful. They pleaded with me to hang on and hope that we would be rescued. They had to whisper and pass notes to avoid detection. They said it meant death for them if the leaders knew of our secret communication. But for them, I would have terminated my existence."

"I don't doubt it," Sam said dryly. He used some bottled water and a handkerchief to wipe blood from his phone and his hands, then began checking his big .45 caliber Glock automatic pistol.

Carolyn took a little pair of scissors from her purse and cut off his pants leg above the wound. It had stopped bleeding but looked messy as hell. She used more of his water to clean it out. She poured iodine from a first-aid pack, then wound some gauze around his thigh. I wondered if there was something developing between them, or was I not reading the signals right? She patted his knee and smiled, despite the trap we were in. Yup. Interest, no doubt about it. Or maybe it was one soldier's respect for another. Hell, I didn't have a clue about much then. Who knew?

Robert and Martha E. Lee were CIA employees, she a semantics linguist and he a physicist. Their home was in Richmond. They were childless and had few family connections, so they were a natural choice for the renegades. They didn't know what a horror show they were getting into, but once in the redoubt, there was no going back. Later on, Jeri and I got to know them pretty well. Nice folks, even if they were both ten times smarter than me.

⁝

The paved crossroad came into sight as we rounded a curve. Two vehicles were blocking access. There were men and women outside the big SUVS, some armed with rifles, some with handguns. Every single one was pointed in our direction. Our driver stopped the van and turned to look at Sam for orders. I'm glad it wasn't me he was staring at. I had no more idea of what to do than a hog trussed up for slaughter. Sam did.

"Everyone outside, except Kyle and the two Crispies. No, Markham, Bergloff and Carolyn. You all stay with them. If shooting starts, cover their bodies with your own. Now listen up, people. We're way outgunned, so keep your weapons out of sight. I'll personally throttle the first person that starts something without my say-so."

"Got it," a medley of voices chorused. Carolyn merely nodded. She understood as well as anyone how important the Crispies were, and in association, my own unlovely self.

"Kyle, Jeri and Ishmael, lie down of the floor so the engine will protect you from gunfire."

"What about that SUV in back of us?"

"Matter of odds. There's more of them in front than back.

That didn't leave very damn many to back him in whatever he had planned. It made me curious. "Just for the record, Sam, what are you planning here?"

"I don't have a plan. All I'm doing is playing for time. Trying to stall whoever those yahoos are and whatever they're up to. I don't think they mean to kill us or we'd already be dead."

There was that. Someone opened the rear door and bodies began piling out. Suddenly the van seemed empty even though there were still seven of us inside. Those in back were probably glad to face something as simple as a gunfight after being crushed by the press of bodies on that lumpy excuse for a road.

Sam ordered all the doors left open so those of us remaining inside could maybe hear what was happening in case the negotiations or fighting or whatever else happened came close enough. I was of two minds about that until I remembered Jeri's acute hearing. The present distance was stretching it but she might be able to pick up parts of the conversation.

⟡

Jeri and I exchanged glances. Neither of us wanted to get down on that bloody carpet. Sam wasn't the only one who had been wounded. There was blood everywhere, coloring the green in tacky pools that stuck to the soles of shoes. In a couple of places it *squished* as the van was vacated. We sat tight. The two big men designated as shields made a move to lay us down by force but Caroline warned them off.

"Jeri should be able to hear. We may need to know when to exit in a hurry." That convinced them, but one moved so he was in front of us and the other stayed back.

We waited. Jeri was concentrating intensely. It was like waiting on the huddle of the last play in a game to break up, where a touchdown was needed to win. I could hardly bear the suspense. Jeri and Ishmael both suddenly turned their attention elsewhere, looking upward as if trying to see the sky through the roof.

"Helicopters, way off," Jeri said.

Damn. That was all we needed. But ours or theirs? We had no way of knowing. We simply huddled and tried to conceal our fear. Everyone, except maybe Ishmael, knew a missile could kill us and probably wipe out Sam and his group in the bargain.

Eventually, after what seemed like hours but was probably only a couple of minutes, I could hear the choppers, too. Choppers? I cocked my ear and listened hard. Yeah, more than one, but I couldn't separate the sounds enough to tell if they were together or not.

I held Jeri as close to me as possible. A thought strayed into my mind: Ishmael had no one to hold on to, yet he was young enough to be afraid. Carolyn must have had the same thought. She moved from her chair and sat down on the stretcher beside Ishmael. She put her arms around him, just as she would have done for a human in need.

I couldn't read Crispy expressions, so I had no idea of what he thought, but I noticed he didn't resist the invitation of her arms. I thought to myself that Sam would be getting a real bargain if he hooked up with her. There aren't many women in this old world who would go out of their way to hug an apparition with his looks.

We all flinched at the sound of an explosion, a normal reaction, even though it comes too late to do any good. Another followed in quick succession, farther away. The van shook from the shock wave as it rumbled past, blowing dust and bits of debris through the open doors. I sucked in a breath of air before thinking to cover my face and got a whiff of smoke and the familiar smell of scorched plastic and composites.

"You guys ought to get on the deck," Bergloff said. At least I think it was him. He and his partner were equally oversized and looked quite a lot alike, with short hair and pug noses.

"Wouldn't do much good if a missile hits us," I said. "If one does, I'd rather go sitting up than lying in that mess on the floor."

"Your choice." The big man grinned.

Nothing else happened for several very long minutes. Most of Sam's group were still outside, but I couldn't locate him. I kept looking and was beginning to wonder when I heard him call.

"Kyle! Outside!"

"Shit," I grunted and did my best to stand up. So did Jeri. "He only asked for me, sweetie," I said mildly.

"Forget it. You go, I go."

If I knew anything about Crispy expressions, her reply drew a strange look from Ishmael. I shrugged, knowing better than to argue. Jeri was worse than a Missouri mule, when it came to us being separated. I climbed down from the back and lifted up my arms to help Jeri down. Instead, Bergloff moved his bulk in front of her.

"Ma'am, we've got orders to keep you inside unless the Colonel says otherwise."

He had his back to me and I couldn't see Jeri because of his broad shoulders, but I could imagine his expression when Jeri spoke to him.

"Mister Bergloff, I know you mean well, but if you don't get out of my way so I can be with my husband, I'll turn you into a dwarf and send you ten dimensions on the other side of the universe."

I couldn't help it. I roared with laughter. His mouth must have dropped open far enough to rest his chin on his chest. He got out of the way. I was still chuckling as I did my best to help her down.

"Pretty good, huh?" She was smiling like a little girl who'd just gone through her first dance recital and not made a single mistake.

"Damn straight. Next time I'm on the losing end of a tough Karate bout, I want you to tell that to the guy that's whupping me. Or gal, as the case might be." I took her hand. We walked to where Sam was stood beside another man, about equidistant from our van and the roadblock.

They were the only two there. Sam gave me the evil eye. I don't think he quite dared to speak to Jeri the way he did to me.

"I thought I gave orders for everyone to stay inside unless I ordered them out."

"Ever try making a woman do something she doesn't want to?" I squeezed Jeri's hand.

"Yeah. Once. That's why I'm divorced now. Never mind, it's done. Someone here wants to meet you." He gave a grudging smile.

Even though the other man had been standing faced away from me, he still looked familiar. I saw why when he turned around. I was staring at the handsome young face of John Lester. He grinned.

"You scoundrel, I ought to be plumb ashamed of the way I let you fool me back in Arkansas." I shook his hand.

"Sorry, John, it seemed like a good idea at the time."

"It might have been—for you. But I caught hell over having you in hand, then letting you go. Along with your new wife, I might add. There's something awfully strange about your relationship. Girls from Albania don't normally leave ten-foot holes in the tarmac of convenience stores."

Be damned! He still didn't know Jeri was a Crispy. Or did he? He did.

"You're the Alien he was hiding, aren't you?" he said to Jeri. "How the hell are you doing it? If all of you can turn into Playboy Centerfolds, I'd want one of you for myself, except I doubt my wife would let me keep her."

"I can guarantee she wouldn't," I said, and bent down to kiss Jeri to prove my point.

"We're wasting time," Sam reminded us.

"Yeah. Okay, Kyle, what's your story? Why did you run instead of asking for protection?"

"Ever have goons from the Russian Mafia after you?"

"No, but I can see your point. Never mind. We want you to come with us. The FBI has jurisdiction over illegal aliens, no matter where they're from."

"Sorry," I shook my head. "No can do. We're staying with the army."

"Uh." His grin had already faded. Then a frown crossed his face. "Kyle, buddy, don't make it hard on yourself or on your friends here. That was a terrorist chopper we just blew up to save your ass, in case you didn't know. You're surrounded, and I have more agents on the way."

"We have more army troops coming, too."

"I've already gotten a ruling from the Attorney General. You belong to the FBI. Don't let this turn into a dogfight." He had acted like a regular field agent when we met before. Now I was beginning to wonder. He must be rather higher up than that. It appeared he had fooled me as badly as I had him.

"John, have you spoken to Senator Benchley in the last half hour or so?"

"No. And what the hell does he have to do with this business? He doesn't run the FBI, or Homeland Security either."

"Neither do you." Like Sam, I was playing for time, but from the way he had spoken we were still going to be outnumbered and outgunned, regardless of the troops on the way. There were only so many soldiers in Army intelligence groups, and they were scattered to hell and gone all over the world. Besides, I had no intention of letting this devolve into a fight between essentially good men, just working for different outfits. I was plain sick of fighting, and running, too.

"Look, I'm going to be real lenient and give you ten minutes to talk it over among yourselves. After that, we'll use force." He gestured to Jeri. "Ma'am, we don't want you hurt, but we *must* get you out of sight and to a safe place. The Homeland security and the FBI can handle this better than anyone else."

"The same way they handled Huricane Katrina? Or the 9/11 terrorists? Or those fanatics who took over that mall during the Christmas rush and killed over a thousand shoppers?" That was stabbing him over events he had nothing to do with, but I knew Jeri wasn't about to go with him, not with his attitude, and even as likable as he normally was.

"That's not fair and you know it. Now for the last time—" His phone rang.

Chapter Twenty-Two

"Shit!" John said, then added, "Sorry, ma'am." He pulled his phone from its case and put it to his ear. "Lester."

After that, about all he did was listen. Carefully. Very. Carefully. Occasionally he said, "Yes, sir," or "No, sir," or "I understand, sir." After he closed the cover and replaced his phone, he gazed at me with an air little short of awe. He took it fairly, though, even forcing a smile that reminded me of a poker player just bluffed out of a big pot when he had held the winning hand.

"You sneaky bastard, you didn't tell me you had that kind of pull in Washington."

"I take it that was Senator Benchley you spoke to?"

"Senator, hell!" he practically shouted. "That was President Morrison himself on the phone!"

"You don't say?" I couldn't help beaming. Shucks, I didn't know I had that much influence, either. "I guess you have orders, then."

"Yeah. Very explicit orders. I'm to have you escorted to..." He lowered his voice to make sure no one but Sam, Jeri and I heard. "...Fort Myer in Arlington, Virginia, at the fastest possible speed consistent with your and the aliens' security and safety. I'm to bring along everyone who's with you, for security purposes. You'll be under the auspices and care of General Shelton, and whoever else he wants to bring in. By the way, he's going to be jumped two grades to Lieutenant General and you, Colonel Haley, will soon be General Haley. One star. And the President wants to reinstate your commission, Kyle, bumped up as well. You'll be given special quarters, freedom of action, access to friends and relatives if they're willing to go into isolation with you, and anything else your little heart desires. Goddamn, I wouldn't have believed this an hour ago if Jesus Christ himself had come down and told me. Now let's get you loaded up and ready to go."

"I've got wounded," Sam said. "We'll need medical treatment."

"Is anyone critical?"

"I don't think so." Sam didn't even mention his own wound, although as John escorted us back to the van, I noticed he was limping slightly.

"We've got medical people with us and a doctor on the way. They'll be taken care of at the base. Now let's go. Leave that van of yours. I'll provide the transportation.

"Wait up," I said as we neared the van. "The other Crispy isn't in human form. No point in letting anyone else seeing him, if we can avoid it."

"Good thinking. We'll throw a blanket or something over him and he can ride with me."

"He has a cloaking device that's still working. I don't know how much power he has left for it, but it ought to get him to your vehicle easily enough."

John didn't bat an eye. It helped me come to a decision.

"Would you like to go into hiding with us as part of the security team?" I asked him.

"You mean that?"

"Why not? We got along all right in Arkansas, and I've got my doubts whether you'd have used deadly force to corral us despite your orders. Besides, I'm not stupid enough to think Army intelligence isn't going to have to work with Homeland Security. You could be bumped to a pay grade with the power to work as liaison to the FBI, maybe even to all of Homeland Security."

"You ever play poker?" he asked as we resumed our stroll to the van.

"Some."

"You probably win a lot. Yeah, I'll go. My boss is going to be awfully pissed, though."

He peeked into the back of the van long enough to get a look at Ishmael, then backed off while Jeri spoke to him in their language. And that took care of our odyssey, or rather it did as soon as we arrived at Fort Myer. Not long after that we were moved to a more permanent location at a place that didn't exist, known only as the Brider Enclave. We got there late the next night. I had argued that we should go to Area 51, just to throw in some irony for all the UFO believers out there. But the Air Force and the CIA owned that place and were very picky about who they let in. We could have pulled some strings, but there was no need. The Brider Enclave was a joint forces intelligence research, development, and acquisition command with an Army three star, Bill, now in charge of it. It worked out fine.

ಬಞ

True to his word, President Morrison and Senator Benchley had most of the arrangements for our comfort taken care of. When the President speaks and invokes the full might of the Office of President of the United States, things happen faster than vodka toasts at a Russian banquet. I didn't know right then where everyone else was housed, but Jeri and I were shown to an apartment roughly the size of the Presidential suite at a five star hotel. We were so tired and emotionally exhausted that we did nothing but grab a quick shower together, brush our teeth and pile into bed. We were content to simply cuddle that night, enjoying the sense of being alone together and safe from harm. It had still not hit me that the President wanted to offer me a commission back, even though Bill—General Shelton—had mentioned it. I was just too tired to absorb it.

"G'night, sweetheart," I murmured.

"Good night, love." She rolled onto her side and backed up to me, spoon fashion. I slipped an arm around her waist and cupped her breast. In a minute or two I was gone.

ಲೂಅಂ

I woke lying on my back, with Jeri on her side next to me. Her arm was thrown casually across my chest. I turned my head just far enough to see her face. She nodded downward at the "tent" I was pitching with the covers, then she gave me a naughty smile and winked.

Without hesitation, Jeri slid my boxers down and crawled over on top of me. Pulling her panties aside, she slid onto me with a wriggle as I reached up and cupped her breasts gently but firmly. She moaned softly as I slipped her t-shirt over her head and pulled her to me. Her long hair swept across my face with her slow rocking motions as our hips ground together. She lowered her nose to mine and gave me a long wet kiss while staring deep into my eyes. Then she smiled and stretched out, squeezing me as tight as she could. In response I held her in a bear hug and rubbed my hands down the small of her back finally reaching a firm grasping place on her buttocks. I kneaded them with my fingers in rhythm with her motion until I let go with an eager, if not early climax.

"Ahhgg," I groaned.

"Shhh. Don't move." Jeri continued to slowly rock her pelvis into me, squeezing me in a way that made me feel twenty again. The new youthful vigor and lease on life she had given me kept my erection rock steady and I held onto her like I never wanted to let her go. Hell, I didn't ever want to let her go.

Amazingly, we made slow languorous love for another hour before getting up. We were both covered in perspiration and we quickly and playfully showered together. I was awake, relaxed, showered, and hungry enough to eat raw meat, but coffee came first. A steward knocked on the door as if he had been watching and waiting. He wheeled in a cart with a big pot of coffee and a breakfast fit for lumberjacks, but it made me wonder how he'd known we were ready for company. Jeri saw my frown.

"There was a tiny spycam. I disconnected the battery from it last night before we went to sleep and reactivated it after we were, mmm, finished with other business. And fine business it was, at that." She wriggled into her t-shirt. Her breasts stretched it in a way that gave me thoughts about going back to bed. They weren't rock hard thoughts, but with Jeri I felt that wouldn't be too difficult to achieve lickety-split.

"Naughty girl." But I was too hungry, and she'd turned the camera back on. I didn't let the fact that there had been a spycam put in our room keep me from enjoying the meal and two big cups of the best coffee I'd ever tasted, but I raised so much hell over it with Bill later in the day that I wouldn't have been surprised to see the culprit who'd had it installed hung up by his thumbs. I'd like to have had my own spycam on the wall when the new three-star and long-time friend dressed down the would-be spy in question.

୫୦ଠଃ

I sat next to Jeri at the conference table, listening to the talk and wearing a uniform again with the CW5 pips adorning it. It felt comfortable to be back in the army, like slipping into a favorite old pair of house shoes that had been lost then found again.

"Somehow, Ishmael, somehow, we must find all of the survivors being held." Jeri held the changing alien's tentacle/hand appendage, that was becoming human-looking much faster than hers had months before.

The two of them had been working in tandem to transmogrify his alien body into a human one, the same way that Jeri had. We'd only been at the Enclave two days and they both had already projected that his body would be fully human within the next week. His oversized head had already begun to have human facial features, with hair beginning to grow on the top of it. From the looks of it, Ishmael planned to be a blond. And from the picture that Jeri had shown me, he intended to look a lot like a male underwear model who was all the rage with the women those days.

"Yes, Jeri. I agree with you. Many of our people would choose not to survive the horror I was exposed to." Ishmael licked at his half-human, half-alien lips with an oversized tongue and then widened his eyes at me. The pupils were most definitely still alien and gave me the willies. "But I cannot leave here until I'm more humanized and prepared for interaction with them. You and Kyle must be the ones to go."

"Now hold on a minute, fella," the three-star at the end of the conference table interrupted. "I'd say that I might have *some* say-so in that. I'm not certain that we want to risk an asset as important as Jeri again."

"General Shelton, if I decide to go to the aid of my people against your wishes, I'm not certain you could stop me. You would most certainly lose my cooperation." Jeri smiled at Bill, in an attempt at making her subdued ultimatum a little lighter.

"Surely, it will never come to that." I could tell that I needed to intervene before things blew out of whack, so I, too, interrupted.

"General...Bill...we can trust Jeri as one of us. And she is a valued asset and resource for the country, true. But, having known her the longest, other than maybe Ishmael over there, I'd say that she'll be useless to us as long as she knows her friends are being held against their will." I scratched my chin as a thought hit me. "Though, I think this conversation is a little bit premature, 'cause I'm not sure how we'd find them. On the other hand, we most certainly don't want them in the hands of hostile nations. I think tracking them down is, or should be, our first priority."

"Why can't we find them?" Bill asked with a perplexed frown on his face. He rubbed at his clean-shaven face as if there were stubble on it.

"Even working in tandem, Jeri's and Ishmael's combined perception is still limited by, say, fifty to a hundred miles," I replied.

"We could put them in aircraft and fly them in search patterns, but that would take a while to cover the entire globe," Sam added from his side of the table. "There has to be a smarter way."

"Okay, fine." General Shelton paused. "We'll make our first priority finding the other aliens. I don't want one of you Cresperians to end up in the hands of the Russians or the Chinese or, God forbid, the damned Jihadists from the Islamic confederation. That means we need a sensor or a concept of operations for finding them. Let's make that our first technology development and operations team effort. Whatever you need, get it, and do it!" There you had it. The lieutenant general in charge of us had made his decree. We *were* going to find the others at all costs.

"Any ideas?" I asked, looking at Jeri.

"The Internet is our best starting place. We also need to work on a power converter for our disintegrators so they can be charged and a communications device that's not susceptible to interception."

The general nodded at Carolyn, the electronics wizard from NSA we'd grabbed at the motel fight. "Get those started."

"Yes, sir." She got up and left the room. Command presence in action.

He turned to the alien. "What's your take, Ishmael? You agree with Jeri?"

"Of course." Ishmael awkwardly placed his half-formed hand thing to his oversized forehead in an attempt to mimic human behavior. "Start with the internet. Any of them should be near enough to a computer that they could gain access via their perception."

"Well, you two were in the United States of America. And what you don't realize is that there are a lot of places in the world where computers are not everywhere you look." Sam rubbed at his wounded thigh as if his stitches were itching him, and then added, "My stint through North Korea assured me of that. I hardly ever found any place to gain access to the web." He rubbed at his leg again. This time Jeri caught notice of it. I could tell she was looking deeper into his wound with her perception. Well, actually, I couldn't tell. Who knew when Jeri was using that alien magical sense of hers? But I guessed she was. I'd come to know Jeri pretty darn good and one thing I knew for certain about her was that she hated to see people in pain.

"What about a satellite in very low earth orbit?" I asked. "Could we put up a bird or use some of the birds already there to communicate with them?"

"Kyle, I used Internet connections to link to satellite uplinks. There would still need to be an uplink on each end." Jeri exhaled through her pursed lips, making a faint motorboat sound, and leaned back in her chair, exasperated. "I guess we start the search in the Internet-friendly geographies first, but I hate that."

"Well, wait a minute." Bill held up the pointer finger of his right hand and almost said "aha." "Do we really have to blanket the entire planet? I mean, wouldn't your ships hit the Earth like a meteor shower does?"

"Of course they would!" Ishmael responded again with the strange hand-to-forehead gesture. "Once the escape pods entered reality space, they followed normal orbital mechanics, and should have impacted along the planet in a single orbital plane."

"So that means that there should be a swath or a band around the planet where the ships would have landed?" I asked. I'm by no means an orbital mechanic but I understood what they were driving at.

"That's right. It shouldn't be too difficult to pinpoint the track along the surface of the Earth where the pods would have come down." Jeri flicked her fingers through her hair and then scratched the back of her head reflexively. "The swath would still be a hundred miles wide or more."

"How many pods could there be?" Sam asked. He had stopped rubbing at his leg. I wondered if it was self-control or if Jeri had taken matters into her own hands.

"That is a difficult question to answer," Ishmael replied. Again those hybrid-looking eyes freaked me out a little. Had Jeri ever looked like that? I guess she had, but thank God, did she ever look different now.

"How so?" General Shelton asked, leaning back in his chair. He wasn't *quite* getting bored with our conversation yet.

"There were thousands of us on the ship, but my guess is that only hundreds of us made it to pods and..." Ishmael paused and his head sunk a bit.

Jeri put her two cents worth in. "I told Kyle I thought no more than a dozen survived to land on earth and probably not that many. I had a perceptive glimpse of the trajectories of only two—the one Ishmael was in and one that came down in Scotland, I think. And, Bill, we have no way of knowing how many of the pods survived the transition from the unreality rift into reality space. The space distortion and control systems of the space drive were failing. There weren't many that made it to earth, though. I can be sure of that much. Ishmael and I and the poor unsuspecting soul that landed in Baja could be the only three, or there could be a dozen, with perhaps as many as three of us in any of them."

"Is there any radar data or anything that might help us narrow that down?" I asked. It was an idea.

"Sam, get us somebody from Space Command on our team that we can trust and see if the orbital debris tracking guys know anything."

"Good idea, General," Sam answered.

"Uh, General." John spoke up for the first time during the conversation. "We checked all of our resources at the FBI and even tapped into the greater resources of the Department of Homeland Security, and found nothing. None of the FAA radars or the National Missile Defense systems detected anything, to our knowledge."

"The makeup of our pods would probably make them very stealthy to your radar technologies. But there is a chance that multi-static radar systems might have detected them." Jeri didn't sound too enthusiastic about the odds of finding the pods from past radar data. And what the hell was "multi-static" radar?

"HUMINT," I said. "We have to have plenty of HUMINT on potential alien landings around the world. The CIA operatives out there must know something. I mean, come on, intel services from several groups around the world tracked me and Jeri down."

"HUMINT?" Ishmael asked curiously, while raising a newly grown sandy brown eyebrow.

"Human intelligence. Real people in the field finding clues and asking questions and going undercover is what HUMINT is all about." Sam nodded. He still wore the brigadier general rank uncomfortably at times, but he seemed more at ease around Lieutenant General "Bill" Shelton than he did anywhere else. The two must have been through some bad stuff to have bonded that way. It was real similar to my relationship with Bill, I guessed. Sam and I were gonna get along just fine.

"We need to tap into more than just the Army Intel," I added. "Bill, I suggest we see if the president might be willing to push the DNI for full cooperation with us. Department of National Intelligence," I added hurriedly for the aliens' benefit. "It might mean we have to give the DNI's office full disclosure, but I don't think that's a problem."

"I can push through the Homeland Security side and the FBI, but that would only lead to contacts with bad guys inside the continental U.S.," John said. His years at the FBI would allow him to query through people he trusted. John was going to be a good asset for the team, too.

"Good. All of this is a start," Bill clapped his hands on the table and rose from his chair. The meeting was coming to an end, apparently. "We have our first line of business actions. From the conversation it is quite clear that we need more smart guys in a whole bunch of different fields. Sam, you start recruiting people we can trust. I want scientists, engineers, mathematicians, doctors, and whoever else you think might can help Jeri and Ishmael figure out how to find their comrades. They have to be clearable. None of these ivory tower egghead hippies that want to give the world all our secrets. I'd prefer it if they were already cleared at a minimum of Top Secret, but we can work with Secret level folks if we have to. Get them investigated and cleared into the program ASAP and before they are read in on what we're up to." Bill paused in thought for a brief moment and then continued with his orders.

"Also, Kyle, you and John, with Sam's help, start putting together some HUMINT teams and some action teams. Anybody you want across any service or civilian agency, get them. If you need Army Spec Ops from JFCOM, get them. If you want a Navy SEAL, get him. If you want a

Marine fighter pilot, get him. If you want a goddamned NASA astronaut, get him or her. Get them quickly and get them here. If you bump into hurdles along the way, I'll call the White House. Get the troops and get us those smart guys quick. We are obviously out of our element a bit. I mean, what the hell is 'multi-static' radar, anyway?"

⳥ﮎ

"Well, Kyle, since you accepted reinstatement of your commission and the promotion the president offered you, you'll have to pass the Army PFT!" Sam grinned at me as he turned to his left to introduce me to a very large young man of oriental extraction. The kid couldn't have been much more than in his mid twenties. He was very muscular, about six feet two inches tall, and had light brown skin. "This is Sergeant First Class Jonas Wu. He and I have been through some pretty serious shit together. His specialty is blowing shit up with reckless abandon, using only household chemicals and duct tape. I personally picked him for our little operation here. He'll be testing you."

"Uh, right, uh, General Haley." I shook hands with SFC Wu and passed pleasantries for a second. "So, Sarge, same drill as when I was in before? Push-ups, sit-ups, two miles?"

"That's right, sir. So, at your leisure, Chief, start pushing the floor." The young SFC grinned slyly and stepped back to give me some room. I had to get used to people calling me chief again. Chief wasn't really correct according to the regs. Mr. or sir is how chief warrant officers are supposed to be addressed. But informally, Chief has been an unofficially acceptable form of salutation almost forever. Personally, I didn't really give a shit. "Uh, General Haley, sir, you, too."

"You, too?" I asked Sam.

"Even us big shot generals have to pass Army PFT. And I'm due, so I thought I'd come along with you."

"I realize that, but your leg?"

"That girlfriend of yours is something else if not easy on the eyes."

"Really," I chuckled at Sam. "I hadn't noticed."

"Uh huh, I'm sure you hadn't. Can't figure out why all your neighbors begged us to double insulate your walls, though? Now let's push the ground soldier." Sam gave me a toothy grin and dropped.

"Yes, General, sir!"

Apparently, Jeri had been working on him and he believed he was fully healed. It was fine with me. Having somebody there more my age made the process seem a little less silly. After all, they weren't going to send me home if I didn't pass, that was for sure. The two of us in our running shoes, Army t-shirts, and shorts hit the ground and started pushing.

Before Jeri had fixed me up, doing push-ups would have seemed damned near impossible, but somewhere around fifty of them I happened to look over and noticed that Sam was starting to sweat at the effort he was putting out. I hadn't even realized I was really doing anything. Hell, I felt like a kid again.

"That's enough for a top score in push-ups, sirs." Jonas tapped at the form on his clipboard.

"You sure? I can keep going," Sam grunted. Sam was a big bulky man and it was quite clear that he had been doing a lot of strength training for most of his life. Even in his late forties he was a physical beast. Hell, his biceps were as big around as my legs at the thigh.

"Me, too," I said, not to be outdone. I began doing the last few push-ups one-handed.

"Uh, sirs, you can do them all day long if you'd like but it won't help with the PFT."

"Right. Sit-ups?" I asked.

"Yes, sir."

I rolled over and started sitting up. Again I could tell that the work Jeri had done on me had made sitting up almost as easy as sitting down. I had come by my fitness the hard way. I had convinced an alien from an advanced civilization to crash land in my yard, convert itself to a hot human female with an insatiable sex drive, then to fall in love with me, and finally to rejuvenate me physically, all the while making mad passionate love to me at a pace Casanova would have envied in his prime. Hard work, I tell you. Nice work if you can get it, though. All Sam had had to do was work out with weights for an hour a day four or five times a week all of his life. Easy.

Once we'd finished the sit-ups we hit the track. Just outside the edge of the Enclave's adit a paved jogging trail had been installed that ran around the facility. The path looped through the trees and over the slight incline of the mound that covered the entryway. I had run on the path a couple times to try out my healed wounds since we moved in. I knew that it was curvy and had a couple ups and downs. And, for the most part the scenery along the two-mile loop in the mountainous terrain was beautiful. It would be an enjoyable run.

At my age I only needed to run two miles at a little over seven minutes per mile each to score perfect on the Army PFT. The minimum was a bit over eight-minute miles. There was no way in hell I could have done that with my shot-up hip before, but then that was before I had met Jeri. The difference in my physical abilities between the last few years of my life and the last few months were like night and day. In fact, I felt more physically fit then than I had at eighteen.

"Kyle, I'm not a fast runner," General Haley started. "I want you to run this thing as fast as you can."

"Why, Sa—, uh, General?"

"I'd like to see what you're capable of. Consider this part of uncovering what all our friends can do for us. We need to know how good you are if we get into a hairy situation in the near future." Sam stretched his neck left and right and shook his arms and legs, getting loose for the run.

"Makes sense to me. I'll give all I've got."

"Whenever you two fine sirs are ready." Jonas Wu held his stopwatch up to give us the hint to stop chatting and start running.

"Ready when you are, Jonas," Sam nodded to him.

"All right, sirs. On your mark, set, go!"

I initially started out slower than I thought I could run, because I hadn't run any distance in a long time and wasn't quite sure what pace I was capable of now. Over the four or five days that we had been moving into the Enclave, I had been running a few miles a day but hadn't tried to run fast yet. After about an eighth of a mile I really started letting go. I could feel my heart pounding in my chest, probably near one hundred ninety beats per minute. I still felt like I could push further. *Thump-thump* my heart pounded.

I crested a small hill near the back side of the Enclave and scared the bejesus out of a white-tailed deer standing there. He jumped off into the trees like a bat out of hell. I made the decision that I'd need to check my shorts as well after the run and that I should talk to Jeri to see if my startle factor could be dialed down. My heart continued to pound like a metronome in my chest. Steady and fast. There was no pain in my body anywhere and I felt better than I'd ever felt in my life. I pushed a little harder. *Breathe in through the nose, out through the mouth.*

Finally, I could see the last turn of the jogging trail and SFC Wu standing at ease near the trailhead. He just happened to look in my direction, and I could tell he was doing a double take at the stopwatch. I pushed harder across the finish and then trotted to a halt and relaxed my breathing. I wasn't sure where I'd learned to control my breathing so easily. I took a slow, deep breath and then relaxed.

"Did I pass?"

"Uh, sir." He looked perplexed. "Let's wait until the general has finished his run and we'll discuss it."

We waited for Sam to finish the run. It seemed like forever before he finally crested the last hill and we could see him approaching us in the distance. He plodded across the line sounding like a steam engine huffing and blowing and puffing for air. He stopped and bent over, placing his hands on his knees, and nearly collapsed.

"Good job, sir! That's a personal best for you."

"Yeah, how fast?" Sam asked, between gasps for air. His face beaded with sweat as he propped his hands on his knees.

"Fifteen fifty-four."

"I passed."

"Yes, sir."

"And Kyle?" Sam, still propping on his knees, panted like a dog.

"Uh, sir, Chief Leverson crossed the finish line a little after seven minutes and a half. Perhaps we should have him retest."

"Sergeant, is that your polite way of saying that you think Chief Warrant Officer 5 Leverson cheated?" Sam stood upright, wiping the sweat from his face with the tail of his t-shirt.

"Well, sir, I don't know of any short cuts, but he crossed the line not even breathing hard at a time that would put him way faster than any world records." He looked down at his pad and chewed at his lower lip. "Uh, much faster than any world records, sir. General, I have yet to log anything for his final time. He could retake the test if you like."

"Well, Kyle, this really pisses me off," Sam said with a smile. Jonas looked as if he were about to be backed up and as if the general was about to lower the boom on a cheater. "I told you to give it your all and I hear that you crossed the line not even breathing hard!"

"Well, Sam," I responded, being more familiar with him than protocol allowed. Sam didn't give a damn and it was better for dramatic impact on our young SFC. He was enjoying playing with the sergeant, who obviously hadn't been fully briefed on our organization yet. "I'm truly sorry. I could run it again, I guess."

"Could you really, Kyle?" Sam asked seriously interested. His eyes widened with excitement at the thought.

"I feel fresh. I'm pretty sure I could run it again just as fast. Maybe faster."

"That is just damned amazing, Kyle." Sam rose to his full height and slapped me on the back. "Jonas?"

"Yes, general?"

"You are to put down that CWO5 Kyle Leverson completed the run a few seconds ahead of me, and will mention this to nobody. The true outcome of his run is now classified above Top Secret. Understand?"

"Yes, general." Jonas didn't look confused or concerned. He simply followed the general's orders without question. Good lad to have around when the shooting starts. I was pretty sure that was why Sam picked him to be there in our little organization.

"Kyle, let's get cleaned up. We've got a briefing to get to."

"Sure you don't want me to run it again?" I said with a grin and a raised eyebrow while looking at the sergeant. "It won't take that long."

Chapter Twenty-Three

"This is Dr. Karen Freeny from Wheeler Laboratories at Princeton," Jeri said, introducing me to the fairly attractive fifty-something woman in a very nice executive style suit. Her hair was dark, with streaks of gray at the temples, and it was neatly pulled up behind her neck. From her appearance I'd have thought of her as a businesswoman in corporate America and not one of the nation's top physicists. But as I was learning, high tech was big business, and there was a certain level of the scientists within the classified high tech world that didn't fit the mold of the nerd with horned rim glasses. Most of them I was meeting seemed more like the alpha of the species: physically fit, well groomed and dressed for success. I found out later that Wheeler Labs meant that she was really working programs for the CIA, NSA and National Reconnaissance Office. And now she was part of "The Group" as we were calling ourselves. I had pushed for a name like "Majestic" or "UNCLE" or "SHADO" but couldn't get any takers. "The Group" just seemed to stick.

"Nice to meet you, Dr. Freeny." I shook her hand.

She gripped it firmly with confidence and smiled. "I've heard a lot about you the last few days. It's nice to finally meet you, Kyle. Please, call me Karen."

"Great, Karen." I turned to Jeri and Ishmael. "So why are we here?"

"This." Ishmael tapped a few keys at a laptop, and a slideshow popped up on the big flatscreen at the end of the makeshift laboratory room. I moved a computer monitor off a chair and sat down. An image of the planet appeared and then three red tracks started tracking from the planet upward into space. "These two red tracks here are my and Jeri's pods. They start in Arkansas at your place and near Thomaston, Georgia, where I crashed. The third track here in Baja is where our poor friend was shot to death by the Mexican Army. We've followed them back to a point of where we think our materialization into reality space took place. Here. Sometime in the future we should go there and look for any remains of the spacecraft or artifacts from it."

"Yeah, wouldn't be good if that cloak or the disintegrator device got into the wrong hands," I replied.

"I agree."

"Disintegrator? Cloak?" Karen asked.

"Sorry, for another time. Y'all were saying about the spacecraft trajectories?" I asked, smiling at my beautiful alien turned human spouse.

"Kyle, we took data from orbital debris tracking radars at Space Command, NASA, and combined it all with data from the National Missile Defense radars, National Weather Service radars, and Air Traffic Control systems," Jeri said. "After some major post-processing we found where our tracks caused very minor disruptions in the radar returns of those systems. It took processing of all of the multiple radar systems and some *a priori* knowledge of the targets—our pods—but we managed to generate an algorithm that allowed us to detect them. After grabbing data from every radar on the planet that we could, uh, implement data from, we managed to collect enough data that might lead us to finding other tracks."

"There is a boundary condition problem, though," Karen added. "I won't, for a second, attempt to explain the algorithms that Jeri and Ish came up with, since I don't understand them, or how in the hell they hacked into all the radar databases, but I understand the basic math. We need a start and an end point for the math to converge on a real solution."

"So, uh, what does all that mean?" I hated to admit that I didn't have a goddamned clue what they were getting at, but I didn't. Bill had been right. We were out of our element and we did need some big brains added to the team. Karen seemed to be one of them, and that was good. "Sounds like you have to know where they landed in order to track them. If we knew that, we'd already know where they are. Or were."

"That's right, Kyle," Jeri flashed her playmate caliber smile at me. "But we can just pick points at random and have the computer crunch the data. If there is a track there, they will converge on it. If there isn't a track there, then the solution should diverge to a divide by zero error with infinite solutions."

"Oh, I see. So why don't we just do that? I mean, run every possibility." As soon as I said it, I knew there had to be a catch.

"Well, we are doing that," Ishmael added.

"But there is a lot of fuzziness about the origin points and the speeds of the pods," Jeri said.

"Why?"

"You see, Kyle, it's because Jeri and Ish here have no idea if the pod propulsion systems were online or not and at what power they were operating at if they were. So, there are about a million possible starting places and velocity vectors. Then the endpoints are along a swath the length of the circumference of the Earth—about 25,000 miles—and a few hundred miles wide. And some of them might have even missed the planet, hit the Moon, or zoomed off into open space, getting trapped in some heliocentric orbit."

"That sounds like a lot of possibilities," I ventured.

"Pretty much infinite," Jeri said. "If you count the ones that might have missed the planet, that is."

"Then let's not count those. Just look at the ones on this planet." No sense in worrying about a problem we couldn't help with anyway. If they were out in space we wouldn't be able to get to them. Humanity could go into orbit and with a lot of effort to the Moon. But that was about as far as our spacefaring went.

"Okay," Ishmael said, and I'd have sworn it sounded sarcastic. "We thought of that."

"Well, it still sounds like a hell of a lot of possibilities," I said.

"About a hundred billion possible boundary conditions to sort through, and one calculation takes several minutes." Karen sat down in a chair by a computer station and tapped a few keys. "It would take, oh, about four years to run all possibilities."

"I see. So what can I do to help?"

"HUMINT and best guesses could help us narrow things down," Karen replied.

"You see, Kyle, this is where your branch comes in." Jeri wrapped her hands around my arm and pulled close to me. "Any intel you might have could narrow the search down. Then we could perhaps enter those regions of the planet somehow, and Ishmael and I could contact them."

"You've had no hits via the Internet yet?" Granted they'd only been trying to find the downed aliens for a week now but no luck. Even the news had quit running the UFO stories and gone on to other things. So there were no leads there. No more monster tales across the Internet tabloids and no more third-world armies playing shoot'em up with alien creatures. The alien invasion buzz had drifted away to the background and conspiracy communities. The prevalent news of the day involved a set of twenty-something billionaire twins caught up in an Internet porn scandal.

"We've had no hits as of yet. It's possible that their stasis fields worked and that they are still hibernating. My pod just failed. That's why you had to rescue me and Ishmael had a safe landing and simply exited his pod.

Others might have crashed with their pod still functioning and chose to stay put. Or emergency systems put them in stasis when their pods failed to disintegrate like you saw mine do. When our ship hit that reality anomaly everything went to hell so many ways that there's no way of knowing." Jeri seemed to be losing her optimism and I could tell that I had to do something to help her out.

"Well, we've chased a few leads but found nothing substantial yet. Perhaps the leads might be all you need. I'll get John in here and we'll dump all the intel and speculation we have on you. John did say something about some new spy satellite data coming in that we needed to see. And come to think of it, we need to ask what our HUMINT assets in that swath might have seen or heard about. It's possible they have helpful information and don't even know it."

"Uh, I'd also suggest we add some other space intelligence folks to the group," Karen added. "I've already put together a list of names for you."

"I've got a meeting with Sam after this. I'll get the names to him immediately."

"That would be great, Kyle."

ಬೇಞ

"So, fifty percent or so of the swath around the planet is over the oceans," I explained to the senior staff. "Give or take. Let's not look there yet. If they're at the bottom of the ocean, we wouldn't know how to get to them, anyway."

"Undamaged pods would steer for land, Kyle," Jeri interrupted, and caused me to remember she'd told me that once, right after we'd met. I still didn't have her memory.

"Well, if any damaged ones hit the oceans, we'll solve that problem later. Besides, if they survived the ocean floor for this long they'll probably be okay a little longer." I raised an eyebrow in her direction. She smiled back at me. "Okay, so that leaves these highlighted areas on the globe." I waited for that to sink in.

"Whew!" John whistled, and shook his head. "Talk about needles and haystacks."

"Exactly," I agreed. "As y'all can see, the swath starts here in Texas, and Arkansas where Jeri's pod crashed, across the Southern States and wraps across the Atlantic to England, Northern Africa, Iraq, Iran, India, China, Japan, and then back across the Pacific through Baja, Northern Mexico, finally back to Texas. That's a lot of hostile territory to look at. John, you want to take it from here?"

"Thanks, Kyle. Actually, I'm going to be brief and then I'll introduce you to a couple of new team members from the National Reconnaissance Office and from the National Security Agency." John switched the briefing slides and then brought up a similar graphic of the Earth with the same highlighted areas. "What we've done is collected HUMINT and various tech-INTs and compiled them into a very large stack of data on anything out of the ordinary. We looked at covert operations, meteor impacts, alien abduction stories, UFO sightings, monster sightings, military presence or motion where it usually isn't, and communications of any nature pertaining to visitors or friends or any other similar subjects. We've also looked at the travel records of respected or known scientists and engineers in these regions. There's some fancy bank account analysis as well."

"Sounds like a lot of data," General Shelton commented.

"Most definitely more data than we could filter through in short order. But we have analysts by the roomfuls going through it and we have special genetic algorithm-driven computers filtering through it for any type of match. So far we've found six immediate possibilities." John clicked the pointer, and the Earth rotated and zoomed to the area of the swath stretching from Libya to Eastern China. Six dots blinked across the region.

"We should immediately run the tracking algorithm on those coordinates!" Jeri nodded to Ishmael.

"I'm already inputting the locations as we speak," Ishmael replied.

"That's all fine. But I'm not sure that's necessary." John nodded to one of the new guys in the back of the room. "This is Dr. Byron King of the NRO. They've been flying high resolution image collectors of various types around the globe for years. Byron, why don't you show us what you have?"

"Hello, it's nice to meet all of you," the NRO scientist said. He came across a lot like Karen: confident, well groomed, nice suit, not too expensive. After all, he was on a government salary. "Here are several high resolution images taken from spy satellites of the six regions shown. We actually happen to have data of the one here in Chongqing, China, that was only a few hours after Mrs. Leverson's crashed pod. With maximum enhancement you can see here that there is indeed a small impact crater."

The meeting went on like this for another hour or two. The details of the impact in China were of the highest confidence because there was actually an image of the impact crater—with a pod in it, as if it had done the same as Jeri's had, failed just before touchdown and fallen the last couple of dozen feet. The ones in Iraq and Iran were less certain, as the optical image was several days later. But new infrared data showed that there was dirt movement along a pattern that looked like a number of vehicle tracks had been covered over. The spy satellite photos of India were much less convincing, as they were in the jungle through triple canopy vegetation. Various types of imagery did hint that there was a newly wiped out path through the trees indicative of an impact, but there wasn't enough data to be even halfway sure.

The tell-all, though, was when the tracking algorithm locked onto pod trajectories in the radar data for each of the six locations. We'd found where at least six other pod locations were! Or had been. Current data showed that they weren't there now, however. That was the problem. How did we find them now? We knew what countries they were likely to be in, though. That narrowed it down some. Didn't it?

Well, the NSA fellow who spoke next had narrowed it down quite a bit. From cell phone conversations and Internet traffic that they monitored daily, the NSA had managed to find several conversations starting on the day the first landings took place, and tracked accents, names, buzzwords, codewords, you name it, from those initial conversations. From there, they managed to narrow the location of three Cresperians down to within a few hundred square miles each. All we had to do was to get Jeri and the now blond Adonis, Ishmael, anywhere near those locations and they could find them with their combined perceptions. Unfortunately, two of the three locations were deep in hostile territory. The third was in India, and that one could be reached through diplomatic channels. The remaining three Crispies would have to be found through HUMINT and alien perception.

We knew where three were at the moment, so we had to focus on saving them from the machinations of hostile countries. We were still negotiating with the British over the one that came down there, while pretending we had none. A dirty trick on a former staunch ally but, damn it, they shouldn't have voted that crazy socialist into power. The problem with the two not in India was that one of them was in China and the other in Libya. Neither of those countries was exactly lovey-dovey with the United States. Despite Jeri's aversion to potential violence, she agreed on the need to try to contact them and bring them over to our side. Ishmael was neutral, not knowing enough yet, but he went along with Jeri.

And I guess this bears mentioning. Once he attained his final form, a big blond good-looking guy with blue eyes and cleft chin, he somehow got the idea that Jeri would automatically ditch me and form a liaison with him. He got his nose a bit out of joint when she politely but firmly rejected his advances, but he got over it after a couple of the female tech specialists taught him that beds had more uses than just for sleeping. The look on his face after that first night was priceless, like waking up a billion dollar lottery winner after just spending the night with the world's leading sex goddess, who fell in love with him after he quarterbacked his team to a Super bowl victory. Something like that.

ഽോരൂ

The day after one of the physics docs finally got a charger working for the disintegrators and invisibility gadgets, Libya came up the winner for our first mission. We were still working out how to manage an ingress-egress for China, but that was partly in the hands of Sgt. Wu, who turned out to speak flawless Mandarin and could even read the Chinese ideographic printing. I put that one out of my mind the minute I heard the news from Sam Haley that the Libya mission was a go.

I immediately started getting the pre-mission jitters like I always did. It was compounded by the fact that Jeri had to go along, of course. Just having her and her weapons would increase the odds of success a hundred percent, at least. Some of the big brains were working with Ish, trying to make duplicates of the weapons with their fabricators but weren't having any luck so far. Jeri would be the only one armed with them this time. Ish couldn't go because General Shelton refused to risk both Crispies at once.

We started a hurried training the day after, mixing briefings with physical preparations, such as going over our weapons.

ഽോരൂ

"You strap the armor across the side here after you slide in with your right side, ma'am." Lieutenant Alex Swavely pulled the Velcro strap of his improved outer tactical vest or IOVT closed around him, demonstrating, again, to Jeri and me how the thing worked. We'd jumped with the armor system once a few days prior but it was still a bit new to us. The vests were different from ones I'd used years ago and were supposed to be more effective. They were a hell of a lot lighter for the coverage they gave. And the way you got in and out of them was, well hell, it was new and different, and the training we'd been receiving for the past week had been like drinking from a goddamned fire hose. We hoped that we retained enough of the water from it to keep from thirsting to damned death!

"Thank you, Alex," Jeri said to the Navy SEAL team's "third-O, third officer."

"Ma'am," he nodded. "Wouldn't want anything happening to the only alien I've ever been charged with protecting."

"Thank you, again."

Jeri and I continued strapping the armor in place and then pulled on the rest of our gear. I snapped the MP-5 on my vest, along with several ammo clips stuck strategically into the vest's webbing. I had a Glock 9mm under each arm, several small bladed weapons placed in other strategic locations, and a baker's dozen of grenades just for bunkum. In front of that was a pack full of other assortments of deadly gear and essentials for survival. On my back were a water bladder and another quite essential piece of equipment—a parachute. One nice thing, with my new improved body, they didn't weigh so damned much!

Shit, I never liked jumping out of planes, especially on short notice. We'd been training for this type of operation for two weeks and had made five jumps so far. My and Jeri's sixth jump would be a high altitude high opening (HAHO) jump operation over Libya, planned just fourteen hours before back at the Enclave. Our NSA reconnaissance teams picked up a transmission that the Cresperian was going to be moved from one location to another, zeroing our search in on his location. The first operation team of "The Group" consisted of a seven-man SEAL fire unit from SEAL Team Five, six marines and two Air Force guys from different black ops units out of Joint Forces Command (JFCOM), a five-man Army team from the 82nd Airborne, John Lester, myself, and Sam.

"The Group" had become the ultimate black ops organization, pulling the best from civil and military. The intelligence community, United States Special Operations Command (USSOCOM), and Joint Forces Command (JFCOM) had become our recruiting grounds. As a standard operating procedure Bill had ordered that only one alien asset, meaning Jeri or Ishmael, could be risked at a time. Ishmael didn't like being benched, but there were other missions that he could go on in the future and thus bench Jeri. I was looking forward to those. Besides, I didn't think Ishmael was quite ready for operations yet. He hadn't had the time as a human to adapt to his new abilities and body and environment that Jeri had. I still hated her being put in harm's way, though.

We all rushed onto a C-130 at the Enclave and were airborne only an hour and a half following the news. We hooked up with a C-17 in North

Carolina and were on our way to the Middle East. We did most of the planning on the sixteen-hour plane ride to Libya. I dozed off briefly every now and then.

We skirted international waters for a bit while Jeri tried to zero in with her perception. The intel we had told us right where the Crispy was supposed to be, but we wanted to be sure. Unfortunately, the alien was moved inland about a hundred miles or so, which was just at the edge of her abilities. After about a half hour of searching, Jeri's final word was that she was uncertain at best. Sam made a command decision and ordered the pilots to follow with the mission plan and prepare to breach the Libyan airspace.

"Okay, team, eyes and ears on me!" Sam shouted.

"Sir!"

"The jump point is at eighteen minutes in. Let's wrap up the gear and put out the camp fires. Any last-minute questions, just keep them to yourselves. It's too goddamned late to turn back now, since our plane just left international airspace. Lieutenant Colonel Gaines, it's all yours!"

"Yes, sir!" the Army Airborne soldier shouted. "Jump team leaders, commence gear check and prep. Let's fall into jump teams and report to the jumpmaster. Move!"

At five minutes out the jumpmaster, an Air Force E7, told us that we would have to go to full time on our oxygen. At the altitude we were going to be jumping and loitering around at, we'd need to be on pure oxygen until we got below ten thousand feet or so. The plane had been slightly underpressured on pure oxygen for the past thirty minutes. If we let the least bit of regular air in we'd have a problem with nitrogen in our blood. So, if we didn't breathe the right kind of air we might die on the way down from the bends or something similar. Even worse, in my opinion, since I hate cold weather, was the fact that the air at thirty thousand feet was cold, real cold. Really, really, cold. We all wore polypropylene undergarments, goggles, and two pairs of gloves to help protect us from it. When we hit the desert floor it would be about a hundred and nineteen degrees Fahrenheit. If we were in the thick of some nasty business we'd just have to sweat it out. Otherwise we could take a few minutes to rethink our gear. The general consensus was to just prepare to be hot. Goddamned desert. Why couldn't there ever be a mission into weather like they have in Hawaii? Probably Murphy, as usual.

"Sam, this is Jeri," Jeri told the general over the com as she squeezed my hand.

"Go ahead, Jeri."

"He's there. I'm certain of it."

"Great. Just as we practiced, you lead us to a couple miles out on the drop."

"Understood."

"I never really liked this plan," I replied not so reassuringly.

"Ninety seconds!" the jumpmaster shouted as the jump lights came on. The red one was lit up as the door in the tail of the C-17 cycled down. The first group—Jeri, myself, John, Sam, and the SEAL fire team—lined up on the ramp of the plane and snapped our chutes on the line.

"Jeri—" I hesitated to tell her I loved her over the open com and I sure wasn't going to pull my mask off.

"I know, Kyle. I know."

"Stay tight on Mrs. Leverson's formation and keep an eye open on the drop," Commander Perry Swain ordered his SEALs. "Swavely, you're on her like glue. If she gets hit, it better have killed you to get there or we'll have words later."

"Hooyay!" the SEALS shouted.

"Ten seconds!" The jump light turned green. "Go, go, go!"

Jeri was off the end of the ramp before I was expecting it, and Swavely nudged me to action. I was right behind her, with him and the others behind me. I didn't really notice the cold at first, as I was focused mainly on not getting killed and making certain that my chute had opened. A few seconds of free-falling, the tether caught, and snap! I was yanked by the chute slowing me down. I looked up at the chords and saw they were all straight and unencumbered. It didn't even dawn on me to gaze at the beautiful night sky from that altitude. The stars must have been brilliant and the Moon bright, but I'm not sure. I was too busy being scared out of my wits. I'd almost be glad when the action started. The jitters would either go away then, or I'd be too dead to worry about them.

"Thank God," I whispered. I know I've proclaimed not to believe in a supreme deity, but looking down at the Earth from thirty thousand feet with nothing but a chute to keep me from smacking into it at a deadly speed tended to inspire bad habits.

As the C-17 pulled away, a string of chutes opened up behind it that I could just see in the poor peripheral vision of the night vision goggles. I searched around and there was Jeri's chute and the tiny little infrared beacon flashing on her shoulder.

"Thank God," I said again.

I kept my eye on Jeri and steered into formation with her, as we had trained. I wasn't that proficient yet, but I wasn't about to leave her up front on the ground without me. So I made myself learn the techniques. I think Jeri must have helped me a little, because it seemed easier than I'd expected. It was almost fun, if you didn't count the fact that I was scared out of my mind. I stayed focused on the job so as not to think about my emotions. I had a job to do and it would take all my abilities to do it correctly.

The team formed up on Jeri and she led us to the ground. The long slow glide seemed uneventful and we covered more than ten miles over the terrain and approached what looked like a small mountain on the horizon. Jeri circled over what appeared to be nothing but empty desert with rolling hills growing larger and more frequent as we approached the mountain. Finally, we could see through the night vision goggles what looked like a gravel road. Then Jeri signaled us and we started circling like hawks, shedding off altitude more quickly until the ground started rushing up at us. Before I knew it, I was rolling across the desert surface trying to break my fall and pull my chute in.

I finally got the chute loose and rolled up to my feet and then I rushed to Jeri and we both set about burying the chutes. There was no sign that we'd been detected by whoever it was that was holding the Crispy, so the two of us quickly started dropping our gear and removing the cold garments in light of the relatively warmer environment we found ourselves in. A desert is cold at night, but nothing like the inside of that plane had been!

"He knows we're coming, Kyle." Jeri slipped her polypro cold suit off and slipped on the Army issue polypro heat and fire retardant under-armor garments back on. It was too dark for me to gawk and we were all too busy trying not to get killed. Oh hell, who was I kidding—if I'd thought of it, I'd have put my night goggles back on so I could've got a better look! Jeri is fun to look at. A crazy thought right in the middle of a combat mission, but I think I've mentioned how my mind goes into a weird zone sometimes. That was one of them.

"Can he help us?" I asked her.

"He's trying to explain the set-up of the place to me as best he can through the perception. But it doesn't really work like talking, so it's just vague notions of the environment," she said.

"Yeah, you've told me that before."

"Ma'am, Mr. Leverson, is everything all right?" Lieutenant Swavely asked from behind me. The young SEAL was as stealthy as a cat.

"Yes, Lieutenant. We're ready," I replied. "Which way, Jeri?"

"Hope it ain't far." Sam slipped up to me and patted me on the shoulder.

"About a mile and a half down this road," Jeri nodded. "I've already keyed in the approximate GPS coordinates to the rest of the teams."

"Not much of a road," I added, and toed at the gravel with my boots.

"Good, the marines and the 82nd guys should be hitting the ground and ready to converge by now." Sam checked his watch and then did a quick radio call to the other teams. "Let's do this before the sun comes up, shall we?" Dawn was already beginning to show over the edge of the mountain horizon ahead of us.

"Yes, general."

"Jeri," Sam started, then hesitated a moment. Had he been giving an order to anybody else there wouldn't have been any vacillation, but he and Bill gave Jeri a more soft-handed approach. "Uh, we know where we're going now. No need in you taking point—"

"Sam, I am—"

"The SEALs will take point, and that's final." Sam became no-nonsense with her and definitely not soft-handed. He turned and started moving forward, not giving Jeri time to argue. She started to, but I grabbed her arm.

"He's right," I told her. "Leave it at that. You're worth more than all of us."

She shut up and soldiered, knowing this wasn't the time for an argument.

Chapter Twenty-Four

The gravel road led up the side of the small mountain where the troops transferring their alien prisoner had stopped for the night, thinking they were safe from interference there. With the night vision goggles the road looked like a bright gray streak doing switchbacks along the face of the barren, rocky precipice. At the base of the mountain was a dug out pit lined with cement, that looked half filled with water, and there were a few construction vehicles about its edge. The thousand-foot-high peak was shaved off flat into a plateau, and at each end of the switchbacks going up the mountain there were other shaved plateaus, made for turnaround spots. The place reminded me of a rock quarry I used to go swimming in when I was a kid.

Barren was the only way to describe it. There was no vegetation—nothing but sand and rock and machines. There was no sign of people anywhere. Our unit stealthily hugged the bank alongside the road leading in, and we took our time as we searched for sensors and maybe landmines. Twice Jeri stopped us because of motion detectors and IR trackers. She fooled them with her perception as best she could, and we kept pushing forward. It would have been nice to have had some spy satellite imagery of the place but there hadn't been time to task any. The best we had was old or taken from commercial spy sat websites. We had nothing at the resolution needed to find the front or back door or any other useful adit for that matter.

The sun must have been peeking over the horizon, because rays of bright orange light stretched out on either side of the mountain's shadow. The marines and the 82nd guys should've been in place by that time on the flanking sides of the facility. Hopefully, they would be able to find other ways in on the sides; otherwise they would just be back-up for our extraction.

On the first plateau about a third of the way up there was a truck entrance into the face of the rock. There was no gate, no guard, no door. There was only a tunnel that led downward and into the rock.

"I don't like this," I said over the subvocal mike to Sam.

"Looks like we don't have a choice. Stay frosty."

"Jeri? Can you pick up anything?" I asked her.

"He's down there about a quarter of a mile," she said pointing down the tunnel with her bracelet hand. "This seems to be the quickest way."

"General, I don't like the fact that there's no guard here," Commander Swain, the SEAL team leader, added.

"Me neither," Lieutenant Swavely agreed.

"Nobody said this would be easy. Maybe this place is being constructed for just a holding cell or a prison. Whatever, this is where they're holding the Crispy now, so let's go." Sam pointed his weapon in the general direction of the tunnel. "Hug the walls and let's move quickly!"

"Sir."

The tunnel was dark even with the night gear, but we managed. Quietly and quickly we made it to the bottom, and then realized why there were no guards on that particular tunnel. It was a dead end.

"Shit. We're closed off, General. I say we shag ass the hell out of here," Commander Swain suggested. "This could be an ambush."

"They don't know we're here, as far as I can tell, Commander," Jeri replied.

I couldn't tell. We were a quarter mile deep in a tunnel in a Libyan rock crusher facility with only one way out. I was beginning to wonder if this was a good idea myself.

"Where is he, Jeri?" Sam asked her as he leaned against the smooth rock surface. It looked to have been made by a tunnel boring machine. The rock was smooth with ripples in it.

"He's only about twenty feet that way." Jeri pointed at a slight angle through the rock wall.

"We could blow it," one of the SEALs said.

"That would for sure wake up anybody that's in here," another one added.

"Yeah, well then we'd get to shoot somebody," the SEAL team's sniper commented.

"No. It might bring the tunnel down on us," I said. "Jeri, your bracelet."

"Of course," she said.

"What about her bracelet, Kyle?" Sam asked.

"We've told you it was a weapon and you've seen it work before. But it can disintegrate anything, as far as I can tell."

"That's right, Sam. I can precisely control it and bore a tunnel."

"Then do it."

"Okay. Everybody behind me," Jeri said as she raised her arm. There was no flash of light and no sound. Just one instant the rock wall was in front of us and the next it wasn't, with only a faintly dusty haze showing where solid rock had been before. She cut through to an open room that obviously had electricity in it. The light was so bright my night gear saturated and I had to flip the visor up in order to see.

In front of us was a Cresperian lying on a cot in the corner of what appeared to be a jail cell. There were bars on the other side of the room. Jeri rushed to its aid and immediately started speaking to it in the alien language. It was clear that the alien had been tortured. The thing looked bedraggled and was missing the tip of one of his, uh, her, long fingers.

"Kyle, help me," Jeri said.

"Right." I grabbed an appendage from the other side and the two of us hoisted it to its feet, pods, uh, whatever the hell you'd call them. The SEALs took up cover positions around the room and were looking through the bars for any threats. There were none, as far as we could see.

"Okay, we got what we came for. Let's get the hell out of here," Sam ordered.

We hauled ass back up the tunnel and outside. The sun was up by this time, and I could see activity further down the mountain. The earthmovers were starting up and there were several men walking around the edge of the pit. From somewhere deep in the mountain, the vibration of a tunnel-boring machine was beginning.

"This place is coming to life, General."

"Yeah. Hold on." Sam keyed his radio. "Package has been acquired. Everybody to the extraction." He waited a minute for confirmation from the other teams and then he turned to Commander Swain. "Perry."

"Sir?"

"Get a couple of guys to slip around the periphery and look for us a stealthy way out of here."

"Got it." He turned to the sniper and one of the others and made some hand gestures. The two men slipped around the edge of the plateau, and were out of sight.

"Any ideas, Sam?" I eased the alien down and let it rest against the ground. Jeri stayed with him—her?—continuously and quietly jabbered in alien with it.

"We could shoot our way out, but we don't have enough intel on this place."

"Sam, Siraounuoliuotls, well, call her Sira," Jeri translated. She pronounced it with a long I like S-eye-ra. "She says that the place isn't operational and that there are only a few guards that were left with her.

She also says that somebody was supposed to be here today to move her to a final holding place." Well, that settled the gender problem. Sira was female, or close enough that it was a she.

"General." Commander Swain nodded that his scout team was back. Sam raised an eyebrow and nodded for him to talk. "Charlie, what'd you see?"

"It's rough going on the other side, sir," Petty Officer First Class Charlie Hodge said. "There's a path that goes down about ten yards or so, then it's a solid drop for about fifty feet. Maybe if we had climbing gear. I bet the other teams couldn't find a way in around there."

"Jeri, you have any ideas?" Sam turned and kneeled beside her and the alien, who was swigging water hard from Jeri's water bag. "And is she gonna make it?"

"She's fine, now." Jeri took the water tube from the alien and tucked it back into her webbing. "We could go back inside, but we don't really know where the tunnels lead. I'm not even sure where the main entrance is."

About that time a dump-truck and a front-end loader started crawling up the switchback and would be up to the first plateau in no time. We pulled back to the mouth of the tunnel and took better cover and were considering hiding.

"Let's take those vehicles and get the hell out of here," Sam said.

"Good idea, General. We got this." Swain nodded to his sniper. "Hodge, take position with the Barrett and be prepared for cover. We're gonna go get us a ride home."

The rest was a big blur. The SEALs slipped over the edge of the road and blended into the rocks and I lost track of several of them. Then as the truck and the loader crested over the edge of the switchback the men swarmed over the vehicles like fire ants on a picnic basket. Silently and efficiently they took out the drivers and then pulled the heavy vehicles in front of the tunnel where we were hiding out.

"Somebody order a cab?" Swain smiled at us through the rolled-down window of the passenger side of the truck. I've yet to figure out why anyone tries to be humorous in the midst of a combat situation but it happens. John, Sam, Jeri, and I loaded Sira into the back and pushed her as far into the empty dump-truck bed as we could to keep her covered. PO1 Hodge appeared from nowhere and crawled up on top of the truck, dragging his mammoth sniper weapon with him.

"Okay, let's roll out of here, and don't start any ruckus unless we have to," Sam ordered. He radioed in our situation and ordered the rest of the teams to stay at the extraction coordinates. "We've got it under control, Major," he said to a protesting marine on the other end.

The dump-truck roared down the gravel road at a breakneck twenty miles per hour but was picking up speed. We'd probably have hit forty by the time we got to the bottom if the road had been safe enough to drive that fast on. The SEAL behind the wheel of the big thing was doing a good job, though. When we hit the road along the edge of the pit at the bottom without any resistance I breathed a sigh of relief—a bit prematurely.

The workers hadn't really paid us any mind. They had tunnels to bore and earth to move. But the handful of guards that were in charge of the alien inside the facility had woken up and realized that their prize was gone. An old sand-colored Jeep with a machine gun mounted on it and two beat up pick-up trucks tore out of a tunnel at the edge of the pit that we hadn't noticed before.

The dump-truck groaned against the road and the engine whined in protest as the SEAL pushed it as hard as it would go. We all took up positions lying down or hugging a sidewall as best we could and tried to take aim on our pursuers. The ancient shocks of the old dump-truck might as well have been nonexistent because they sure as hell weren't helping smooth to out our ride. I could barely hang on and I couldn't imagine how Petty Officer First Class Hodge managed to stay put on top of the cab, but he did. Somehow he turned rearwards so he could take aim and then I heard a horrendous boom from the Barrett sniper rifle. Several of us followed suit with shots from our own weapons. I fired a couple of bursts, but it was a close range weapon. I didn't expect to hit shit. And I didn't.

The Jeep pulled in closer to us and began peppering us with the machine gun rounds. A rider in the passenger seat was also firing a Kalashnikov AK-47 out the side of it at us. Several of the 7.62x39 mm rounds pinged into the sidewall of the truck just above my head. I dived for cover against the floor and then crawled back to Jeri.

"Stay down!" I yelled to her and Sira.

"I could use my weapon," Jeri offered.

"We can handle this. Stay down."

The Barrett fired again and then again. Several more rounds pinged around inside the bed of the dump-truck, throwing bright sparks and molten hot shards of metal into John's face. He fell over swatting at the burns they left.

"Fuck this," I muttered, and drew a couple grenades from my webbing, pulled the pins, and tossed them out the bed of the truck. They exploded just behind the Jeep and in front of one of the old pick-ups. That just seemed to piss them off. The pick-ups swung around the Jeep and pulled up to either side of us, with their occupants firing Kalashnikovs through the bed of the truck and into the cabin. I took a sudden liking to that bumpy road because while it spoiled our aim, it did the same for our pursuers, and Arab armies have a well deserved reputation for being lousy shots anyway. Nevertheless, a round came through the bed and hit dead center of my chest. It knocked me flat on my ass but it didn't really hurt. The IOTV armor did its job. The steel dump bed had absorbed a lot of the round's momentum, too, before it hit me. Had it hit me in the head, though, I'd have been in trouble.

I tossed another grenade at the Jeep, this time waiting for the grenade timer a little longer. I missed again. But PO1 Hodge didn't. The Barrett fired right through the windshield of the Jeep. It swerved off the road and flipped into the sand, but the pick-ups on either side of us continued to fire. Several rounds hit home, wounding more of our team. One of the SEALs caught one in the neck splattering blood across the soldier beside him. His teammate quickly slapped a bandage on it, but from my viewpoint it looked lethal.

The dump-truck swerved hard to the right and ran off the road into the sand. As it hit sand it slowed but the driver managed to pull it back under control and keep the wheels rolling. Then I realized I hadn't heard the Barrett fire in a bit. I looked up and Hodge wasn't there. He must've been thrown off. The dump-truck swerved again in response to another round of AK-47 fire and this time it got stuck and came to a stop. We were fortunate it didn't roll over with us.

"Everybody keep firing!" Sam shouted.

A grenade bounced into the edge of the truck and rolled back to where I lay.

"Grenade!" somebody shouted.

Without thinking, I reached down and picked it up and threw it over the edge of the truck bed. It exploded on the other side, sending shrapnel into the steel with a deafening *clang!* The Libyans kept pouring on the Kalashnikov rounds and another grenade bounced into the truck. One of the SEALs grabbed it and tossed it back out. I started throwing my own grenades as fast as I could over the side in both directions. They didn't really help much but it did give us brief pauses to reload.

We took turns rising up over the sidewall and shooting down at the bastards on the other side and then we would quickly dive back down for cover. I took two rounds into my armor doing this. Several of us had been hit multiple times and were beginning to wear down. But we couldn't stop or we were goners for sure.

"Somebody's got to do something! We're pinned the fuck down!" I yelled.

"Keep it frosty, Chief!" Lieutenant Swavely shouted back at me as he rose to fire.

"Fuck frosty!" It suddenly clicked that I had what amounted to super powers and there wasn't a reason in the world not to use them. I grabbed my MP-5 in my right hand and a Glock in my left and dived headfirst out the back end of the truck bed. Swavely and another man had to use all their strength to keep Jeri from following, but I learned that later. I rolled across the gravel onto my feet and then ran firing the automatic weapon in my right hand at the banged up old pick-up. Four men in it each were shooting at me with AK-47s. The Russian-made weapons banged deadly reports in my direction but seemed to miss each time. Or rather, it was as if I could see them aiming at me just as they started to fire, and I serpentined or ducked out of the way at just the right moment. I raised my left hand and took aim on the lead Libyan in the bed of the pick-up as I leaped more than five feet high and covered twenty feet of distance, landing in the bed of the truck as the first guy fell with a hole in his head. I sprayed the MP-5 through the cabin and took out two more of them.

My momentum carried me into the top of the cab a little too fast and I lost my balance slightly and rolled over the front of the truck and clumsily onto the ground. I heard a weapon fire behind me as the fourth occupant of the truck slumped to the ground next to me. I jumped up to my feet and slammed my back against the front driver's side quarter panel of the dump-truck. Then I heard the weapon fire again. In the commotion and over my heartbeat and the AK fire I hadn't realized what I heard, but this time it was quite clear what that sound was. It was a Barrett sniper rifle.

Several more shots fired and the AKs stopped. I eased around the front of the truck with my weapon at the ready, but they were all deader than hell.

"Clear!" I yelled.

"Clear!" I heard from the rear of the truck.

I rushed around to the back and jumped straight up into the dump-truck bed with one leap. I landed beside Jeri and knelt beside her.

"Jeri, you okay?" I hugged her to me.

"I'm fine, Kyle. But I need to focus right now." She had a serious look on her face and there was blood across her armor. "It's not mine."

I turned, and could see Lieutenant Swavely's throat covered in blood, while one of the other soldiers worked on him. It looked like a major artery in his neck had been spewing blood all over the bed of the truck. I looked down and realized that I was standing in a pool of red. Jeri crawled forward a bit and took Swavely's hand.

He looked up at her and tried to whisper. He managed "God help me..." and then he slipped into unconsciousness.

Jeri just squeezed his hand and focused that perception on slowing down his heart rate and forcing the wounds to heal rapidly. I wasn't sure, but I thought that Sira was helping, too. Who could tell what kind of expression Crispies have on their faces? They're just too damned alien.

Several of the SEALs were hit, but none as bad as Swavely. John's face was burned pretty badly, but it was superficial, just painful. Jeri and Sira and the team medic were doing all they could to keep Swavely alive. The SEAL administering first aid to him was rapidly pulling bandages from his kit and he shoved an injection of something into his leg. I looked down at the Crispy, at Sira. She seemed no more worse for the wear. Then I nearly shit my pants as a C-130 dropped out of nowhere, almost clipping the truck and landing on the road just in front of us and coming to a stop about a thousand feet away.

"I'll check on everybody else and see what I can do to help," I said, and patted Jeri on the armored shoulder. Overhead, I heard the thunder of Raptor fighter bomber jets providing cover. It was certain that our calls for help had gotten out.

"Kyle!" Sam shook his head at me. "You crazy sonofabitch!" He shook my hand and patted my back. "Good job!"

"Should've done something sooner as far as Swavely is concerned."

"Yeah, and Peterson and Swain. They're both dead. Probably, because we swerved the way we did. They probably got Peterson, who was driving, when we swerved the first time and then they got Swain. Goddamnit. We've gotta move to the plane quickly."

"Mr. Leverson!" A voice from behind us startled me a bit. Sam and I looked up at Petty Officer Charlie Hodge. His left leg was bloody as hell, with a makeshift bandage on it, and he was limping pretty badly. The large sniper rifle rested on his shoulder and there was a big bruise on his forehead that would look pretty nasty for a while. I guessed he had a concussion at the least.

"Hodge! You saved my ass!" I took the rifle from him. The goddamned thing was heavy. Then I patted him on the shoulder and shook his hand.

"You okay?" Sam asked him.

"I must have hit my head really hard, General. Because I'd swear that through my sighting scope I saw Mr. Leverson here moving almost faster than I could see and he had to have jumped at least twenty feet or more through the air."

"Uh." Sam turned and looked at me.

"I dunno. I just did what I had to do." I shrugged my shoulders.

"PO Hodge?"

"Yes, General?"

"As far as Mr. Leverson is concerned, what you *think* you saw is classified and *nobody* has a need to know, even other members of The Group. If they need to know, they know. Is that understood?" Sam ordered mildly.

"Yes, sir, General, sir," the navy sniper replied.

"Besides," Sam said, more lightheartedly, "who'd ever fuckin' believe it?"

"We'd better get moving," I said. "We still have to pick up a bunch of marines and Airborne and get the hell out of Libya."

Chapter Twenty-Five

Navy SEAL Lieutenant Alex Swavely died in Jeri's arms on the C-130. She stayed focused on him for the entire flight from Libya to Qatar and then with him for the next hour and a half. And that was even though doctors had told her that he was dead and his brain had gone way too long without oxygen for him to be normal even if she did bring him back. The ischemic cascade of his brain had already happened, and unless Jeri knew just what his brain had looked like before the cascade it was unlikely that he could be repaired back to normal. But Jeri just wouldn't give up. Sam and I had to go in and drag her out of there. She cried and screamed when Sam pulled a sheet over his head.

"Jeri, there was just nothing you could do," I told her.

"Kyle, he took that bullet for me. One of the Libyans stuck his rifle around the end of the truck, and when he did Alex dived on top of me and Sira. He sacrificed himself to protect me."

"He was a hero, Jeri," Sam said. "That's what heroes do. And if he were here, I'm sure he'd tell you that he'd do it again if he had to."

"I thought that I could repair the damage just enough to keep him alive or rejuvenate him." Tears rolled down her pale cheeks.

"It took months for me, and days to heal Sam when he was shot. You just didn't have time, Jeri." I hugged her. "You need to go take care of Sira right now."

"Yes. I do." Jeri continued to cry for a moment and sniffled into my chest as she hugged me to her. I held her as tight as I could without hurting her. She had seen killing and death recently, but none that was so close and that included such a sacrifice for her. It was hard for her to deal with it. Understanding why soldiers do what they do is really hard for most people. For an alien turned human, who had only recently started understanding the ins and outs of humanity, I'm sure it was really difficult to cope with.

"Jeri," Sam patted her arm. "You should go to Sira now. Kyle, we need to check in with Bill."

"Roger that, General."

ഇരുൻ

We almost immediately took a C-17 back to the Enclave. Sam had to commandeer one from the Air Force while we were there. Sooner or later we were going to have to get our own set of planes. Or maybe our science and engineering teams could come up with something better and faster. But as it was we trucked along in the C-17, headed for home. Jeri didn't speak to me much along the way. She spent all of her time with Sira, teaching her English and convincing her that she needed to start a transformation to human. Sira was more reluctant than Jeri or Ishmael had been. For some reason, converting from her current physical form seemed emotionally difficult for her.

Hell, I guess so. If I landed on a planet of Crispies and I had the ability to change, it'd be damn hard to convert myself over to something so alien, when I'd been human all my life. But Jeri and Ish had made the choice to take on human form and make humanity their new home.

Finally, Sira came around after Jeri convinced her that the odds of rescue from other Cresperian vessels were effectively zero unless by some small chance one of the unreality drive engineers had survived. Not likely, considering Jeri had told me that they, like the navigators, had stayed at their posts, trying to save the ship. Besides, she could always revert if she wanted to, from the core of their original form that they keep regardless of what they might change to or from, or when going from male to female or vice versa on their own planet. But I think what finally convinced her was Jeri using her perceptive sense to give her an idea of what sex would be like as a human. And love, too.

I found a seat next to Sam and John, whose face was all bandaged up. One of the men was complaining about missing all the action, as had most of the other two teams' members.

"Good thing," I said as I sat down in the nearly empty C-17. "It really fucking sucked." The young sergeant didn't respond.

"You got that shit right." John nodded his head groggily. The pain meds he was on had him fairly incoherent. I'm sure he was hoping for time with Jeri or Ishmael.

"Don't worry, son. There's going to be other missions real soon, I feel sure," General Haley said. And then he turned to me.

"Kyle, I think you and Jeri need a vacation."

"Yeah. Okay, I'll bite. Where to?"

"Tell you later." Sam leaned back and closed his eyes without saying another word, leaving me to wonder, damn him. Jeri and I exchanged glances, but neither of us was up to trying to worm any more information from him just then. In fact, I closed my eyes, too, while Jeri and Sira continued to chatter away in Cresperian, and they were also using their perceptive senses, I was sure.

I decided to put it out of my head for a while. My ribs hurt where I had stopped several AK-47 rounds with my armor. I took the pain meds the docs gave me but I knew I would heal up faster than normal. Jeri had seen to that. I was now probably the fastest healer in the history of mankind. But the ribs still hurt and the pain meds might make me drowsy. I downed them without hesitation and drifted off to sleep. The next thing I knew the loadmaster was shaking me.

"Sir. Sir, wake up, Sir. We've landed and offloaded." The young E5 shook me gingerly and smiled.

"Huh?" I squinted at the light coming in through the lowered tail ramp. "Oh. Sorry, uh, Staff Sergeant."

"No problem, sir. I just thought you might want to get off with the rest of your crew."

"Yeah, thanks. Hey, what time is it? Hell, what day is it?"

"It's Tuesday, sir. 5:22 pm," he said, looking at his watch.

"Right, Tuesday." I dragged my carcass up, grabbed my pack, and then sauntered down the ramp, clearly the last one off the plane. Why nobody else had bothered to wake me I wasn't sure. I guess they had their own business to attend to, and I knew Jeri was helping Sira.

I was hungry enough to eat a mule's ass without ketchup but I also wanted to find Jeri and see how she was. I guessed she had stayed with Sira. A shower would probably be a good thing to fit into the schedule also. I figured that Bill or Sam would be tracking me down soon, too. I walked the hundred yards or so from the airstrip to the Enclave's side entrance, and had to rummage through my pack for my badge because there was a new set of guards there who didn't know me. After a few seconds I produced the badge and then swiped it over the turnstile and punched in my pin number. The light turned green, the thing dinged at me, and I walked on through. The guards looked back down, paying me no more attention.

I made it up to our quarters and found Jeri, Ishmael and Sira in the living room area. Sira had already changed dramatically. Having three Cresperians to work on her body must have sped up the process of going from alien to human pretty darn fast. There was a laptop open with pictures of naked women on it and there was pornography playing on the widescreen panel on the wall.

"Uh, doesn't the Army firewalls block those sites?" I asked.

"Sure, we unblocked them," Ishmael said nonchalantly. "Sira needs all the information she can gather about human capabilities in order to choose her appearance."

"If it bothers you, Kyle, we can go somewhere else." Jeri smiled up at me.

"Oh, hell no. I'm just gonna hit the shower and go grab something to eat then." I looked at Sira closer. Her head was already taking human shape and hair—she apparently wanted to be a strawberry blonde—was starting to grow there. Her alien appendages were forming into arms and hands, and her foot pads looked more like feet with normal toes. It took Jeri weeks to get that far and Ish about a week. Jeri had worked with her on the plane ride home and Ishmael had been helping from the instant the plane flew into his perception's range. Most of the progress, to hear Jeri explain it, had taken place over the last couple of hours.

"Oh, Bill called. He said to drop by when you get the chance. And Ishmael has some important information to show you. But it can wait."

"All right, then." I closed the bedroom door and started removing my sandy, sweaty clothes, and exhaled with a long, slow sigh, letting my shoulders slump. The digi-cam uniform fell to the floor as quickly as I could get my boots off. "The shower is gonna feel sooo damned good."

৪০৪৪

I put on civilian clothes—jeans, an Army Knowledge On-Line t-shirt that the IT guy had given me when he hooked up my common access card reader for my laptop, and my running shoes—then I was out the door to the cafeteria. Unfortunately, I needed to kill two birds with one stone. Bill and Sam were sitting at a table already and waved me over. I bought a cheeseburger, fries, chicken fingers, and a peach cobbler, along with a salad and a large glass of sweetened ice tea, and then joined them.

"Hungry, Kyle?" Bill chuckled.

"Uh, yes, sir. I've found that I require more food these days."

"Drop the sir shit and have a seat," Bill told me.

"Right."

"Kyle," Sam looked at my tray of food again. "Do you think you need the calories because you went super speed, maybe?"

"Hadn't thought about it, but I'll bet you're right. We ought to test that." I thought about it. Every time I had run really fast in the past week or so—I'd only recently begun to realize I had the capabilities—or done something requiring more than typical human abilities, I did recall being really hungry later on.

"Super speed?" Bill looked wide-eyed at us. "I knew you were fast, but how fast? Sam hasn't had the time to keep me well briefed, and you've been on the go."

"Well, Bill, the SEAL sniper claims that he saw Kyle here dodging bullets and then jumping more than twenty feet over a pick-up truck."

"No shit?"

"That was yesterday, Bill. And I wasn't really dodging the bullets and I didn't make it all the way over the truck." I consumed the salad in a couple of bites and started in on the fries and burger. As an afterthought I added, "Maybe if I'd have tucked my legs. But I wasn't dodging bullets. That's just silly."

"Then what were you doing?" Sam asked.

"I'm not sure how to describe it, but it was like I could see everything more thoroughly. They just seemed much, *much* slower to me, and I could see when they aimed at me and that they were about to pull the trigger of their weapons. So I moved out of the place they were aiming at really quickly." I ate several fries in one bite and then washed them down with the tea. "Bill, could you hand me the ketchup, please?"

"Jesus, Kyle, three months ago you could hardly walk." Bill shook his head in disbelief as he slid the ketchup bottle over to me. "We've got to figure out how to bottle whatever it is she's done for you."

"Bill, if you could bottle a tenth of what all Jeri has done for me you could make a billion dollars overnight."

"I'll agree with that." He chuckled, almost choking on a swig of coffee in the process. "Sam, he sure as hell ain't as old and ugly as he used to be. He's even changed since we made it to here."

"Right. Come to think of it, you do look a lot younger, Kyle." Sam laughed and wiggled his brows.

After a brief pause, during which I had time to finish off my cheeseburger and fries and the chicken fingers, the two generals started getting more business on me. My heart wasn't really in it at the moment, but when two generals are talking at you, there's not much choice but to buck up and do your job.

"Listen, Kyle," Bill started. "Among other things, Ishmael and Dr. Freeny have been working on some sort of unreality detector thing, whatever the hell that is, that can supposedly detect the presence of active power systems for those lifepods."

"How long till they get it working?" I asked.

"Oh, apparently it was just a modification of the gear on his bracelet and parts of Jeri's survival package plus some other laboratory gadgets, but it's already working." Bill sipped at his coffee and let that sink in.

"Have they already found a pod?"

"No." Again he paused. I could tell he was playing poker with me.

"Okay. So what did he find in Hexixincun, China?"

"Well, it was really in Jiuquan, at the space launch facility. There's some kind of anomaly, as they put it, in the vehicle assembly building at the south launch complex not far from the tower for the Long March 2C/D or 4B rockets." Sam slid a folder over to me. It was marked Top Secret/TG, which we all knew was the special access marking for "The Group." The folder had several images of the facility, with each of the buildings labeled. We weren't worried about reading the information in the cafeteria, because the entire facility was a special access and sensitive compartmented information facility, and only people read into our program were allowed in. Some people might not be fully briefed yet, but that was because they were coming in faster than we could handle, with all the recent operation prep and everything. We'd probably grown to well over a hundred at the time, what with the special ops teams.

"Well? What is it if it's not a pod?"

"They believe it's a prototype for an unreality drive," Bill said.

"A faster than light engine," Sam added.

"No shit?"

"No shit."

"But that doesn't make any sense. Does it?" I wasn't sure what that meant. The Chinese hadn't had time to reverse engineer an engine, especially up from the tiny ones in the lifeboats to what would be needed for a spaceship. Or so I assumed. But it had been months now since the aliens arrived in their lifeboats. Could the one that landed in China have found the Chinese government tolerable and allied itself with them? That was the only thing that made sense to me, almost.

"We can only surmise that a Crispy is behind it. Maybe he's trying to build a system to go home with. Maybe he's become loyal to the Chinese. Who the hell knows?" Bill picked his coffee cup up and looked into the bottom of it. Then he set it back down. "I don't give a shit. The Chinese can't get FTL. But if they did, that type of technology would destabilize our superiority over them. Just think of an FTL intercontinental ballistic missile with a nuke on it."

"Our missile defenses would be useless," I said. "Hell, Bill, they wouldn't even need a warhead. Just slamming something the size of a baseball at FTL speed into the U.S. would probably be enough energy to take us out completely."

"Hadn't thought of that. Shit."

"Yeah, shit. Not to mention that they'd start colonizing the stars before we do." I finished the last bit of my tea while Bill & Sam were both silent. I'd poleaxed them with the colonizing business. I leaned back in my chair, looking at the spysat imagery of the facility more closely. "There should be satellite dishes and other hi-tech stuff there. Why hasn't Ish been able to contact the Crispy using his perception control of the electronics?"

"Ishmael says that he's tried but the Crispy won't pick up the phone, so to speak," Sam responded. "He's gonna brief us more thoroughly tomorrow morning."

"What do you suggest we do, Kyle?" Bill asked me, still fiddling with his coffee cup.

"Well, I guess we have to do two things." I thought for a second and ticked off on my fingers. "One, start our own rapid development FTL drive technology program. Two, Jeri and I need to go there and talk to this Crispy, but you better have a damn good ops put together before we risk it."

"Good." Bill finally put the cup down. "I thought as much. You'll leave ASAP, then."

"Uh, yes, sir."

ജ൝

"Hexixincun, China," Sam repeated to us the next day as soon as he sat down in the small conference room with a fresh cup of coffee. That first day spent going over the China mission was a closed meeting with only Sam, Jeri and me, Ish and Sgt Wu.

"Yeah," I said glumly. I was having lots of second thoughts about this business.

"Right. Okay, other than a small town full of rocket scientists, there's a manned launch facility for Long March rockets just outside town, in Jiuquan. Also, as you might guess, Ishmael believes our friend is there. More than that we'll have to let him tell us. Today, we're just going over the broad outlines of a plan to get you in and out, preferably with the Crispy coming back with you. Jonas thinks you could pose as a honeymoon couple, with no problem."

I wasn't sure Jeri was ready for another mission. Maybe Ishmael would rather go on this one. Nah, if it was to be an undercover mission, Jeri and I on a honeymoon vacation would make a hell of a lot of sense. Wasn't quite sure, though, how anybody thought we could get onto a Chinese rocket launch facility. I mean, sneaking into an under-construction and mostly abandoned Libyan underground facility was one thing. But a Chinese launch facility was a whole nother ballgame, especially one so far inside the country. I said so.

"It turns out that we have some human assets there," Wu said. "There's a scientist on the very inside of operations who's passed the layout of the place to us. And we have a couple of soldiers who're going to let me and a pal inside to provide backup for you. We're going to pose as soldiers guarding you."

"Who, me and Jeri? Not likely! They'll never let Caucasians in that place."

"Nope, you wouldn't fit the role even if Jeri and her friends went to work on your bodies and made you look Chinese. You're going to be visiting IC scientists, since you speak Arabic and Jeri can learn it right quick. I'll leave first with another man who speaks Mandarin and make contact with the soldiers. After they get us inside, they'll also wait on us to come out with the Crispy. The scientist will get you further along to a meeting with the Crispy after we take you to him. After that, it's up to you to convince the alien to come home with you. The soldiers will have clothing and other equipment ready for us and will lead us to the coast. By then we'll all be posing as peons looking for work. There's plenty of them wandering around these days, and most of the authorities are susceptible to bribes if we're stopped. A stealth submarine will drop a SEAL team off at the coast to pick us up and take us back to the sub."

I didn't like it right off the bat, and made it clear. "I can tell without even asking that this whole op is based on the idea that the Crispy will be sympathetic to our goals, and if not, would at least not blow the whistle on a fellow Cresperian and her husband. But we'd be bearding the lion in his den without knowing how sharp his teeth are or whether he's friendly or not. And then there's the Cresperian perceptive sense. Our quarry will sense us as soon as we get close, and if he's unfriendly, that would be it." We knew it was a he from the internet and we also knew from it that he wasn't communicating with us, but we didn't know why. It could be because of fear of getting caught or it could be he was on the Chinese side. We just didn't know. I let my fears about that be known right away, too. I was willing—well, maybe not willing but ready—to risk my life on a mission vital to national security but not Jeri's, not again. I was worried that all the killing and fighting was affecting her adversely.

But perhaps I was wrong, because she made her feelings known. "I feel as if I can convince him that our way is best, Kyle. And as you said, I'm sure I can at least get him to let us go without harm even if he won't come with us. Just as I do here, he's certain to have a lot of influence there."

"Our scientists have been busy while we've been gone, too, Kyle," Sam said, trying to ease my fears. "Otherwise I'd have to give this some long thought and probably turn thumbs down on it. As it is, they've come up with a little device that'll mask the Crispy's perception of Jeri right up to almost face-to-face distance, yet without affecting hers. And she'll have her cloak and disintegrator, as well."

"Not only that, but the rest of us have orders to get you out at all costs," Jonas said.

I knew what that meant. The others were to die defending us if necessary. I looked over at Jeri. Her eyes were puffy and red from lack of sleep, despite using her perceptive sense to dispel some of the fatigue poisons. But not all of them. She'd told me her human body functioned better with some sleep and the normal process of recuperation from stress and overwork and tiredness.

"How soon do you want us to leave?" I asked.

"A week from today. That'll give us time to get Sgt. Wu and Captain Zeng into place."

That was just what I wanted to do, sign up for another long-assed international flight while I was still lagged from the two I'd made in the last few days. My internal timepiece was so damned confused that I wasn't sure when I'd flown where. But I knew one thing was for certain, I wanted to get to bed again. As soon as we could, Jeri and I left the generals and went straight to the room. Sira was still there, using the spare bedroom until she felt comfortable enough being human to be assigned a place of her own. I focused on her transmogrification. Sira's head looked completely human now and her body looked like a slightly misshapen and overweight human. I was guessing that by morning she'd be fully humanoid-looking.

"Jeri, I need to talk to you," I said.

"Ishmael has already told me about China, Kyle. I need to rest." She looked exhausted and I knew that she must still be conflicted about Lieutenant Swavely dying in her arms.

"I agree with Ish. You're human now. You need to eat and sleep."

"There's a good way to put me to sleep, if you're up to it, sweetheart." She managed a grin.

I was, and it worked beautifully.

Chapter Twenty-Six

We spent the next week on preparations for the mission. Once during that period, I brought up the subject with Jeri of the unreality generator apparently having been built in China. "Sweetheart, it seems to me like I remember you told me, while we were still in Arkansas, that it was highly unlikely you or any of the other survivors could construct a FTL spaceship. What's the story now?"

She mused for a moment, then explained. "First, I didn't know then just how many truly brilliant scientists earth had, especially here in the United States. And secondly, I doubted anyone who knew much about spaceship construction would have survived. Apparently at least one did, someone at least familiar with unreality engineering at any rate. And since Ish has recovered, we've been comparing notes, and between the two of us, and now with Sira, I believe we've come up with plans at least worth testing. We'll see what they've been up to in China, too, if the person there is friendly."

"You think he's converted to human form?"

"Oh, yes. I guess Ish forgot to mention it. Sorry."

"No problem. I still don't like the way this operation is put together, though. Too many possibilities for Murphy to rear his ugly head."

"I agree, dear, but Bill has convinced me it's necessary."

"Yeah, me, too," I sighed. "Damn it to hell."

ഇൻ

We took a commercial flight from Dulles through Atlanta then on to Shanghai. I was severely jet-lagged, just as before. During that leg of the flight Jeri and I had time to hold hands and talk and sleep, and we even watched a movie that I would normally never have watched in my life. But, hey, we were a captive audience. Jeri was having a hard time getting past Lieutenant Swavely and I was hoping we could clear the air on some of that.

Somewhere over the Atlantic Ocean I decided to be brave enough to bring up the topic. What I got in response was something that was so different from what I expected that I'm still not sure I understand it.

"But I understand sacrifice, Kyle. Or at least I thought I did."

"Sometimes sacrifice is harder to grasp when it's right on top of you than it is from miles away," I tried to reassure her. But I was way off base.

She leaned close to me and lowered her voice so we couldn't be over-heard. "No, that isn't what I mean. The navigators of our ship sacrificed themselves so we would all have time to get on the lifeboats and away through the unreality rift. I understand and have been close to the actual sacrifice part." She squeezed my hand lovingly, as if placating her poor, dumb, slow husband.

"Then what? I'm confused."

"I'd talked to Lieutenant Swavely several times over the week of training up to the mission."

"Yeah, so had I. He was a great kid."

"Well, did you know he was an atheist?"

"Uh, no. Never got past who was gonna win the Super Bowl." I shrugged my shoulders. "So what?"

"His last words were 'God help me', Kyle. But...he was an atheist."

"Sweetheart, as human as you have become, you still have a lot to learn about being human." I finally began to understand what was bothering her. I even began to wonder if she had tried to bring him back to life just to ask him why he had gone back on his belief. Nope, Jeri had a bigger heart than that. My guess was that she wanted to save him from nonexistence because he thought God was there to help him and she knew better. Boy, was I wrong!

"Have you ever heard of a theory called quantum consciousness?"

Interestingly enough, I had. I recalled doing some research on the topic a few years back, while I was planning to write an article about it. The general idea was that all things in the universe were supposedly once a teeny-tiny single thing called a quantum singularity, and then due to a Big Bang that singularity was spread out into everything within the universe. Well, that meant from a mathematical standpoint—and I had to take the physicists' and mathematicians' words for it because the math was way, way over my head—everything in the universe was somehow quantumly connected to everything else. A growing number of scientists believed that once your corporeal self was no more, your wavefunction was still part of this quantum-connected universe, and that everybody and everything were all connected to everybody and everything else. The big question was whether the universe itself had a consciousness as a result of all of the subsets within it that had at least been conscious at some point in time. It was a lot of what I thought of as metaphysics, rather than real science. Apparently, I might be wrong.

"Yeah, I do know about it. A bunch of boogie man mumbo jumbo was my take," I told Jeri.

"No, Kyle, it isn't. It's mathematically sound. It is only the interpretation of the math that involves any philosophical or theological implications." Jeri paused briefly and I thought for a second that she was going to tear up, but she didn't. I still wasn't sure what this was truly about.

"Then what is it that is bugging you so strongly?"

"What if my people were wrong in the interpretation of the proof that God doesn't exist? I mean, since we don't even recall our history, perhaps we lost sight of the interpretation and what it really meant?"

"Don't you know the proof you've talked about?" Okay, now she was pulling the rug out from under me. I had blindly accepted that an advanced alien race had proven mathematically that there was no god. Now that same alien was backpedaling on me.

"Oh yes. I understand the proof completely. We're all taught it from the very beginning of our lives. It's one of the things we do each recall. Perhaps it's like a religion to us. I'll confess I've never thought of it this way before. And the more human I feel, the more and more I'm feeling a need to question the proof's meaning." Jeri was conflicted about life, death, and God. Couldn't get any more human than that.

"Jeri, sweetheart, now you know what it is like to be a thinking human. Even those with the most unwavering faith in whatever it is they believe, still have doubts, whether they want to admit it or not. There's an old saying that there are no atheists in foxholes. It originated sometime during World War II and nobody truly knows who started it. There are generals and colonels and chaplains and authors credited with the statement. The point is that many religious folks believe that in the end, under the stress of dying, even the most dedicated atheist will grasp for some chance at faith rather than accept that they will soon cease to exist."

"But is it true?"

"What? That there are no atheists in foxholes?"

"Yes."

"I dunno. How could you test a statement like that? I think it depends on the individual and how truly and deeply he or she believes their philosophy. I know when I lost Gwen I wanted her to be some place other than just no longer existing. I wanted it so much that I almost gave up not believing in God. But, my long history of not believing still tugged at my very being. So I just decided then and there that we can't know the answer without proof one way or the other. A logical argument either way is that both religion and irreligion is a belief. At least where humanity is concerned, there is no way of knowing which one is really true. At least the Cresperians have a mathematical proof, whether it's wrong or right."

"This is all so confusing."

"Well, the really religious say they feel God's presence, or something similar, and that they truly know God exists. But my grandma believed in ghosts and spooks, too, and assured me that she had seen them." The flight attendant smiled at us as she passed and asked us if we'd like a drink or a snack and I told her to bring us some wine. Oh, I hadn't mentioned that since this was our "honeymoon," we were flying first class. No government per diems would make sense for our cover. I had to approve this with Bill, but we had budget for whatever we wanted.

"What concerns me, Kyle, is that I know all of this. I've read it. I was trained in the mathematics of the proof. But now, for some reason, I'm wavering in the interpretation of the knowledge that I've understood for centuries. Why?"

"My guess is that you ain't what you used to be."

"I don't understand."

"Your brain is in a human-sized container now and functions like a human brain. Oh sure, you have that core of your Cresperian self and your perception tucked away in you somewhere, and you've fixed your human brain to function more efficiently and effectively than we humans know how, but it's still a human brain. It will reach conclusions and emotions and the like the way all of us do. We try to learn and use logic to overcome overwhelming stresses and emotions without going nuts. Welcome to humanity, gorgeous." The flight attendant returned with some wine, and both Jeri and I took long sips at it. I hadn't had a discussion like this since I was a freshman in college.

"This is an extremely encompassing feeling, Kyle. I can see why humanity is so conflicted with itself."

"Yeah, well, add to that, not knowing if there's even more advanced sentient life in the universe and you'll really be onto something." I smiled at her lightly. I wasn't sure that the feelings were good for her, or me, but at least she was talking through them. Mortality has the tendency to make people think about such deep, unanswerable questions.

"Well, I should warn Ishmael and Sira about this. I shouldn't have pushed them into becoming human so soon without truly understanding what it means to be human. If they're not expecting this it could lead them to a very unhealthy downward spiral." Jeri frowned.

"They'll adjust and get used to it, same as you're doing. Besides, with the Cresperian input maybe we can solve some of these great unknowns and help humanity with its self-conflicts." I asked for some more wine. Jeri leaned over and kissed me.

"I was lucky to have crashed on your farm," she said.

"I doubt it. You'd have been better off crashing at Harvard or Princeton or some damned place where you'd have had an educated person to help you. You sure didn't need a depressed old codger like me that doesn't know shit from shinola," I responded to her with a grin, and then I squeezed her hand as she rested her head against my shoulder. "If anybody was lucky, it was me."

"Yes, you're probably right." She smiled back at me, teasing.

By the time we landed in Shanghai we'd let the metaphysics filter on to the backs of our minds. We were in China and still had a long way to go to find the Cresperian. To my surprise, sometime during the night, or whenever, Jeri had managed to teach herself how to speak Chinese. She stepped off the plane speaking broken Chinese well enough to get us a cab to our hotel.

Assuming our cover as a honeymooning couple on a sight-seeing venture held, we'd spend the night in Shanghai hitting some hot tourist spots. From there we would take a circuitous route to the Jiuquan space facility. We spent a couple hours at the hotel showering and napping and eating. The entire time Jeri had the television on. Before we were ready to go out on the town she spoke Chinese like a native.

Hexixincun was only about fifteen hundred miles away. On the way, we passed through Zhengzhou, where we spent most of a day. As soon as we got there, Jeri's perception on our end and Ishmael's on the other fiddled with the internet to make it seem as if IC scientists would be arriving at Hexixincun in a few days. Tiayuan was interesting and it had a satellite launch complex as well. We visited it to add to our cover of rich American tourists interested in reserving seats on a future orbital flight. Lanzhou was next, and we stayed overnight there. Then, after another day's traveling, we made it to our final destination.

Hexixincun, China, is the Cape Canaveral of the Far East. It is pretty much just like the Cape except that it is in the northern region of China, in the westernmost part of Gansu, and south of Mongolia by a couple of hundred miles. There is no beach, and as far as I could tell, the weather wasn't near as pretty. So come to think of it, it wasn't a goddamned bit like the Cape, other than the fact that humans had launched from Earth and gone into space from just a few miles outside of town. Unfortunately, we didn't get to do much sight-seeing there. We spent our time switching identities and making forged papers using Jeri's fabricator. She had kept this device with her by deleting custom officials' short-term memories a couple of times, although we'd had one scary moment. I wished like hell her fabricator could make a disintegrator for me, too, but the energy source defeated it.

I almost didn't recognize Sgt. Wu and Captain Zeng in their Chinese Liberation Special Guards uniforms, complete to the snow-white gloves. I could hardly tell them apart, dressed like that. Sgt. Wu and Captain Zeng had already changed clothes and been allowed inside by our undercover guards shortly before we arrived at the gate of the Jiuquan complex and presented our newly forged IC papers. Wu and Zeng were masquerading as special guards and escorts for the important IC scientists we now were.

Everything was going fine, and I was thinking Murphy might have stayed in bed that day. We were escorted into the presence of a well-dressed, handsome, and seemingly muscular-looking Chinese man; it was clear to me that Jeri immediately recognized him as the alien, for she suddenly became more alert and concentrated all her attention on him. There were several others in the room with him. He barked orders in Chinese to his companions and our "guards" and they withdrew. I was thinking then and there that he probably recognized Jeri for who she was, despite the suppressor, and was in the mood to talk friendly with her. Well, one of two ain't bad, except we were a long, *long* fifteen hundred miles from our ride home. And at the time I thought we were two out of two because he introduced himself as Lao, still giving no indication that he recognized Jeri as a Crispy.

∞⟡

The next thing on the agenda was a real surprise. We got a really good tour of the South Launch Facility, riding in a car with a guide designated by Lao. He told us he would see us after the tour. The only reason I can think for him doing this was from an inflated sense of his own ego and prowess, assuming he could talk Jeri over to his side. And I guessed he planned on letting me stay with her, if I was good.

There was a Long March rocket with a Shenzhou capsule and shroud that had been rolled out to the launch tower and people were scurrying around it like ants. They were a ways off but it was clear they were getting ready for a launch. I wondered why they needed a launch vehicle. Why not just fly the FTL drive from Earth? Maybe it was a safety thing? Or maybe it was some damned physics thing about gravity that I didn't understand.

We continued on across the parking lot for the Vehicle Processing Building and the Launch Control Console building. We paused there for a few minutes and our guide got out of the car and went inside for a few minutes. Jeri took the opportunity to brief me. Possibly it was intended.

"FTL," she whispered, and pointed her eyes toward the rocket. I figured she meant that the FTL prototype was atop that rocket and that they were planning to launch it soon.

"Right," I whispered back.

Our guy came back from the Launch Control Console building and got back in the car. We started and he pulled us around at a slow pace past the Solid Motor building and came to a halt at the Hazardous Operations building. Finally, we were joined by a gang of what I supposed were scientists converging there in a couple more vehicles. Everybody got out of the cars and some guards appeared who pushed us along to the interior of the tall white complex building.

Once inside, we were led to what looked like a conference room and suddenly things began to get rough. It had guards outside it. We were ushered into chairs, then the guards stepped outside, leaving us alone. I was certain we were being watched via the video sensors for teleconferencing over the top of a big flatscreen on the wall at the end of the room.

"Does the FTL thing work, do you know?" I whispered to Jeri in bad Arabic, trying to turn my head from the camera and move my lips as little as possible.

She took a moment to adjust the perceptive suppressor. It could also serve as a privacy guard, but could not perform both functions at once. I guess she figured he was already on to our deception, and now the privacy of our conversation was the most important thing. Let him sense her if he wanted to. I just wondered what in hell he was up to at that point.

"I think there's a mistake in the power coupling to the unreality generator. It's likely to go critical and explode when they activate it. Even I know that much, Kyle," she replied in perfect Arabic. "Lao isn't going to be friendly, sweetheart. I can sense that already. Any idea how to get out of here?"

"I'm working on it." I thought for a moment. "If you know what's wrong with the unreality generator thing, could you fix it?"

"Oh yes, it is a simple fix. In fact, I could do it from here. If they activate it, the unreality drive could go critical, with a release of energy as powerful as a hydrogen bomb. I'm surprised he hasn't figured it out, but he hasn't, so he couldn't have been an engineer, I don't think. The thing is, I can't tell who he was, now that he's in human form. He certainly doesn't fully understand the machinations of the FTL system. Not that I do either, but I do know it's coupled wrong, from a tour I was taken on by a friend on the ship. I was a unreality drive enthusiast of sorts, while I was a companion of Brstulliantrst, but not all of us were. I didn't understand the navigation system at all, for instance."

That's the moment when Murphy stuck his head in the door and gave us a big raspberry. A phalanx of guards came into the room, surrounded each of us, and had us handcuffed before we could decide whether to resist or not. Then they left us alone again.

Jeri began to wriggle against her cuffs, then saw how tight they were and quit struggling.

I grinned at her and winked. Having been in similar situations undercover in the past, I had an ace up my sleeve that I wasn't prepared to reveal yet. A good intel operative follows the Boy Scout's motto for as many scenarios as he can.

"He hasn't tried to perceive me at all, Kyle. And he is continuously blocking me from perceiving him. At least he could talk to me."

"I'd say it's clear that he doesn't want to be rescued."

"I have to agree. So what should we do?"

"We came all this way, we should at least get to say hi." Then the door opened and in walked our guy.

"Hello again," he said to us, then turned to Jeri. "You might know me as—" and he said something in Cresperian.

Jeri nodded and spoke her Cresperian name, then continued, "I'm now Jeri Leverson and this is my husband, Kyle."

"Husband?" He paused. "Intriguing."

I answered him. "We're on our honeymoon, and Jeri here has been trying to find all the Cresperians that arrived safely. We guessed one crashed in China somewhere but had no idea where you would be." I adlibbed on our cover, hoping Jeri's perceptive sense kept him from sensing my mendacity.

"I have seen the Internet searches. How did you know to come here?" Lao asked.

"If you saw the searches, why didn't you respond to them?" Jeri asked.

"I wasn't sure who was doing the search and what their motivation was. Now answer my question. How did you find me?"

"Well, we just got lucky," I said.

"Doubtful."

"Okay, we built a Cresperian detector and found you that way," I replied.

"A Cresperian detector or an unreality detector?"

Okay, enough of the bantering. That was getting us nowhere. He knew how we found him and he knew that we knew that he knew. Typical Mexican standoff. Somehow we needed to diffuse the confrontation.

"Look. America has no need to start any hostilities with China, and I'm sure China feels the same," I said, but I didn't really believe it. I had once had a cat that the Chinese poisoned to death with their damned tainted cat food. Was that on purpose or was it bad quality control? I doubt the poisoning was on purpose, but the economic warfare was certainly planned.

"What would you suggest?" Lao asked. I thought he sounded sincere.

"Look, why don't we work together? You could come back to America with us or you could stay here and work with us as an ally. Who knows, it might improve the peace relations between our countries." I wasn't sure he was buying any of this.

"Dah, dah!" he grunted. "America is riddled with philosophical infestations and conflicts that it can never overcome. I bet you have already poisoned Jeri with them. 'America is the only true superpower and the best hope for mankind' you have no doubt told her."

"Uh, I didn't tell her that exactly—"

"I came to that conclusion on my own, Lao." Jeri interrupted me. "The Americans have their problems but they are also tolerant of all philosophies, for the most part. I didn't come here to debate this with you. I came to make certain you were alive and well and didn't need any help. I see now that you are happy where you are. So why don't you let us go and we'll be on our way never to bother you again?"

"Perhaps. First I must tell you, Jeri, that we were wrong. I don't know what these Americans have taught you, but the Tao and the Shangdi have shown me that we were truly wrong in our interpretation of deity. I plan to construct a vehicle and take the truth of the Shangdi back to Cresperia and give it to our species."

"So, the Chinese are happy-go-lucky and willy-nilly funding you to build a starship so you can become an evangelist to the stars, Lao? Come on. You expect us to believe that?" I didn't know what the hell the Shangdi was and I only knew what Tao meant because I'd studied Bruce Lee's *The Tau of Jeet Kun Do*. Tao meant "the way."

"I am not so naïve, Kyle. In return for my starship, I'm giving the Chinese government the expertise to reproduce the propulsion and energy technology of unreality physics, in a reduced sort of way so that they will be no threat to our home world. That should sufficiently enable them to shift the balance of power on earth. Besides, it is the American *way to take from those who do not have enough and to give to those who already have too much. With wise leaders, all can exist in unity, each with the other, because no being should feel that he exists, only as a shadow of his brilliant brother."*

"What the hell was that? Sounded like some sort of communist propaganda to me." I grumbled. Lao had spoken his piece like an evangelist.

"It is the Tao Te Ching, my friend Kyle. You see, the Shangdi is the all-encompassing personality of the noncorporeal omniscient Heaven. The Cresperian proof on no deity failed to account for the fact that all existence might be God itself. The Heaven is indeed the Shangdi and the proof can be shown to allow thus."

What was it with the Cresperians turned human that they had to focus on religion? Maybe it was some sort of mental and emotional trauma or side-effect that hit them. But was it that big a damned deal that this guy was going to give the Chinese the means to rule the world? Well, it was to Lao, and I knew how much it had impacted Jeri. I could see this as a crisis with the Crispies that Bill had to know about. My guess was that therapy was called for in at least some of the ones who converted to human, assuming we could deduce what type would be best for them. It reminded me of kids on Ritalin. They would seem normal right up to the point where they hacked their parents up with a butcher knife. This was a ticking time bomb that had to be diffused.

It was interesting that this Shangdi thing sounded a whole hell of a lot like the quantum consciousness. The shit made my head hurt, though, and I was beginning to see that we weren't gonna talk our way out of this situation. There is no way that the Chinese were gonna let us walk away with this knowledge. Lao might, but the Chinese government, no way. I slipped the cuff pick from the hem in my sleeve and started on the handcuffs.

"Look, Lao," Jeri pleaded with him. "I have come to similar conclusions, but that is not a reason to allow the entire balance of power of this species to be thrown topsy-turvy."

"*Nature acts without intent, so cannot be described as acting with benevolence, nor malevolence to any thing. In this respect, the Tao is just the same, though in reality it should be said that nature follows the rule of the Tao. Therefore, even when he seems to act in a manner kind or benevolent, the sage is not acting with such intent, for in conscious matters such as these, he is amoral and indifferent.*" Lao spouted more of the Taoist doctrine. I was beginning to think he was a little off his rocker. Jeri at least admitted an uncertainty in her musings of metaphysics.

"So that is your justification for probably starting a war?" I asked.

"Amoral and indifferent, that is the Tao of Shangdi." He paused. "I'm growing weary of this talk. Let me show you what I came to show you and then it will be up to Colonel Zhang what will happen to you."

I didn't know who the hell Colonel Zhang was, but I wanted to be ready for him. With that, I paused from working on my cuffs and slipped the pick back up my sleeve. Lao helped Jeri up and then led us out into the hallway. We were flanked on either side by an armed soldier. Lao led us down to the end of the hall and into a stairwell. We went down to the ground floor and into a high bay area on the back side of the building. Inside the high bay was another Shenzhou capsule without the solar panels and a lot of the other things I'd recalled seeing on the exterior of the manned spacecraft from Chinese public relations photos. Any good science writer or science fiction fan has kept up with the space race. This Shenzhou was fairly standard, minus some of the more clunky extremities. Above it was a large retractable roof panel that was an obvious new modification to the building. He planned to fly the thing right out of there when he had it ready.

The hatch to the capsule was open at the top where the crew would enter. The thirty-foot-tall spacecraft had three sections. A small cylinder was the orbital module, a cylinder with a round top sat in the middle and was shiny metal-colored. It was the re-entry module. A larger white cylinder at the base was typically the equipment or propulsion module. There were no rocket nozzles at the base, as far as I could tell. I suspected the modules were rearranged from what their original purpose had been, and were most likely redesigned inside. Had to be, if this was truly a starship, in order to give more room for living quarters, but still... There were several catwalks and scaffolds around it, and equipment racks spread out as well. This was Lao's starship, but small as it was I suddenly decided it almost had to be a model, regardless of what he said, made for testing purposes. Otherwise why a reentry module? Jeri had told me their reality drive spaceships could take off from the ground and land the same way. I wondered if it worked yet. Or was he just plain crazy? He wasn't even a navigator, because Jeri had told me they all died. If he planned on going home he had to be planning on a long search for the home planet.

"With the *Lao Tzu* I will take my message back to our people, Jeri. Come with me." I was surprised he offered her that, but was willing to bet he'd had sexual encounters and didn't want to go on a long voyage without a woman, preferably one from his own species originally.

"Thank you, Lao. I might take you up on that, but I can't let you disrupt the balance of power of this species so nonchalantly." Jeri turned to the craft and looked it up and down. "Is it ready?"

"You wouldn't ask that if you didn't already know, Jeri. I assume you ask for Kyle's benefit. Yes. I believe it is ready for a test flight, as I'm sure you know."

"If this is the starship, then what is that thing out there for?" I nodded in the direction of the Long March rocket.

"Ah, that is my gift to humanity, among other things. Our wonderful space agency is testing the first human-built unreality drive in an unmanned flight test in a few days. They have all of the blueprints and diagrams to reproduce it. When it works humanity will have a new option in superpowers."

I had kept a careful an eye on the two guards on either side of us as we entered the high bay area. They had taken up positions about ten feet behind us. I also spotted Captain Zeng and Sgt. Wu in the distance. Apparently they hadn't been found out for what they were yet. I had also been thinking about how we were going to escape from Jiuquan. I realized now that coming here had been a very bad plan. But I had one for getting out, and hoped Zeng and Wu would realize we couldn't go back the way we'd planned and would join us. The pick finally ticked the lock in the cuff. I grunted and cleared my throat to cover the click. The cuffs sprang loose and I turned, tossing them hard, like a Frisbee, at the guard farthest from me. That distracted him long enough to give me an instant to rush the other one.

I leaped at him, covering the ten feet or so between us with one jump. I slammed him with my knee up through his chin as I pulled his head down at the same time, squashing my kneecap through the bone in his jaw. It cracked like a rifle report. I tore away his weapon and turned it on the other guard and clicked the trigger. The safety was on.

The other guard pulled his pistol during the time I worked the safety. I turned quickly to avoid getting shot in the chest and managed to move away almost enough. The bulled ripped through my right shoulder, splashing blood in droplets that seemed frozen in the air to me as I flipped the safety and pumped two rounds through his head.

I immediately spun to Lao, who was already on top of me. He kicked me in the head, really fucking hard! I saw stars and dropped the gun on the floor. But somehow, I managed to stay out of his way just enough to dodge a barrage of kicks and fists that were at least as fast as I could move. I heard shooting, and knew that our companions had joined the fight without even knowing yet what we intended.

"*Like the sheltered, fertile valley, the meditative mind is still, yet retains its energy,*" Lao said as he continued to kick my ass. I was beginning to feel woozy from the gunshot wound despite my enhanced body, and taking more hits from him sure didn't do me any good.

"Shit." I ducked as a knife hand strike from his right hand whipped through the air where my head had just been. I followed up with an uppercut into the air where his chin had just been and then I caught a knee to my left side cracking several ribs. "Fuck!"

"*The Tao is abstract, and therefore has no form.*" He shifted and tossed me with a Kung Fu maneuver that I'd never seen. "*It is neither bright in rising, nor dark in sinking, cannot be grasped, and makes no sound.*"

The crazy son of a bitch was quoting philosophy at me while toying with my life, stringing it out on purpose, possibly just showing off in front of Jeri. I rolled across the floor, banging my bloody shoulder on it and hitting my head on an equipment table. Screwdrivers and a power meter flew off it in front of me. I forced myself to my feet and barely managed to duck a tornado roundhouse kick. I stutter-stepped backwards, blocking his advance as best I could.

"*Great good is said to be like water.*" Lao continued with his Tao and a barrage of punches and kicks that were beating me senseless. I was beginning to lose control, barely able to defend myself. Even an enhanced human is no match for a Crispy human, also enhanced but also having that perceptive sense to call on. If he caught me with one more hit to the head I was gonna go out like a light. *"Sustaining life with—"*

The sound of the gun firing forced him to pause. It fired again and the side of his head exploded scattering blood and gray matter on me. I was too stunned to move. Lao's eyes rolled in the back of his head as his body collapsed to the floor. Jeri stood behind him with the pistol in her grip, her cuffs hanging from her left hand.

"Why don't you just shut up!" she screamed. I could see tears streaming down her face and then I collapsed on the floor.

The next thing I knew Jeri was dragging me up the scaffolds to the *Lao Tzu's* hatch. I was still staggering and mostly incoherent but I could tell that Jeri was trying to get me through the hatch and into the taikonaut couch. Below, I saw Captain Zeng and Sgt. Chu running toward us, pausing to whirl and fire at security guards, then running again. I winced as I saw Zeng take a fatal wound and Sgt Wu go down with both legs shattered. I wiped at my face and felt my busted lips and broken nose. They hurt and that bit of pain brought me back around. Wu managed to wave a hand at us to go on without him, then rolled over and began firing past the prostrate form of the Captain.

I looked away. "What are we doing, Jeri?"

"We're flying out of here."

"Good. Will it work?"

"Do you have a better idea?"

"Nope. Did you fix the FTL drive out on the launch pad?"

"No, I didn't," she said.

"Good, don't." I helped her get us strapped in and sealed off and she started cycling through the launch sequence. She used her perception to figure out which switches had to be flipped when and how. The unreality engine spun up and we were thrust up through the ceiling of the high bay and then through a ball of whirling orange light. My senses went nuts and I lost all notion of where up, down, left, right, here, or there was. Then I promptly vomited.

"Uh oh," Jeri groaned, as a green swirling pool of light seemed to consume the ship and then disappear in front of me. It could have just been the dizziness and my mind going nuts or maybe that combined with the agony of seeing our friends die. Then there was a *bang* from beneath us somewhere.

"That can't be good," I groaned, trying not to be sick again.

"Like I said. Uh oh," Jeri replied.

"What's going on?" I shouted.

"The unreality drive is failing. I'm tossing the drive module. Hopefully, it won't explode. I'm trying to keep it from doing that. We have to get into the reentry module, now!"

We struggled into the reentry module and sealed off the docking ring, while still accelerating, I thought, even though we were weightless. Well, it was billed as an unreality drive, even though it was a small test model with the means for emergency reentry—and thank Boogram for that! Then Jeri fired the release for the module. At some point I managed to look out the viewport and could see the Earth beneath us. Jeri had managed to steer us across the Pacific Ocean on a ballistic trajectory back to North America somewhere toward the western part of the continent. I was guessing we might hit somewhere in the Rockies, if we survived reentry.

"Are we gonna make it, sweetheart?" I wasn't sure about our odds.

"The reentry vehicle can handle it. But we're coming in fast. I hope the chutes hold when they pop. Lao had inertial dampeners installed but they are only working at about twenty percent. We'd already be dead if they hadn't been functioning."

"Okay, can they handle a crash?"

"Maybe. Hold on. And pray."

Chapter Twenty-Seven

The chutes popped after we passed through the ionosphere. The pre-chutes slowed us slightly and then failed because they weren't designed for that type of trajectory. The secondary chutes popped and dragged us down to a few hundred miles per hour. The g-forces on us were already around ten or so gravities and that was with an inertial dampening system. The weightless sensation had disappeared as soon as we sealed off the reentry module. The capsule bucked and rattled violently as one of the chutes tore open in the middle, ripping until it spun round and round, entangling the others. The ship twisted and fell at over a hundred miles per hour.

"Kyle, I love you!"

"I love you, Jeri! You are the best thing that ever happened to me." I squeezed her hand, thinking this was going to be it. I caught a glimpse of a forested slope through the porthole, then felt the capsule tearing through a canopy of trees as if through paper. We slammed into the earth but that didn't end it. The capsule was tossed and tumbled across the ground, while my eyes were glued on the section in front of me. It was being crushed closer to my body with each impact against a tree trunk or boulder. At one point I felt a sharp pressure on my legs and was certain they had been horribly mangled. My already aching ribs snapped as a piece of the hatch was flung free and jammed into me as we finally rolled to a stop.

"Jeri!" I tried to move but I couldn't. I was pretty sure that my back was broken.

"Kyle...I'm alive and so are you. You're hurt very badly and I must focus to help you. Try not to distract me."

I tried to tilt my head to see her but I couldn't. I couldn't feel her hand or anything. I could see, breathe, and hear, and that was about it. I could barely hear Jeri's rasping breath and her occasional soft moaning.

"Jeri, how bad are you?"

"I'll live."

"Somebody will find us soon. Can you use any of the gear to contact anybody for help?"

"Everything is damaged beyond any use, Kyle. We have to hope we're found soon. Please be quiet and let me work."

A long time passed that seemed like hours but I had no way of know-ing, until it started getting dark in the crushed little capsule. At some point I passed out or maybe Jeri turned me off. I wasn't sure. The next thing I knew it was getting light again.

"Why haven't they found us yet?" I asked out loud. "Jeri?"

"Hold on, Kyle. They'll find us." She didn't sound too sure. But then I felt a squeeze on my hand. I hadn't felt my hand since the crash. I hoped that was a good sign.

"Jeri, if we don't make it you have to—"

"No, don't talk like that," she interrupted me. "We're going to make it. Just fight and stay alive..." She didn't sound real good and her voice trailed off in a gurgling cough.

"But just in case, Jeri. You have to know that just meeting you and knowing you and falling in love with you made my life worth living since Gwen died. If I don't make it, then you have to know you gave me a new lease on life that was wonderful even if it was short." I cleared my throat and tried with all my strength to squeeze her hand back. I wasn't sure if I did it or not.

"Kyle, I could have never been as happy as I am with you had we not crashed on Earth and had you not been such a wonderful being to accept me into your life. I'm so proud that we've been together, too, and that I made the choice to be human." She gurgled again, and this time she wheezed as she coughed. "If I had it to do over, I'd do it again every time. All of it." Then she was quiet. Her breathing reached a point that was practically inaudible.

"Jeri?"

"Jeri!" I tried again to squeeze her hand but still wasn't certain if it worked. "Jeri!" I could feel tears on my face or maybe it was still blood. I know that I felt like crying. That was all I could feel. Then I whispered, "Oh, God! Please let her live. Forget about me, just let her live."

I lost all sense of time for a while but Jeri never answered my peri-odic pleas to speak. When I came back to my senses there was nothing but silence and birds outside chirping and the wind howling through the broken spaceship. From the direction of rays from the sun through the broken port I knew we must have been there for hours without Jeri making a sound.

"Jeri?" I whispered. There was no response as the moment stretched to longer moments and the silence continued. "Oh God, please?" I whimpered. Then there was a squeeze in my hand and a surge of strength. I felt better almost instantly.

"Kyle!" Jeri said abruptly even though her voice was barely audible and still rife with the pain she was suffering in order to keep me alive. "I feel them!"

ഇരു

They're still with us, but barely." I heard Sam's voice, though I wasn't sure if I was hallucinating or what. Jeri hadn't made any sounds for what seemed like hours and I was beginning to think that she had used herself up to keep me alive. This alien from another world had come to earth and given me a new lease on life and a new vigor and taste for it. And then the alien gave up eons of heritage to become human: human by choice, and to live alongside us—alongside me, in particular. And now I was beginning to worry that finally she had given her last effort, to keep me alive. I didn't want to lose her. I couldn't stand losing the woman I loved, not again. I just couldn't.

"I love you, Kyle," I heard a faint whisper and felt a nudge against my hand.

And then there was Ish and a doctor I recognized and Sam's unlovely face. I wasn't hallucinating. We were saved. Jeri was alive and nothing else mattered.

That wasn't the end of the story, of course. A few days after our rescue, when bursts of diplomatic outrage were still being directed our way, there was a gigantic explosion centered on what was then the Jiuquan space facility in China. I doubt seriously that the Chinese will be a space power again for many, many years. And the diplomatic protests and threats abruptly ceased.

By the time Jeri and I recovered, I learned we still hadn't located all the aliens. However, Britain's socialist government had fallen and the Brits were cooperating with us again. We would be working together, developing ships using the unreality drive.

India was still being cagey, but we knew they were holding two Crispies from a lifeboat that had landed in their country. And after going back over the data again for about the tenth time, some highbrow specialist thought he'd located an area in the Rocky Mountains where a lifeboat may have come down. We're still looking for that one, but I doubt if I'll be around when they find it, if they do. You see, Jeri and I are leaving earth on the exploratory ship USSF Zeng Wu. One of the Crispies from

England had a passing interest in navigation and thinks he might be able to locate the Cresperian home world, *might* being the operative word. Of course, we'd be going exploring, anyway. America is a nation of pioneers and explorers, built on the shoulders of some great ones in the past, and I'm not just talking about physical exploration. Our scientists are still at work, and on the whole they're the best in the world and have been for the last century and a half.

Bill isn't going, but Sam Haley is, as Captain of the ship. His wife, the former Carolyn Blanchard, is coming along with him.

Other ships are being built. Another great age of exploration, like the world hasn't seen since the American continents were rediscovered, is just getting underway. Even if we never locate the Cresperian world, we're bound to find a lot of surprises out there among the stars.

I can't wait, and neither can my wife, who is *human by choice.*

- The End -

Darrell Bain

Darrell is the author of about three dozen books, in many genres, running the gamut from humor to thrillers and science fiction to non-fiction. For the last several years he has concentrated on science fiction, thrillers, and short fiction. He is currently writing the sixth novel in the series begun with *Medics Wild* and working on the sequel to *Human By Choice* as well as another novel with Travis S. Taylor.

Darrell served thirteen years in the military and his two stints in Vietnam formed the basis for his first published novel, *Medics Wild*. Darrell has been writing off and on all his life but really got serious about it only after the advent of computers. He purchased his first one in 1989 and has been writing furiously ever since.

Visit Darrell's web site: http://www.darrellbain.com

Travis S. Taylor

Travis S. Taylor—"Doc" Taylor to his friends—has earned his soubriquet the hard way: he has a Doctorate in Optical Science and Engineering, a Master's degree in Physics, a Master's degree in Aerospace Engineering, all from the University of Alabama in Huntsville. He also has a Master's degree in Astronomy from the University of Western Sydney, and a Bachelor's degree in Electrical Engineering from Auburn University.

Dr. Taylor has worked on various programs for the Department of Defense and NASA for the past sixteen years. He's currently working on several advanced propulsion concepts, very large space telescopes, space-based beamed energy systems, and next generation space launch concepts.

In his copious spare time, Doc Travis is also a black belt martial artist, a private pilot, a SCUBA diver, races mountain bikes, competed in triathlons, and has been the lead singer and rhythm guitarist of several hard rock bands. He currently lives with his wife Karen, daughter Kalista Jade, two dogs Stevie and Wesker, and his cat Kuro, in north Alabama.

Visit Doc Taylor's web site: http://www.doctravis.com

Don't miss any of these
other exciting SF/F books

➤ Angelos
(1-933353-60-0, $16.95 US)

➤ Burnout
(1-60619-200-0, $19.95 US)

➤ Monkey Trap
(1-931201-34-X, $19.50 US)

➤ The Focus Factor
(1-931201-96-X, $18.95 US)

➤ The Melanin Apocalypse
(1-933353-70-8, $16.95 US)

Twilight Times Books
Kingsport, Tennessee

Order Form

If not available from your local bookstore or favorite online bookstore, send this coupon and a check or money order for the retail price plus $3.50 s&h to Twilight Times Books, Dept. LS909 POB 3340 Kingsport TN 37664. Delivery may take up to four weeks.

Name: _____

Address: _____

_____

Email: _____

I have enclosed a check or money order in the amount

of $_____

for _____ .

Breinigsville, PA USA
09 March 2010
233878BV00001B/75/P